JEPP, WHO DEFIED THE STARS

JEPP,
WHO DEFIED THE
STARS

✴

KATHERINE MARSH

HYPERION
NEW YORK

Copyright © 2012 by Katherine Marsh

All rights reserved. Published by Hyperion, an imprint of Disney Book Group. No part of this book may be reproduced or transmitted in any form or by any means, electronic or mechanical, including photocopying, recording, or by any information storage and retrieval system, without written permission from the publisher. For information address Hyperion, 125 West End Avenue, New York, New York 10023-6387.

Printed in the United States of America

First Hyperion paperback edition, 2013

10 9 8 7 6 5 4 3 2 1

V475-2873-0-13244

Library of Congress Control Number for Hardcover Edition: 2011053065

This book is set in Adobe Caslon

Designed by Marci Senders

ISBN 978-1-4231-3786-3

Visit www.un-requiredreading.com

SUSTAINABLE FORESTRY INITIATIVE

Certified Chain of Custody
Promoting Sustainable Forestry
www.sfiprogram.org
SFI-01054

The SFI label applies to the text stock

To my mother, Elaine Milosh Marsh

*The soul of the newly born baby is marked for life
by the pattern of the stars at the moment
it comes into the world.*

Johannes Kepler

*The fault, dear Brutus, is not in our stars,
But in ourselves.*

Julius Caesar
William Shakespeare

Book I

MEMENTO MORI

Chapter 1

Being a court dwarf is no easy task. I know because I failed at it.

But before I tell you how I failed, and how I ended up imprisoned in this star-crossed coach, bumping up and down bone-rattling roads, I will tell you a little about myself. My name is Jepp, and I was born fifteen years ago in the town of Astraveld, twenty miles south of Utrecht.

To call Astraveld a town is probably not quite correct—it is more of a crossroads, and a dangerous one at that, set among lands claimed by both the Spanish Netherlands and the Protestant North. Astraveld was a real town once, when my mother was young; with long, flat stretches of green fields, cows and chickens, a harvest festival, a small church, and a dirt square where farmers traded eggs and barley, and visiting merchants plied spices

3

and cloth. But when the Protestant North rose up against Spain, most everyone fled except my mother's family and three or four others. My grandparents realized they needed a different livelihood, independent from their pillaged lands, so they opened an inn that served both Catholic and Protestant alike, until the day my grandfather was stabbed in the heart by a drunken Spanish soldier who mistook him for a spy. Even after this tragedy, my family stayed: bound by the stars, my mother said, to a town that had been their home for as long as anyone could remember.

A few years later, my grandmother died, and my mother become the sole mistress of the family establishment. She proved a formidable businesswoman. As the traffic of war flourished, she hired the remaining families of Astraveld in various capacities, and her inn, like the Ark itself, sustained the inhabitants of our much reduced town.

It was at this inn that I was born, as skirmishes continued around us between the Spanish Netherlands and the Protestant North. My mother would not talk about my birth, just that she loved me from first sight. She was broad-shouldered and stout with a brown mole on her left cheek. Her eyes could flash stern enough to shame the rowdiest drunk or—upon viewing a mewling kitten or another of the hapless creatures she so enjoyed—crinkle with mirth. The remaining families of Astraveld, who felt deep gratitude toward her, showered me with affection and praise. As the popularity of the inn grew but I did not, I attributed the laughter and smiles of passing travelers to the love owed me as prince of my mother's spirited kingdom.

Our inn consisted of two stories—the first contained an open room in which the eye was immediately drawn to a large hearth, where orange flames crackled and roared under a great cauldron of bubbling porridge. Circling the fire were mismatched chairs and tables—abandoned by various townsfolk as they fled the uprising—and beneath them, always, gaming cats—their eyes squinting gaily as they scanned the floor for mice. Two or three girls hired by my mother carried pewter mugs of ale from behind the bar and delivered them with loaves of black bread and small bowls into which they ladled the porridge. The ale was watered down, the porridge bland. The rich, pungent odor of sweat and hops soaked into a traveler's hair and clothes. And yet, especially after a long journey, such as the one I am forced on now, the cozy room and its companionable smells offered the very respite a weary soul desired.

Although fealty to my mother prevented the Astraveld families from ever remarking upon my condition, my mother could not always control the yaps of travelers, especially after they had emptied several mugs of ale. I remember still the first time this happened—I was seven and playing with one of the cats, dragging a piece of string before it by the fire. Two men in dirty burlap coats, their potato noses red with ale, were watching me and, in my mind, admiring the industry with which I drew the creature after its prey. With hearty laughter, they calculated something on their fingers and then, with a red-faced grin, one of the men called me over. I walked up to them fearlessly, expecting some kind word or compliment. But as soon as I reached him, the man hoisted me up on his lap. Then he seized my string and, dangling me in the air by the ankle like a hare, began to measure me with it.

"Three feet and an inch!" cried his companion. "That's what the dwarf is. I am sure of it!"

I did not have to struggle and cry out, as I would at other times ahead, because in a flash my mother was there, slapping the man who held me with such force that he dropped me, and I tumbled into her apron. The terror I felt ebbed as she enveloped me in her arms.

And so I learned the word that would come to supplant my name. But I thought not of myself as a dwarf. I was Jepp to my mother, Jepp to the families of Astraveld, Jepp to the regular travelers who greeted me warmly and brought me gifts. My favorite among these was an alphabet primer with which I taught myself to read. But there was also the body of a spiny mer-creature with a tiny snout; a wooden knight; a yellow finch that escaped its cage and was eaten by one of the cats; a pair of stilts that allowed me to tower over all. The sea of humanity that passed through the inn was my school: I heard stories of the New World, of sea monsters, of men who gazed upon the celestial spheres, of foreign courts, of new dyes for paint, of cities teeming with pageants and universities, of churches that soared up toward God like the tower of Babel itself.

My height was just a fact of life—the real mystery that captured my imagination as I grew in years was my paternity. When I was very young, my mother had insisted that I had no father. She claimed that she had conceived me after staring at a turtle that had come between her and the well. But gradually, when I developed no hump or shell, I began to doubt this provenance, and my suspicion turned to the few remaining able-bodied men of Astraveld.

There was Pieter, our brewer, a quiet, pockmarked man, who carved me a small wooden horse. But he had sired two burly, red-haired sons, who lifted barrels of ale over their shoulders as lightly as the horizon heaves up clouds. With my dark hair and eyes, I could not imagine these fair Atlases to be my brothers.

There was Farmer Helmich, whose rough hands were oversized for the rest of his short-limbed frame. His wife, Jantje, was so full of chatter that she gaped in between tales like a fish gasping for air. But Helmich only had eyes—or rather, ears—for his wife, beaming at her like a perpetually amused audience. They had no children.

Willem, who could read and write figures and helped my mother keep track of what was bought and sold, told me tales from the Bible and about the pagan heroes of Rome. Long and thin as a flute, he lived with us at the inn; and of all the men, I would have liked him best as father. But when I hinted this to my mother, she averred that he had no interest in matters of the flesh and laughed so merrily that I knew it to be true.

I turned my attention to the cast of travelers who paraded through the inn—the soldiers, merchants, scholars, farmers, monks, gentlemen, servants, fortune-tellers, and musicians. I did not know what I was searching for—a familiar look in a stranger's eye, a tender gaze at my mother? By some sign, I believed, my true father would reveal himself.

As I waited, I envisioned each man in the fated role, and how my resulting life would be in court, on stage, in university, or on the battlefield—as the son of a king, a hero, a man of action—a son reclaimed to live a life of adventure and renown. These were my boyish fantasies, but in my bed at night, the stars unblinking in the cold sky and my candle crying waxy tears, I would have been happy enough with a simple country man, so long as he claimed me as his own.

At fourteen, I was not much taller than I had been at seven, though my thoughts and feelings took up a much greater part of me. My mother and Willem alone seemed to understand this;

visitors to the inn continued to proffer toys and pat me upon the head. I began to spend less time there, retreating to the barn with the cats or settling myself in the crook of a tree root with a book about the lives of the saints, which I had collected in addition to my primer. The urgency of finding my father seemed to wane. When I dreamed, it was of perfect loneliness—a hermit in a cottage, a monk in a cell—a sublime vision of what I already felt and assumed to be my lot.

My mother thought my melancholic humor was the result of idle hands and put me to work. I sat in a corner of the great room, in view of the hearth, washing mugs and bowls in a wooden bucket. But even though I labored now in the heart of the noisy inn, I was as removed from the commotion and stares as I had been in the field or barn. I kept my head down, focusing on my task, reciting stories in my mind to while away the time. When spoken to I spoke, but I did not seek out company. "What ails Master Jepp?" my mother was asked. "Growing up," she would say. Some would laugh, thinking this a jest, but some understood.

It was on a busy autumn night as I dragged my rag over the dregs of porridge stiffened in a bowl, that I became aware of someone staring at me. There was nothing unusual about this—I was accustomed to stares from new visitors. After glancing up at a dapper, bearded man with a feathered cap and a ruffed collar, I concluded him a stranger and his curiosity the familiar sort. But his dress struck me as uncommonly fine, and his manner odd: unlike most strangers, who after a time lost interest and turned away, this man continued to gaze upon me, his mug of ale untouched. When one of the girls brought him porridge, he waved it away and then stopped her to ask a question.

"Jepp," I heard her say.

"Jepp," he repeated. He stood up, removed his cap, and bowed grandly in my direction.

With pulsing heart, I recalled my boyhood fantasies. Though I did not see my features reflected in the man's face, I felt certain that he was the instrument of my fate. Of this, sadly, I would not be mistaken.

Chapter 2

A few moments later, this gentleman approached me, just as I knew that he would. "Jepp?" he said.

I barely managed to answer, so stricken was I with anticipation. "Yes?"

"Please join me at my table." He smiled as if my assent would bring him great satisfaction.

And so I did, clambering up onto a chair, feeling from this vantage like a guest in my own home. He introduced himself. He had a name, a very long one that he presented as if rolling out a carpet of words. But I quickly fell into the habit of calling him by the Spanish title Don, and from this he did not dissuade me.

As Don chatted about the rigors of travel and praised the flavor of my mother's ale, I waited for him to arrive at the true subject of our conversation. Finally, I could be patient no more.

"Do you know my father?"

Don stared at me in confusion. "Your father?"

"My mother never revealed his identity to me. I thought perhaps—"

Don interrupted me with a laugh. "I know nothing about this."

I looked away, attempting to conceal my disappointment.

"But you are right to guess that there is an important matter I wish to discuss with you," he continued. "Have you ever pictured yourself at court?"

I shook my head, not wanting to reveal my own foolish dreams.

"There is a place for you there," he assured me. "As a court dwarf."

Though I had imagined myself being summoned to court many times, it was never for the distinction of my height. As I pondered this surprising turn of events, my mother rushed over from across the room, her face creased with worry.

"Good evening," said Don, greeting her with a sweeping bow as he repeated his lengthy name.

"He wishes me to go to court," I blurted out.

I expected her to dismiss Don's overture promptly, for it wasn't the first time a stranger had made an offer to take me on his travels for companionship or show. But with a respectful nod to Don, she took a seat and listened as he spun fantastic visions of what such a life might entail: I would hobnob with princes, diplomats, church officials, and painters; feast on stuffed game and almond cakes; dance the galliard to the strains of viol and lute; and be schooled in ancient languages, new sciences, and the secrets of the spheres.

"This is indeed a fine life," my mother said when he was done.

Although my impressions were much the same, I felt betrayed. Surely she wished to keep me by her side? Had I become so sullen that she wanted to send me away? But when I sought counsel from her eyes, they evaded my own, looking downward.

"I don't want you to go, Jepp," she said, as though reading my thoughts. "But what this gentleman promises . . ."

"Our family has always been in Astraveld," I protested. "I have a good life."

This remark seemed to touch her deeply, for she grabbed my hand beneath the table and held it fast in her own. I would have stayed by her side all my days had her words not clashed with this gesture.

"You can have so much more, Jepp. You can see the world, learn your place in it." She hesitated, looking at Don for assurance. "And when you're done, you can come back, my love. I will be here."

Don squinted his dark eyes and grinned agreeably at her. "None of us would ever keep a boy from his mother's breast."

At this tender remark, my mother withdrew her hand from mine and nodded at Don, her eyes wet with tears. I understood then that she did not wish me gone but only to have the greater life of which I dreamed. That she was willing to part with me no longer seemed an insult but a testament to the depths of her love. I thought back to the pretty scenes Don had painted of court. Even though I had been invited there under the auspices of my stature, I would be a member of this world. And Don had promised my mother that I could still come home. It was this homecoming that made the journey seem enticing, for on my return, I imagined telling her and Willem of all the astonishing things I had seen.

But before I could agree to this adventure, I had one more question. The primer upon which I had taught myself to read and the legends of the saints had whetted my appetite for more than just feasts and finery. "Will there be books?"

"Books!" Don said with a laugh. "There will be an entire library for you. Like nothing you've ever seen!"

The next day, with my mother's blessing, I departed with Don for Brussels, the capital of the Spanish Netherlands, and the court of the Infanta Isabella Clara Eugenia and her husband, Archduke Albert of Austria. There I would join the Infanta's retinue as her court dwarf. The journey would take three days in Don's coach. I had never traveled so far, and never in a conveyance so elegant and fine. A cloth of red velvet hung over the hard wooden seat. Silk pillows, ornamented with gold brocade, softened the jostles of the road. Pelts of fox and sable prevented drafts, and a hot coal wrapped in a sturdy burlap blanket on the floor warmed our feet. Satchels of rosemary hung from the ceiling to freshen the air, and a repast of candied almonds and honey cakes banished the smallest shadow of hunger.

I felt like Apollo, flying over the ground, my thoughts as buoyant as my chariot. I was only vaguely aware of the horses' hooves dancing over the red and yellow leaves; the drowsy sun glinting over streams; the peasants, industrious as bees, harvesting their fields of peas and barley, rye and beans. Next to me, Don tunelessly hummed a madrigal. Over the course of our journey, he offered no further details about my future life, preferring to silently pick at his teeth with the sharp-edged splinter of a chicken bone. By the third afternoon, I could not help but deluge him with questions.

"Will I have duties? As a member of the court?"

Don pulled the chicken bone out of his mouth and looked upon me quizzically, as though he had forgotten I was there. "Your only duty, Jepp, is to be yourself."

This did not satisfy me in the least. I bit into a honey cake and determined to prod him more. "What are your duties, Don?"

Don tugged at his beard, considering this for a moment. "To satisfy the wishes of the Infanta and her court."

"Where were you headed when you discovered me?"

His dark eyes blinked rapidly. "Back to the court . . . from . . ." His voice strained to sound merry. "This is not your business, Jepp."

I flushed, not intending to irritate my patron. "All I meant is that it is lucky you found me."

Don leaned close to me. His breath was surprisingly rank, and I struggled not to draw back. "There is no luck," he confided. "There are only the stars, Jepp. That is where our fortune or lack of it resides."

"Not with God?"

"God made the stars." Don looked around as if checking to see if someone had joined us inside the coach, an angel or demon in the deepening shadows. "But it is the celestial bodies that make us. I am born in the month of the Scorpion. My element is water. I can transform myself just as water can become steam or ice."

This should have been a warning to me. But I sought to draw this slippery figure closer. "My mother says I am the sign of the water bearer."

"Aquarius," said Don, musing upon this. "Despite being the water bearer, it is an air sign. I suppose there is something airlike about you."

"Airlike?"

"Driven by the head. You ask too many questions."

My feelings wounded, I struggled to find the proper words with which to respond. "But I am being myself, Don."

"You do not know yourself, Jepp," he replied somewhat wearily.

I felt confused, for how could I be myself if I did not know myself? As the sun sank below the horizon, I began to have doubts concerning my destination. Perhaps, like Don, everyone at the court spoke in such indecipherable riddles. Perhaps I would fail to impress, and they would send me back home. The thought was not entirely an unwelcome one.

As the coach hurried forward through the cooling afternoon, my thoughts raced back to Astraveld, to my mother's kindly eyes, to Willem's stories, even to such chores as bringing water from the well and sweeping ashes from the hearth. Like all things left behind, they appeared even dearer in memory.

I opened my primer, one of the few mementos I had brought from home, seeking comfort in the familiar words and pictures. But instead of reading the pages before me, I recalled my mother's embrace, her parting words. No longer had she deigned to suppress her grief at my departure. Her cheeks stained with tears, she had bent down on her knees and cupped my face in her hands. "You were born for a better life, Jepp. Now it is yours to claim," she had said. But it was my past that I longed to recover, and my future that loomed frightening and cold.

In the dark, our coach reached the city wall. My apprehension was great as we drove through a gate in a huge stone fortification and turned up a lane. On either side of it were tall houses, each one blazing with light. Dogs roamed the street, and the smell of night soil fouled the air. We rumbled past a large square filled with peddlers' stalls where groups of bundled figures shivered around small fires, and then past a church that rose and rose, disappearing in the night like a ladder to the stars. Though it was near time to sleep, Don seemed more awake—his dark eyes flashing at the city sights.

The coach hurried along a street lined with grand brick and stone houses and then began to climb a hill, ascending over the city as if to some Olympian mount. Don adjusted his hat. The road leveled out on top of a promontory, and we drove through enormous gates, by many gardens, and toward a palace, illuminated by torches, that appeared as great as any mortal-made structure I had ever seen or imagined. It was at least four stories high and seemed to me endless, a labyrinth of arches, gables, and windows. "Coudenberg," announced Don in the same grand manner that he had first introduced himself.

I whispered the name of my new home—*Cold Hill*—and, as though I had uttered an incantation, my doubts vanished. I suddenly understood that, if anything, Don's words had failed to do justice to the wonders of the life that awaited me. I felt as if I had passed into a dream.

Don, watching me, smiled. "Just wait, Jepp, till you see your quarters."

Chapter

3

Our coach proceeded along a cobblestone promenade to the side of the palace and then stopped. Don sprang out, as jaunty as a grasshopper, and lifted me down after him. My legs felt stiff and my nose cold, but it hardly mattered. In front of us was a small, arched door. I peered up at Don eagerly, awaiting his instruction. "Go ahead, Jepp," he said. "Open it."

For the first time in my life, I did not have to reach up for the handle. I pushed open the little door and stepped into a white marble hall illuminated by a pair of elegant brass candelabra. Don followed me inside, hunching beneath the doorframe, and when he straightened up, I noticed that the top of his head nearly brushed the ceiling. At the end of the hall was a staircase. Voices drifted down it.

Don gestured for me to follow him along the hall and up the stairs. It was the first time I had climbed so steep and winding a staircase. Halfway up, my head began to spin, and I made the error of gazing back down. I ceased my climb and leaned against the wall, watching Don take the stairs ahead of me three and four at a time. It occurred to me that, like the little door and low-ceilinged hall, they too had been fashioned for a smaller-than-normal inhabitant. "Come along," said Don from the top of the staircase, mistaking my inexperience with heights for hesitation.

I steeled myself and continued to climb until I had reached his same aerie platform. We passed through another small door and into a second hall. The voices were louder here. They beckoned from an illuminated chamber to our right. Don bent beneath the low doorframe to enter the chamber, and I followed after.

I will never forget the sight that greeted me. Inside this apartment were two ladies and one gentleman of approximately my own stature. The gentleman, who was elegantly dressed in green vest and breeches, a lace ruff, and a scarlet cape, stood in front of a dressing mirror designed to his dimensions. The older of the two ladies, a dark-haired woman with a stout face, sat on a miniature throne, sipping from a tiny silver goblet. Between them, a girl—but a few years older than myself—with golden tresses nearly as long as she was, stood beside a low, round table, upon which lay a lily, a beetle, a half an orange, a seashell, and a small, white skull. Next to her, on the floor, was a large gold birdcage. In the far corner of the room, a giant as tall as all three of them together sat on the floor, bent over a tiny lute, adjusting the strings with his enormous fingers.

"You're not supposed to be here, Robert," said Don, bravely

shaking a finger at the giant. He spoke in Spanish, a language I had learned easily at my mother's inn.

"I am fixing Mademoiselle's lute," the giant replied in a low French-accented rumble.

It wasn't the giant, however, that held me spellbound at the entrance. It was the sight of the apartment's three small inhabitants. I had never in my life seen anyone like me. I knew there were others—travelers to the inn had told tales of tiny sailors and shepherds and monks—but it was altogether different to gaze upon them. I felt great kinship with these fellow beings, a certainty that their dreams and heartbreaks were my own. And yet, there was also a touch of disappointment that I was not the only one at Coudenberg. Don had not mentioned these others, and my status as courtier seemed less singular now.

"This is Jepp," said Don, continuing to speak in his native tongue. "The Infanta's new court dwarf."

The gentleman in the red cape was the first to approach me. He had a handsome face with small features, a jutting brow, and a dark beard trimmed in the same fashion as Don's. I smiled, but he glowered at me and positioned himself at my back. "Who is shorter?" he demanded.

"You are, Sebastian," said Don. "By a finger's length at least."

With a jeering look, Sebastian returned to his mirror and busied himself adjusting his red cape.

Don laughed heartily at this exchange.

"Ignore Sebastian," said the older woman. "You'll be perfect for a pie."

The giant shook his massive head disapprovingly. His jaw, I noticed, was enormous. "You are frightening him, Madame Maria."

"Not at all," said Maria. "Come have some hippocras, Jepp."

She held out her tiny goblet, which I presumed was filled with this light wine spiced with honey and cloves.

Though I did not know what to make of her comment about turning me into a pie, her voice was gentle, and I walked over to her. She stood up, revealing herself to be the tallest of our number. Only her limbs were short. Her large face was round and lumpen like a piece of kneaded dough, and she wore a black dress, trimmed with white lace. She seemed near my mother's years.

"Here," she said, handing me the goblet. "You've had a long journey."

I raised it to my mouth. But the liquid that entered tasted not like any hippocras I had ever drunk. It burned my throat, and I felt a brief flicker of fear that I was being poisoned. As if to assuage my panic, Maria put her hand on mine; and I forced myself, out of politeness, to swallow her potion down.

She gestured at the mirror. "You have met Sebastian."

"Robert." The giant bowed his head.

"And Lia," she said, pointing to the golden-haired girl, who shyly smiled at me before arranging the objects on her table. Lia was as small as Sebastian, but her form, unlike his, was in perfect proportion. She had a dainty head, milk-pale skin, and large blue eyes that I thought more enchanting than any I had ever seen.

"Now that you are acquainted," said Don, "I will fetch Hendrika. She is very eager to see Jepp."

He slipped under the doorframe and departed.

"Who is Hendrika?" I asked Maria.

Maria took back her goblet and poured herself a generous drink of her acrid hippocras. "The mistress of us all."

Sebastian snorted.

Maria turned to Robert, who was still adjusting the strings on the lute. "You had better go."

Robert stood up, crouching so as not to bang his head on the ceiling. He handed the tiny lute to Lia. "I regret, mademoiselle, that it is not altogether repaired."

"You will come back?" she asked him in Dutch-accented Spanish.

He nodded and, bending himself nearly in half, managed to squeeze his fearsome frame through the door.

No one spoke after he left. Maria continued to drink her hippocras. Sebastian tried on various stern and offended expressions in his mirror. Lia leaned the lute against the empty birdcage and resumed arranging the objects on the table. I was plagued by many questions but had the distinct impression that no one was in the disposition to answer them. I approached Lia and observed her labors. She placed the beetle on a petal of the lily and moved the skull closer to the orange. "What is this?" I asked her in Spanish.

"A memento mori," she said without looking at me.

I shook my head. The expression was then unfamiliar to me.

"It is a tableau of life and death," said Sebastian crossly.

"It is a reminder of death," corrected Maria.

Sebastian stamped his foot. "That is what I said."

Lia pointed to each object. "The beetle eats the lily; the orange rots; the sea dries up and leaves the shell; the body decays and leaves the bone."

"And how about the bird?"

Lia looked at me oddly.

"What does the cage mean?"

Lia opened her mouth to speak, but at just that moment a woman darted beneath the doorway into the room.

"Jepp!" the woman announced, bending down to gaze at me. She was tall and raven-haired, with the long, elegant face that so often signals high birth. But her beauty was faded—not so much by age, for her hair was untouched by the cobwebs of gray that time had spun in my own mother's hair—but by the fretful knit of her brow. With spidery fingers, she squeezed my shoulder and stroked my hair, then hastily drew back as if she had discovered something that displeased her. "Jepp," she snapped. "What kind of name is Jepp? A country name."

Her sudden venom took me aback. "My mother named me. It is a fine name!"

"Your mother doesn't matter here," she said coldly.

The long journey, the shock of my new company, the unkind words now directed at my only parent, lost to me just three days ago, all conspired to bring tears to my eyes. I felt ashamed by this uncharacteristic display of weakness and turned away. But Hendrika, for this woman was surely the mistress of us all, saw my tears. "There, there," she said gently. "You are home now."

I shook my head. I felt farther from home than ever before.

Her failure to soothe me seemed to trouble Hendrika further. She stood up and, as if noticing them for the very first time, surveyed the other inhabitants of the room. "Maria, did you give him something to eat?" she asked.

Not wishing any blame to fall on my new friends, I spoke up. "She gave me some of her hippocras."

Maria's doughy face colored. "I was about to order him supper."

For the first time since he had measured himself against me,

Sebastian was no longer looking in the mirror. "He drank very little," he said.

Hendrika ignored him. "No wonder his humors are imbalanced." She firmly took my hand and led me to the door. "Come, child, I will put you to bed."

I did not look at Maria, Sebastian, and Lia as I followed Hendrika out of the sitting room. I realized that I should not have mentioned the hippocras, but I was too tired to figure out how to make amends. Instead, I let Hendrika lead me down the hall to another low-ceilinged chamber, inside of which was a child-sized bed covered with silken pillows and velvet blankets edged with fur. She seemed distracted and offered me no meal, but the hippocras had tempered my hunger anyway, leaving my eyelids heavy and my mind dull. I curled up in the bed, and she blew out the candles. The smell of smoke drifted through the chamber. Hendrika made no motion to leave but instead brushed her fingers against my brow. "Sleep, child," she whispered. "Tomorrow your new life begins."

Chapter 4

For a brief moment, before a bump jars me fully awake, I forget where I am. My arms are no longer fastened behind my back, the bruises on my face do not throb. I am in my bed in Astraveld—the rooster crowing, the dawn light seeping across the sky, my mother singing softly as she teases awake the embers of a fire. I have never seen one of the great cities of the world, never imagined luxuries more rich than a three-week-old kitten dozing in the palm of my hand, never truly known the cruelty of men. But then, as my body awakens, the cold and the pain—and worst of all, the memory of my final days at Coudenberg—return. Astraveld vanishes and, like Prometheus chained to his rock, I once again feel the loss of my innocent self.

There was some small premonition of my fate that first morning at Coudenberg as I awoke from a tender dream of home, my mouth dry and my head sore. For a moment I knew not where I was, perched on top of a mound of silken pillows, the silence putting me in mind of a tomb. But slowly, the events of the previous night came back to me—Maria's spirit-laden hippocras, Lia's memento mori, Hendrika whisking me away—and as I mulled them over, I became aware of footsteps beating a steady rhythm down the hallway toward me. I shrank back, wishing not to see Hendrika.

To my relief, a bowlegged man appeared at the door, a measuring string draped over his shoulders. "Señor Jepp?" he inquired.

His arrival marked the beginning of a most unusual day. Throughout the morning and well into the afternoon, servants visited me at nearly every moment—tailors, cobblers, seamstresses, ladies-in-waiting, valets, and various other figures whose exact duties were a mystery to me. They measured me for knee breeches, linen shirts, buttoned vests, lace ruffs and cuffs, short capes, gloves, and heeled silken slippers; bathed me, washed and curled my hair, scoured my nails, fitted me for plumed hats, altered and realtered the handsome garments that appeared so fast they seemed made by an army of angels rather than by human hands. At the same time, one lady-in-waiting brought me a mild hippocras that banished my headache, while another delivered pears and marzipan on a silver platter. Later there were tender spiced meat pies with flaky crusts that threatened to drift like golden snowflakes onto my new clothes, greatly distressing the tailor.

This symphony of activity was so continuous that I had no opportunity to leave my room or explore my environs. At first, I enjoyed my captivity. I had never had others wait upon me, nor had anyone ever tended so rigorously to my appearance or my appetite. I was struck too by the servants' lack of reaction to my form—they never commented upon its peculiarities or stared agape, even when I was naked. But increasingly, as I was forced to stand, arms out, for minutes on end, or tilt my head this way or that, the production grew tiresome, and I felt restless and eager to explore. The only way I could do so was with my eyes— for a single window in my room overlooked a garden. Even there, nature was not left to its own devices but carefully orchestrated into shapes and colors, classes and types—an orchard of forty stunted pear and apple trees grew in four rows, shrubs were cut and trimmed into geometrical order, water was carefully contained in a string of ornamental ponds.

Though many classes of travelers frequented my mother's inn, we treated them equally. It was in this spirit that I attempted to engage the servants in conversation. But I was surprised to discover that they seemed reluctant to depart from anything but the most basic pleasantries. The task at hand was preparing me for the evening's festivities, and they focused on it with unflagging resolution. As the afternoon wore on, a new set of servants appeared: two men, one thin and one stout, with a dusting of white powder upon their hair and eyelashes. They measured me height-wise and width-wise, and conferred with one another in whispers.

"I see you enjoyed your repast?" the thin one asked, pointing to the empty platter where the spiced meat pie had once lain.

Grateful for a question other than "Too tight?" or "Too loose?" I averred that I had. The man smiled, but to my regret, he readied himself to go and did not carry on the conversation.

As shadows fell over the garden, the activity in my room reached a crescendo. The tailor dressed me in the finest of several outfits sewn that day—a vest and breeches of such blinding yellow that they appeared to be fashioned of pure gold. The cobbler shod my feet in a pair of yellow silken, heeled slippers; the valet adjusted the groomed curls upon my head; the haberdasher combed the ostrich feather atop the hat that he then placed atop my head. And then everyone stood back and viewed me in silence. I felt the urge to laugh but did not want them to construe my mirth as an insult to their efforts. Most of all, I longed to sit down. But before I could take a step toward the small chair that beckoned my aching feet, a commotion erupted.

"The feather is too tall!" exclaimed the thin man with the dusting of white powder who, unbeknownst to me, had reappeared. This set off a flurry of frantic adjustments to the hat, to the great dismay of the haberdasher, a man with a long face and drooping eyes.

And then—after I had almost become accustomed to being the center of this hive of industry—they all left. I hobbled over to the chair, for the slippers pinched my toes, and gratefully sat down. But, at just that moment, Hendrika appeared. Her hair was swept up and elaborately plaited, and she was dressed as a lady of noble birth in a black gown with a white millstone ruff. She nodded approvingly at my own more elaborate transformation, and I imagined her glad to see no longer the country boy who had offended her.

"We must go!" she announced, rousing me to my feet. Behind her a servant wheeled a cart with a large wooden box on top of it. Hendrika removed the box to reveal a small chair. "This is where you will sit for the first part of the evening. You must be concealed, for you are to be a surprise."

"A surprise?"

Hendrika stared at me as if I were daft. "A surprise to the Infanta. But you can watch the others through these holes," she added, pointing to two small circles cut into the box.

I did not care for the idea of being enclosed, but I did not think it wise to object. Hendrika hastily directed me onto the chair, and the box was placed over me. The two holes admitted only a little light, and the air inside was stuffy. The cart began to rumble beneath me. I could see that we were turning into the corridor, and for the second time that day, I was tempted to laugh. I was finally able to leave my room—but in a box and with peepholes far smaller than my room's single window.

The cart stopped moving, and I could hear the bustle of several new attendants. "The servants are now going to carry you down the stairs," Hendrika announced as I felt myself lifted into the air.

I held on to the chair for dear life as the cart dipped and swayed. The spiced meat pie lurched in my stomach. A moment later, I was relieved to feel the wheels of the cart touch down on solid ground. Through my peephole I could see we were in another hall, this one with higher dimensions. The walls were lined with tapestries. Although I could not see her, I could hear Hendrika's shoes click on the marble floor next to me. "A few minutes before you are to be presented to the Infanta, you will be moved to the . . ."

But it was hard to hear her with the rumbling of the cart's wheels.

". . . you must leap up and shout 'Surprise!'"

Before I could ask her more, Hendrika made a loud shushing noise. "Not a word until then."

We continued down the corridor in silence. Legs moved around us. I could hear the swish of ladies' dresses and their laughter, then the bugling of a trumpet. Peering through my peephole, I could see a great arched door and ladies and gentlemen rushing in wearing silken, lace, and gold-embroidered garments much like my own. We followed behind them, starting and stopping. The noise—a cacophony of viols, bells, trumpets, and voices—increased, as did the heat. In my mounting excitement over my very first view of court, I leaned forward, nearly tipping over the box. A hand steadied it and rapped a reprimand against the side.

At last my cart ceased moving, and a clearing permitted me a better vantage point. In the front of the room was a canopy held up by pillars swathed in scarlet cloth embossed with purple leaves. Beneath the canopies were two large wooden thrones upholstered in velvet. In one of them sat a striking dark-haired woman, not old but past the first blush of youth, with a ruff so large and lacy that she resembled a flower. On top of her head was a scarlet pointed headdress decorated with teardrop-shaped black pearls. A large cross on a necklace of white pearls hung down over the golden bodice of her dress, which was embroidered with red and blue flowers in uniform rows. I was so mesmerized by the Infanta's appearance that it took me a moment to notice a third small throne to her left—and Maria, dressed in a similarly large ruff, and black gown, sitting atop it.

To be considered even a minor member of the court was heady enough; but to imagine myself as Maria was, at the Infanta's very side, was exhilarating. I ceased to be aware of my box, liberated by my fantasies of occupying just such a throne, of looking down upon the rest of court. As the courtiers settled into position, I gazed at them: noblemen in fur capes, ladies in black lace cuffs, bishops in long, embroidered copes, envoys from distant lands. Flanking the royal canopy was a score of musicians in matching costume: trumpeters, viol players, lutenists, and a swarthy man with a mandolin, who appeared to direct this mighty ensemble.

At some signal invisible to me, he silenced them, and the crowd's murmur died down to a hush.

A red-haired youth with a mischievous expression trotted into the clearing. After a sweeping bow to the Infanta, he turned to the rest of the court and proclaimed:

> *"A bird that sings and plays the strings*
> *May be the finest of God's things*
> *Most worthy of our Queen's delight*
> *This captured creature of the night."*

At the conclusion of this pretty speech, Robert strode into the chamber. His enormous face was expressionless, and he carried a rounded object draped in cloth that I hastily recognized from its shape and gleaming handle as the golden birdcage. He set it down before the Infanta with a solemn bow and then lumbered to a spot beside the musicians whom he towered over by two heads at least. A high-pitched, eerie voice began to emanate from the cage, and the entire court fell silent to listen to it.

> *"From distant lands I have come*
> *To sing a song of home*
> *Weeping for the love I left*
> *Upon those gentle shores.*
> *I have flown o'er mountains cold,*
> *And forests dark and silent seas,*
> *I fly now captive in this cell,*
> *Till Death erase these memories."*

This song had a profound effect upon me—the plaintive lyrics, the meandering and almost tuneless melody, the disembodied voice. In contrast to it, the bright colors of the court seemed garish; my ambitions of just a moment earlier hollow. I thought of home, of my mother and Willem, and I was filled with a terrible longing for them. Glancing at the faces of the courtiers, I surmised that I was not the only one who was so moved. The song, as it drifted away like smoke, had left behind a common sadness that softened faces and deepened glances, encouraging each and every listener to nurse secret longings. Gradually I became aware of the rising and falling strums of a lute, like a dreamy epilogue.

This brief interlude was followed by the lone, thundering applause of the red-haired young man. His extravagant ovation seemed to make a mockery of the performance. I sensed I was not alone in my annoyance, for at first everyone just stared at him. But as the song's spell abruptly shattered, self-conscious grins crept across the courtiers' faces, and they began to clap too.

As the applause died down, the Infanta addressed the red-haired youth. "What have we here, my dear Pim?"

"Behold the enchanted bird!" Pim declared, whisking the cloth off the birdcage. Inside, wearing green wings fashioned out of feathers, a yellow beak fastened with a string around her head, and holding a tiny lute, was Lia. She shyly smiled at her audience through the golden bars.

The Infanta roundly applauded, laughing merrily at the spectacle. "Release her!" she ordered.

To the cheers of the courtiers, Sebastian rode in on a small white pony. Dismounting his steed, he opened his palm to reveal a key. It was clearly ceremonial—he opened the cage door by undoing a simple latch. Lia stepped out and fluttered her wings to the delight of several ladies, who waved their fans in tandem. With a sweep of his hand to his brow, Pim feigned lightheadedness as he gazed upon her.

The Infanta tapped the toe of her elegant leather shoe on a footstool, beckoning Lia to sit upon it. "Come, my beauty," she said.

"I could have sung a more favorable tune," Sebastian groused. "Her Royal Highness has made a poor choice."

I cringed—certain that Sebastian would be punished for his impertinence. But the Infanta merely laughed. "You can sit at Maria's feet, Sebastian."

"I will not!" said Sebastian, stamping his foot.

"He prefers his ladies tall," stage-whispered Pim.

Though I knew Pim was only performing his duties as jester, his mockery of Sebastian's stature made me wince. Laughter rose up from the Infanta and her courtiers.

"Be quiet, curly-locks, or I will smite you in two!" Sebastian said, glaring first at Pim and then at the crowd. But his threat was only met with more mirth. Turning his back on the audience, he jumped onto the royal platform and clambered up onto the empty throne beside the Infanta's.

"So you shall be my consort, the archduke, while he is away," declared the Infanta playfully.

"And now, Your Royal Highness," declared Pim with a sweeping bow, "we have a surprise for you."

At just this moment, the cart beneath me jerked back to life, and I was wheeled hastily into an anteroom. The box was lifted, and before I even had a chance to breathe fresh air, the stout man with white powder in his hair lifted me up and set me down inside a large metal dish. "What are you . . . ?" I cried out.

But as soon as I saw the thin man carrying the top crust of a pie, I knew.

"On three, leap out," said the thin cook as he deposited this pastry sheet over the dish, entombing me in crust.

There was no time to determine whether I should laugh or cry at this development in my fortunes. Once again, the cart beneath me was on the move. I could hear the muffled murmurs of the crowd as I was wheeled back into the central chamber. Pim—for I was sure it was he—began to count in a theatrical voice. "One . . . Two . . . Three."

For a brief moment, I stayed curled inside my pie, my eyes closed. "Three!" shouted Pim again, his voice no longer playful. Upon this warning note, I jumped. The crust broke over my head to the shouts and applause of the court. I had forgotten what, if anything, I was supposed to say.

Don appeared and bowed obsequiously before the Infanta. "Her Royal Highness is hereby presented with a new dwarf."

The Infanta delightedly clapped her hands. "He's nearly as small as Sebastian," she said, "and just as handsome too!"

"Not so," grumbled Sebastian.

The Infanta ignored him. "What is his name?"

I opened my mouth, but Don cut me off. "Titus Maximus."

"I shall write the archduke all about him!" The Infanta leaned forward on her throne to indicate she was talking directly to me. "Welcome to Coudenberg, Titus Maximus."

In my surprise over my new name, I managed nothing more than a nod.

"Among his many fine attributes, he is also a mute!" Pim declared with a wink at the audience.

"This is his first time at court," said Don. "He has been rendered speechless by the wonders he has beheld."

"Poor dear! Maria," the Infanta ordered, "give Titus Maximus your throne."

Maria stood up, stumbling slightly as she stepped to the side. Don gave me a small push, and I awkwardly climbed the platform stairs and sat atop the throne beside the Infanta. Her Royal Highness smiled down upon me as the courtiers, led by Pim, applauded. I had to force myself to smile back. I could see I had won their affections. But I had lost my name.

Chapter 5

The following morning as I finished my breakfast, an insistent rap sounded on the door of my chamber. I feared it heralded the beginning of a fresh onslaught of tailors and bakers, but when I answered, I found only Pim. "Good day, Titus," he said, and with amiable countenance, sauntered past me into my chamber.

I knew not what to make of this forward behavior and so stood by the door as he took in the view from my single window, snatched a pear from the silver platter that had been delivered to me yesterday morning, and inspected my primer. He was no more than a few years older than I, but he moved with a grown man's confidence, a thick build and a rounded burgher's girth adding to this illusion of years. His eyes—brown but flecked with the feverish orange of his hair—had an impish quality, as if with each blink, he were newly amused by some thought or scheme.

"You are a man of letters," he said, as he paged through my primer.

I assumed he was mocking me and did not reply.

"I do not read myself," he said.

This admission took me aback both in the casual way it was proffered and because I had assumed his quick wit was the result of a learned upbringing.

"My memory is most prodigious," Pim explained, as though he guessed at my surprise. "I grew up in a traveling theater, a child actor. Mine is an education of the road."

"Why are you not still upon it?" I asked.

I feared my question impudent, but Pim seemed pleased to have drawn me out. He wedged himself into my armchair.

"The particulars of my temperament are better suited for comedy than tragedy. I care little for the latter."

"Is there no tragedy at Coudenberg?"

Pim laughed. "There is no tragedy for me. And one hopes for you neither."

I recalled the warning note in Pim's voice the previous eve when I did not jump upon his order, and felt I was hearing its echo. "What exactly is your position here?" I asked, trying to determine as politely as I could his intentions.

But though I thought my question benign, Pim's smile dissolved into a long frown. "I am tasked with seeing that the Infanta is amused. Beyond this chore, I serve no master and care not to play one. I have simply come to welcome you to Coudenberg."

Pim's sense of offense seemed so genuine that I wondered if I had perceived ill will where none was intended. I felt ashamed then of my uncharitable greeting and tried to dismiss my wariness—ignoring the whispers of my intuition. "Well then, this is most kind."

Pim accepted my words with a forgiving nod. "Where are you from?"

I welcomed this interest for, in truth, I was lonely and eager to speak of home.

"A small village outside Utrecht," I replied. "My mother has an inn there."

As I spoke, Pim thrust out his black-heeled boots, assuming a posture of leisure made preposterous by my ill-fitting chair. "You and I are much alike."

I could not help commenting upon this. "My chair begs to differ."

Pim's orange-specked eyes regained their merry fire. "Ignore its groans as it bears witness to my argument," he countered.

I grinned. "Let us put this jest behind us."

My own mood had lightened considerably by this time, buoyed by our verbal jousting and Pim's evident appreciation of my wit. I even began to feel sympathy for this churlish figure whose labors mocking others must have made him unlikable.

Perhaps my growing ease emboldened Pim, for when he next spoke it was more pointed. "Now, Titus, your wit may not outstrip mine. I am first among all in the art of tongue-lashing. Win your laurels in some other sport such as tongue-tying—I believe you showed a native talent for that the other night."

This stinging allusion to my previous evening's performance reminded me that Pim was no certain friend. He must have noticed my hesitation return, for he laughed as if to show he meant no malice. "No, I am glad you have come, for my sense is that you are much like me. Neither of us belongs here, but we deserve this life more than those who were born to it."

I would not so easily allow Pim back into my good graces. "Perhaps you, with your talents," I said coolly.

"Everyone has talents, Jepp. Yours may be other than wit. You will discover them."

I was caught off-guard by his use of my true name. I had not even been aware that Pim knew it, but it added a measure of sincerity to his words.

He dislodged himself from my chair and rose. "You have a lovely view of the orchards," he said, as he passed my window. "Remember to enjoy Coudenberg. For so long as you prove your value here, you are free to do as you like."

After Pim departed, I wondered exactly what he meant by my value: did it lie in jumping out of pies for the Infanta's pleasure, or in something more? But, despite this uncertainty, his counsel reawakened in me the sense of possibility that Coudenberg had first inspired. For if a figure as humble in origin as Pim could prosper here, so, I allowed, could I. I resolved to set aside my uncertainties about life as a court dwarf and enjoy the freedoms I believed Pim had promised.

I quickly discovered that Coudenberg offered many opportunities for self-improvement. As prized members of the court, Lia, Sebastian, Maria, and I were encouraged to develop our talents. Lacking any in music or art, I was assigned a tutor to further my education. His name was Master Kees, and he was a rheumy-eyed and kindly old man. I remember still the first time he brought me to the court library. As Don had promised, this grand room was filled floor to ceiling with volumes from across the ages. Each book seemed to me a treasure—a conversation through time, a journey to foreign lands, an answer to some mystery of existence—and I felt amazed that all of this wisdom was mine for the taking. As the days passed, I spent many hours there—devouring these volumes with an insatiable hunger.

Master Kees took pleasure in my appetite for learning and sought to broaden my palate by teaching me Latin and Greek. I had an innate talent for these ancient languages, and my swift progress began to unlock more of the volumes on the library's shelves. As it did, my tutor introduced me to the studies of mathematics and science. From him I learned that the heavens—the planets and sun—revolve around the earth, God's most beloved creation. I learned to calculate the date upon which Easter falls and to distinguish the chief constellations. I learned about the effects of eclipses and comets upon history and the affairs of men.

Master Kees even told me something of my own history. From him, I learned that as long as there have been courts, there have been dwarfs collected and prized by the monarchs who ruled them. The Ancient Egyptian kings kept dwarfs, as did the emperors of ancient China. A century ago, Isabella d'Este, marchioness of Mantua, who owned vast collections of classical writings and paintings, also collected dozens of dwarfs at her court, sending her favorites to family and friends as gifts. Of all the European courts, Master Kees related, the French and Russian treated their dwarfs most cruelly—mocking them and locking them up lest they escape.

From this I concluded that life for dwarfs at Coudenberg was better than at most courts. We were permitted to roam the palace and grounds freely; we were fed abundantly to the point that my new garments had to be let out more than once; we were treated fondly by the Infanta, who even commissioned a portrait of herself with Lia, whom she favored and often requested in the evenings at her bedside. Indeed, Don's promises were largely true. Diplomats and high officials readily conversed with us, and the court painter allowed us into his studio, where Sebastian was a favorite model. We were welcome at any and all court functions.

I was even—in a fashion—able to preserve my name. Though at court I was Titus Maximus (a name I constantly had to remind myself to respond to), to Maria, Sebastian, and Lia, I was still Jepp. There was never any discussion of this decision, just as there was never any discussion of the weekly humiliations we were expected to suffer—performing acrobatics or engaging in mock weddings, dancing upon tables or donning the costumes of beasts or birds. Before these performances, Pim would pay us a visit wherein he would inform us of the Infanta's newest fancy and coach us in how to bring it to life. He was most masterful at the art of stagecraft and directed our ensemble—especially Lia, our most gifted player—with a shrewd eye. Though I struggled to remember cues and showed little skill at music or dance, he patiently instructed me. In the beginning, Hendrika assisted him at these rehearsals; but my bumbling efforts seemed only to vex her, and she soon left the duty of training us solely to Pim.

If there was any shadow upon me those first weeks at Coudenberg, it was cast by Hendrika. She occupied a chamber in our quarters and, although she emerged from it mainly to issue the Infanta's orders, I twice caught her spying upon us in the sitting room, her stern gaze fixed upon me. I had the distinct impression that, as a woman of high birth, she thought me unworthy of court life and was waiting for me to make some grievous error that would prove this.

But the company of my peers made it easy for me to forget Hendrika's inhospitable manner. Although Maria, Sebastian, Lia, and I had free rein of the palace, many nights we chose to spend together in our sitting room. So long as there was no sign of Hendrika, Robert would join us, hulking in the corner as he tuned Lia's lute or mended its strings. He lived in another part of the palace, alone, and for this I pitied him.

Our gatherings were gay. With her decanter of bitter hippocras, Maria was a lively raconteur. In her youth, she had served at several other courts: she told tales of their histories and intrigues and shared gossip about the courtiers in our own. From her I learned that, despite Don's grand airs, it was his elder brother, who had died the previous spring, who had possessed the title and riches. I learned that Pim carried on dalliances with the servant girls, and that Hendrika had been a lady-in-waiting from a noble Brussels family. She had refused to marry—reputedly choosing between tending to us dwarfs and the convent—but was not, Maria whispered, the virtuous old maid she seemed. Sebastian tried to pry more out of her, but Maria, with a devilish smile and wink at me, refused. I was relieved, for I did not care to imagine that joyless woman in the arms of some aging secretary or captain of the guard.

Some nights, Maria would tell us about others the Infanta had once collected—a three-armed Austrian woman, a man from Poland who was just a head. The man who was just a head, she explained, was tied to a wooden pole, upon which he would chatter and sing for the courtiers as if on a pike. The woman with three arms was an expert juggler. But one night, the man who was just a head rolled onto a cart of cabbage leaving the palace and escaped. The three-armed woman, who had been secretly in love with him, strangled herself—one arm squeezing her neck, the other holding down the struggling third arm.

I quickly realized that these stories were untrue, and yet they were among my favorites. Sebastian and Lia oft requested them as well. It was oddly comforting to imagine deformities and humiliations worse than our own. Laughing at the image of the three-armed woman strangling herself, we felt bound by a common understanding of our condition that I knew I could never find among the people dear to me in Astraveld. And so I might have settled into this life, grown fat on meat pies and wise in ancient tongues, accustomed even to my new name, were it not for what happened with Lia.

Chapter 6

Lia's story leads here, to this wretched coach that races through night and day, as if driven by the Devil himself. Though the driver makes haste, I know not where. Twice, we stop to change horses, but wooden slats obscure the view, and my hands are bound behind my back so I cannot lift them. I must travel onward in ignorance, my wrists chafing, my gut gnawing upon itself. But if I am to be kept alive, I know my circumstances must soon change. I counsel myself to stay vigilant so that when they do, I may gather clues to my destination and perhaps even escape.

On the second night of my journey, the coach rolls to a stop and my door opens. Standing before me is the hefty, red-faced driver. He unties the rope binding my hands and goads me out of the coach with the end of his whip. But I see no more than a pair of mud-covered wheels and a sliver of star-speckled sky before he shoves me into a cage and tosses a horse blanket over it. He carries me inside and procures a room speedily—for I know I must be the object of some curiosity—then sets the cage down on the floor with a clatter.

A moment later, he relieves himself loudly. Then I hear him depart and lock the door behind him. I rub my wrists for the first time in two days. My mouth is parched, but the cage is warm beneath the blanket. Thankful for this comfort, I lie on my side and slumber.

I am awakened by the sound of footsteps. As the driver draws the blanket from my cage and holds a candle to my face, the sharp vapor of drink fills the air. Yet it is he who wrinkles his nose. "Take off those rags," he orders.

He watches as I disrobe, gaping at my form.

"Cursed creature," he says, and shoves a blanket through the door. As I cover myself hastily, he takes from his pocket a half loaf of bread and tosses it into the cage. He follows this with a mug of watery ale. Whilst I tear at this meager supper, he fishes out my once fine traveling costume, now soiled and ruined, and departs with it. After some trouble born of too much drink, he locks the door behind him.

With the blanket drawn up, I can now inspect the cell that holds me captive, but there are no clues to be gleaned from its simple straw pallet and dusty floors. There is only the sharp stab of memory, for my mother's inn had travelers' berths much like this one. But it is how this room differs that pains me most—the smell more of hay than hops, the floorboards lacking the knots and swirls that my mother claimed were the marks of fairies. So small—and yet so exact—are the comforts of home.

I have barely digested my bread, never mind these musings, when the driver returns. Without a word, he blows out his candle and collapses onto his pallet. Before I can formulate the proper question about my fate, or even that of my only garments, he buzzes with snores. I curl up inside my cage and try to join him in this slumber, but the bread and ale have revived me. I cannot help but think of Lia and the night, when in a humor much like this one, I began to write a letter home.

It was early one evening, as a late winter storm battered the palace, that I positioned one of the small chairs in our sitting room in front of the fire and took up paper and quill. In my first couple of months at Coudenberg, I had written my mother several letters detailing the wonders and luxuries of palace life— though I omitted my labors of dressing in indecorous costumes and jumping out of pies—and received in return one of a most loving nature in Willem's hand and my mother's voice. But since then, for reasons I could not quite explain, I had become a less diligent correspondent.

That evening, however, seemed to present a perfect opportunity to rectify my lapse in filial duty. I was alone, for Maria was distempered with headache, Sebastian's company had been requested by the Infanta, and Lia and Robert were off together. This moment of solitude was a rare one, and it provoked in me thoughts both sad and sweet of home and the distance I had traveled from it in soul as well as body. For a long time my quill rested on the paper as I stared into the flame, unsure how to put these emotions into words.

I was so preoccupied that until I heard the grating of a chair against the floor, I was unaware I had company.

"I thought I would sit by the fire too," Lia said in Dutch, catching my eye from behind the chair. "My presence won't disturb you?"

I rushed to reassure her in our native tongue—"Not at all"—and scrambled down to help her position her chair beside mine.

I had never until that time been alone with Lia, though I often found myself wishing that such an opportunity would arise. I envied Robert her attentions. With the rest of us, Lia wore her shy smile like a mask, revealing nothing except through her music and the memento mori she arranged and sketched. I longed to pierce her reticence, but I felt plagued by it myself as we sat silently side by side.

It was Lia who spoke first. "To whom do you write?"

I looked at the empty sheet in my hands. My letter suddenly seemed inconsequential. "My mother."

I had spoken freely of her and my life in Astraveld, a topic that tired Maria, who had no patience for rustic life. But Lia had always smiled at my tales.

"That is good, Jepp. I imagine she wishes to hear from you."

These words pricked my conscience.

"Do you correspond with your family?" I asked.

I knew Lia had come from a city farther north, and like me, had never been part of a court before. But that was all. She never spoke of her life before Coudenberg.

She shook her head. "I do not write."

"I can write for you," I eagerly offered. I imagined serving as her secretary, our friendship deepening, as we spent several hours each week alone.

"It is not necessary," she said.

I was not sure what to make of this response—whether I had misunderstood and she could indeed write herself or whether, like Maria, she did not care to correspond with her family. But before I could ask her more, she smiled and said, "Do you like Coudenberg?"

The blunt way she introduced this topic made me realize how much she wished to abandon the previous one. Though my curiosity was piqued, I felt eager to oblige her. "Everything but the pie."

I instantly regretted making mention of the forbidden topic of our indignities, but she rewarded me with a high-pitched giggle.

"Do you?" I asked, regaining my customary boldness.

"Everything but the cage," she said.

We grinned at each other. I was surprised not only by her wit, which she normally concealed, but by her candor. As the fire crackled before us, I found myself speaking freely to her.

"It is most strange here."

"You have just noticed this?"

Lia smiled, but her eyes did not. She stared into the fire. "There are ways to survive here, Jepp. Shall I tell you?"

I nodded eagerly.

"Do not anger Hendrika."

"I fear she does not care for me," I confessed.

"She takes her duties of overseeing us most seriously. Luckily, since your arrival, she has stayed away. But she was in a foul temper before it."

"What else?"

"Do not take Maria's hippocras, which she taints with powerful spirits and potions. Even a thimbleful."

"Unless she offers it."

"Especially if she offers it." Lia's eyes crinkled with mirth, reminding me briefly of my mother.

"And Sebastian?"

"He will rail at you no matter what you do, but never mind it. He can speak freely here."

"So I have noticed," I said, trying not to betray my envy. "Why is he permitted this privilege?"

"This is no privilege," Lia corrected. "He is not taken seriously. That is why he can say what he wishes. The Infanta considers him a clown."

"Like Pim?"

Lia shook her head most vehemently. "Pim is no clown."

"I am not sure what to make of him."

Lia stared into the fire, her expression stern. "If you dislike him, you must not show it. He is a great favorite of the Infanta's."

Thinking her envious, I rushed to reassure her. "As are you."

"I am a smaller favorite," she said softly.

"I'm afraid there is no altering that."

Lia laughed, and I felt pleased to have revived her good humor.

"And what of the Infanta?"

Lia shrugged as if this topic held little interest. "Her fancies are our own."

"What do you mean?"

"She wishes a bird in a cage who sings in a human voice, or a living pie, and it is we who must become them."

"Even if it is the Infanta's fancy, your song is most beautiful."

I felt myself blushing, for I was not practiced at delivering such compliments to a girl.

Lia looked down demurely into the folds of her dress. "The song is mine. I composed it."

"Then you are indeed a song bird!"

Lia shook her head. "I am merely fortunate that it pleases the Infanta."

Her modesty made my confidence grow. "It pleases us all," I proclaimed.

Perhaps it was the fire, but Lia's face had colored most prettily. "You sound like Robert."

I did not care to be compared to Robert but smiled as if this were handsome praise.

"He is fearsome in appearance but not demeanor," Lia said. She caught my eye and frowned. "He is treated more cruelly than us, for people fear him. But he is the kindest soul here—kind even to those who mock him."

"He can afford to be so when no cage can hold him," I quipped.

Lia barely seemed to hear me, so lost was she in her enthusiasms for Robert.

"It is you who are kind," I said, wishing not to dwell on Robert's virtues. "Offering me your guidance—"

"I hope it may be of some use but I fear I have distracted you from your task." Lia abruptly stood up. "You must finish your letter."

"I can do so tomorrow," I protested. "Please stay."

Lia shook her dainty head. Despite her size, the gesture was firm, hinting at a stubbornness I would later come to know. "Good night, Jepp."

After Lia departed, I did not follow her instruction and return to my letter but instead stared into the fire, reflecting upon our conversation. That Lia shared my uncertainties about Coudenberg, that we had voiced them together, made me feel close to her in a way I had felt with no one since my arrival.

But with the others usually about, the chance that we would be soon afforded the same solitude to share our thoughts again was slim. This I could not accept. As I retired to bed, I wondered if I might summon the courage to ask Lia to join me on a walk through the palace. Little did I know that Lia and I would soon be thrust together in a way that would change both of our lives forever.

Chapter
7

A few days after I had spoken with Lia by the fire, Maria, Sebastian, Lia, and I were engaged in a discussion of oysters, a dish that Sebastian and I extolled but that the ladies found wanting, when Pim sauntered into our sitting room.

Since his initial visit to my chamber some three months earlier, Pim had not sought out my company nor showed me any special consideration based on our conversation. For this I was mostly relieved. As much as I admired Pim's lightning wit and independence of spirit, I was not sure I wanted the mantle of being his favorite, especially since Lia did not seem to care for him.

As was his habit, Pim joined our conversation as if he were already a part of it. Plucking an apple from our platter, he petted

Lia's head, and said, "Oysters are most succulent."

Pim often touched us during our rehearsals—moving us about by the shoulders or placing a hand upon our heads, then removing it, like a chess player considering among pawns. But this caress discomfited me—for I saw the brief pucker of Lia's lips, the bitterness caught and swallowed, as if she had just tasted a despised oyster. She composed herself quickly, though, and I wondered if I had misjudged her reaction, for the others seemed to pay no heed.

"One more for our side!" Sebastian replied jauntily.

"Not fair," Maria said, with an exaggerated pout.

"Doubly fair," Pim said. "For in this company, I am worth two votes."

"Nonsense," said Maria.

"We hereby anoint His Majesty, Oyster, as king," Pim said. "Hurrah! Now, onto some business."

Pim paused for dramatic effect—biting into his apple—as he scanned our faces. "The Infanta wishes a dance recital in miniature," he said as he chewed. "I have been appointed to play dance master and teach the small couple a new series of steps that have become popular in France."

"Very well," said Sebastian, standing and adjusting his hat with a peeved look. "Though I see not why I can't just lead Lia in the pavane."

"Not you," Pim said. "Titus."

Sebastian glared at Pim. "Jepp! Is the dance to be performed atop a pie?"

Pim ignored Sebastian. "Titus and Lia will meet with me starting today at noon in the dance hall."

Sebastian continued to grumble, but I felt emotions of a more confusing variety. The thought of taking Lia's small hands in my own filled me with pleasure. I also hoped that the lessons would serve as occasion to further our friendship apart from the others. But I did not trust Pim, and wondered why he had chosen me, so unschooled in the art of dance, to be Lia's partner. I looked to Lia but could make out no reaction, for she had retreated to her paper and chalk. After Pim departed, the presence of the others prevented me from voicing these doubts. But even if I had had the chance, I might not have questioned our assignment for fear of losing the chance to be alone with Lia.

As the pendulum of the clock in our chambers swung to and fro, my own heart beat anxiously. At last, shortly before noon, I suggested to Lia that we make our way to the dance hall. With a sigh, she placed her drawing into her notebook, bound it with string, and readied herself to go.

"Good luck, Jepp," Maria said, tipping her goblet with an amused grin.

Sebastian did not turn from his mirror, into which he glowered.

Lia and I made our way in silence to the main hall of the palace, stopping often to curtsy and bow to passing courtiers. In between these encounters, her mien was most serious. Though I suspected that it was Pim who troubled her, I could not abandon a more selfish fear, and finally blurted out my true sentiments.

"You wish not to have me as a dance partner," I said. "This I understand. I am not gifted. But I will make every effort—"

Lia touched my hand and, in my surprise, I nearly stumbled over my feet. "This is nonsense, Jepp. I am pleased to have you as my partner." With a smile, she confided, "Sebastian fancies himself a fine dancer, but he is most abrupt in his motions."

"And in his moods," I added.

Lia gave me a knowing look, and I felt the return of the clever girl I had met by the fire.

"Why do you think Pim has chosen me?"

"I do not know." Lia shrugged as if this question little concerned her, but she could not disguise the uneasiness in her voice.

I considered whether to mention the sensitive matter of Pim's caress, but before I could figure out how to broach it, we had reached the dance hall, a large room lined with tapestries. It was not uncommon to find musicians or actors at practice there, but the midday meal was being served then, so this chamber was abandoned.

As we entered, Pim appeared, seemingly stepping out of a tapestry of a royal hunting party.

"There you are," he said. In his hands was a small viol. "The musicians are otherwise engaged," he said by way of explanation.

He began to fiddle a jaunty riff, stopping in front of Lia and dipping his bow playfully toward her. A strand of her blond hair nearly caught in the bow, and she drew back as it flew out of harm's way. Though Pim's serenade was not yet complete, I began to applaud heartily to remind him of my presence.

Pim lowered his bow and turned to face me. "Ah, Titus," he said, as if noticing me for the first time.

"I never knew that you possessed such talent," I said, hoping to distract him with my banter.

"A life on stage teaches many talents, some of which I keep secret. Though the Infanta of course knows the full range of instruments upon which I play."

Pim laughed merrily. Though I did not, in my innocence, fully understand his meaning, the color rising in Lia's cheeks told me that it was bawdy in nature.

"May we begin our instruction?" Lia asked curtly.

"Indeed," said Pim with an agreeable grin. "Let us first learn the steps, and then I will supply the tune."

Our footsteps echoed as we strode to the center of the floor. Pim locked the doors and then followed. "We wish no one to see the dance till it is well rehearsed," he said.

I did not relish this enclosure and looked to Lia for confirmation that she shared my unease; but she seemed distant now and did not meet my gaze.

At first, Pim treated our lesson most seriously. He pranced before us, demonstrating the three springing steps, the hop, and turn that formed the basis of the new dance. As we tried to mimic these motions, he trailed after us; and his hands fell often upon my shoulders or Lia's, directing us in our efforts.

I had barely mastered these simple steps when he once again took up his viol and began to play. As I blundered through the dance, I kept expecting him to stop and correct me. But he focused his attention solely on Lia, though her steps were in little need of improvement. Her carriage erect but without the taut posturing that signals effort, she moved with an exquisite grace. When not nestled in mine, her tiny hands waved in time to the strains of the viol. As she turned, her long blond tresses swung about her; and where she stopped, silence itself seemed to gather as if waiting for her to take flight again. I quickly realized that I could have stood as still as stone and, so long as Lia moved about me, I would have seemed a fine dancer.

Pim never did press me to master my steps, reviewing them at the conclusion of our lesson in but a cursory way. This lapse in his theatrical standards added to the troubled impression I had formed of the lesson and his intentions toward Lia. Still, I figured that as our performance neared, he would be forced to turn his attention away from her and to my graceless efforts.

Lia and I did not discuss any of this as we walked back to our quarters. I did not wish to discomfort her or needlessly stoke her fears. But I felt I must speak to her.

"It is fortunate that your performance will blot out mine," I said, trying to give her cheer.

Lia spoke softly. "The fortune may be more yours than mine."

In such a way, the matter was broached. But before I could come up with a suitable response, Robert appeared, loping from the direction of our quarters and carrying Lia's lute. He looked most relieved to see her, and I greeted him warmly; though, in truth, I felt no such amiable response.

That night I retired to bed early, but memories of the dance lesson prevented me from falling asleep. Like seeds borne by the wind, thoughts of Lia swirled through my head. When I finally did succumb to slumber, these fancies sprouted into dreams, and nightmares—Lia and me dancing by my mother's inn in Astraveld; Lia and me inside a pie as Pim tried to cut and serve it; Robert crushing a fly in his hand, except that it wasn't a fly but me.

I woke with a start. As my consciousness returned, I had the feeling that there was someone in my room. I peered into the darkness. Just as I was about to dismiss my fear as fantasy, I saw her. It was Hendrika, wedged into the small chair in the corner, her spindly figure hunched and distorted. Her bony white feet were illuminated by moonlight through the window, and her dark hair snaked in a girlish braid down her nightdress. She stared out into the night as if under some trance of memory or longing. Afraid that her gaze would fall upon me, I closed my eyes, willing her away.

In the morning, the room was empty, and I concluded this fearful apparition must have also been a dream.

Chapter 8

From my present nightmare, I cannot awake. When I open my eyes, the driver is crouched before my cage, unfastening the lock. Though it is still dark, the contours of our cell are beginning to emerge, and I can hear a rooster outside trumpeting the dawn. The driver tosses something at me, and I flinch before I realize that it is my garments. They are clean and faintly damp, as if laundered by the dew.

A heel of bread follows and, as I gnaw upon it, I feel most grateful toward my captor. But then I remember I am still in a cage, that my face is mottled with bruises, that I am being ferried against my will to a destination unknown. I scold myself for falling into the docile habits of Coudenberg and resolve to stay sharp—and ready for escape—in the hopes that my fortunes may continue to improve.

And, thankfully, they do. A few minutes later, the driver covers my cage with a blanket and carries it out of the inn into the chill winter morn. He sets it inside the coach, springs the door, and orders me to crawl out. But though I expect him to be waiting with a rope to bind my hands, he carries none. Knowing not whether this is by accident or on purpose, I tuck my hands behind me so as not to draw attention to their freedom. The driver, not seeming to notice, slams the door. As soon as the coach sways, signaling he is mounting his seat, I gently take a small, spiral seashell out of my pocket and clasp it to my breast. Then I try the doors, but find they are locked. Still, I can pull up the wooden window slats and, for the first time, gaze out at the surrounding country.

The inn, as I had pictured in my mind, is thatch-roofed and small. Swine mill outside in the dirty snow, and a few thin curs slink around them. A peasant girl carrying a pail has stopped to watch my coach, her breath blooming white in the frozen air. I wonder if she saw my cage and is dreaming of what is inside it—a magical songbird, perhaps, or a fairy king, certainly not a boy as humble and forlorn as she.

I am but the dream of a dawn moment, for the coach starts up, speeding quickly past the girl and the inn. We pass the rest of the town—more thatched houses, a dirt square, a frozen canal, a stone church with a bell tower that gives little hint of whether it is Catholic or Calvinist. But though the church does not aid me in my search, the heavens do; for as the sky lightens behind the bell tower, I realize that we are heading into the rising sun at an angle that suggests our course is toward the northeast.

This intelligence is meager, and yet it comforts me greatly. To know where I am—relative to the sun, to the stars, to the edges of the earth—gives me faith that I won't disappear into nothingness. I know, too, that I am not headed for Spain, the Infanta's cruel and mighty birthplace. And though I am certain that Astraveld now lies south of me, I find solace in the fact that on those first wretched nights of my journey, I must have passed near my mother and home.

The flat sweep of snow-covered fields, the dun-colored windmills, the spindly trees lining the frozen roads reveal no more. And yet I am momentarily comforted, for now it is not only my heart that knows the way home.

There was nothing to comfort me or assuage my unease at our second lesson: as Lia danced and I stumbled alongside her, Pim continued to show little interest in my progress. His attentions were fixed solely on Lia, whom he stopped twice, once to adjust the velvet bow atop one of her heels, another time to refasten a silk rose that had fallen from her hair. Lia accepted these ministrations dutifully, though her eyes darted about like those of some innocent beast in a trap.

It was as Pim's fingers were knuckle deep in Lia's hair affixing the rose that I decided something had to be done.

"What about me?" I said, affecting Sebastian's insouciant manner. "I have little skill, and yet you barely instruct me at all."

Pim looked over at me in surprise. "You complain because I give you no labors?"

"I will look like a fool beside her," I said, pointing at Lia as if I envied her Pim's attentions. "You must instruct me!"

Pim laughed. "But how then will I preserve your natural lack of talent? Truly, Jepp, if I had wanted Lia to have an able partner, I would have selected Sebastian."

It was then that I realized that I had been consigned a comic role in this nouveau dance—a left-footed foil to Lia whom Pim would mock during our performance. Pim turned back to her, but his words continued to sting. I felt cruelly used. Pim's revelation kindled in me a spirit of rebellion, one further inflamed by the liberties I had seen him take with Lia.

On the walk back to our quarters, I turned to Lia and pleaded with her to instruct me in secret. "Let us make Pim feel like the fool! He will expect one act and get another."

Lia's eyes narrowed with the larking smile I had nearly forgotten she could summon. "It is a tempting scheme."

"Then say yes."

"What if he tells the Infanta?"

"The Infanta will be amused by our cunning. And so long as we amuse her, we can do as we like. Pim told me so himself."

Lia hesitated.

"It is not right what he does to you," I whispered.

She stared at me. Then she took my hand and silently led me to her room.

I had never been inside it before. It was much like mine—low-ceilinged, lit by a single window and fitted with a small, canopied bed and proportional furnishings—save for one difference. Upon a rounded table with peg legs were Lia's models—the fruits, dead insects, flowers, shells, and bones that she arranged for her memento mori. Though I knew that they were supposed to be a reminder of death, they teemed with life, of the sea and field, of the earth and sky, as though Lia had grown a garden of the world's delights.

But the greatest delight of all was Lia's instruction. For once she had closed the door, she led me, with great vigor, through the dance, gently correcting my errors. Of these there was no shortage. My arms were slack, my tempo slow, my eyes cast down upon the floor instead of up at her. I tried to remedy these flaws as she named them, but all I could think of was the touch of her hand, the first that did not belong to a child and yet still snugly fit into my own. I felt a part of me awaken that belonged not to the world of manners but to the objects upon the table, an urge of the flesh that both enraptured and shamed me. This distraction further confounded my wayward limbs.

"Close your eyes," Lia commanded.

I feared that in my blindness I would tread on her delicate feet—shod in their silken heels with velvet bows—but even more I feared her discovering my discomposure. So I closed my eyes and tried to succumb to the rhythm of her step. I stumbled, but she caught me with surprising strength and righted me.

"There now," she said, in a tender voice. "You didn't fall."

My face burned. "Only because you caught me."

"You will catch me in return."

This comment did not then strike me as prophetic, but it nevertheless stayed with me, for kindness seemed a rare debt to owe at Coudenberg. For a brief moment, as I envisioned catching Lia in return, my feet moved unthinking and my form felt in harmony with the space around it.

"You have it, Jepp!" Lia said.

She danced me over to the rounded table, where she released my hand and picked up a small, orange seashell from her memento mori.

"Here," she said, handing it to me. "By this, you may remember the moment of your triumph."

I took the shell in my hand, wondering at its construction. It was spiny outside, with what looked to be delicate stone thorns, but was smooth as glass within.

"Surely you need it for your drawings?" I said, though I wished never to part with this gift, which seemed a token less of my triumph than of her affection.

"I have others," she said, pressing my hand around the shell.

This seashell was not the only thing that bound me to her. We now shared a secret, one we carefully concealed from Pim. During his lessons, I would stumble about, feigning such incompetence that Lia would cough to disguise her amusement. Once his lessons were over, we conducted our own. Twice, Pim announced that our performance had been postponed according to the Infanta's whim, yet he continued to rehearse us. But this did not trouble me. So long as Pim's lessons continued, so did Lia's. I wished them never to end.

With Lia as my tutor, the French dance soon became as natural to me as walking. Lia even added little variations and, with each turn and bow, our rebellion seemed to fade in importance. We no longer danced to deceive Pim—or even to please the Infanta—but perhaps, most rebelliously of all, for ourselves.

Chapter 9

When I had first arrived at Coudenberg the previous fall, the palace had seemed to me as large as the universe and with as many wonders. But as winter progressed, this universe shrank till everything wondrous was contained in Lia. This is the power of love—to capture all that is precious and good in a single soul.

In the first blush of love, I did not doubt that Lia would someday be mine, that I would catch her when she fell. For I soon had faith not only in the constancy of my devotion but in the prophecies of the stars. One evening, Don arrived at our quarters bearing a satchel and, with much fanfare, gathered us around. "I have had an astrologer of great renown draw up your horoscopes. Thereby you may know what fortune smiles down upon you."

This occasioned in all of us much excitement and speculation. Even Sebastian, who averred that he was nothing like his sun sign of Sagittarius and thought the stars a poor window into his soul, showed curiosity in the scrolls that Don unloaded from his satchel. "Even if you have had a star chart made up before, the accuracy of these will astound you," Don said, handing the first scroll to Maria.

Maria, a great devotee of the astrologer's art, possessed a star chart that had been devised for her at the Spanish court. She peered at it often, especially after having had her fill of hippocras. Perhaps dissatisfied with what she saw there, she seemed glad for another. Don gave Lia and then Sebastian their scrolls next, and they took to quietly studying them. Turning the satchel inside out, he pulled out the final two. "This one—" he said, unrolling it briefly, "is for Titus Maximus."

The name, as it still had a habit of doing, jarred me, and I almost imagined that the fortune—drawn up under this false appellation—could not be my own. "Who is the other for?" I asked.

Don looked upon me strangely. "It is for you as well, Jepp. But it is a copy for me." With that, he returned it to the satchel.

I was unsure whether I should be flattered that Don wanted a copy of my fortune or troubled by his interest. There were no other scrolls, indicating that he had made no copies of the others' horoscopes. But as with many happenings at Coudenberg that did not entirely make sense, I chose not to dwell upon it and unrolled my chart instead.

Master Kees had tutored me in the basics of astrology, showing me the charts of several great kings. Each consisted of overlapping squares marked with ancient symbols that represented the planets and their placement in the cosmos on the day of the sovereign's birth. The chart I unfurled was different in design—instead of squares, there was but a single wheel portioned into even pieces like a pie. In the innermost core someone had written the date and place of my birth (February 17, 1583, Astraveld, Utrecht province), and around this were interlapping lines that formed triangles and squares. Some of these lines were marked with symbols, a number of which I could recognize—the sun cross of Earth, the sliver of a new moon—others of a more mysterious nature that were scattered along the edges of the pie. In the lower corner of the scroll the astrologer had written in Latin, *Suspiciendo despicio*, which I knew from my studies meant "By looking up I see downward." But I could translate few of his tidings.

"Jupiter conjunct Mercury," noted Don, who had leaned over me to offer his services as interpreter. He laughed. "This explains why you like to gab."

I did not care for this estimation and sought to direct Don to more favorable interpretations. "How about my prospects for fortune?"

"Leo is lord of the second house. You will most certainly have riches, for you have the support of powerful allies."

I was eager for the others to hear this lofty prophecy, but being more skilled in reading heavenly tidings, they were still immersed in their own scrolls.

"My brother had this aspect as well," Don mused. "He was a Taurus, sign of the bull. His chart was blessed in every way. Like yours."

This struck me as most flattering for, from Maria's gossip, I knew Don's brother to be a man of great power and wealth. But before I could take pride in such a comparison, Hendrika, who unbeknownst to me had entered the sitting room, stared glumly over my shoulder.

"Jepp's nativity is no doubt less fortunate," she remarked.

This jab at my humble beginnings infuriated me, but before I could defend my mother and home, Don bristled as if offended for us both. "This is a true Capricorn, Titus," he said, speaking of Hendrika as if she were not with us. "Always dark in spirit."

Then he turned to look up at her. "I have already given you your horoscope, have I not?"

"It fails to interest me," Hendrika said.

"Well, do not become overly interested in others," Don said.

Then he turned back to me and began to trace a square on my chart, his expression most serious. "Now, it is true that the influences of home constrain you, Jepp. You must not allow your attachment to home and mother to interfere with your future."

It pains me to recall how I nodded dutifully, pretending to agree with this poor counsel. In my defense, my mind was elsewhere, for there was yet another topic that I longed for the stars to advise me on.

"How about matters of the heart?" I asked more quietly as Hendrika drifted away.

Don's good humor returned, and he winked at me. "Jupiter rules the seventh house. You will make a good marriage to one helpful and true."

I was even more pleased by this than by the propitious news of my future wealth. For I was certain that the object of this luck in love was Lia.

Chapter
10

It has been two days since my hands were released. By now I am convinced that this was no slip, as the driver has not retied them. But I am still nightly imprisoned in my cage, and the coach doors are always locked. The driver does not look at me while he does these things, and I wonder if he is ashamed to treat another of God's creatures so, even one as strange in form as me. But it is hard to tell, for he is laconic and often altered by drink, with powerful hands and a nose as bulbous as a pile of stones.

One night, as we are stopped at a tavern, the driver returns to our room from the inn, opens my cage door, and slams down a bowl of porridge. "Couldn't finish it myself," he mumbles gruffly.

The porridge raises my hopes. I want to devour it, but I hold back, sensing an opportunity in this brief interlude of kindness. "Please. What is your name?"

The driver takes a step toward me, his eyes bloodshot. I shrink back in my cage, holding tight to the porridge.

A look of pity crosses his face. "Matheus."

"I am Jepp." Though I imagine he already knows my name, I hope that by offering it, I can establish the illusion of friendship. "Can you tell me, Matheus, where I am headed?"

He stares at me uncertainly as if he has been instructed not to reveal such information.

"North," he finally says.

He takes off his boots and lies down on the bed. I know I have just moments before he succumbs to sleep. "Where north?"

He holds a bent copper in his rough hands, turning it around and around, before he shoves it back into his pocket. "To Tycho," he says.

From my studies with Master Kees, I know Tyche to be the Greek goddess of fortune. But, beyond this, the name means nothing to me. "To where?"

But his buzzing snore has already begun.

The next morning he is cross and refuses to speak to me. As our coach rumbles northward in the chilled and starless dawn, I close my eyes, trying to dream my way back to spring.

If there was ever a moment when Coudenberg seemed to bestow the full flower of fortune that Don had promised me, it was that spring when the gardens began to bloom. Over two months had passed since Pim had begun rehearsing us. We had practiced longer for the French dance than any other performance at Coudenberg, and though this struck me as curious, I was in no hurry to perform. As the weather grew more temperate—the

Infanta's small orchard in bud, the songbirds on the wing back north—Lia and I moved our lessons from her room to the palace grounds. So as to not to attract inquisitive eyes, we met twice a week in the early morning when even the Infanta's gardeners were not yet at work rooting out toadstools and propping up wayward flowers and trees. Only the creatures of the garden were full of industry—the ants on a march, the robin darting for her worm—and Lia would narrate their labors as we danced, for she was much taken by even the smallest creatures.

Our afternoons were different, though not without pleasures. Freed from our lesson with Pim, we joined the others. When the sun bathed the gardens in dappled light, Maria and Sebastian would picnic beneath the small pear and apple trees. Hendrika encouraged us to join them in this activity—the Infanta enjoyed coming upon us all with her entourage, and the servants made sure we had tables and chairs, and straw sun hats for the ladies, that complemented our stature. Robert joined us only when the Infanta was occupied inside the palace, for word was that she did not care for his distorting our tableau.

But it was the mornings that burn brightest now in my memory. I remember one such dawn when Lia and I danced among the pale yellow lilies and stalks of iris, still speckled with dew from their nightly ablutions. The moon was fading in the purple sky and an orb—perhaps Venus—twinkled faintly. Lia's hands were snug in mine, her breath warm against my cheek. I held her close before she drew away and sighed.

"What troubles you?"

I feared that she did not care for my embrace, and wished in the urgency of youth to know the worst.

"I am thinking of home."

That she was not thinking of me at all took me by surprise

and nearly wounded my pride before I realized the true wonder of her statement. In all our conversations, intimate as they had become, Lia still never spoke of her life before Coudenberg. Though I felt this mystery keenly, I had never again asked her about it for fear of driving her away.

"Tell me," I said.

"I miss the sea," Lia whispered. "The sweep of the waves. That was the lullaby of my childhood years."

I thought of Lia's shell, which lay on the table by my bedside. I now understood why she had several in her collection. "I have never seen the sea," I confessed.

Lia smiled sadly. "It is the hearing of it you never forget."

I wished to ask her more: who had rocked her to that watery lull, who had nursed her and caught her as she toddled, who had given her away to this landlocked court. But I sensed from the downcast sweep of her eyes that the moment was not opportune. So I endeavored instead to bring her comfort by sharing my own deepest longings.

"I miss my father," I said, "though I never knew him."

Lia thought upon this. "It is strange how our hearts can long for both that which we know and that which we can only imagine."

"It is what drives us through the world—our memories of the past and our hopes for the future."

I did not look upon her as I said this, for I feared to do so would be to reveal that it was she who had become my greatest future hope. But Lia seemed not to divine my meaning. She looked back at the palace, her thoughts elsewhere.

"I like that, Jepp. You speak of life with a pretty tongue."

Her praise greatly pleased me, and though I had not solved the mystery of her early years, I felt closer to her than ever. Like the farmer who with gentle hand tends the first tender shoots in his field, I coddled and cherished my newborn love. For her benefit, I continued to muse upon the world. I sought to describe all I saw and thought in the elevated manner that impressed her and, in doing so, felt myself clever and bold. Half of Cupid's gift is the love a lover feels for himself.

I think now that this self-love gave me courage. As we returned to our quarters, a plan hatched in my mind. I would declare myself to Lia after our performance of the French dance for the Infanta. I counseled myself to practice my steps and tender words equally, for I was certain that my heart would burst if I did not soon reveal its intentions.

But Coudenberg, as I would learn, had a way of confounding lovers' plans. A few nights later, a thunderous knock sounded on my door. I opened it with haste—fearing it to be Hendrika—but instead discovered Pim. He sauntered into my room and took his place upon my tortured chair as if to resume our conversation of six months earlier.

But six months earlier, I had not known him. Now I did. I met his mocking orange-flecked eyes with a frown.

Pim responded by lodging himself more deeply in my chair. "Did I disturb your slumber?"

I shook my head.

"Oh, Jepp, you are still cross because I would have you play the fool. But only a wise man can play a fool."

Though I was tempted, I did not give voice to the other reason I detested him. "You give most strange compliments," I said.

To my dismay, Pim looked encouraged by my retort. "If this assignment is your grievance against me, I come bearing good news. All can be forgiven. The dance never happened."

I looked at him uneasily, struck by the oddness of his language.

The performance had not yet happened, but it seemed as if he was suggesting that our lessons had never happened as well.

"What do you mean?"

"There will be no more lessons," he said.

I did not immediately follow his meaning. "We will perform soon?"

"No," said Pim. "The Infanta has tired of the whole idea. She no longer requests the dance. I have already informed Lia."

Though I knew the Infanta's fancies were wont to change, I felt a keen disappointment in this turn of events. Pim would no longer get the chastening he was due. More important, Lia and I no longer had cause to dance. Gone in an instant were our secret lessons and private plans. I knew not how to declare myself now. The French dance had been the only performance at Coudenberg that I had actually looked forward to delivering.

It pains me now to think that I believed Pim, how the next day I remained in my room, moping as the noon bells chimed. I had not yet realized just how skilled he was in the dissembler's art.

Chapter 11

The spell was broken. Or at least that was the way it seemed after Pim ended our lessons. When I finally ventured out of my chamber, determined to find Lia and convince her to keep me as a pupil (for happily, I had realized, there were many dances in which I was still deficient), I discovered only Maria and Sebastian playing draughts in the sitting room. Maria had learned the game as a girl in Spain, and I could tell from Sebastian's furrowed brow that her growing pile of red draughts was making him cantankerous.

"Have you seen Lia?" I asked them.

Sebastian glared at me. "Can you not see that we are in the midst of an important game?"

Maria jumped three more of his draughts, adding them to her captives.

Sebastian stomped his black boot on the floor.

Maria fought to conceal a smile. "She retired to her room not long ago with a headache and plans to take her supper there."

I wondered if this headache was a pretense, one meant to conceal Lia's own disappointment in the demise of the French dance. But when I knocked on her door and softly called out her name, she did not answer, and I soon abandoned my efforts for fear she was truly indisposed. I returned to my own room to gaze forlornly upon Lia's shell, disappointed that I could not immediately act on my resolve and also troubled by foreboding. That night I did not seek out the company of the others but instead gazed upon my horoscope, looking for reassurance in the symbols of Venus's favor that Don had discovered there.

But Venus seemed not to favor me the following day either. Shortly before noon, I joined the others in the sitting room, relieved to find Lia among them. I tried to catch her gaze, but she remained studiously focused on Maria, who listed for her benefit the many cures for headache, and then Sebastian, who boasted of his robust constitution, which he attributed to his sanguine humors and a daily tincture of horseradish. As our companions' mouths were finally silenced by their need to chew the meat and cakes set out for us, I turned to Lia.

"I am disappointed that we are not to perform."

"The French dance has been called off?" Sebastian said excitedly.

"It is over," said Lia, still avoiding my gaze. She did not offer regrets of her own.

"The Infanta has come to her senses," Sebastian said. "Jepp can return to his pies and you and I to dancing the pavane—"

But I was barely listening, as Lia's response had filled me with panic. So blinded was I by love that I could only interpret her words in relation to myself. I feared that she wished no more to do with me. This made me only more desperate to press ahead with my plan.

"We can still continue our lessons?" I whispered as Sebastian prattled on about his love of the pavane.

Lia spoke quietly, yet her voice was firm. "There is no need now, Jepp."

I wished to tell her how I enjoyed dancing with her and hoped she had enjoyed it too, but was uncertain how to put these tender thoughts into words, especially in the presence of the others.

Before I could say anything, Robert bent his monstrous head beneath our doorway and asked Lia if she might join him for a walk. She nodded fervently and, with a haste that suggested she was eager to escape her present company, slipped off her chair to his side.

In the weeks that followed, it was just as Pim had promised— as if the French dance had never happened. But this was a dark sorcery, for Lia seemed to vanish with the dance. As the days lengthened and the gardens blossomed into a tapestry of colors, Lia spent more and more time with Robert. Even Sebastian and Maria commented on his faithful presence at her side. She joined fewer of our sitting-room gatherings and met my seeking gaze with a blank stare, as though nothing had ever passed between us.

Though I knew the ache of a missing father and a mother separated from me by countless miles, I had never known the pain of missing someone sitting right before me. It seemed to me an exquisite torment and one that, even more than leaving home, marked the end of my childhood years. Some nights I took out my primer and wished myself a child again; but the simple words and pictures seemed a relic of another life, one I felt that had been lost to me forever.

If I had not been so consumed by my own heartbreak, I might have put together the pieces of the drama that had begun to unfold. Instead, I retreated to the library and its many books, searching in the stories of the ages for a cure to my wounded heart. I had never imagined it capable of suffering so grievous an injury and feared this delicate organ would never mend. Though I was finally left with ample time to renew my neglected correspondence with my mother and Willem, I made no progress beyond the greeting, for I did not wish to reveal the disappointment I had suffered but could think of nothing else. Instead of composing my letter, I would sit and mull over what qualities Robert had that I did not, beyond a greater span of inches and years.

On the loneliest of mornings, as the hot summer began its approach, I slipped out to the garden, trying to avoid the places haunted by memories of Lia. I took refuge in the rose garden, which was in resplendent bloom. The Infanta employed a special gardener just for the roses, and they were the great pride of all who called Coudenberg home—some as large as cabbages, some as dainty as buttons, in shades that ranged from ruby red to the tempered white of a moth's wing. Even more lovely than the appearance of the roses was their perfume—potent and drowsy, like a fairy's spell.

But as I crossed beneath the trellis, itself adorned with cascading pink blossoms, I beheld a sight that stopped me from advancing into this realm. On a stone bench sat Robert, and beside him, sheltered in the crook of his enormous arm, was Lia. Her face was pressed against his shirt, and his other large hand stroked her hair, as delicate in its motions as if petting a mouse.

I fled, for I was certain of what I had uncovered, and it wounded me anew. But as I hastened back to the palace, this scene forced me to recognize my hopes as foolish. As my longing transformed into anger, I resolved to think no more about Lia and to forge ahead with my life at Coudenberg. Back at the palace, I found Sebastian and badgered him into a game of draughts; later I dressed in my finest and joined a gathering of courtiers, making jests about my amorous aspirations with the ladies and amusing all.

Over the summer, I focused my attention on becoming a favorite of the court. I attended nearly every function—from reception to feast to falconry—learned the name, position, and proclivities of every courtier, and humored even those whose amusement came in slighting my stature. Word of my efforts must have reached the Infanta, for one night, Hendrika came to my chamber and said that, instead of Lia's presence, Her Royal Highness had requested mine during a spell of ennui.

The Infanta's room was the size of my mother's entire inn, but instead of a crackling hearth, visitors gathered around her enormous canopy bed, carved with the rearing lions of the Hapsburg crest. This is where she lay in a pale imitation of her public self, stripped of her largest jewels and ruff like a plucked bird. As I bowed, I recognized several of her favorites assembled before her: her secretary, a long-faced, bearded man with a habit of clearing his throat as if to brush aside the lesser words of others; a slender, dark-eyed lady-in-waiting who wisely distracted from her own beauty by incessantly fawning over the Infanta's; an older, heavyset lady-in-waiting with a mustache, who trafficked in court gossip; and Pim.

"Titus," the Infanta said, peering down at me from the height of her bed. "Come sit beside me."

She offered no hand, nor did any of the others. I knew not how to scale her bed.

"Your Royal Highness, I am too small to take advantage of such an honor," I finally said with a bow.

Pim laughed merrily. "He means he cannot reach."

The two ladies in waiting rushed to hoist me, like a sack of flour, onto the bed. I toppled onto my face.

"He is better served as a pie," Pim remarked dryly.

The Infanta smiled briefly, revealing tiny creases around her mouth and eyes. As I righted myself, her long fingers emerged from the tips of her black sleeves and petted my hair.

"Lia no longer amuses me with her melancholy songs," she said, staring at me but speaking loudly for the benefit of the others. "She has taken them too much to heart."

"I wearied of them long ago," said Pim.

Though the topic of Lia and her songs still pained me, I could not help defending her. "They are heartfelt, Your Royal Highness."

"Certainly a heart can also feel joy, Titus?"

The scene in the rose garden came to mind, but not wishing to attest to what I had seen, I let the Infanta's question go unanswered.

"Not all hearts are as joyful as our beautiful Infanta's," said the slender lady-in-waiting.

The Infanta sighed deeply, though I could not tell whether she was still dissatisfied with Lia or simply wished this representation of her own heart to be true.

The secretary, assuming the former, cleared his throat. "The other dwarf, Maria, has a more amiable temperament."

"So long as she is not thirsty," said Pim.

The heavyset lady-in-waiting tittered appreciatively.

The Infanta fixed her dark eyes on Pim. "It is Hendrika's job to correct these flaws in my dwarfs. And yours."

Pim bowed deeply. "Believe me, Your Royal Highness. I have tried."

I found this curious, for Pim had done no such thing.

"I have given them everything so they may be happy," the Infanta said.

She seemed so childlike in her disappointment that I felt compelled to comfort her even if my words were as false as Pim's and those of the slender lady-in-waiting. "We are happy, Your Royal Highness. We think only of your generosity."

The Infanta nodded sternly. "You feel joyful, then, Titus?" she pressed.

"I—"

"Of course he does. The pleasures of Coudenberg invite no other emotion," Pim interrupted with an impish smile.

I thought of Pim's caresses of Lia and despised him anew. But I was surprised to hear another voice sound a disapproving note.

"Pleasures indeed," said the heavyset lady-in-waiting.

The Infanta turned to her. "What now, Lady Francisca? Has our Pim been causing trouble again?"

"This fox has been among the hens of the kitchens," Francisca said.

Pim shrugged as if it were pointless to defend his own nature.

I expected the Infanta to punish this admission of roguish behavior, but Lia had been right about Pim's status as favorite. The Infanta merely wagged a finger at him. "You should marry, Pim. Consider me. I was an old maid before my father would allow it. But marriage suits me in every way."

Pim bowed. "I am married to serving Your Royal Highness."

"How he evades! It is lucky for you, Pim, that you amuse me."

The talk turned to gossip about the courtiers, including how

Don Diego strived for his brother's success in court, but the Infanta thought him neither as dignified nor as charming. Then it wandered off into a new painting of the Virgin and Child she had commissioned, and her wish to extend the street that ran outside the Aula Magna, Coudenberg's grandest hall for receptions and parties, all the way to the St. Michael and St. Gudula Cathedral. No one ever returned to the question of whether I was joyful.

I must have made a favorable impression, for the Infanta requested my presence several more times that summer. Though I took no pleasure in divining her moods or watching her favorites compete to flatter and amuse her, my duties there helped distract me from thinking about Lia. By late summer, I had become a favorite of the court. But as fall approached, a situation arose that made me question the worth of this achievement.

Chapter 12

I have never felt such cold as this, our seventh day upon the road. Bright sun and a clear sky give the illusion of warmth as the coach lurches past snow-covered fields and wind-bent beeches. But the only clouds are fashioned from my own breath and the cold shoves its loose-boned hands beneath the blanket that serves as my coat, prickling the hairs on my neck and arms, and rattling my teeth. I think about Willem and the stories he told of the North, of pale giants and castles of ice, of creatures blind from lack of sun—for it is to these dark lands I fear I am headed.

It is so bitter that we stop to change horses only twice, and then retire to an inn several hours before sunset. Though our day's travel has been considerably shortened, by the time Matheus unlocks the door of the coach, I am shivering uncontrollably. His face is wrapped up in strips of cloth as if his head were in a poultice, but his eyes, which peek through an opening, widen at the sight of me, and I can hear a muffled curse as he ushers me into the cage and carries it inside. I no longer care where I am headed—northward, Tycho, even hell—so long as I may find there a spot of warmth.

The fire in our room has died out, but Matheus does not hasten to revive it. Instead, after depositing my cage on the drafty floor and unwrapping his chapped face, he rushes out. Though I know not from what wellspring of heat it derives, I feel a sudden anger that his lust for ale is so great that he would abandon a fellow man half-dead with cold. Though his form would raise no eyebrows, it is he, I tell myself, who is truly a beast.

But before this ire can reawaken my sluggish blood, I hear something heavy battering against the door. Matheus has returned, followed by two strong-armed maidservants, one carrying a wooden basin and the other a kettle.

I look at this party in no less amazement than they do me. As Matheus unlocks my cage and says in his rough voice, "Come out, come out," one of the maidservants points to me with excitement and says something to the other in a foreign tongue. I realize from this clue that we have landed in a kingdom that is not beloved by the Infanta—that of the Danes. But while the Danish tongue is similar to my own, it is different enough that when the other servant answers back, then leans over to peer at me, it is her curiosity I understand more than her words. I crawl out and stand shivering in the drafty room.

As Matheus points to the hearth and then the basin, the women abandon their gaping and set to work lighting the fire, hanging the kettle. They steal glances at me as they wait for it to boil, then pour the water into the basin and fetch more. A glorious heat, like the warm crook of my mother's arm, stills my chattering. Soon I am no longer emitting clouds but breathing them in as steam billows out from the basin.

Matheus pretends to sip a cup and dip a spoon into a bowl, and the women nod in comprehension and bring him ale and porridge. He watches me carefully each time they open the door but, for the moment, I have no hunger to escape.

When the basin is full, Matheus gestures for the women to depart. They leave reluctantly, slowing gathering the kettle and glancing back, seemingly in hopes that they might see me disrobe before them. He waves them away, and the door finally closes behind them.

"Go ahead," he says, turning away as he drinks his ale. "Bathe."

I strip off my clothes, not minding the brief blast of air upon my naked limbs before I clamber into the basin. The hot water stings my numb feet and hands, boils my skin pink, envelops my head in steam. I stare at Matheus's back and am touched most by this simple kindness, by his allowing me to take my bath alone.

It is a good thing his back is turned, for once my body warms, so too does my heart. I start to cry, silently, my tears mixing with the water around me.

There is no midwife of sorrows to pull me out of these waters and dry my tears. But there is a quarter-portion of porridge and ale awaiting me in my cage when I emerge. Matheus locks the door behind me, then repairs to his pallet to thumb his bent copper. With my belly warmed inside and out, I fall into a deep and blessedly forgetful slumber.

One September morning, Pim sauntered into our sitting room and announced that in several weeks time, important members of the Holy Roman Empire, to whom the Infanta and her husband were closely related, would be coming to Coudenberg. The archduke, who was often away overseeing the military campaigns to the north, would be in attendance, and for his and the Austrians' pleasure, the Infanta wished us to perform her favorite amusements, in addition to acrobatics and songs.

Pim began to rehearse us, but Maria, Sebastian, Lia, and I were not the only ones caught up in the ensuing frenzy of preparation. For weeks before the Austrian royals' arrival, the entire palace was abuzz with activity: artists and craftsmen brought their finest tapestries and paintings for the Infanta's consideration, the cooks procured rare edibles from the farthest reaches of forest and sea and perfected their recipes (I generously devoured many of their mistakes), the tailors worked around the clock creating garments of the finest silks and jeweled embellishments, the musicians practiced their celestial tunes till the early hours of the morning.

But there was a less pleasant aspect to the royals' visit. To the dismay of us all, Hendrika began to emerge more often from her chamber to correct flaws in our appearance and enforce the importance of performing our duties without incident or error. She thrummed with the same nervous energy as the rest of the palace and seemed particularly unkind in her estimations of us. Sebastian had failed to lance a blemish on his chin, giving him, she chided, the look of a pox victim; Lia and I had both increased a size and were forbidden to eat on the day of our performance; Maria stank like a sailor and was admonished not to have her hippocras in the presence of the royal guests. As Hendrika finished this dressing-down and stood glaring at us, Robert crouched through the door.

"Why do you come here?" she demanded.

I could see he was caught off guard. "To see Lia," he said honestly.

"Why?" Hendrika said. "You might step on her and crush her!"

Robert retreated back through the door. I noticed Lia wince as if the smart had been directed at her.

"Oaf!" Hendrika shouted after him. "Stay away!" As soon as Robert's heavy footsteps faded down the hall, she swung around so she was facing me. "You!" she ordered. "Do not permit him in here."

I was most surprised by this command; it was the first time she seemed to favor me above the others. I wondered whether my efforts at court had sufficiently impressed her, or whether she was laying a trap so that if Robert was found among us, she might later blame me. But even if the latter were true, I had no intention of following her orders. Though it would have afforded me a thrill to exercise such power over Robert, I wished neither to make an enemy of Lia nor be regarded as Hendrika's lieutenant.

After Hendrika departed, it was quiet in our chambers. Finally, Maria spoke up. "As soon as the Austrians leave, all will be well again."

I wished to believe her. But I felt that all had not been well for some time.

Ten days later, in a dozen carriages pulled by teams of white horses, the Austrian royals and their servants arrived. The Infanta could not have been more proud of the palace and the grounds, of her servants and courtiers, all of them groomed to perfection. But there was one thing she could not control: the weather. A stifling heat had settled over Brussels, and even atop Coudenberg's promontory, there was nary a breeze to stir the heavy air. Beneath our gold threads and jeweled finery, every one of us was drenched in an uncouth sweat.

Our first performance of acrobatics and songs was set for that evening and, as the appointed hour approached, I dreaded it. Even though I had ably demonstrated my wit and charm to the Infanta over the past months, she had once again commanded that I make my entrance by leaping out of a pie. She thought this spectacle—like Lia's cage and Sebastian's pony—most amusing. Though it was cooler within the walls of the palace, it was still airless, and the thought of being encased in my box and then entombed inside the warm piecrust was most disagreeable. But when the time came, I obediently took my place inside the box, attempting to breathe deep and slow to keep my spirits calm.

The Aula Magna, the palace's banqueting hall where the Austrian royals were being received, was more crowded than I had ever seen it, as if the entire city of Brussels had turned out. Adjacent to the Infanta sat two men and a woman being fanned by servants beneath a yellow flag with a two-headed eagle. The Infanta absently fingered the pearls on her large cross as she smiled at the Austrian royals and leaned in to whisper something to the archduke. Maria sat on her throne looking wilted and—doubtless because of Hendrika's prohibition of hippocras—cross. Drops of sweat trickled from the musicians' foreheads and rolled onto their instruments.

A moment later, Pim appeared, his face flushed the same color as his hair. "Greetings to our royal guests!" he declared to a thundering of applause. After a deep bow in the direction of the Austrians, he continued, "The Infanta wishes to welcome you with some enchantments."

The heavier of the two Austrian princes waved his arm in the air to signal a speech. "The hospitality of our hosts . . ." he began.

I could barely listen to his words. My hair felt wet with sweat, and my temples ached from the heat.

The Infanta replied with gracious words of her own.

"And now . . ." said Pim.

I had never been so relieved to hear his voice. Lia would sing, and then I would jump out of my pie. We would trill and tumble, and then my playing the bumbling fool would be over. As Pim recited, *"Most worthy of our Queen's delight/This captured creature of the night,"* I pictured myself opening the small window in my room and sticking my head out into the evening air, though I feared even this would bring meager relief. In Robert strode with the birdcage. Setting it gently upon the ground, he retreated to his spot where he towered above the musicians. My head throbbed as I waited to hear Lia's voice. *"From distant lands,"* I mouthed, spurring her on.

"This captured creature of the night," Pim declared loudly.

I realized then that it wasn't my headache that was making the wait seem interminable. Despite Pim repeating Lia's cue, the birdcage was silent. Not a single note emanated from it.

A fear gripped me, blotting out my aching head.

"Lia!" Pim hissed.

Again, silence.

The courtiers stood fixed in their places. Even the Infanta was frozen on her throne. The only one of our number who moved was Robert. In two loping strides, he was beside the cage and whipped off the sheet. Inside, Lia was slumped over, her face ashen, her eyes closed.

"Lia!" he cried and, in a single motion, ripped the door off the front of the cage. As he pulled out her limp body and laid it on the floor, his huge face twisted up in misery like a gargoyle's. The Infanta's personal physician, with Hendrika on his heels, rushed forward. I toppled the box from above me and slipped over to Robert's side. But no one noticed or seemed to care. All eyes were on Lia and the physician.

"She's alive," the physician said.

The courtiers murmured in relief. But Robert's expression, I noticed, was slow to unfix itself.

"She has just fainted," the physician continued loudly for the benefit of the crowd. He produced a vial of smelling salts from his pocket and waved them under Lia's nose. She started and opened her eyes.

At this moment, Sebastian rode in on his pony. "What happened to our songbird?" he asked.

Either the mere sight of Sebastian or his comment or the combination thereof caused the fatter of the two Austrian royals to bellow with laughter. For the first time, I looked at the Infanta and glimpsed a childish frown just as it metamorphosed into a surprised peal of laughter. It was then I realized that, by sly design, Sebastian had tempered her displeasure.

"My deepest pardon," the Infanta said to the Austrian royals when the laughter that had risen up to join hers died down. "My dwarfs are sensitive creatures; their delicate physiques cannot take the extremes of heat like our own."

Seeing my opportunity to join Lia and make certain her constitution was not more seriously altered, I piped up. "Your Royal Highness. I confess to feeling ill as well."

No doubt uneager to have a repeat of Lia's misfortune, the Infanta nodded. "Hendrika, you and the doctor will accompany Lia and Titus Maximus back to their quarters. Tomorrow, perhaps, it will be more temperate, and we can enjoy their company."

I feared that, when we arrived back at our miniature quarters, Hendrika would send me back to my chamber and I would not be privy to the doctor's report; but thankfully she seemed distracted by the events that had just unfolded, and failed to dismiss me. While the physician examined Lia in an adjacent room, Hendrika loomed over a chair in our sitting room.

"It was too hot for you to be so enclosed," she said, shaking her head vehemently.

I had never before seen her troubled by our treatment, but her concern seemed so genuine that I found myself reassuring her. "Lia will be fine."

"And you, Jepp?" she said, almost angrily. "Will you be fine?"

I realized that she had used my real name, though she did not appear aware of it.

"My headache is abating."

Hendrika frowned as if my answer did not satisfy her.

"I fear . . ." she began but then stopped, turning away from me and toward the room where the physician was examining Lia.

In my own mind I finished this thought for her; despite my reassurances, I too feared that Lia was truly ill. The thought of losing her evoked in me such panic that I was forced to admit that I had been feigning my indifference. But before I could make sense of my reawakened affections or Hendrika's newly revealed ones, the physician rejoined us.

"It's not just the heat," he said to Hendrika.

Hendrika still seemed lost in thought. "Pardon?"

"The little dwarf," he said. "She's pregnant."

Chapter 13

It was late at night when Maria came out of Lia's room, but neither Sebastian nor I had retired to our chambers. Sebastian had spent the past hour modeling his collection of feathered hats before the mirror, but his expression lacked its usual impudence. I had devoured a plate of cold, spiced meat pies, which had abated my headache but done little for my troubled spirits.

Before rushing out with nary a word to Lia or me, Hendrika had convinced the physician to wait until morning to reveal Lia's condition to the Infanta. Tomorrow, we would learn how this news would be received. But worse than the prospect of the Infanta's displeasure was my own selfish grief. No sooner had I confessed to myself that my affections for Lia had remained constant than I had lost her—and in a way I had not previously imagined.

Though her door remained closed after the physician departed, I knew I should endeavor to speak with Lia. Yet, to my shame, I sat unmoving. I was most relieved when Maria returned and—showing an admirable calm—took upon herself the duty of comforting her. For the last hour Maria had been in her chamber, and her voice, rising and falling cheerfully through the closed door, had lessened my sense of dereliction.

"How is she?" Sebastian and I both asked in unison as Maria emerged.

She settled herself on her small throne and poured herself a generous cup of her hippocras. "She is in shock."

Sebastian shook his head most woefully. "Did she not realize the consequence of Robert's affections?"

That Robert's role was so readily apparent to all only deepened my gloom. I wondered, too, whether Hendrika would hold me partly to blame for not following her instructions to bar him from our quarters.

Maria leaned toward us and spoke in a hushed voice though there was no one around to overhear. "She will not reveal the father."

I suddenly envisioned Pim with his fingers twined in Lia's hair and felt a wrench in my gut. "Are you certain he is Robert?"

"Of course he is Robert," said Sebastian. "Are your eyes not open, Jepp? You think he comes here every day to see us?"

"And why else would he have run up to her in front of the entire court?" Maria added. "He must have guessed her condition. Besides, when I asked her about him, she would not say he was the father, but neither would she deny it."

This seemed most convincing, especially when I thought back to what I had witnessed in the rose garden. A vague unease still troubled me, but I attributed it to a different fear.

"Will Lia be all right?" I asked Maria. "Bearing a child?"

She took a long sip of hippocras. "There are dwarfs who manage to give birth."

This comment was meant to reassure me, but all I could hear in it was that many did not. And Lia's child would be part giant. How would she birth such a creature?

Maria must have read my face. "Do not fear, Jepp. The Infanta will take care of her. The physician will take care of her. *We* will take care of her."

During this speech, Sebastian returned to his mirror, where it seemed he labored to frighten away the dark horseman of Death himself by striking a fierce pose in a red-tufted hat. Then he spun around back to us, his dark eyes glowering. "They will want to interview us."

"Why us?" I asked.

"To ascertain what we have seen. To gather evidence of Robert's guilt."

I realized at that moment the power I wielded, for I alone had witnessed Robert and Lia's assignation in the garden. Maria had told us of wicked courtiers and sinful servants whom the Infanta had locked up in her dungeon, a place of legendary sorrows, or even banished from Coudenberg altogether. On my intelligence, Robert might suffer the same fate. That I thrilled to these prospects troubled me, for my mother had raised me not to relish the misfortunes of others. Besides, Robert, of all the denizens of Coudenberg, had never shown ill will toward me. I thought back to his admonition to Maria not to frighten me by mentioning the pie, the care he took in tending Lia's lute, the fearless way he had ripped off the cage door to free her.

But then I envisioned Lia struggling to birth some monstrous child. I could not fault Robert for being struck by Cupid's arrow, as I had been, but I could blame him for endangering Lia's life.

The following morning, Don appeared and requested that I might join him for a walk through the gardens. Such a gambol would normally be agreeable to me, but with the Infanta by now likely informed of Lia's condition, I sensed that his purpose was not merely to be amiable. Before I followed him out of our quarters, Sebastian slyly winked at me, and I felt certain that the inquisition had begun.

The air had finally grown cooler, and a mist shrouded the familiar paths. Don kept up a steady stream of friendly banter, asking me about the comfort of my quarters and my impressions of the court. I participated in the conversation in a cursory way, providing pleasant answers that I imagined he wished to hear. Our walk continued for some time without incident, and I began to wonder if Don had not heard the news and had simply taken me out for a friendly stroll.

As we passed through the stunted orchard, an oversweet stench filled the air. Under each tree, a few apples lay rotting on the ground, and one of the Infanta's gardeners trod on his knees carefully collecting them. No one harvested the fruits still hanging, as they were just for show. In the midst of this wasted crop, Don halted and crouched down to face me. "I know about Lia," he said, staring me square in the eye. "Did you do it, Jepp?"

"No," I stammered.

I prepared to defend myself further, but Don laughed and

stood back up. "Of course you didn't," he said. "Though you should have."

"Pardon?"

"The Infanta would have been far less upset if you or Sebastian had done this mischief. Instead it is likely the child will be of average size—a mean of his parents."

This comment combined with the smell of the rotting apples to sicken me. "We are not dogs being bred for the hunt!" I cried.

Don's lips curled into a smile. "Do not take offense, Jepp. We know who the culprit is. I imagine you do as well. Have you seen them together?"

I looked down at the ground, fixing my eyes on a wormhole in one of the apples. Don's comment still smarted, and the indignities of life at Coudenberg suddenly weighed upon me. As I thought of them, I knew that I could not betray Robert. Not when those who controlled our fates valued our feelings less than our forms.

"Have you seen them together?" Don pressed.

"Who?" I pretended.

"The giant," said Don, slightly irritated. "Lia."

"Yes," I said, but elaborated not.

"Robert is in your quarters often?" Don pressed.

I nodded. Robert's frequent visits were hardly a secret.

Don grinned. He made for a poor inquisitor, likely because he was already certain of Robert's guilt. "You should have had a go at her," he said.

I turned away. "I need to leave," I said.

Don looked at me and laughed. "Are you a man, Jepp, or are you still the child you appear?"

I hurried back to the palace, but my legs were too short to enable me to escape Don's mocking. "A child still," he said, loping alongside me. "Never mind. The Infanta will realize yet that there is value to this coupling."

Don turned out to be right. Within days, Lia's condition became the talk of Coudenberg. As it turned out, even if I had revealed what I had seen in the rose garden, it could hardly have further incriminated Robert, for in the minds of the courtiers and servants he was already guilty. They needed no evidence, because the idea of a giant coupling with a dwarf appealed to them—not only as a romantic fancy but as something entertainingly grotesque. Pim made many gibes, too bawdy for me to repeat, at Lia and Robert's expense. The Infanta, who, as Don reported, had initially been displeased with the affair, began to see its benefits as both amusement and scientific experiment.

Despite all our expectations that Robert would be punished, the Infanta left him unmolested. If anything, he was treated more kindly at court than before. He came to our quarters to see Lia often—seemingly immune to Sebastian's barbs and Hendrika's scowls as he retreated to the privacy of Lia's chamber.

Hendrika never did blame me for failing to banish Robert from our quarters. Perhaps she realized that even had I followed her orders, Robert and Lia would have found another place to pursue their affair. But since our brief conversation in the sitting room, I began to notice, if not quite warmth from this sullen woman, a kindness toward me and, especially, toward Lia. Uniquely among the courtiers, Hendrika seemed to find no amusement in her situation. She stopped in upon Lia daily, bringing fine dishes she had commissioned from the Infanta's cooks and, as the weather finally cooled, soft blankets to banish the chill.

Excused from her duties, Lia spent many a day in her room. When she emerged, she no longer arranged her memento mori but stared into the distance with a wan smile. The others attributed this to her delicate condition, but her melancholic humor revived my unease. For it struck me as strange that neither Robert's attentions nor the court's acceptance of their affair seemed to make Lia happy. As a result, I was the only one who was not completely surprised by what happened next.

Chapter 14

Ten days into our journey, in the middle of a chilly, sunless morning, the coach stops, and Matheus opens the door. He carries no cage. But when I gaze past him, I no longer see a road but a vast expanse of water. Thick, brooding clouds hang above the horizon and a brisk wind whips up white-tipped waves, carrying with it a scent that reminds me of birth and death all at once. I have never seen the sea before, and tears well up in my eyes as I finger the seashell. Lia's face and voice seem painfully near. I understand now why, despite the wind and the crash of the surf, she sang of the seas as being silent.

Matheus gestures for me to disembark, and I clamber down onto a wooden wharf where several other figures, huddled against the wind, are silently waiting. It is a relief to be out of my cage, allowed to walk about. But I know that any real sense of freedom is an illusion. There is nowhere for me to run save into the freezing waters.

"Where are we?" I ask.

"Nyborg," he says in his curt fashion, handing me a blanket to wrap around myself.

This Danish name means nothing to me, just as Tycho means nothing to me. All I know is that I am as far away from home as a soul can be. As we stand on the wharf, I make out a ship moving toward us, teetering across the waves. It is a small sailing vessel, and as it nears, I can see that the deck is crowded with bundled souls. It occurs to me that our journey is about to continue on this watery road and beneath these threatening clouds.

An hour later, I am standing on top of my cage, heaving over the side of the ferry as it tosses me more wildly than any chariot. There is ice on the deck, and snow has begun to fall in a dizzying rush. As the other passengers stare, Matheus rubs his bent copper and watches me with a worried frown, grabbing on to my shoulder when we pitch so violently that I threaten to topple overboard.

"What is the meaning of your copper?" I shout over the wind.

"It brings good luck," he says.

Closing my eyes tightly, I pray that this is so and our voyage may end safely. But when I open them again, the watery plain is the same, the sky unforgiving. Since God is everywhere, since He walks on the seas, I know He has heard me. But the Lord has refused to listen. I think of Robert then, and I am filled with shame.

The last time I was permitted inside a church was on All Hallows' Eve, when the entire court gathered for a vigil to pray for the souls trapped in purgatory. It was a clear, cold night, and the bishop's benedictions echoed through the towering St. Michael and St. Gudula Cathedral, which was illuminated by hundreds of candles.

Beside me, Sebastian was counting the buttons on his coat as if making a show of his unbelief. Maria fingered her rosary, though her eyes were occupied with the more earthly task of reviewing the assembled courtiers, no doubt in search of fresh gossip. Although attendance at Mass was required, Lia, feeling unwell, had been permitted to stay in bed. Across the aisle, I spotted Hendrika kneeling on the cold stone, her hands clenched together in prayer, her eyes closed tight. I wondered whom it was she so fervently prayed for.

Turning away, I tried to think of the souls I knew in purgatory. Back in Astraveld, farmer Helmich and his wife Jantje had lost several children, but they were mere infants. Having been baptized, they must have passed directly on to heaven. My grandfather had been murdered, but my mother assured me his soul was at rest, for she had never seen him wander. I wondered then where purgatory was, whether it was cold, or whether—dangling between heaven and hell—it had seasons like our own. I resolved to ask Master Kees how long a soul might be trapped there.

My thoughts were still concerned with these weighty matters when we arrived back at our quarters. Though the others went to bed, I felt restless, and it came upon me that I must talk to Lia. I had not tried to speak to her alone since she had found herself with child, but the service—with its tidings of mortality—made this conversation seem most urgent. I wished to tell her I understood now why she had no longer wished to dance with me, but that I was still her loyal friend, one who wished only to ensure her happiness. I knocked softly on her door, but she did not answer. I almost did not knock again, fearing she was asleep, but my need to tell her these noble sentiments overwhelmed my restraint. I gently turned the knob and took a step inside. Blankets were strewn atop her bed. "Lia?"

A shadow cast itself over me and I started, imagining a lost soul come to haunt. But when I turned to face its source, I realized it was only Hendrika, standing behind me in the doorframe.

"Where is she?" she asked frantically.

"I don't know. I just came to—"

I wished not to describe my intentions to her. But she failed to notice my hesitation for, at that moment, there was a commotion down the hall. Hendrika and I ran toward the voices. Several of the Infanta's guards rushed toward us.

"What is it?" Hendrika asked them.

"The giant," said one of the guards. "He's gone."

As the Infanta's guards descended into Brussels in search of Robert and Lia, I awoke Maria and Sebastian to share the news. Maria was certain that they would not get far, but, as the hours passed, the hunting party did not return with their quarry. A part of me was secretly glad that Robert and Lia had escaped, but a greater part of me wished them to be caught so I could see Lia again.

In the early morning hours, I sat in my chamber, staring out of my tiny window and thinking of Robert and Lia. What perplexed me was why they had fled. This question did not seem to trouble Maria or Sebastian, who saw this elopement as the natural progression of their affair. But if it were nuptials they sought, I was certain the Infanta would have provided them, and in a grand manner. My thoughts returned to Lia's melancholy, and I wondered if this, rather than her passion for Robert, had driven their flight.

I fetched a quill and paper and began to write a letter to Willem and my mother, thinking it would distract me from these cogitations. I had continued to neglect my correspondence with them and, after a lavish apology, I intended to share my impressions of the cooks' finest dishes and my progress as a student, which Master Kees had praised just the other day. But I found I could not write of Coudenberg without writing of Lia. And when I wrote about Lia, I found myself telling the story of our friendship in minute and unabashed detail. I wrote about the French dance and our secret lessons, I wrote about their sudden and disappointing end. I even wrote about coming upon Lia and Robert in the rose garden. But as I committed this scene to the page, it seemed different in nature than it had appeared at the time, Robert's caress less romantic than consoling.

With growing consternation, I reread my depiction of how Lia had acted after Pim had ended the lessons, for the first time absenting my own hurt feelings. The headache, her retirement from my company and that of the others, her vacant manner— they no longer signaled anything about Lia's affections toward me but only that Pim's nefarious end had been reached. Had the Infanta ever even requested a performance of the French dance? I suddenly doubted this just as much as I doubted that Robert was the father of Lia's child. Pim had chosen me—the most innocent of our number—to give the lessons an illusion of propriety, for I could not say I had seen him alone with Lia. But I had a strong suspicion that, while he had canceled the final lesson for me, he had not for Lia.

The few remaining hours of that night I barely slept, so troubled was I by the crime I belatedly realized had taken place, and my own blindness in the face of it. I tore up the letter to my mother and Willem, not wishing a servant to intercept it; but even without the words of the tale before me, I felt myself a great fool, and rightly undeserving of Lia's affection. Though I had not prayed at the cathedral, I prayed most fervently now that Lia and Robert would escape. The knowledge that Lia was not the first of Pim's marks and that the Infanta was little bothered by his saturnalian escapades, made me only the more anxious for Lia and Robert's success.

As I lay restless in my bed, I thought about the man who was just a head, and the story of his escape from Coudenberg on a cart filled with cabbages. But Maria's tale, I knew, was not true. Besides, Robert, whose head was attached to an assemblage of arms and legs as tall as a tree trunk, could not be so readily concealed.

And indeed, it was as Maria had foretold. Early the next morning, shortly after I finally fell asleep, Sebastian burst into my room.

"Wake up!" he said. "They've caught them."

I dashed after him, into the main part of the palace and down several flights of stairs to where an arched door opened onto a small stone courtyard. In a corner of it sat Lia, her face buried in Maria's lap. Robert lay sprawled on the ground in the center of the courtyard, surrounded by four guards, Don, and Pim. Each guard held a rope that was fastened to one of Robert's wrists or ankles and pulled taut so he could not bend his arms or legs. The side of his face was purple and bloodied, and his large jaw looked misaligned.

"Out of my way!" shouted a voice behind us.

I jumped to the side just as Hendrika raced past us and

toward Lia. Scooping her up, she turned to Don. "How dare you let her see this?" she said. "In her condition . . ."

Before Don could answer, Hendrika hurried off with Lia then abruptly stopped at the arched door and turned back. "Jepp!" she said. "Come along!"

But though she ordered me to her side, I could not leave Robert and made no motion to depart.

"I shall come," Maria said, rushing over.

Hendrika scowled but, before she could chastise me for my disobedience, Lia sobbed, and she did not summon me again. As they disappeared into the palace, Robert struggled against his ropes and gaped his broken jaw; but the resulting nonsensical cries made him sound more like beast than man.

"I cannot watch this," said Sebastian, and he turned and left.

One of Robert's eyes was swollen shut. But the other eye was wide open and for a brief moment, it locked upon my own, pleading.

I ran over to Don. "Release him!"

"He issues orders like a king," said Pim. "King of the dwarfs."

The guards laughed, but Don did not look amused at my intrusion.

"He is innocent," I said to Don.

I expected this revelation to have a great effect but, just as on stage, Pim was quick to divert his audience. He laughed heartily. "He has great powers of persuasion, as well, for he suggests to these fine gentlemen that they did not see the giant at the city gate absconding with the Infanta's prize dwarf. Perhaps it was you, Titus Maximus, casting a large shadow. Is this your confession?"

"No," I stammered, tongue-tied by my anger.

But before I could renew my allegation, Pim plucked me off

my feet. "Shall we toss this rascal?" he said to one of the guards. He began to pitch me back and forth as if preparing for a most spectacular throw.

I was certain his plan was to dash me upon the stone. He would make it seem an accident, as if he had dropped me midair. My words lodged in my throat. This was not like the inn, where my mother would appear with apron to catch me.

"Cease your jesting, Pim," Don said, his tone sharp.

Pim put me down but, as he did, his hand squeezed me about the neck. I knew then that I had not imagined the violence he threatened.

"Jepp, listen to Hendrika. Go back to your quarters," Don ordered.

I feared that Don had failed to understand the implication of my words, but I also feared that he simply did not care. In any case, I did not dare repeat my charge; I felt powerless to make it effectively amidst such hostile company. Under Pim's watchful gaze, I turned away from Robert and, to my great shame, left him to his tormenters.

When the maidservants brought the noontime meal, we learned from their gossip that the Infanta, reconfirmed in her original enmity toward Robert, had ordered him locked away in the palace dungeon. I might have gone there to seek his forgiveness were it not for the fact that later that day, on the Infanta's orders, locks were installed on all the doors to our quarters. That evening, Hendrika gathered us in the sitting room. On a chain around her neck hung a key.

"The locks will be removed once Lia gives birth," she said in a reassuring voice.

But her eyes would not meet our own, and left unsaid was that in the meantime, all of us were imprisoned along with Lia.

Chapter 15

Very little changed. We were still dressed in the finest silks, still fed spiced meat pies and almond cakes, still carefully tended by ladies-in-waiting. The locks did not bring with them cruel hands or meager fare. Nor were any of our possessions taken from us—we still had books, paper, chalk, quills, musical instruments, decanters of hippocras. But though there had never been a prison so fine, we knew it still to be a prison. The servants now entered our quarters only during set times of the day, when a guard unlocked the door from the main part of the palace. At night, the guard retired, and this traffic ceased.

Although the key Hendrika wore day and night around her neck suggested that she was no fellow captive, she remained constantly with us and busied herself with the task of seeing to

Lia. During this time, I endeavored to speak with Lia, but she remained in seclusion, admitting no one.

In the meantime, I did not tell Maria and Sebastian what I had realized. I told myself that I needed to be certain I could convince them, but in truth, my discretion rested on fear. Every afternoon, Pim would pay us a visit and, under the pretense of lessening our isolation, share tales from the court. His face would color with mirth, his laughter echo most jolly, but his orange-flecked eyes would fall sternly upon me when the others were distracted. "Be good, friends," was his parting salutation. "Do nothing foolish."

"How can we do anything foolish in these confines?" Sebastian groused the first time Pim took leave from us in this manner.

Maria laughed as if Pim's words were meant in amusement. But I took them to heart and abandoned a plan I had briefly formed of sharing what I knew with the Infanta. I was certain that if Pim got wind of my request for an audience with the Infanta, he would find a way to discredit or even harm me. The risk might have been worth it if I had had faith that the Infanta would expel or imprison Pim, but judging from the blind eye she had turned to his previous debaucheries, of this I was doubtful.

During this week, the first wet snow fell. Though the garden offered but a dreary respite, I longed to visit it. Our quarters—which had once appeared just right for my stature—now seemed too small. During the idle days, Maria overindulged in her hippocras, and she and Sebastian bickered constantly. At night, I thought of Lia, but even were she to see me, I felt powerless to comfort her or offer any help. Her secret seemed to me another lock upon us.

When I fell asleep, I dreamed about the wide expanses of

Astraveld and the winter wind blowing through my hair. I awakened each morning feeling newly entombed. Even the storybooks Master Kees sent me (for my lessons in the library had been suspended) failed to distract me from our captivity.

One November night, around the feast of St. Cecilia, I set out to write a short letter to my mother and Willem. By this time, having torn up my last missive, I felt most delinquent in my filial duties. As I did not wish her to think that I had forgotten her, I concocted some harmless banter to set her heart at ease.

Dearest Mother, I began.

> **Forgive me the long delay in our correspondence, which is a reflection not of my affection for you—boundless as it is— but of the many obligations of my new life. The court is like heaven—I am cosseted like an angel and feast upon dreamstuff.**

Here I hesitated and then struck a line through these false sentiments.

I am imprisoned here and I want to go home, I wrote beneath them.

"Jepp?"

I instinctively covered the letter with my arm. Standing in my doorway was Lia.

"Lia," I stammered.

"I know you've wished to speak to me," she said. "But first I must speak to you."

I stood and gestured to my chair. "Please! Sit down."

She closed the door and walked with heavy gait to the little chair. It had been seven months since Pim had ended our lessons, and her form had grown increasingly rounded. I tried to imagine her dancing, but the dancer was gone.

I had imagined a speech, full of delicate allusions to what had befallen her, but instead I blurted out, "I know it was Pim who did this to you."

Lia's silence spoke for her.

"You could have told," I said softly.

It was as if Lia had been waiting for me to say this. She struggled to her feet, her face red. "So the Infanta could punish him lightly and make an exhibition of my condition? So that rascal could punish me greatly? He says if I tell, the Infanta will marry us off, and he will beat me nightly. I have told no one, Jepp, and I pray you will not either."

I had never seen her like this—almost fevered—but I pressed my point, evoking a justice that I myself no longer truly believed in. "But they have punished Robert severely."

She jabbed at her girth. "Not for this!" Her eyes brimmed with tears. "What crime is Robert being punished for? For giving me a breath of air. For this he suffers, Jepp. For a breath of air."

She collapsed back into the chair and began to weep.

This piteous scene affected me greatly. I fell to my knees before her and took her hands in mine. "Lia, I am your friend—"

"I want to be free of this place, Jepp," she sobbed. "I want my child born free of it. If you are my friend, you must help us escape."

It shames me now to remember my initial response to her entreaty. Though I was moved nearly to tears myself, all I could picture was Robert lying in the courtyard, bound and beaten, and myself in his place. "Lia," I said gently, "even your Robert, as strong as a dozen of me, couldn't spirit you out of the city."

Lia stood up again, her voice frantic. "We left too early, when there were still curious eyes about the streets. They caught us by the city gate, where we had arranged to meet a coach. If we had left later—"

"The driver would have turned you in. Let us wait till you birth the child, till they remove the locks—"

Lia's face turned red with anger. "So they will take it? Just as they have taken us! Just as they have made us their playthings!"

Fearing that these exertions would harm her babe, I tried to calm her. "No one will disturb you. No one will take your child."

Lia remained silent. But after a moment, she pointed to the letter lying on my bed and said softly, "Were you not taken from your mother?"

"It was my choice to come to Coudenberg," I averred, but her words troubled me. In the thirteen months since I had arrived, I had learned not to trust the way things seemed.

"There is no choice," Lia said darkly.

My mind whirled. Would Don have brought me to Coudenberg against my will? I brushed this troublesome thought away, for I realized that Lia was finally revealing something about her life before Coudenberg. "Did you have no choice?" I asked.

"I was told that there was nothing for me but to come here," she said. "But, as with life itself, it may not be our choice to come, but it is our choice to leave."

Lia's words unsettled me. I feared that she might take her own life if I did not help her. But I also couldn't stop thinking of Don's promise to my mother that he would never keep a boy from his mother's breast. Locked in my quarters, I knew this to be a lie. Lia was right. That I had chosen Coudenberg was—like the life of pleasure and freedom we had been promised here—an illusion. We were captives, possessions, playthings, toys.

It was at that moment that I decided to rebel and quit my

life as court dwarf. I thought of Don's words to me in the garden: *Are you a man or still the child you appear?* He had claimed I didn't know who I was. But I did. I was the man of action I had dreamt myself to be before he had snatched me away to this counterfeit paradise.

"Lia, I will help you," I said. "I will find a way out."

Chapter 16

Just when I think I can heave my innards no more, a coast appears through the snow, and our bark pitches toward it.

"Is this Tycho?" I ask Matheus, emboldened by this glimpse of terra firma.

He shakes his head. "From here, we continue by coach."

Though our journey appears far from over, I greet this as welcome news, for I wish never again to venture upon the sea. As soon as we are on land, I counsel myself to think no more of the wind and water but of the comforting rumble of our new coach's wheels upon the solid earth. But when I touch Lia's shell, phantom waves still toss me.

The following day, we arrive in a port town of cobblestone roads and brightly colored houses. Judging from the Babel of tongues inside it, the inn we lodge at is crowded with travelers from shores both near and far—Danes, Scots, Holsteiners, Germans. As the driver carries my cage through a noisy room that reeks of herring and ale, I even recognize a few fellow Dutchmen, discussing the trade in grain and salt.

That night, Matheus is in an uncommonly bounteous mood. He brings me a full plate of herring, a half loaf of rye bread, and a mug of ale. After nearly a fortnight of meager fare, this counts as a feast, especially since he permits me to eat it on the bed beside him.

"I have never seen Kronborg," he observes midway through our meal.

He punctuates this musing with a belch, and I realize he has momentarily mistaken me for his supper partner rather than his captive. This is where we must be—in Elsinore, home to the great castle of Kronborg, where the King of Denmark and Norway holds court.

"Is Kronborg where you are taking me?" I ask.

As my viscera roil, I envision doing acrobatics or being stuffed into the costume of some beast. I would rather the dignity of hard labor than serving again as some monarch's fool.

Matheus looks at me quizzically and then, realizing what he has revealed, frowns.

"I told you," he says, more gruffly now. "You are going to Tycho."

"Where—?" I press.

But Matheus interrupts. "You will learn soon enough. We will be there tomorrow."

And so I learn that my journey is close to its end. That night, as I lie in my cage, I am gripped by such apprehension that every familiar thing—Matheus's lucky copper, even his buzzing snore—feels dear to me. But it is not just the unknown that frightens me. It is the known—most of all, the memories of my flight from Coudenberg with Lia.

As soon as Lia left my chamber, I felt a great sense of trepidation, not because of the dangers that awaited me, but because I feared I could not deliver on my promise to her. I had never been the receptacle of someone's hope, and found this weightless thing to be a heavy burden.

I knew where I would take her, where they would hide us both. I no longer believed Don's reading of my star chart that I should beware the influences of mother and home. It was mother and home that would save me. Astraveld would be our sanctuary. Instead of Hendrika, I pictured my mother warmly tending to Lia and her babe, her eyes crinkling at the sight of her small charges. And if Don came to snatch us back, the families of Astraveld would secrete us in their houses, protecting us with the fierce loyalty my mother inspired.

As for escaping Brussels, Robert and Lia's failed attempt proved instructive. We would need to leave after midnight when our unique presence was less likely to attract notice. And it would behoove us not to arrange to meet a coach at the city gates, where guards assembled. This question of how to arrange a driver without a spy at the stables alerting the palace, and how to ensure his reliability, plagued me. I had seen but little of Brussels in my year at Coudenberg; my impressions were mostly formed by my ride through the city that first night with Don. But as I thought back upon this trip, I remembered the peddlers and their carts camped in the square. A plan began to form. I would convince one of them to spirit us out of the city by offering him something precious in return. Though it was true I had nary a coin to my name, as I catalogued my worldly possessions, I realized that Lia and I possessed a small fortune's worth of jewel-encrusted costumes. The pearls alone would be handsome recompense for our driver.

My spirits buoyed, I turned to the question of how to escape from Coudenberg itself. If we wished to escape at night, Hendrika's key seemed the only way out. I knew it must open one of the doors—most likely the one leading back into the palace. But I did not trust that Hendrika would willingly aid us in an escape; for although she seemed most sorry about our plight, she had also consented to playing our jailor. I would have to steal the key—but how to do so from her very neck? I could slip into her chamber and try to remove it as she slept, but chances were that my efforts would rouse her. And if I somehow managed to steal it while she was awake—say, at her bath—she would realize it was missing before we had a chance to escape.

I pondered this problem late into the nights, lying sleepless in my bed. In this fashion, a fortnight passed. I knew Lia had to be anxious for word of my plan, but I avoided her as much as possible. Finally one evening I could stand it no more and decided to confess my failure. Before I left for her chamber, I heaped abuse upon myself—how I was just a child, as Don said, how I was good for nothing but leaping out of pies. Perchance, I thought bitterly, I could someday rise to Sebastian's role of pretending to save Lia with a false key.

At this instant, I froze, my self-pity abruptly forgotten as I considered for the first time Sebastian's key. Fashioned to look like one of the palace keys, it was almost exactly the same size and shape as the one around Hendrika's neck. If I substituted it for hers, she would be unlikely to notice the imposter until she actually attempted to use it. Although this did not solve the problem of how to pull off such an exchange, I felt my hope renewed.

As I rushed into the hall, I could hear Sebastian and Maria squabbling in the sitting room. I sneaked past them and into Sebastian's chamber, where I knew he kept his props. It was far less orderly than my own—costumes and hats littered the floor, no doubt thrown there that very afternoon as the servants straightened our rooms every morning. Or perhaps, I wondered, as I rummaged through drawers overflowing with scarves and buckles and buttons, Sebastian was allowed this level of disorder because he played the child whose tempers must be indulged, a role that—like my own as bumbling innocent—amused the Infanta.

In a drawer of pony bits and white leather bridles, I finally found the key. Holding it up, I felt most elated, for it was indeed a close substitute to Hendrika's.

"I always knew you would try to take it," said a voice from behind me.

I swung around to find Sebastian standing in the doorway, his arms crossed over his chest. He took a menacing step toward me. "Barely a year you've been here, and you think you can play the hero?"

I was perplexed by how he had figured out my plan to flee. Had he overheard me that night reassuring Lia? "How did you know?"

"I know your scheming type," he spat out. "But you must learn your place. I free the lady! You, sir, leap out of pies."

I started to laugh, which wasn't a wise idea. Sebastian threw himself at me. We tumbled to the floor as he pummeled my head.

"Stop! Stop!" I cried. "You've misunderstood. I'm not trying to usurp your role."

He continued beating upon me as if he were deaf.

"Please, Sebastian! Stop!" I said, grabbing his arms, thankful that I was slightly bigger and stronger. "I just need the key."

He thrashed about in my arms, glaring at me. "Why?"

There was no way out of the situation. I had to tell him the truth. "I'm going to free Lia."

"I knew it!"

"No," I said. "Not as an amusement. For real."

Sebastian stopped struggling as I quietly revealed the story—how Lia had beseeched me, Hendrika's key, my plan—omitting my and Lia's secret. But when I explained how my plan was to substitute the fake key in exchange for the real one, Sebastian snorted. "Don't be a fool, Jepp! Think upon Robert."

This engendered a passionate response in me. "I think upon him every day! We wronged him, Sebastian. He was innocent!"

"Innocent?" Sebastian mocked. "How can he be innocent when the child is his?"

I hastily recalled my promise to Lia not to betray her secret and tried to dissemble. "Innocent in spirit, I mean."

My face felt warm and my words unconvincing even to me. Sebastian narrowed his eyes. "What do you know, Jepp?"

I looked away.

"You must tell me," he insisted.

I felt I had no choice to but to reveal the truth. I swore him to secrecy, made him promise to make no mention of what I had told him to anyone, especially Lia. Then I leaned over and whispered what I had seen and what I knew.

Sebastian stood up and began to pace the room. For a long

time he spoke not, and this silence struck me as more genuine than any of his rages. At last, he squatted down beside me. "And how do you plan to plant this decoy?"

"Perhaps when she is sleeping—?"

"You think Hendrika will slumber through this? She is the lightest sleeper among us."

"There may be another way . . . perhaps she removes the key to bathe?"

"No," Sebastian said, waving me off. "You simply need to make sure she slumbers soundly."

"Pray how—?"

"Maria takes a sleeping tincture of poppy called laudanum. She puts a few drops of it in her hippocras." Sebastian grinned. "If you place it into Hendrika's wine at supper—"

"Sebastian, you are brilliant!" I bowed my head toward him.

At this show of gratitude, Sebastian's face clouded. "Take care of our songbird, Jepp."

"I will protect her with my life," I solemnly swore, though my conscience pricked me as I thought about how I had revealed her secret. Perhaps she would be more forgiving of my betrayal if Sebastian joined us? "But why don't you come?"

Sebastian shook his head. "As much as I hate the imbeciles and miscreants who surround us, I hate the rest of the world more."

I smiled at Sebastian's familiar choler but then grew serious again, imagining the punishment that might befall him if the Infanta thought he had aided us in our escape. "If I succeed, you must tell them I stole your key."

Sebastian snorted. "You think I was planning to implicate myself? You will be the first I blame."

We shook hands, and I started for the door.

"Wait, Jepp. You should tell Maria what you are up to. It is unwise to attempt to steal her laudanum. She guards it most closely. And she is unlikely to believe it is for either of us."

I thought uneasily of Maria's faith in the Infanta. "But what if she does not approve?"

Sebastian's eyes met my own. "You must remind her of Robert . . . and tell her of Pim."

Chapter 17

The next morning, I went to Lia and told her my plan. Still troubled that I had betrayed her secret and not wishing for her to know that the others would be involved, I claimed that I had stolen the key from Sebastian's room and the laudanum from Maria's. She seemed not at all surprised by my ingenuity and most pleased with the charming picture I painted of Astraveld and the succor we would find there. The border between the Spanish Netherlands and the Protestant North was a three-day drive from Brussels, and Astraveld only five miles farther if we took a northwesterly route. We settled on a night four days later when the moon would be new and the sky darkest.

In truth, I had not yet secured the potion from Maria. Despite Sebastian's encouragement, I remained apprehensive about confiding my plans to her. It was only on the morning of our departure, after I had finished—with a tinge of sadness—my last morning repast of cakes and jam, that I knocked on her door.

Maria opened it still in her dressing gown. Her brown hair, threaded with gray, was piled high above her lumpen face.

"Why, Jepp, come in!" She gestured me toward a small divan.

Though Maria was the queen of the sitting room, directing affairs and telling tales from her small throne, when she retired to her chamber, she never invited anyone to follow. In this way she was more solitary than the rest of us. Her room was neat and airless, tinged with the slightly acrid smell of her hippocras, as though the window had not been opened for some time.

"Forgive my intrusion," I said. My eyes scanned her small wardrobe and chest of drawers, wondering where she hid her laudanum.

"Not at all." She sat down beside me on the divan and stared at me. Her eyes had a mother's way of delving. "Is something troubling you, Jepp?"

I took a deep breath. "It's Lia," I said.

Maria shook her head and sighed, enjoying as some women do the dramas of others. "Poor Lia."

"I'm going to help her escape."

I had not meant to reveal my intentions from the start and immediately regretted my words.

Maria looked at me in alarm. "After what befell Robert? Are you mad, Jepp?"

"She does not want the child born here—"

"She does not know what she wants!"

"But she does!" I continued. "She wants the child born free. It's her desire!"

"And you want to fulfill this desire?" Maria snapped. "The freedom to die? She is far along with child. You endanger her and yourself with such a foolhardy escapade!"

The thought of Lia's death took me aback.

Maria saw this. "Stay here, Jepp," she added, more gently. "Here she is safe."

My life would have been very different had I dropped my argument and followed this logic. But it was too late. I had seen too much of Coudenberg to believe this place offered any of us refuge. How could it, when it housed the very monsters that tormented us?

"Safe?" I repeated angrily. "She is not safe here. It was Pim who did this to her."

I felt another pinch of guilt for revealing this confidence, but I also felt it the only way to convince Maria of the righteousness of my plan.

Maria's dark eyes flickered, but she betrayed no surprise.

"Robert is innocent," I said in case she had failed to understand the import of my revelation.

Maria walked over to her chest and pulled a glass decanter from the bottom drawer. She poured its contents into a goblet that had been sitting on a tray with her uneaten breakfast. Then she drank it.

Her calm disturbed me.

"Think how they laughed at her and Robert, a dwarf and a giant, mocking them!" I continued frantically. "We are kept for their amusement, Maria. Does the Infanta really care if Pim has his way with Lia? Or just that we sing and jape and jump out of pies?"

Maria put down her goblet and waved me off. "Jepp, you are young. You think only of your pride."

My countenance must have betrayed my consternation, for she continued, "I know I seem unfeeling, but my intent is kind. I have seen the world, Jepp. It is cruel to those like us—"

"It is cruel here—" I countered.

"What do you know of the world?" Maria said harshly. "You know nothing. Let me tell you how I ended up as a court dwarf. My own mother sold me to a court. She said I was too ugly to marry and too costly to feed. The day I left was the only day I pleased her.

"I tell you this not to make you feel sorry for me. I have had a wonderful life. I have sat beside queens, conversed with kings and princes. I have danced the galliard in dresses embroidered in pearls and gold. I have slept on soft beds and eaten the finest meals.

"I would be lying if I did not admit that there have been humiliations along the way. But all of them are worth soft clothes, Jepp, a warm meal, a chamber of one's own"—she held up her goblet—"a decanter of hippocras. Out in the world, you and I can never belong. At court, we have a place. Lia's child will as well. Lia will come to realize this."

"I won't."

Maria looked at me pityingly. "Your mother—"

"Was nothing like yours! The world is not as cruel as you say. Nor is Coudenberg as kind. Think of what they did to Robert!"

"You think of it too. Robert endangered her by taking her—"

"—*Pim* endangered Lia! Robert came to her aid."

Maria sighed. "Give up your plans, Jepp. They will only lead to trouble. As a dwarf—"

The word rankled me. I thought of my mother, who loved me but not as a curiosity or a prize. "Have you ever thought of yourself as just one of God's creatures?"

"I do not follow," said Maria, but her face said otherwise.

"Lia deserves to live or die as she pleases. She deserves the freedom God gave her."

"But we are not free, Jepp." Maria held out her shortened arms. "This is our fate. It's in our stars. It's the curse we've been burdened with."

"God did not curse us. The people who mistreat us curse us."

Maria shook her head wearily. "Jepp, I cannot reason with you—"

I caught a note of defeat in her voice. "Then don't," I begged. "Just help us. I am taking Lia away. We leave tonight. We avoid the city gates—"

Maria held out her hand. "Do not tell me."

I felt great relief, for I knew then that she would keep our confidence. "I need some of your laudanum, not for us."

Maria studied me as she considered this request. "You cannot escape who you are," she finally said.

"But I only wish to escape Coudenberg."

"Coudenberg is who you are, Jepp."

This angered me. "You are mistaken!"

She sighed wearily. Then she turned and walked to her door. "You'll find the laudanum in the drawer. It is yellow in color. One vial will give a night's peace. Take no more."

Without another word, she left, closing the door behind her.

My cheeks still burning with the fire of my argument, I ran quickly to the chest of drawers, for I feared Maria might yet change her mind. There in the bottom drawer was a collection of vials, some larger and filled with a clear liquid, others smaller and containing a yellow tincture that I knew must be Maria's laudanum. I plucked out a single yellow vial, then closed the drawer. Gripping it tightly in my trembling hands, I raced out of Maria's chamber and back to my own.

That evening, as the shadows began to fall, I poked my head out of my door and began my watch. At seven thirty, the guard opened the door for the final time that day. A trio of servants proceeded into our corridor, carrying our supper and various sundries for the night. A few minutes later, as we had agreed upon, Lia called for Hendrika and kept her occupied as I dashed into her chamber and poured the tincture into her wine.

Although I had been served my favorite supper—a guinea hen garnished with parsley and turnips—for the first time that I could recall, I had little appetite. I was beset by fears that Hendrika had not drunk her wine or had tasted the laudanum or that Maria had not permitted me a strong enough dose. But, as the ten o'clock bell struck, I realized that I had not heard Hendrika's voice in the hall, bidding Lia good night, nor any sound from her chamber. With Sebastian's key and my candle in hand, I tiptoed toward it.

After a light knock on her door elicited no answer, I slowly pushed it open and peered inside. In the flickering light of my candle, I made out Hendrika's prostrate form upon the bed. Her dark hair was still pinned on top of her head and she had not bothered to undress, so overwhelming must have been her need to slumber. Her pale skin seemed waxen, as in death, but the slow rise and fall of her breast—and the key that so temptingly lay upon it—reassured me that she was yet among the living.

Still, she seemed a different creature in this tranquil state and in her own forlorn lair. As I gently closed the door behind me, pausing to make certain that this sound did not rouse her,

I allowed myself—as I had not before—to study her chamber. Although, like the rest of our quarters, the walls and ceilings had been built to a miniature scale, her furniture and bed were of average size, giving the room a cramped and disconcerting feel. On a table beside her bed lay her rosary and, more surprising to me, a small painted likeness of a dark-haired man dressed in a fur cape. As I crept closer to her bedside, I recalled what Maria had said about Hendrika not being the virgin she seemed. I stared at this gentleman but did not recognize him from court. Lying open beside the likeness was a star chart that I concluded from its sun sign of Capricorn must be Hendrika's own. Despite insisting to Don she had no interest in her own stars, many feverish jottings had been made upon it. These objects—with their intimations of love and longing—filled me with pity, and I suddenly felt sorry to betray her. But I also knew she would never willingly free us, for she seemed not free herself.

As quietly as I could, I hoisted myself onto her bed, then kept as still as the deer in sight of the hunter, my heart thumping. But she slept on, and with trembling fingers I unfastened the gold chain from about her neck and lifted the key from her breast. I slid it off the chain into my clammy hand, then replaced it with Sebastian's. But just as I clasped the chain back around her neck, she stirred, and with an incomprehensible murmur, gripped the decoy key. I froze, certain I had been apprehended, but her eyes remained closed, and I realized that she was dreaming.

A few minutes later, my hands still shaking but the real key nestled in my pocket, I knocked three times on Lia's door, the signal of success we had agreed upon. Then I returned to my room and, full of apprehension, made final preparations for our journey. I had thought it safest for us to wait till midnight, when there was less chance of our being intercepted in the palace halls.

Naturally, there was a risk Hendrika might arise from her stupor before then. I could only hope that the decoy key would convince her that nothing was amiss.

As a result of this fear, these final hours passed interminably slowly. I harvested the pearls from my and Lia's finest garments, stowing them in a purse inside my sack; stuffed several pillows beneath my blankets in a semblance of my form; and donned a dark gentleman's costume, slipping Lia's seashell into a pocket.

Just before midnight, weary of pacing my room and eager to be on our way, I heaved up my sack and ventured into the quiet hall. To my surprise, Lia was already waiting. She wore a long, black hooded cape that concealed her condition. Upon seeing me, she took my hand and squeezed it. Though she said nothing, I knew exactly what this gesture meant, and gave thanks to God that I had not failed her.

I slid the key from my pocket to show her. She nodded and we started toward the door. But just as I reached up on tiptoe to put it into the lock, a door opened and someone stepped into the hall. I whipped around, key in hand, expecting Hendrika to seize us both. Standing there instead was Maria. I wondered if she had changed her mind and was about to raise an alarm or stop us.

"Godspeed, children," she said softly.

Lia looked as stunned as I felt as Maria rushed up and embraced her.

Maria kissed the top of Lia's head and then turned to embrace me. I could smell the stench of her hippocras on her breath as she whispered in my ear. "If you run into trouble, go to the Dubois family house—their coat of arms bears a tree—on Rollebeek Straat. Ask for Annika. She used to work at Coudenberg and knows me. Tell her you are . . . my family."

Then, with a kiss to my head, she turned back to her chamber.

I looked at Lia. A tear was wending its way down her cheek. I felt stricken by similar emotions. Though Coudenberg was not our home, we were still leaving the ones most like us, the ones who understood. Maria seemed the most imprisoned of us all, and I wished, at that moment, that I could take her with me.

"Are you ready?" I finally asked.

Lia nodded.

I shoved the key into the lock—relieved when it fit. Then I turned it, and opened the door into the darkened hall of the palace.

Chapter 18

I barely sleep, certain that our destination the following day is Kronborg, that Tycho is some wing of the great castle, which Master Kees once told me about during a lesson on the world's most powerful kings. My only hope is that I might escape to a boat of my countrymen, who would surely take pity on a prisoner of the Spanish crown and spirit me away. But Matheus has locked my cage, his kindness apparently subordinate to his sense of duty.

The following afternoon, my cage is covered once again with a blanket and Matheus hoists it into the air. Once he carries me outside, onto streets that smell of horse dung and smoke, I expect my captor to unlock the coach door and shuttle me into the back. But instead, with a clatter, I am placed, cage and all, on what I guess from the cold air is the back of an open cart. This strikes me as an unceremonious way to arrive at a court—but then again, I am a castaway from another realm, not some celebrated visitor.

Too soon, the cart stops. I can hear Matheus hop off, and then my cage is lifted and put on the ground. He draws up my blanket, and as I blink in the late afternoon sunlight, he unlocks the door and orders me out. To my surprise, there is no castle in sight, only an old peasant standing beside a skiff that lies half on the shore and half in the water before us. Though I swore I would never again journey by sea, I am so relieved that I am not going to Kronborg that I scramble into the skiff upon Matheus's command.

As the waves pick up, I wait for my gut to churn, but all is calm. I am so grateful for this reprieve that I gaze upon the watery road with renewed vision, taken by the beauty of the undulating waves, the light of the setting sun seeping through the clouds, the splash of spray and lashing wind through the skiff's sail. Although my fate is still uncertain to me, for this brief moment, whatever misfortune may befall me next troubles me not; this world is not against me, but mine.

Just such a moment as this Lia and I shared after we slipped ghostlike through the empty palace halls and emerged through a side door into the night. The sky above us was still and clear—without breeze or cloud—the only blemish a sprinkling of distant stars. Although the frigid promontory of Coudenberg lived up to its name, the cold did not trouble us but rather, in signaling that our journey had finally begun, invigorated our spirits. To avoid any guards, we slipped through the gardens on our way to the road into the city. As we passed the stunted orchard, the apple and pear trees pruned and propped to keep their shape through winter, Lia took my hand and entwined her fingers through my own. "I am the happiest of all creatures," she whispered.

And so too was I, though I gave no voice to my heart.

Past empty trellises and snow-covered topiaries, we joined the road, which sloped down through the city from our aerie prison. We saw no soul—quick or otherwise—and yet still we whispered, so as not to break the hush of night. It was different talking to Lia there, the night concealing our forms but freeing our feelings. I spoke of my mother, my longing to see her.

"Why did you agree to leave Astraveld?" she asked.

"You said I didn't have a choice," I reminded her.

"The court would have compelled you one way or another as they did me. But you *believed* you had a choice. So why did you choose to leave?"

A year earlier, I would have said, to seek my fortune. Now I said, "Because I feared to be alone."

"And yet you never were," she mused. "You were loved."

"But there were none like me there."

"Why seek out like? God made the creatures of the earth in great variety."

I thought of Lia's memento mori—the delicate shell snug in my pocket, the orange, the flower, the skull—they were reminders of death but at the same time, they were reminders of life in all its colors and forms. Even the four of us—Sebastian, Maria, Lia, and I—were expressions of God's infinite creative variation. And yet Maria's view troubled me still—that we were cursed to a life of loneliness and revilement by what made us different. "But before Coudenberg, did you not feel alone?" I asked.

I had not meant to broach this forbidden subject. But Lia's hand was warm in mine, and our escape from Coudenberg had emboldened me. As we continued down the lanes of the city, past tall, silent houses, it seemed we could talk freely about anything. And yet, my question hung in the cold air.

"I did not mean to pry," I said. "If you wish not to say—"

Lia stopped, loosened her hand from mine, and touched her girth.

"How do you fare?" I asked.

She did not seem to hear me. "Like you, Jepp, I once had a home and parents who loved me. Their death is what made me feel alone. They and my three brothers—strong boys, each nearly thrice as big as me—died of fever over a single week. I do not know why I was spared, but I tended them all to their graves."

I suddenly understood the reason for Lia's memento mori, her song, her dolorous manner. She continued walking with a weary gait, and I slowed my pace at her side.

"We lived in a village close to the city of Sluis. The Spanish laid siege to the city when I was a child, and rule it to this day. A fortnight after my family died, a local Spanish officer claimed to have pity upon my plight and arranged for my transport to Coudenberg. What choice did I have? If my parents or my brothers had lived . . ."

She blinked rapidly, warding off tears. I wished to console her, for I did not yet know that grief is a burden that no man can carry for another.

"Lia," I whispered, "you are still loved."

She smiled faintly. "I am tired, Jepp."

Her face, I noticed, was flushed. "It is not far to the square," I reassured her.

We spoke no more as we made our way through the sleeping city. Lia's tale stayed with me, and I thought of my own mother longingly. A veil of clouds appeared over the stars as a few flakes of snow drifted down to the street. A shutter clattered open; a dog trotted shadowlike behind us, then disappeared; a candle flickered on in a window. We passed a stable, where the hollow tap of the horses' hooves, shifting in their stalls, reminded me of home.

Twice Lia stopped and leaned against me, her expression briefly disconcerted before she took my arm and murmured, "All is well." I was anxious to reach the peddlers' square and end her exertions.

The square was smaller than I remembered from my ride with Don, but then again I had become accustomed to the grand spaces of Coudenberg. Peddlers' carts jammed the main part of the square, and in between them a few hearty souls stoked fires and kept watch over their wares. The rest of the peddlers had no doubt taken rooms at the city's inns. At the square's edge, I instructed Lia to sit in the shadows of a cart, for it was best that the other peddlers remembered only me. From there, I peered out at their lot. Their faces were hunched over their fires and unreadable. I finally chose the one closest to the edge of the square and the road, and took out my purse.

The man looked up upon hearing my footstep, and his mouth fell open at the sight of me. It had been some time since my appearance was gaped at, but it did not put me in foul temper as it was yet another reminder of my approaching freedom. I smiled at him, but his gob remained open. I began to wonder if he were simple until I realized that it was darkest night and such a traveler as I might seem otherworldly. "I am human," I called out softly. "Just small."

The peddler closed his mouth then. He was young and sandy-haired.

"I would like to buy something," I said, holding up my purse.

"A fine hour for that it is," he said, eyeing me from head to toe.

I opened the purse to show him the pearls.

A fire flickered in his eyes as he caught sight of them. "Let me see, friend."

I dared not hand him the purse but instead gave him one pearl. The peddler glanced around to be sure no one was watching, then rubbed it against his tooth and grunted.

"I will give you a dozen more," I said. "For a ride."

The peddler laughed. "Is this some trick?"

"No, I need you to take me and my—" Here I faltered. "My wife to a town near the border. She is with child. We are in a hurry and must leave now. If you do not wish this deal, I will bring it to another."

"No need for that, friend!" he said, rolling the pearl in between his fingers. "I will take you."

I pointed to the spot where I had left Lia. "You must help my wife into your cart."

Stomping out his fire, he followed me. But before we could reach the spot, I heard a moan and Lia appeared, staggering toward me as tears streamed down her face.

"What is it?" I exclaimed. "I have found someone to take us! We'll go to Astraveld—"

But even as I spoke, I knew from the sight of her that these exhortations were useless. The child was on its way.

Lia fell into my arms. "Please," I pleaded, stroking her hair. "We can go—"

"Jepp," she gasped. "I can't—"

In the storm of her sobs that followed, the peddler snatched the purse out of my hands and dashed off. But it hardly mattered. I could not have chased after him. I was dragging Lia through the streets of Brussels to the only place of refuge I knew.

Chapter 19

on and I had passed Rollebeek Straat when he first brought me to Coudenberg. It was a long street of tall houses, which was made longer not just by my stature but by my charge. Every few moments Lia crouched in pain, and so I had to coax her along. When we at last reached a gabled house with a tree upon its coat of arms, I was dismayed to discover that I could not reach the handle of the gigantic door. I knocked and kicked at it, but it was only when Lia began to wail that a gray-haired woman in a dressing gown appeared. From the pot of water in her hands, it was clear she had mistaken Lia's shrill cry for that of a lovesick cat, and she stared at us in wonder before I shouted at her to find us Annika.

"Hush," she said, pointing up at the windows. "The master and mistress slumber." I understood then that she was a servant to the Dubois family, the fine people who occupied this grand dwelling.

"Is Annika your mistress?" I inquired in quieter tone. "For if so, I need—"

"She serves this house. She is nurse to the children." She eyed Lia. "Your need for her is clear." She said this in a way that was not unkind and held open the door, allowing us shelter in the parlor from the elements, which some hours into our journey had lost their enchantment.

"Thank you," I said, truly grateful to deliver Lia behind solid walls.

"Wait here," ordered the old woman. "And try not to raise the rest of the house." As Lia writhed silently in my arms, I whispered to her that all would be well, but I feared my words provided scant comfort. After a few minutes, I was relieved to hear footsteps descend the stairs. A stout woman with a wide peasant face and flaxen hair appeared. "I am Annika," she said, surveying us with dismay.

"I am Jepp," I replied. "Maria sent us. We are family."

At this, she reached down and stroked my face. Her broad hands reminded me of my mother's, and I felt oddly calmed. But her caress did also confuse me, and I felt compelled to direct her to the true patient. "She is having a child," I said, pointing at Lia.

Annika's fingers withdrew. "I can see." As she crouched beside Lia, pressing her swollen girth as if testing a fruit, I briefly regained hope. Surely this woman, so gentle in temperament, would see Lia safely through the trials of childbirth.

"Mena," she inquired of the older woman, who had reappeared breathless behind her. "We will be less likely to wake the master in your quarters. May we go there?"

Mena opened a door off the parlor, holding it open as her

answer. "She looks to be but a child herself," she remarked as Annika heaved Lia up and carried her inside.

I followed behind, unsure as to my duty. Mena led us through a large kitchen and into a small room off of it that smelled of the tinctures of old age. A rumpled bed served as the centerpiece and the only warmth came from the dying embers in the hearth. Mena lit a candle and stoked the fire, though this did little to increase the warmth. Then Annika set Lia down before the hearth, exhorting her to stand upon her feet; but Lia lay down and curled into a ball like some animal protecting itself from violence.

The women whispered in each other's ears, and then Mena took me by the hand. "This is no place for a boy," she said, leading me out. I would have corrected her but, truth be told, in this frightful circumstance, I did not feel like the man of action I had so recently been.

Mena directed me to the kitchen, where she busied herself with the tasks of childbirth, boiling water, preparing a caudle of wine and herbs, stuffing the keyhole of the door to prevent evil spirits. The kitchen seemed a peaceable kingdom compared to the one we had just left—a pot hung over the hearth, potatoes and turnips lay in ordered piles on a table, a bouquet of dried herbs had been suspended above the chopping block, chickens slept in a cage. Mena moved about with purpose; it was clear that this realm of spice and spoon, larder and ladle, was her domain. "You knew that Annika once worked at Coudenberg, didn't you?" she asked, as she swept by me.

I shook my head, wondering if this was her way of signaling to me that she knew that we were from Coudenberg too.

On the heels of this odd exchange, Mena disappeared into the bedroom with the caudle and boiling water, and I was left alone. But I had little time to ponder her intent, for but a moment later she reappeared, clad in cloak and hood, a most troubling costume.

"How is she?" I begged.

"We need shepherd's purse," she said, barely looking at me, and scurried out.

My thoughts were a jumble. From my mother, I knew this herb to be useful in childbirth. But was Mena's errand different from the one she acknowledged? I felt troubled by her intelligence that Annika had worked at Coudenberg and wondered if that was her true destination. If so, I realized that there was nothing I could do to prevent our capture. In Lia's state she could not flee, and I would rather be sent back to the palace in chains than depart without her.

A loaf of bread sat on the table, but I had no appetite. My ears strained to hear Lia's exertions, though when she did wail or cry through the door it comforted me not. I knew not how long I waited, expectant with worry, as I stoked the fire and paced the kitchen. The winter night seemed longer than any I had known, and my prayers and promises to my Maker lost in that darkness.

When a door finally opened it was not the one to the outside world I expected, but to Mena's bedroom. Annika stepped out, her broad hands stained with blood, her hair disheveled. She looked at me with such pity that I feared that fate had conspired against us.

"Go in, Jepp," she said. "She wishes to speak to you."

To my shame, I stood wedded to the floor.

"There is not much time!" she said, pushing me toward the door. "Go!"

Even now, I cannot describe my emotions as I comprehended what she meant. I could not breathe. I could not see. My feet were like another's, walking of their own accord; my hands a stranger's, opening the door as I stepped inside the dim bedroom. The sight before me was monstrous, yet I saw it as if from afar. Lia in the bed, her face gray, her body shrouded in a bloodstained blanket. A red-haired child lay in her arms. She sang to it, her voice barely rising above a whisper.

"From distant lands I have come
To sing a song of home
Weeping for the love I left
Upon those gentle shores.
I have flown o'er mountains cold,
And forests dark and silent seas,
I fly now captive in this cell,
Till Death erase these memories."

But the child did not stir to her tune, for it was blue and lifeless.

"We shall be buried together," she said, looking at me for the first time upon the song's end.

"In many years, perhaps—" I said frantically.

"Jepp, you must listen to me! I have not the strength to speak twice."

I ran to her side. "You cannot die," I whispered.

She did not appear to hear me. "I do not wish for them to bury us at Coudenberg, but in my town, by the sea, beside my family."

Even on her deathbed, she wished to go home. I began to cry.

"I am free, Jepp," Lia said gently. "There is no cause for tears."

"I have killed you!" I cried.

"Let no one tell you that. You have saved me."

Outside, as if day had swiftly arrived, I heard the wheels of a coach and then voices.

"Please, listen. Tell Robert—"

A door opened in the next room.

"Tell him I loved him."

The door to the bedroom flung open, and the Infanta's physician dashed in, followed by two guards and Don.

Before Lia and I could exchange another word, Don grabbed me by the scruff and dragged me out of the room. I feared he might have broken my neck right there in the kitchen had Annika not stepped before him. "I summoned you trusting that you would be gentle with him. He understands not what he has done."

Annika was my betrayer, my Judas—of that I was now certain—and, yet, she was defending me. Adding to my confusion, my angels and demons were the same.

Though he could have scolded her for her impudence, Don released his grip upon me. "As Maria surely noted in her message to you, it is best Jepp return to those who can protect him from his own foolish nature."

I realized then that Maria had not given me Annika's address as a refuge but as a trap. But I could not be angry with her, too worried was I about Lia and whether the Infanta's physician could save her.

Don took my hand and led me out of the kitchen, past a wide-eyed Mena. A crowd had assembled in the hall—among them a stately couple sure to be master and mistress Dubois, no doubt awakened by the coaches and commotion. "Business of the Infanta," he explained, tipping his hat and smiling affably at them as we passed.

Don led me out into the gray, dawn light of Rollebeek Straat, then picked me up and shoved me into a coach beside him. As the driver set off for Coudenberg, I waited for Don to strike me, but the only violence he performed was to his teeth, scraping at them with his familiar splinter of a chicken bone. I sat beside him and thought not of my own fate, but of Lia's. Closing my eyes, I bartered with God. If the physician could save her, I would happily bear any torture that the Infanta's guards could devise. I would forgive Maria. I would even stay at Coudenberg forever.

As we began to ascend the cursed promontory, Don cracked his knuckles. "Did you know, Jepp," he said, "that Mars, the God of War, rules your house of home and family?"

It was at this moment I knew that he planned to personally administer my torture.

Chapter 20

Not long into my second sea voyage, a shore appears: a range of rugged cliffs that juts up from the sea like Neptune's brow. As our skiff blows toward this outcrop, the only sign of civilization is a crumbling fortress with a half-collapsed turret, perched atop the headlands. We pass beneath this ruin, rocking tremulously as we round a bend into a small harbor. There, in the growing shadows, several skiffs similar to our own lie on the beach. As the old peasant who ferried us drags his beside the others, I wonder if I have finally reached Tycho. My fear returns, apprehension of what kind of place I have landed in and who my new master will be.

The old peasant directs us to a set of steps worn into the cliffside. Although Matheus allows me to walk, my legs, cramped these last two weeks in coach and cage, are unused to such exertions. By the top, they are sore and I am panting. But I am rewarded for my efforts with a view of a small village set on a gentle, sloping plain. The low, half-timbered buildings with their thatched roofs remind me of Astraveld. For an instant, I imagine that Lia is with me and that we have arrived home. As I have a hundred times since her death, I lose her again—a moment's blessed forgetfulness dashing into grief.

Although this humble village in this desolate place suggests my new life will be one of hard labor, I do not fear the prospect. I long for the blankness of mind that a tired body brings, the small peace of a hard-worked day. With Lia gone and my mother and home denied me, it is the only tranquility I can envision.

When we enter the village, the old peasant takes us past farm-houses, wherein I imagine crackling hearths, and hams hanging from the blackened rafters. But instead of taking us inside, he brings us to a stable, where he leads out an old nag and hitches her to a cart. He gestures for us to climb in, and as we bump along, winding our way past the shades of farmhouses and crofts and then larger fields lying fallow beneath the snow, I realize that my journey is not yet over. We are leaving the village for somewhere else.

I had never before seen the Infanta's dungeon. In the days when I could freely roam, it had never occurred to me to seek out this drear hall, and by the time Robert was imprisoned there, I was myself a captive. All I knew was that the dungeon existed deep beneath the savory kitchens and marble halls and gold-dusted chambers, a seed of sorrow at Coudenberg's core.

It was to this place that Don took me, by means of a crude staircase that descended behind the guards' quarters. The stones were rough hewn, the way narrow, and Don made me stumble down first as he carried a candle behind me. The air had a fetid smell—of human waste and sodden earth—that grew most powerful as the stairs ended. As my eyes adjusted to this shadowy realm, I could see we were in a corridor lined with cells. The floor here was neither marble nor wood but dirt and, in places where water had trickled down from the stone walls, mud.

Human forms lurked behind the bars. As Don led me along the corridor, I looked among them for Robert. But though a few faces stared out, the whites of their eyes flashing in the light of Don's candle, I did not see his enormous jaw and soft eyes.

When we reached the last cell, Don unlocked the door with a key and held it open.

"Go ahead, Jepp," he said, directing me inside with a flourish of his hand. It was a sinister repetition of the introduction he had given me to Coudenberg over a year earlier. He followed me inside, then shut the door behind us. He removed his hat and his gloves, twining them neatly through the bars. Then he crouched down so as to peer directly at me. "You have shamed me before the Infanta," he announced.

His stillness put me in mind of a snake coiled to strike. But though my stomach curdled with fear, I found my voice. "That was not my intent."

He butted my face with his knee and sent me sprawling on my back.

"Get up!" he shouted, dragging me to my feet. But I let my legs go limp, falling to the floor. He climbed on top of me and began to rain blows upon my head. I tried to cover my face, but he tore my hands away and renewed his efforts, pounding upon me like a baker upon dough. My face felt wet but not from tears. I would not let them flow. As my head throbbed and my skin tore and bruised, I thought not of my torment but of my mother, who had always protected me from violence, from the cruelty of men like Don. I began to call to her, though the words that came out of my swollen lips were unintelligible.

"Stop!" her voice cried, as she pulled at Don's arms. "Let him be!"

My sight was clouded, for blood had spilled into my eyes, yet I soon became aware that I was not imagining this scene. As the blows ceased, I was cradled against a woman's bosom, but it was not soft and wide but bony and long. I felt unsettled, as if I were in a dream when the familiar mutates into something strange. The woman holding me was not my mother but Hendrika.

"What have you done?" she asked me.

At first I thought she alluded to my betrayal, to the sleeping tincture and theft of her key. But her voice was not angry, only mournful, and her dark eyes were wet.

"Lia is dead," she said.

An anguished cry echoed across the dungeon. At first I imagined it to be my own, my grief assuming its true proportions, but from its deep tone I realized it was Robert's. The sound of it was more painful to me than any blow I had yet received. Only then did I begin to cry, my tears mixing with blood.

"This is all your fault!" Don shouted.

For once, I agreed. I looked up, wishing he would strike me again.

"Please, Don Diego!" said Hendrika. She clasped me tighter to her breast as wisps of her dark hair, wet with blood, clung to my face. "It can't be undone now."

"You have ruined me with this business!" he roared, glaring at me.

Hendrika clambered onto her knees, lifting me into her arms. "Go!" she pleaded. "I beg of you, Don Diego. It is over now. Just go!"

This quarrel, though over my very fate, concerned me not. I did not wonder or give thanks that Hendrika defended me. All I could think about was Lia.

"Damn you, Jepp!" Don said, ripping me out of Hendrika's arms and grasping me by the neck.

I closed my eyes, waiting for him to break it.

Instead, he dragged me back down the corridor, past Robert, now visible weeping in his cell, and up the stairs. This ascent was so rapid that I was halfway up the stairs before I thought to tell Robert what Lia had wished him to know. "She loved you, Robert!" I cried out to him. He had won our rivalry—for my instincts were not wrong, it was him she loved—and yet we both had lost. There was no response to my cry, and I couldn't be sure he had heard me.

"Quiet!" Don yelled, slamming me against the wall.

At the top of the stairs, we ran into one of the Infanta's guards. "Her Royal Highness wishes to see you and your charge," he said to Don. Staring at my face with a grin, he added, "Your improvements to his countenance may soften her heart."

"I will be there expressly," said Don. But as soon as the guard had passed us, he shoved me out a side door and back into his coach. After giving the driver directions, Don joined me and we rode in silence. My head ached, and I could feel my face throb and swell. I thought of Lia, but my tears were exhausted and my heart felt numb.

As we pulled up before a grand gabled house near the Cathedral, Don bound my wrists behind my back and then disembarked, locking me in behind him. Some minutes later, the man I would come to know as my driver appeared, carrying the cage that was to be my home. "Make certain he remains in it!" Don ordered. "He may try to escape but cannot return here again."

Under Don's watchful eye, the driver readied the coach for our journey. Just as he closed the door, I remembered my other promise to Lia and banged on the door. "Don, you must make certain Lia and her child are buried in her village, near Sluis! It was her wish."

The door flew open, leaving no question as to whether he had heard me. "She will go home," Don hissed. "But you will never know home or mother again."

Chapter 21

As I stroke the shell in my pocket and the little village recedes, I think of Lia. Did I do her wrong or right? This question has haunted me every step of the journey. Sometimes I believe—as Maria would—that it matters not that Lia died free, only that she died. Other times I remember how we were treated at Coudenberg and regain faith in Lia's dying words. But this is not a question I can answer to any satisfaction. Fourteen months after leaving Astraveld, I am no longer certain of right and wrong. I am certain only of my own sorrows and doubts.

The road behind lies heavy on my heart, so I turn my gaze forward—and this is when my eyes alight upon a sight most startling. On a hilltop in the distance is a castle crowned with an onion-shaped dome and flanked by cylindrical towers, like the strange offspring of palace and cathedral. At first, I wonder if it is an illusion of the growing dusk, for this intricate construction seems entirely out of keeping with the spare, empty kingdom around it. As we near, wending up the hill toward this structure, its features only grow more fantastical. I see golden spires, cupolas, balconies, and, it appears, a series of turrets in the shape of ladies' skirts that jut from the castle's sides.

"This is Tycho?" I ask, breaking the silence.

The old man spits on the ground as if trying to expel a bitter taste. "Tycho's," he answers.

It seems that my new master, this Tycho, is no humble country gentleman but a man of means so great and tastes so peculiar that he would build this diabolical castle in this desolate spot. My dreams of simple work vanish and a feeling of trepidation overtakes me. Will I be forced again to jump out of pies for some rich man's pleasure? Will the powerful once again mock me and abuse those I come to love? The thought of my own humanity, my will, being forever subjugated by those who deem themselves superior has become as unbearable to me as it was to Lia. I wish to jump out of the cart and flee. But there is nowhere to run, for as we ride up to the castle, I take in a view that would be lovely to most but to me appears a prison. In every direction is the cold, blue sea. My new home is an island.

Above the turrets and domes of Tycho's castle, the first stars of the long winter night begin to shine through the firmament. Although I know Don to have been an untrustworthy interpreter of their influence, I cannot help but think of the one prediction I was certain he had no cause to contrive: that I would marry one helpful and true. As the cart hastens toward my new home, I gaze angrily up at the sky. But the stars give no answer for their betrayal, blinking and shining with ancient indifference.

Book II
SUSPICIENDO DESPICIO

Chapter 22

"Uraniborg."

This is the name the old peasant utters as he takes a hand off the horse's rein and jabs his finger toward the gatehouse of Tycho's castle.

As I recall Master Kees's lessons, I realize the irony of my fate: Lia is dead, my home and mother lost, my father still unknown to me. The heavens have deceived me. But it seems I cannot escape the stars, for I have been sentenced to the castle of Urania, the Greek muse of astronomy.

In the deepening shadows, I hear a chorus of frantic barking and follow the sound to the flat-roofed top of the gatehouse, where a half dozen kenneled mastiffs hurl themselves against metal bars. This Hadean welcome is cut short, however, when a servant boy appears and, with a shout to the dogs, unlocks the gate. Matheus explains that he is here to deliver me to Tycho, but it is only the mention of his master's name that seems to animate the boy, who must not speak Dutch.

As he leads us onto the grounds, I can see that the castle's name was not bestowed lightly. Uraniborg has been laid out so meticulously that it looks as if it were designed using its patron muse's signature compass. The gatehouse sits at the meeting point of two enormous ramparts, which appear to form a ninety-degree angle. A pin-straight path bisects this angle, leading from the gatehouse to the front entrance of the castle.

As we follow the servant toward it, we pass an orchard, the spindly fruit trees arranged in as orderly a formation as the Infanta's, though there seems to be a greater variety of shapes and sizes. Past the orchard, is a plot of even more elaborate design—a series of snow-encrusted shrubs cut into the forms of stars, circles, and squares. Since I know this Tycho is no king, I wonder whether he is a sorcerer to have conjured such an intricate universe.

This impression is only heightened when we pass a circular formation of wooden palings and enter a round clearing, in the center of which lies Uraniborg castle. Atop the highest spire, seeming to fly up into the darkening sky, is a rotating statue of Pegasus, the horse's wings spread as it spins in the cold breeze. Beneath this lies a limestone crown of domes and cupolas. The turrets that reminded me of ladies' skirts now seem even more fantastical as they appear to be attached to the sides of the castle's red brick hull by little more than slender poles. Reclining above the door is a statue of a half-naked Titan resting his hand on a globe of the earth and looking to the heavens.

Even Matheus stops to gaze at the palace in wonderment. I forget my fears and join him until, from the side of the castle,

I hear a cacophony of birdsong, a tangle of chirps and whistles and caws. It seems that my new master keeps an aviary, and the birds' wild tune returns me to my sorrows. For the singing of the trapped creatures reminds me of Lia and how, because of my actions, her voice is absent from the world's song.

It is with heavy heart that I follow the servant boy under the statue of the Titan and into a long hall illuminated by torches. I expect it to lead to the sorcerer's room, a study exhibiting the same misplaced faith in order as the rest of Urania's kingdom. But what I see instead is so miraculous that I blink several times to be certain I am not dreaming. In the center of a rotunda at the end of the hall is a large bronze basin with the heads of the four winds arranged at equidistant points atop it. Even more extraordinary is the water spraying out of the winds' howling mouths.

"How the devil . . . ?" Matheus says before he catches himself.

I am just as perplexed. Even at Coudenberg there was no such thing as a sculpture that sprayed water, never mind indoors in the dead of winter. I stare at the winds, trying to figure out where this water is coming from.

The servant boy watches us, all but ignoring this magic.

Matheus looks uneasily around the rotunda, fingering his lucky copper. Judging from the identical halls that depart around us on all sides, we stand at the very heart of the castle. Adding to the eeriness, there is not a single soul in sight.

"I have business with Lord Tycho," he says to the boy, his voice commanding but his eyes darting from side to side. "I demand to see him."

The boy points to the basin of water and holds up his hands— gesturing for us to stay where we are—then disappears down one of the corridors and through a door. Matheus paces, staring at the enchanted sculpture, then turns on his heels and walks nearly the length of the hall we first entered, as if contemplating his own escape. While he does this, I walk up to the basin and hoist myself over the rim. I dip a finger in the burbling water and feel a stab of longing for Lia. She would have loved this tiny sea, its mist of spray.

Footsteps sound behind me, and I hastily lower myself back to the ground. The servant boy gestures for us to follow him down a hallway that lies perpendicular to the one we first came through. When he comes to the end, he opens a massive wooden door.

The scene that I behold is even more wondrous to me than the one we have just left. Inside this circular room, a dozen men labor by the blazing light of candelabra, oblivious to our entrance. Some study a brass globe as large as a bale of hay that rests on a base by the far window; others hunch over wooden desks, their quills dancing; still others search a vast library. For the first time since Lia's death, I feel my spirits rise. The shelves are lined with hundreds of volumes of every size and kind. Even the Infanta did not possess so extensive a collection.

I gradually become aware of other curiosities as well—a life-sized metal man and lion stand at attention, flanking the door. Music plays, though I see no musicians. But it is the books to which my gaze returns. I wonder if some of these volumes are devoted to whatever dark arts allow water and music to appear out of thin air. Most of all, I hope that I, too, will be permitted to study them.

A barrel-chested man with a white ruff breaks away from the group gathered around the globe and marches toward us. His reddish blond hair and beard are mixed with gray, a scar bisects his forehead, and there's a more frightful detail—part of his nose seems not to be pink, like the rest of his round face, but reddish brown.

"Lord Tycho Brahe?" asks Matheus tentatively.

I have no doubt that, although he does not acknowledge his name, the man who glares at us is Tycho. "No one is supposed to interrupt us until supper," he grumbles in Dutch. "We are working."

"We have come all the way from Coudenberg," says Matheus.

Tycho seems barely to register this defense. Instead he peers down at me. As he does, I get a closer look at his nose and realize that the reddish brown part—the entire upper half—is actually made of copper.

"Another dwarf?" he says wearily as I try not to stare back in horror.

"I have a letter," says Matheus, as if this explains all.

Tycho impatiently reaches out a hand as Matheus fumbles for the letter. Upon finally securing it, Tycho tears open the seal and glances at it hastily. "Fine. Fine. Let's proceed." Switching to a tongue I recognize as Latin, he shouts, "Longomontanus, Severinus, come here!"

Two young men obediently rise from the tables. The first to reach us is a tall youth with a head of golden curls and long limbs that seem to amplify the shortness of my own. From the confidence of his step and the easy smile upon his face, I wonder if he is Tycho's son. Following in his wake is a smaller fellow with a servant's watchful eyes and a scraggly beard.

"Severinus, paper," Tycho says.

To my surprise, it is the tall youth who plays the servant, loping off to fetch paper and quills and sharing them with the smaller man.

"'Dwarf jester,'" Tycho dictates to them. "'Six-year minimum. No library access or scholarship privileges. No notes or letters to the outside. No revealing any aspect of our pursuits at Uraniborg.'"

I am certain my new master assumes that I am unable to follow this ancient tongue. But I do, and the portrait of indenture he paints fills me with despair. My position upon this sorcerer's rock is no different than at Coudenberg. I am once again a "dwarf jester," a plaything of the powerful, a fool whose task is not to study or learn but to amuse those around me. I am barred from this maginificent library, and the books and learning that could have sped the progression of six slow years. To make matters worse, I am not even permitted to correspond with my mother and Willem, who must be wracked with worry over my long silence. I cannot live such a life. I resolve to find a way to escape and return home to Astraveld.

The scribe with the scraggly beard, Longomontanus, crouches down before me and holds out the paper upon which the terms of my service are written, and a quill. Blemishes dot his pallid forehead, and his teeth are yellow.

"What is your name?" he asks in Dutch.

"Jepp," I say.

"Can you write, Jepp?"

"Just have him mark the contract with a line," Tycho says impatiently in Latin.

I am tempted to answer my new master in Latin, to tell him that not only can I write but that I understand his every word, and care not for the servitude and hard conditions of my employment. But I have little faith that such a revelation would alter my fate. I am certain that these men, like the courtiers at Coudenberg, are capable of seeing me as little more than an amusement. Better that I play the fool so that they do not suspect I have the cunning and intelligence to escape. Still, I hesitate, for I do not wish to legitimate this devilish contract.

"Time is wasting," Tycho says in Dutch.

"Perhaps he can read Latin?" the handsome youth, Severinus, says in Latin, then grins.

I hastily mark the contract in a rude hand, not wishing the others to guess how close Severinus's jest is to the truth. Longomontanus takes back the quill and folds up the contract.

Tycho hands Severinus the letter that heralded my arrival. "Put that with my correspondence," he says in Latin.

Then he swings around and points to Matheus, who is staring at the enormous globe. "And get this man out of my house!"

Just as he says this, something shiny flies past me and lands with a clatter on the floor. Matheus begins to back out of the room, and when I look up, I can see why. My new master has lost part of his nose. The top, from the middle to the bridge betwixt his eyes, is a gaping hole. However no one but Matheus seems aggrieved by this, including Tycho himself. He merely sighs as if a crumbling nose is his lot in life.

"Jepp, your labors start now," he says to me in Dutch. "Pick up my nose."

I never thought I would look back fondly to the days of donning the costume of a beast or being concealed in a pie. But retrieving a man's nose is a far less savory business. As I squat down to scoop up the copper proboscis, Matheus says, "Goodbye, Jepp. Good luck to you."

I can tell from the pitying look in his eyes that he means it. Unexpectedly, tears well up in my own. Matheus has been my jailor but, faced with the uncertain cruelties of my new home, the memories of his small acts of kindness loom large. I wish for him not to go.

"Good-bye, Matheus," I say.

He reaches out his rough hand and gently pats my shoulder. Then he turns and follows the servant boy to freedom.

As the door closes behind him, I pass the copper nose up to Tycho. He takes a small box from his vest pocket, dabs some ointment from it onto the back of his nose, and affixes the nose to his face. When he seems satisfied that it will hold, he releases his grip on it.

"You are not to come in here again," he says. "Jonas will help you prepare for supper, where you will entertain us."

A few minutes later, a burly valet with a curly thatch of yellow hair opens the door. Tycho issues him instructions in Danish, then peers down his copper nose at me and adds in Dutch, "There is a particular task, Jepp, I believe you well suited for."

With this, my master smiles; and I am left to wonder what new misery awaits me and how quickly I can devise my escape.

Chapter 23

Jonas silently leads me back into the hall. Near the basin of water, I spot a bent copper on the ground and hastily snatch it up. In his fear and confusion, Matheus must have dropped it. But it is too late to return it to him now, besides which I need its auspicious tidings even more than he. Although the water continues to flow from its magical source, there is still not a single soul in sight. But, just as we pass the basin, I hear hooflike clops on the marble floor. Someone must have ridden a horse into the castle, although why Tycho would allow a beast inside to soil his floors and guzzle from his bronze basin is a mystery. When I listen more closely, however, the clops sound more delicate than those of a horse, as if its hooves are cloven; and I wonder if what I am hearing could be human or even, in this mad castle, a mix between beast and man.

This mystery, like the invisible music and flowing water, is left unsolved as Jonas ushers me down the hall and through a door at the end of it. To my relief, this room is nothing stranger than a kitchen. Flavorful clouds of steam hover in the air, and fish and game of numerous sizes and shapes lie on a large wooden table, waiting for the cook's alchemy of fire and spice. The cook, a large man with cheeks so round they look as if they have been stuffed with apples, shouts orders at a bevy of women. He greets me with but a brief look as if, not being hare or goose or boar, I am of little interest to him. But several of the women allow their eyes to linger, their red faces giving them the appearance of being stewed along with their dishes.

Jonas says something in Danish, but all I can make out is my name, Jepp, which the women repeat softly over their pots and dough like an incantation. I notice their straw-filled pallets stacked in one corner of the kitchen, and I hope that I will be stowed along with them in this warm and savory realm. I imagine growing plump in my melancholy, a creature of appetite whose loneliness and grief is dulled by his gut.

But, to my regret, Jonas leads me into a chamber dim and chilly by comparison. Although pallets cover nearly the entire floor, proof of an invisible army of servants, not a single soul inhabits the shadows. As Jonas searches through a sack left on one of the pallets, I cannot help but think of Lia's song—of love left on a distant shore, of silent seas, and being held captive— and how it has become my own. I run my fingers along the spiny seashell in my pocket.

A short while later, Jonas finds what he is searching for—a many-pointed cap that jingles with bells. At the sight of it, my despair deepens, for it confirms that I am yet again expected to humiliate myself for the pleasure of the rich and powerful. But I fear what will happen to me if I openly resist and, as he gestures for me to do, I put the cap on.

We sit silently side by side in the darkening gloom until a knock sounds. At this signal, Jonas leads me back into the blazing hall, where we stop before a door next to the forbidden library. A great din of voices and tongues issues from inside, as if Tycho has transformed the birds in his aviary to human form. Jonas opens the door wide and pushes me through.

The room before me is generous in its proportions and richly appointed—in one corner is a towering tile stove; in another a curtained four-post bed, where Tycho and his wife must sleep. In the center of the room is a sideboard laden with silver vessels for drink, all of them engraved with the same coat of arms. But it is a long oaken table against the far wall that commands my attention. Sitting on benches on the far side of it are at least forty souls, chattering with vigor as the cook's dishes lie steaming before them—a slab of what looks to be venison drenched in sauce, a whole fish, a tureen of stew, a side of rare beef, a platter of tongue, chicken, eggs, and eel, and heaps of sugar cakes.

Lording over this feast, on a seat higher than the others, is my new master, his copper nose glinting in the candlelight. A plump, flaxen-haired woman sits on the elevated perch beside him, and a gaggle of fair-haired children flank him—ranging in age from shrieking infant with nurse to noisy young woman banging her fist on the table to emphasize some point. I am relieved for their sakes to see that all of them have inherited their mother's sturdy, upturned nose.

"Jepp," Tycho says, waving a tankard in the air. Then he says something in Danish, and his company bursts into laughter. I steel myself for more insults.

One man pipes up and then another follows; but both speak

Danish, and the only words I catch in common are "per gek."
But whatever the men have said, Tycho seems little amused by it.
He grimaces and shakes his head. Then he points at me.

"Under the table," he says in Dutch.

I wonder if I have misheard him, or whether he has made a
slip in a foreign tongue. Surely he wants me to sit *at* the table,
not *under* it. I walk hesitantly to the edge of it, the smells of the
banquet making my stomach tighten.

"Now, under!" says Tycho impatiently.

I stoop beneath the edge, expecting him to stop me. But he
does no such thing. A long, straight finger descends under the
table and points to his black leather shoes.

"Sit at my feet," he says.

I wonder if this is the task he has envisioned me well suited
for. I can hardly stomach the indignity of this arrangement,
but Don's bruises are newly healed, and I fear the price of disobedience. As I crouch at my master's feet, I feel as if he has
transformed me into a hound. Above, there are delicacies, laughter, the company of men; while below, I quiver, my gut rumbling.
This impression is only strengthened when Tycho's ringed hand
slides under the table with a morsel of venison. As he waves it
before my face, I realize I am meant to take it. I briefly consider
refusing, but my hunger triumphs over my pride, and I snatch it
from his hand. My obedience is rewarded with another morsel—
a slice of eel.

As I chew it, I hear a tankard pound the table above my head.

"A few words on the great work of Uraniborg!" Tycho says
in Latin.

Though I dare not bite my master's hand, I can at least take
satisfaction in eavesdropping on his labors, which he seems so

eager to keep secret from the world. Perhaps I will even glean some intelligence that will aid in my escape.

"Severinus, please share our most recent progress."

I see a pair of long feet shift as their owner rises. "Thank you, my lord," says Severinus in a voice nearly as bold as his master's. "As of this day, we have collected seven hundred and ninety-three stars."

The table thunders above me as fists pound it in applause. But I am perplexed. How does one collect a star? I imagine Tycho's army of scholars flying through the sky with nets. I wonder where Tycho stores all these stars, and whether it is they that power Uraniborg's magical water sculpture and fill his study with music.

"This is work well done," Tycho says when the applause dies down. "But we must hasten our efforts while maintaining the precise standards that Urania has set for us. To a thousand stars!"

"A thousand stars!" echoes the table. Their cheer is so rousing that if Tycho's nose had not tumbled off and clattered to the floor in front of me, I might have forgotten myself and joined in. I pick it up just as an empty palm impatiently appears before me, and in a strange reverse of our eating ritual, I drop the nose into it. I can see Tycho's other hand dig into his pocket for his box of ointment.

A moment later, when the nose is doubtless back in place, Tycho bangs his tankard yet again.

"To celebrate our continued progress, my new dwarf, Jepp, will amuse us," he says in Latin.

I feel the toe of a shoe drive into my back, and I crawl out from under the table. Forty pairs of eyes watch me expectantly as I stand beside my new master.

"Well?" thunders Tycho. "What can you do?"

My true talent is books and languages. But this I will never reveal and, thankfully, Lia has given me another.

"I can dance."

"Jacob!" Tycho says.

A dark-haired lutenist appears and strikes up a lively melody. Though I have not danced since Lia's death, I am relieved to discover that my feet remember what my mind cannot. But I take little pleasure in the applause and cheers that follow my performance. For I think only of Lia and how it pains me to perform the French dance without her.

Tycho laughs heartily as I bow. "What a sight!" he says in Latin.

He hands me an oyster and sends me back under the table.

Jacob begins to play a ballad and for a brief moment, I imagine that Lia has been brought back to life by the magic of Tycho's seven hundred ninety-three stars. But Jacob's song is long and far less beautiful than Lia's. Tycho continues to proffer me tidbits, which by the lengthy ballad's end leave me feeling as if I have actually consumed a meal. Still, each bite fills me with shame and, as Jacob plucks the final strings of his song and servants appear to take away the dishes, I pray that the banquet is over and Tycho will release me. But as more servants appear and more savory smells fill the room, I realize that the supper is merely beginning. Above I can hear the splash and hiss of ale and wine being poured, the thunderous laughter of my master, the clatter of silverware. A bite of roast lamb with beets is handed to me under the table, then a few crumbs of almond tart. One of the scholars recites a poem he has composed on the glories of the heavens, and later another man sings.

As the voices above grow louder and merrier with drink, Tycho's children race wildly around the table. A boy of perhaps five, though no taller than I, with a round face and wispy blond hair, dodges under the table and sticks his tongue out at me before he is hauled back out of my realm by a disembodied hand. Then a second face appears, that of the young woman who I had first seen banging her fist on the table. That she is in so indecorous a position, crouched on her knees, seems to cause her no shame, though her form is most womanly. Her round face hangs over me like a moon, cratered by a few white smallpox scars. She appraises me with a bold, unapologetic stare, then says something in Danish.

"You don't speak our language," she says in Latin when I fail to respond.

I almost shake my head in reply before I stop myself. I have never heard a woman speak this ancient tongue, though it does not surprise me that a sorcerer's daughter would have this skill. Why she thinks I possess it, however, strikes me as most curious.

"My name is Magdalene," she continues in Latin. "I am sorry on my brother's behalf."

Though I wish to acknowledge her, I instead hold up my hands and smile foolishly as if to indicate I do not understand. Magdalene shrugs as if I no longer warrant her interest and disappears.

Before I can make head or tail of this odd conversation, the door opens, and I hear the strange clopping sound of the creature I heard earlier. Merry shouts issue from the table, Tycho's loudest of all, as I behold four brown legs, moving with the wobbly motion of a man on stilts. As I peer out from beneath the table, I can see Jonas lead in the rest of the creature, a massive mix of horse and cow. Enormous antlers, like the bones of an angel's wings, protrude from its head, and a brown, wattlelike beard hangs down from its neck.

Reaching the table, it bellows pitifully. Then the bellowing abruptly stops, replaced by wet, slopping sounds and the occasional snort. I crawl out from beneath the table and peek over the edge. To the delight of Tycho and his boisterous company, the beast is muzzle deep in a tankard of ale.

"Jepp!" Tycho says, as if recalling my presence. His nose, I notice, is not properly affixed but tipped to one side. He draws himself up in his chair as if to make some grand declaration, and I wonder if he means to reprimand me for abandoning my post.

"This is Ulf," he says in Dutch. "My moose. He is tame and exceedingly partial to a draught of ale."

Though I would not have been surprised if the creature had turned to me and issued a proper Latin greeting, Ulf takes no notice of our introduction. He instead clatters the tankard against the table in his efforts to devour its dregs.

Tycho's nose loosens further as he leans toward me. "The great disadvantage to Ulf's appetites is that on occasion he has broken free and wandered the halls in an inebriated state. This is quite dangerous for him. But you, Jepp, can prevent that! As his bedmate!"

I smile wanly, certain that my new master is playing some trick upon me for his amusement.

"It is good fortune indeed that you were sent to us," Tycho concludes. "Now, you and Ulf may retire for the night."

Pulling a rope around Ulf's neck, Jonas tries to lead him away from the table; but the moose—its muzzle still wedged in the tankard—won't budge. Clearly this is not the first time Jonas has met with such obstinate behavior, for he next takes the tankard with him, using it to entice the beast forward. The moose belches, filling the air with the smell of hops, and stumbles after it.

Tycho gestures for me to follow him, which I do at a safe distance. Even though my master waves as though he does not expect to see me again, I wager that this is but a jest, and Jonas will send me back as soon as the moose is secured in its stable.

But the room to which he leads Ulf is no stable but a small, doorless chamber off the kitchen covered with straw and reeking of animal fur and dung. Jonas ties the creature to a post on the wall. Ulf guzzles from a small basin into which flows another mysterious stream of water, whilst Jonas sets a straw-filled tick on the floor, tossing a coarse blanket onto it. It is only then that I realize that Tycho fully intends for me to sleep with this creature. Jonas points to the pallet and then to me, confirming this impression, then departs.

After studying it for some time, I conclude that the pallet is just far enough away that, so long as Ulf does not break his tether and embark on one of his drunken nocturnal gambols, I should escape being trampled. This gives me little comfort, however, as I lie on the pallet and stare at Ulf's massive rump. Tycho is most certainly another cruel and capricious master. I take out Matheus's bent copper and rub it between my fingers as he did. I cannot accept that this—a life of ignominy, loneliness, and loss—is what fate intends for me.

When at last I fall asleep, I dream Lia and I are trying to escape this diabolical island, chased through the night by Tycho's stars.

Chapter 24

The following morning when I wake to the wet smacking sounds of Ulf's lips as he guzzles from his basin, I catch a sweet odor, like a reprise of the previous evening's meal, mingling with the musky scent of moose. I sit up to find a woman hovering over me, holding a warm sugar cake on a plate. She appears to be some thirty-odd years, lean as a boy, with luminous gray eyes that seem mismatched with her bulbous nose and thin lips. A dark linen coif covers her hair.

"If I sit, will this beast tread upon me?" she asks in perfect Dutch with a wary glance at Ulf.

I am as pleased by the sound of my native tongue as the cake she holds out to me. "You speak Dutch?"

"My father is Danish but my mother was Dutch," she replies. "My name is Liv. Liv Larsdatter. I am a housekeeper here."

"Jepp," I say, introducing myself.

She appraises me with a sad smile.

"You are even smaller than Per Gek."

Per Gek, I suddenly realize, is the name of another dwarf who must have met some unfortunate end at Uraniborg. But before I can inquire further, calls of "Liv, Liv!" sound from the hall, and she springs back lightly to her feet.

"I must go light the furnaces."

As I consume the cake Liv has brought, I allow myself to imagine the pleasures of a friend in this desolate place. But Coudenberg has taught me the dangers of trusting those around me, and I remind myself to be careful about confiding my true feelings. If I am to escape, I must chart my course of action carefully, watching and discerning, and most of all, keeping my own counsel. I must learn everything about Uraniborg, but Uraniborg must learn as little as possible about me.

Armed with this sense of purpose, I find my labors easier to bear, as they enable me to secretly school myself in the daily rhythms of Uraniborg—and of Tycho. I am still not certain that my new master is entirely mortal. No matter how late his revelries extend and how many tankards of ale he imbibes, he is always awake by four, whereupon a servant brings him a breakfast of warm beer and herring. After this repast, he adjourns with his bevy of scholars, with their foreign tongues and Latinized names, to the museum—his name for the wing of Uraniborg that houses his library, chemical laboratory, and observatory.

During the second meal of the day, which is served around nine or ten in the morning, I am required to sit at my master's feet and entertain his companions with acrobatics or dancing. Tycho takes this meal with his family—his wife, Kirsten, and their children—and the scholars in his living quarters. Although the rich dishes and copious drink leave most of his companions drowsy—a snore erupting from the table is not uncommon—Tycho is always keen to return to his work when this meal is done. He and his scholars take up their studies again till four or five in the afternoon, whereupon I am called to return to my place at his feet for supper. This meal, with its three or four courses, endless tankards, stories, Latin orations, the ale-drinking moose, and general mayhem can last up to eight. Sundays are little different. Though I can see an old church set on the cliffs below Uraniborg, Tycho prefers his personal chaplain to conduct brief services in his chamber. In comparison to the Infanta, he seems little concerned with the fate of his soul.

And even on those Sabbath nights when the heavens are propitious for star chasing, Tycho will sometimes repair to his library with Severinus and Longomontanus. Though Severinus's native German tongue quickly puts an end to my impression that he is Tycho's son, he is clearly from a family of similar importance and means. More curious to me is Longomontanus, who wears simple smocks and cleans his plate hastily as if unaccustomed to leisurely meals. Was he a servant who wormed his way into his master's affection? This seems doubtful, for his Latin is even more elegant than Severinus's and his script graceful. He is most devoted to Tycho, and yet there is something about him—a watchful quiet—that fills me with unease.

One morning, curious to learn more about the nature of Tycho's work, I slip into the library. But I catch only a glimpse of the tempting books and the scholars hunched over the brass globe before Longomontanus rushes me out, explaining in his halting Dutch that I am not permitted there. After this, Jonas ensures I am not idle. My new caretaker is not rough with me, but neither does he make overtures toward friendship, for we do not speak the same language. During the many long hours when the scholars are at work, he gives me odd tasks—helping peel the shells of spiny sea creatures in the kitchen, mixing the ointment that my master uses to adhere his nose to his face, cleaning up Ulf's waste as he leads the beast about the castle grounds. I observe, to my dismay, that the gates leading in and out of Uraniborg are always locked, besides which Tycho's infernal hounds sound the alarm whenever anyone even approaches them.

It seems that the only possible way out of Tycho's kingdom is through the forbidden library. For this room contains not only books, each page a tunnel through which I might escape my present torments, but quills and precious paper too. Though Tycho has forbidden any correspondence, I decide that I must get a letter to my mother and Willem, who know nothing of the dire change in my fortunes. When they learn the fate that has befallen me and how desperately I wish to return home to them, I am hopeful they will find a way to rescue me. Perhaps, I imagine, my mother will even summon the man who is my father to help secure my freedom.

My careful observation of the household routine leads me to conclude that the safest time to sneak into the library is the hour after midnight, when even Tycho has retired to his bed. To further improve my chances of entering undetected, I choose the evening of Candlemas. After a brief service by Tycho's chaplain, the wine and ale flow particularly freely, and the supper banquet is double its usual size. That night I lie awake on my pallet, fighting slumber as I listen to Ulf guzzle from his basin and shift his cloven hooves on the straw.

When the midnight bell tolls, I check to make sure that Ulf's tether is secure and then slip out of our quarters, treading as lightly as I am able down the dark corridors to the library. The castle smells like beeswax candles, which Uraniborg's chaplain blessed earlier that day, and which the island's peasants, who are more devout than their master, light to ward off winter storms. Though I can only faintly see it, I can hear the spray of what I now know to be called a fountain, whose burbling song has been constant since my arrival.

I slowly turn the brass knob of the library door and push against it. It opens easily, but finding it unlocked fills me with alarm that Tycho is within. I freeze, expecting a voice to call out or a pair of heavy footsteps to march toward me. But the only sound is a faint rustle, and when I listen again, I hear nothing but my own ragged breath. I open the door wider and slip inside.

Here, too, is the faint whiff of candle smoke, the lingering scent of Candlemas. A waxing moon shines through the windows, which look out over the silenced aviary. Its light fills the room with incongruous shadows—the globe eclipsed upon the floor, quills casting knifelike shapes, the metal man looming over me. I hear a floorboard creak, but when I look around, all is still—not a soul about. I stare at the metal lion, whose silver eyes reflect the flame of my candle. I reach out my hand and touch his mane, which is ice-cold and smooth.

The beast springs to life, and begins to walk jerkily toward me.

I leap back, covering my mouth lest a cry escape it. The lion rears on its hind legs, towering over me, and with its metal paws opens a door in its own chest. In place of the bewitched creature's heart is a silver fleur-de-lis.

The lion remains frozen in this posture whilst I remain frozen in mine, my heart beating so frantically, I fear it might spring out of my own chest. It is only after some minutes that I gain the courage to step forward and poke its haunch. But whatever life Tycho seems to have given the lion is spent, for it responds not to my advance but remains motionless on its hind legs, the door to its fleur-de-lis heart ajar. This poses its own threat, however, for Tycho will surely notice that the lion has changed its position during the night and suspect there has been an intruder. I calm myself with the thought that there are many others in the household whom Tycho could suspect before me.

The sight of Tycho's books, hundreds of them arranged along curved bookcases, tempts me. I creep over to inspect them. Many of them are in Latin—treatises on philosophy, astronomy, astrology, and alchemy. On a shelf above my head, I spot a volume entitled *De Stella Nova* composed by Tycho himself. My curiosity compels me to stretch high on my tiptoes and pull it down so I can inspect it.

Inside are illustrations of compasslike instruments, mathematical formulae and calculations, astrological predictions, and diagrams of the heavens. These make little sense to me, however, and so I prepare to close the volume when on its final pages, I discover a poem called "Elegy to Urania." In it, Tycho describes how he is wandering in the forest one evening around sunset when the muse of the heavens comes to visit him. Though I have been little impressed with my master's previous poetic endeavors, which he delivers with a surfeit of emotion at his banquets, I read the elegy to its end:

> *The stars that far in advance know our fate,*
> *Fate—often good, often bad;*
> *The stars that silently exercise justice among you.*
> *Much do they grant with grace. They hinder too,*
> *But do not force the soul that has a mind,*
> *For he does all according to his will.*
> *But few will take the way of the mind on earth,*
> *So, very few can bend the heavenly force.*

I carefully close the book and mull over these words. I want to believe them, but I know the raw power of fate, know how will and desire are not enough to change its course. The idea that I can choose my destiny is as cruelly fantastical to me as the rest of Tycho's kingdom. For if this were so, I would have chosen Lia. I would have bent the heavens to keep her alive, realigned the stars. Does not Tycho understand that, in all but the smallest ways, we are powerless? This Urania who whispers in his ear is merely the illusion of his own importance. He may lord over this island now but, like Lia and me, he too is made of flesh and bone. One day, when he is least ready, he will be returned to ashes and dust.

I angrily thrust the book back on its shelf and walk over to the enormous bronze globe, which is inscribed with hundreds of small dots. I spin it on its axis, faster and faster.

"Be careful with that," says a voice in Latin.

My first thought is that the lion has spoken, but the voice is girlish; and when I whirl around, I see a figure emerge from beneath one of the scholars' desks. Magdalene rises, her woolen peasant-style dress carelessly draping her figure, her pale hair in a nimbus around her face.

"What are you doing here?" she asks.

The tone of her voice is inquisitive, not sharp, but I still fear she is moments away from dragging me off to her father. I quickly decide my best defense is to shrug as if I cannot follow what she is saying and know not myself why I have wandered in here.

Magdalene comes closer, the small scars on her face reflecting the light of my candle. Her sturdy brow and chin jut out defensively like the cliffs that surround the island. She is much taller than I. "I know you understand me," she says.

I decide that I care not for this odd girl and her blunt manner, and hesitate, wondering if she is engaged in some trickery meant to get me to reveal what I know.

She shakes her head. "It will not serve you well in this household to pretend ignorance. And besides, I have read the letter."

I wonder if she is referring to the letter the driver handed Tycho upon my arrival. My curiosity gets the better of me. "What letter?" I murmur in Latin.

Upon this admission that I understand her, Magdalene smiles, an act that involves not just her lips but her pale blue eyes, which narrow in satisfaction. I instantly regret having confirmed her suspicions.

Magdalene lights her candle with mine then walks briskly to a desk, opens a drawer, and pages through its contents till she finds a piece of paper that she holds up triumphantly. Then she begins to read:

"'To the honorable Lord Tycho Brahe, Urania's chosen servant, et cetera, et cetera . . .

"'Please accept my gift of this dwarf, Jepp, for your amusement, et cetera, et cetera. . . .'

"Here it is," says Magdalene.

"'Unlike some of his stature whose minds only develop in proportion, he is cunning in intelligence and has been versed in Latin and Greek, befitting a man of your station.'"

Upon hearing this, I do not feel very cunning at all. "Your father has known all along that I understand Latin?"

"Likely not. He would hardly bother to read a letter like this in full."

Though I am relieved to hear that Tycho still thinks me a fool, I do not know where this revelation leaves me with Magdalene.

Still holding the letter, she draws closer to me. "Why does Don Diego de la Fuente not wish you to return to Coudenberg?"

she asks, easily pronouncing Don's full name, as if she has spoken it before.

I must have looked askance at this question, for Magdalene once again holds up the letter and begins to read.

"'If the dwarf does not satisfy you, I ask only that you not return him to the Infanta's court but inform me that I may send him elsewhere to serve another master.'"

At first, this sentence inflames me, for it makes me think of how I have been exiled while a miscreant like Pim continues to bask in the Infanta's affections. My anger makes me careless.

"I was defiant," I tell Magdalene.

I expect this answer to intrigue her, but she waves her hand as if brushing it away. "And yet Don Diego does not appear to want to lose you."

Magdalene's presumptuous tone irritates me, and yet I am startled by the verity of what she says. It strikes me that it was not truly the Infanta who exiled me. The guards had told Don that the Infanta wanted me delivered unto her. She might have locked me up in the dungeon like Robert, or merely chastised me before returning me to Hendrika's care. But she had no chance to do either, for it was Don who disobeyed her orders and sent me away. I think of how he said, as he struck me, that I had shamed him before the Infanta. I cannot fathom why a man who cares so much for his reputation would then risk injuring it further by disregarding the Infanta's wishes.

While I am lost in thought, Magdalene offers her own interpretation. Bending down so she may look me straight in the eye, she asks, "Are you a spy?"

This leaves me newly dumbfounded. "A spy?"

Magdalene narrows her pale eyes and smiles as if she has

caught me in the act. "It has happened before. A scholar named Ursus stole my father's ideas and passed them off as his own. Perhaps Don Diego has sent you to steal the fruit of my father's labors so the scholars of Spain can claim it. In exchange for this, he will secure your future after you leave here."

I now understand the reason for the final dictum of my contract, that I will not reveal any aspect of Tycho's pursuits at Uraniborg. The gravity of my situation frightens me. It was bad enough to be caught trespassing, but now, thanks to this meddlesome girl, I am in far worse danger of being branded a traitor. I rush to my own defense.

"I am no spy! I do not even know exactly what your father does."

"Then why are you in the library?"

As the clock tolls one, I realize I might ask the same of her. But it is not my place. The only response I think to give is an honest one. "I have been on this island some three weeks. I fear my mind grows dull. I long to read and write."

Magdalene considers this with more care than I imagined.

"If you are a spy, you are a clever one," she finally says. "But I am clever, too, and I will be watching you."

It appears that she is not going to wake her father or apprehend me for my misdeed. I nod as if to accept this condition.

Magdalene straightens to her full height and walks over to the lion. On a nearby desk, I spot a piece of paper beside a pot of ink and a quill. This may be my only chance to take them, but I fear her catching me and using this theft as proof that I am a spy. I watch as Magdalene turns to face the metal beast and places her hand upon his head. With a whirring sound, the lion shuts the door to his fleur-de-lis heart, lowers to all fours, and walks jerkily in reverse as I quickly stuff the paper, pot, and quill into my smock. When the lion is back in its original place, Magdalene turns to me.

"You *were* frightened by the automaton," she says, as if consoling herself for not catching me in a full-out act of espionage.

I fear that my smock looks disordered, so I attempt to distract her. "What did you call it?" I ask. "An automaton?"

"The lion has a mechanism inside, a motor, to make it move. My father collects automata. He likes to use them to frighten guests. The man is also one. There is a switch on his head that makes him clamber about."

For a moment, she seems almost friendly, and I think how there are many more mysteries of Uraniborg that I would like to ask her about. But I do not trust her and fear my curiosity will be misinterpreted as spying.

"You had better go," Magdalene says, gesturing toward the door.

I know I should bow, as she is my better, but I do not want her to hear the crinkle of the paper pressed against my chest.

"Good night," I say.

I am in the hall, my smock wet with sweat under the arms, when I hear her summon me. I turn to see Magdalene's head, illuminated by the candle in her hand, hanging out the library door as if disembodied.

"Only come when I am here," she whispers.

I am unsure whether to count this as an invitation or a trap. Either way, I have no intention of returning to the library when she is there. And yet, I nod in agreement. With a click, the library door closes, and I am left to navigate the shadowy Candlemas hallways alone.

Chapter
25

That night, as Ulf bellows and shifts beside me, I work on the letter to my mother and Willem. With but a single piece of paper at my disposal, I am determined not to waste a jot. This is made easier by the fact that I no longer endeavor to disguise my situation with pretty words. Instead, I write about my predicament in the plain language of my heart.

I tell them of Lia and my feelings for her, of how we tried to escape Coudenberg, of how Don banished me to Tycho's strange island deep in the kingdom of the Danes. I tell them how I long to escape my new home and be reunited with them, my mother most of all. For the first time since I left Astraveld, I tell her how much I love her and have missed her.

I reread the letter, then fold it up and hide it behind a loose brick I have discovered in the wall. But though it comforts me to know it is there, I still have no plan for how to get it off the island. The next day, Magdalene watches me, peering under the table at supper with a knowing look. I am certain that if she found out about the letter, it would only contribute to her misimpression that I am a spy.

As my desperation mounts, I conclude that I must find an accomplice, preferably one who has duties outside the castle grounds. At first, I doubt this can be achieved, for the denizens of Uraniborg have demonstrated little interest in befriending me. I assume this is because I do not speak Danish, besides which, I am quartered separately with Ulf. But then it occurs to me that I do have a friend. For every few mornings, I still find a warm sugar cake on a plate beside my head.

The following morning, I wake early hoping to catch Liv and discuss the matter with her. As I wait, I study Ulf, who sleeps standing up, like a horse. He smacks his muzzle, dreaming perhaps of some forest home, far from the desolate island we are both stranded upon. I am about to close my eyes, my mission losing its urgency, when I hear the light patter of footsteps, and Liv appears with my sugar cake in hand.

"You are awake," she says with a smile. "Hungry, too?"

I am heartened by her amiable manner.

"There is something I wish to ask you."

But before I can continue, one of the kitchen servants passes by, and I fear we will be overheard. "Is there someplace we might speak in private?"

Liv's gray eyes fix upon me, blinking as she schemes. "I will request that you be allowed to assist me this afternoon in the botanical gardens," she finally says.

Before I can even nod my assent, she is gone. I read the letter one last time, then seal it with candle wax and conceal it in my pocket for later.

Liv is true to her word. Just after noon, when the February sun is at its zenith, Jonas fetches me from my labor of mixing Tycho's nose ointment (a paste my master himself devised of boiled sturgeon bones and pickling lime). He hands me my cloak, then leads me out of the castle, past the ornamental gardens with their patterns of star- and square-shaped shrubs, to the orchard. We pass several rows of barren winter trees until we come upon a small wooden house with abundant windows that I first noticed during one of my walks with Jonas and Ulf. I can see Liv standing inside it, in between long tables covered with clay crocks and tubs. Jonas nudges me toward the door, then departs.

I knock, and Liv gestures me to enter. Inside, a stove warms the sunlit air, as if the occupant of the house is a midsummer's day.

"I brought you a stool," says Liv, pointing beside her.

I clamber up so I can observe from her vantage. Each crock is filled with green shoots, which poke out of the dirt, oblivious to the frosts and gales outside. Liv plays the rain, drenching them with a watering pot.

"This is where we grow the master's herbs. Come spring, they will be planted in the knot gardens." Her pot dips from receptacle to receptacle. "Here is angelica and gentian. Here prunella and blessed thistle. Here wormwood, sweet flag, valerian, and bloodwort. They are all medicaments, some to cure ague, others to cure weaknesses of the liver or digestion."

I am genuinely impressed by her knowledge. "You seem well versed in their properties."

But Liv merely nods as if this is a known fact. "I also sometimes help take measurements in the chemical laboratory."

That Tycho permits a woman—and a mere housekeeper at that—to perform such scholarly duties surprises me. But I do not doubt her intelligence; I know how a supple mind can be concealed in an unlikely body.

"We must plant elecampane seeds in these pots," she says, pointing to a half-dozen barren ones. She hands me a packet filled with seeds that resemble a child's tangled hair. "It aids in ailments of the lungs and helps expel melancholy. We can talk as we plant."

As I gently separate one seed from another, I carefully consider how to broach my letter. I am torn between making the kind of friendly conversation that might compel her to help me and being forthright. But before I can decide how to proceed, Liv pins me with her eyes.

"I take it no one has told you about Per Gek."

I shake my head. "He was another dwarf?"

Liv sighs. "He was a gift of the Hapsburgs, a merry little soul. He became a great favorite here. But one night, he tried to run away. He did not make it far before he was captured. Lord Tycho was most displeased and locked him in his prison."

Per Gek's story is beginning to sound all too familiar. I feel a bead of sweat drip down my temple. "Uraniborg has a prison?"

Liv nods. "Lord Tycho mostly uses it to punish the villagers if they refuse to work for him."

That it is the villagers who are the usual victims of my master's ire gives me but little comfort.

"After a month, Lord Tycho released Per. And for a few weeks all seemed as it had been. But then Per escaped again. This time he succeeded in procuring a boat from one of the villagers.

He set sail on a winter evening, hoping the early darkness would obscure his flight. But a storm blew in."

Liv pauses, giving a particularly rough shake of her watering pot. "His body washed up on shore the following morning."

Though I did not know this man, I feel as if his death is my own.

"Lord Tycho pronounced him a fool," Liv continues after a moment, "but I wager he was as heartsick over Per's death as the rest of us."

There is so much I wish to say: how it is preposterous for one man to subjugate another, feed him scraps beneath the table like a dog, and then expect his loyalty and affection. But I do not know Liv well enough to give voice to my true feelings. Instead, I think of Per alone in his skiff on those storm-tossed seas. I wonder if, like Lia, he was able to find some small measure of freedom, if even for a moment, before the winter waves dragged him to his grave.

"Lord Tycho is not a cruel man," Liv continues. "But he is quick to take offense. The villagers despise him."

I hesitate, wondering if what I mean to ask is too forward. "And you?"

She squints up at the sun, seeming to considering it as if it were Tycho himself. Then she looks back at me. "I have served his family for nearly seventeen years, since shortly after his daughter Magdalene was born. I could never despise Lord Tycho, but I understand why there are those that do."

I nudge an elecampane seed beneath the dirt with my finger, trying to feel emboldened by Liv's answer. There are not many seeds left in my packet and, as Liv lowers her empty watering pot, I fear my opportunity to enlist her aid is slipping away.

"Liv, do you have any family?" I ask.

"Not on solid earth."

I must look bewildered, for her thin lips press into a tight smile. "My father and brothers are sailors. My mother and I were the ones who preferred earth to water."

I seize upon this. "Your mother—?"

Liv crumbles a clod of dirt between her fingers. Her gray eyes briefly close, and without this crowning feature, her face appears careworn. "She died in December of 1583, when I was nineteen. My father and brother were at sea, and so I was left alone. I did not care to marry, so I applied for a position in Lord Tycho's household."

If there is any moment to appeal to her sympathy, it is now. "My mother—" My voice trembles.

"Go on," says Liv. She reaches out to pat my hand, and this gives me courage.

"She does not know what has become of me. It torments me night and day. I must send her word of what has become of me."

I am nearly out of breath, afraid to stop my plea, afraid she will say no. I take the letter out of the pocket of my breeches and hold it out to her. "I know I am not supposed to send letters but . . . Can you help me, Liv? Please?"

Liv glances out the window at the gardens. Then she turns back and takes the letter. I suddenly fear that she will give it to Tycho, and that all my secrets will be revealed, including that I have escaped before and long to again. I can already feel the moss-covered prison walls, the dank air.

"My mother is all I have in the world." I feel my face color as I confide this to Liv, who is little more than a stranger. "I miss her."

Upon these honest words, my eyes flood with tears.

"There now, child," Liv says, taking my hands in her own much larger ones. "You will stunt the herbs if you water them with tears. Lord Tycho does not control every soul on this island. I will see to it that the letter is sent. We'll have your mother reply to one of the villagers who knows me and can deliver it here."

"Thank you," I say over and over. Looking at Liv's gray eyes, stormy with tears of their own, I wonder if I owe some part of this good fortune to Per Gek. But whatever its source, I am grateful for it. The letter is my seed: I pray that, like Tycho's herbs, as winter turns to spring it will grow into a cure for my wounded heart.

Chapter 26

With my letter entrusted to Liv, I have no choice but to wait. I estimate that it will take at least two weeks for the letter to arrive in Astraveld, and at least two more before anyone is able to travel to this island to free me. Though a month—the transit of a single moon—is but a short span, my own impatience seems to slow the very course of the heavens. With each passing day, it seems as if Tycho's elaborate meals grow longer, my duties such as mixing his ointment and tending to Ulf more tedious, even the poems and stories that Jacob or the scholars recite at supper less of a distraction. I think often of Lia and home. As Tycho and his scholars discuss their latest bounty of stars, I wonder how it is that longing can seem to change time itself.

At night, I allow myself to return to my boyish fantasies.

I imagine my father has heard of my plight. He finds his way across sea and town and field to rescue me and bring me home. But these dreams are often sullied by unbidden memories of Don, and his threat that I would never know mother and home again. It is on such a night, a little less than two weeks into my wait, that my restlessness compels me to rise. I find myself thinking of Don's letter to Tycho requesting that I be returned to him if I displease—no doubt so he can beat me again. It angers me that Magdalene believes I would willingly work for such a man as his spy.

Though I have sworn to keep my distance from Magdalene, I want to tell her about Don. I want her to know she is wrong. But she did not even name the hour upon which she would be at the library, and her invitation may be a false one meant to send me to Tycho's prison. I am about to give up on this foolish idea when the tolling of the midnight bell reminds me that it is upon this same hour that I found her last. After a quick check of Ulf's tether, I creep through the darkened halls of Uraniborg toward my master's library.

When I reach the library door, I knock lightly, waiting for a response lest Tycho himself be at work. When no one answers, I gently turn the knob and step inside. The library is dark, the sliver of a new moon barely illuminating the brass globe hulking by the window.

"Magdalene?" I whisper.

Silence is my only answer.

"Magdalene?" I repeat, taking a few steps forward.

I nearly jump as something crinkles beneath my feet. I light my candle and draw it down to the floor, where I discover several scattered pages. They are covered with mathematical calculations and diagrams, and I have the distinct impression that I would end up in Tycho's prison if he found me perusing them. I hastily arrange the pages in as neat a stack as I am able and rest them on the closest desk, hoping they will not seem misplaced there. Then I peer beneath the table where Magdalene crouched the first time I encountered her. But tonight there is no one beneath it. Although it is no doubt for the best that I not find her in my present rash mood, I feel strangely disappointed.

Sensing someone behind me, I turn around but see only the automata, man and lion, lurking in the shadows by the door. The faintest creak of the floor sends me whirling in the opposite direction. But again there is no Magdalene, only the sickle-shaped moon tearing through the veil of a passing cloud. I feel as if the library is playing tricks on me, and I wonder if the real reason Magdalene admonished me to visit only when she was present was to protect me from some sinister force bound within it. I turn and beat a retreat to the door. I close it firmly behind me, but it is not until I reach the fountain that my heart stops knocking in my chest.

By morning's light, my fears seem childish and I regret my flight, wishing I had taken advantage of my solitude to inspect Tycho's books. That no one the following day makes any mention of finding Tycho's papers out of order seems to further confirm that my trepidation was unwarranted. That night, I goad myself to face down the demons of my own imagination and return to the library. I resolve that if Magdalene is not there this time, I will examine my master's books. In the dark, my fears of the otherworldly regain some of their potency, but as the midnight bell tolls, I rise, single-minded, and creep back past the fountain to the library door.

I rap lightly. Once again there is no answer, and I am all set to venture in when the door swings open.

I leap back, terrified that my master has discovered me.

Magdalene peers down at me with a bemused smile. "I thought you might be you," she says in Latin. "But you did not think I was I."

She is wearing another woolen peasant dress, her pale hair in two long braids like one of the village girls'. There is nothing that distinguishes her as a lady of the household. It strikes me that Uraniborg is indeed a mixed-up place, where a housekeeper does the tasks of a scholar, and a noblewoman dresses like a housekeeper. But whereas I approve wholeheartedly of the former, I know not what to make of the latter.

I find myself attempting a stiff bow. "I hoped you were here."

But Magdalene waves me off as if there is no need for false sentiments.

"Come in," she says.

She closes the door behind me, and I follow her over to the same desk where I had placed the scattered pages. A candle rests atop it and a quill, the ink upon it still wet, lies beside a page. Magdalene takes a seat at the desk and picks up the quill. I open my mouth but find myself unable to unleash the tirade I had imagined the previous evening.

Magdalene stares at me. "What is it?"

"I am not a spy," I finally manage to spit out. "Don beat me. I would never serve him."

Magdalene looks unsurprised. "That is what you've come to tell me?"

"Yes," I say. I feel unsettled by her seeming lack of interest. Does she not believe me?

She cocks her head toward the library shelves. "Would you like to look at the books?"

I wonder if this is some trap. If so, I will not be so easily ensnared. I decide that it matters not if she is my master's daughter. I will confront her directly. "Do you still think me a spy?"

I expect her to take offense at my belligerent tone but, to the contrary, Magdalene smiles and puts down her quill.

"After you left the library that night, I thought, What if he is not a spy? And indeed, as I watched you over the following days, you gave me no cause to think you were lying. But then I began to wonder, Why else would he conceal his intelligence? Perhaps, I thought, because you had been punished for it, even harmed. This made more sense to me than that you were a spy. I'm sure it threatens the rest of the world that someone like you has a mind."

That she—a noble, a person of ordinary stature—is able to intuit so much about my situation amazes me. But though I am struck by her perspicacity, I do not feel entirely comfortable with this girl who seems to gaze into my very soul.

"Uraniborg is different from the rest of the world," she continues. "So go on. Look at the books. I have my own labors to attend to."

She picks her quill back up and waves me off with it. Though I am tempted to protest that Uraniborg is no different for me, her invitation seems genuine, and I decide not to argue lest she change her mind. I hurry over to Tycho's collection. Just on the few shelves I am able to reach are hundreds of books in Latin about the heavens, about the human body, about God and nature, philosophy and love. But perhaps this bounty is too rich for one who has been as starved of wisdom as I. Fingering the leather and vellum spines and handwritten names of their authors—Aristotle, Ptolemy, Copernicus, Regiomontanus, Sacrobosco—I find that I am too overwhelmed to digest any of them. Instead, I find myself watching Magdalene, her mouth moving silently as she writes.

"What are you working on?" I ask.

Magdalene stops writing and peers over her desk to inspect me.

"We have established that I am no spy," I say. "But I understand if you should wish to keep it secret."

Magdalene considers this, then shrugs. "It is a horoscope for King Christian's son, Frederick, who was born during the second week of Lent. My father furnishes all the royal family's horoscopes, but he has been occupied with his observations, so I am drawing up the prince's chart for him. He prefers that the others do not see me do these labors for him, so I work at night."

"Are the prince's fortunes propitious?"

"Jupiter rules his chart, but Saturn is lord of his sixth house. In other words, his constitution is weak, but he may overcome it."

As she speaks, I find myself walking toward the desk till I too gaze at the prince's chart. It is wheel-shaped, symbols affixed along its many spokes. But it is the lower corner of the scroll that makes me realize what this royal chart has in common with my own. For written there are the very words that graced my own horoscope, *Suspiciendo despicio*: "By looking up I see downward."

"Does Lord Tycho draw up horoscopes for other courts?" I ask, though I already have a strong suspicion as to the answer.

"He has no time for commissions," Magdalene says, and my heart drops as I wonder if this Latin phrase is customary. "He is trying to record the positions of a thousand stars. So I also draw up these other horoscopes for him."

I stare in wonderment at the authoress of my chart, for I am certain now that Magdalene is she.

Magdalene narrows her eyes. "You must have seen my charts at Coudenberg. Don Diego de la Fuente requested some last winter. Was one of them yours?"

"Two of them, for he requested a copy for himself." This detail troubles me even more now that I know from Don's letter that his interest in my fate has not waned.

"He must have made the copy on his own, for I drew up five charts for him, all of them different. When were you born?"

"February seventeenth, 1583."

Magdalene smiles in recognition. "Yes, in Astraveld, Netherlands. An Aquarius, Venus ascendant, a favorable chart with good fortune, though considering your diminutive stature, I am surprised I did not find Saturn squaring your sixth house—"

I cast a longing glance at Tycho's books, certain that I am about to sacrifice the privilege I have just been granted with my insolence. Still, I cannot stop myself. "The horoscope you drew for me was wrong," I interrupt.

"Wrong?"

I hesitate, not wishing to tell her about Lia. "My fortune has been far less favorable than you suggested."

"How so?" Magdalene asks, peering down at me inquisitively as if my current station beneath her father's table were not misfortune enough.

"I wish not . . . I'll only say . . ." I sputter, torn between telling her about Lia and my intuition not to.

"Tell me," Magdalene orders.

"If the stars promise something and it does not come to pass, then astrology is flawed!"

I expect Magdalene will be offended by this display of intemperance for her art, but it seems only to further intrigue her. "This is quite a charge," she says, leaning back in her chair as if to ponder it. "As a defender of astrology, am I not entitled to know its basis?"

I reach for the seashell in my pocket. "Your chart shows I will marry one helpful and true. But she was lost to me."

"Lost in what way?"

Her tone is so direct that I cannot help but answer. "She died."

For a moment, Magdalene does not respond, and I imagine she must be gathering words of comfort and sympathy. But when she finally speaks, she offers nothing of the sort.

"Your birthday is but a couple of days away. You will be sixteen, will you not?"

"Yes, sixteen."

"A year younger than I. How can you be so certain the stars are wrong? Your life lies ahead of you. You may meet this girl yet."

Her words make sense, but I wish not to hear them.

"I already met her! She was small like me but beautiful. She taught me to dance. She sang like a nightingale. She—"

I cannot go on, for I realize that this is the first time I have spoken to anyone about Lia since my exile from Coudenberg.

Magdalene slips off her chair and sits beside me. "How did she die?"

"It matters not. Only that she did. There can be no other—"

"You cannot know this yet."

"My heart knows it."

"Do you think the heart does not heal and change?"

I feel a flash of hatred for this strange girl, the way she wields the truth, the way she presumes to know me. I leap to my feet. "I must go."

Before Magdalene can say more, I dash out of the library and into the hall.

Had I not been in such a rush to get away, I might have noticed the footsteps sooner. But by the time I do, Tycho is already in sight, marching toward me with a grave expression. I know it is he not only by his forceful step but by the hole in his face, for he has not bothered at this hour to attach his copper proboscis. I frantically try to devise a suitable lie as to why I am prowling the halls of his castle at this ungodly hour, but the fearful sight of him makes every excuse I try to devise ring hollow. Just as he bears down upon me, I hear a different type of step, the tap of cloven hooves, and Ulf appears, rounding the corner toward us.

Tycho turns to face his enormous pet.

"He is found!" he says in Dutch, throwing open his arms in delight, then swooping down as Ulf passes to grab the rope that trails behind him. It is only then I realize that I forgot to check whether my bedmate was securely fastened to his post before I left.

Ulf bellows mournfully at me as his master drags him to a stop.

"I searched for him everywhere," I tell Tycho. Fate, in the guise of this dumb creature, has saved me, and my relief gives credence to my lies. "He broke free as I slept."

Tycho barely seems to listen, so engaged is he in trying to direct Ulf back to our quarters. But the moose is as obstinate as his master. At last, Tycho cries out, "Jepp, you must go ahead or the beast will not budge!"

The urge to laugh forces me to purse my lips as I follow his command. And indeed, as I scamper ahead, Ulf walks in a most docile spirit after me. Tycho follows beside him. We make for a most odd procession.

When we reach our stall, I expect Tycho to scold me for this lapse in my duties; but once I have secured Ulf to his post, my master departs without a word. Ulf dips his square muzzle in his basin and guzzles the stream of water that flows within. As I gratefully stroke his massive brown flank, my thoughts return to Magdalene. I should take heart that the girl who draws up horoscopes for the King of Denmark himself believes my fortune is still good. But instead I feel dispirited by the truth of her words: that Lia was never meant to be mine. I resolve to visit Magdalene no more.

Chapter 27

When a child falls down, only his mother can comfort him—her soothing words and caresses seem to him a balm like no other. Though I am far from those childish years, I long just the same for my mother and the comfort only she can give. For she would not dismiss my sorrows as Magdalene has done but allow them with a mother's heart to be her own.

But my birthday passes and the moon comes and goes and still no one appears to take me home. I mean to ask Liv whether any letters have arrived for me; but my apprehension keeps me awake late into the night, and I slumber through her fleeting and infrequent deliveries of sugar cakes. During the day, she labors either out of sight—perhaps in the chemical laboratory—or else in the botanical garden. In the hope of finding her there, I lead

Ulf past the little house of seedlings. He now follows me like the calf does his mother, and I feel my own fondness for this dumb creature and his loyal companionship grow.

Once or twice, I spot Liv through the windows, but I dare not call out to her for fear of arousing the suspicions of Jonas, who always accompanies us. One day, however, as Jonas is yanking Ulf away from the window of the little house, I manage to catch her eye and, early the next morning, I feel a hand gently shaking me awake. My heart beats fast in the hope of news.

"Has a letter come for me?" I whisper.

"I'm afraid there is no answer yet," Liv says.

I try to disguise my disappointment. "I am sure it will arrive soon."

But my own words do little to reassure me.

"I will be back tomorrow," Liv says. "Perhaps there will be news then."

She opens my hand and places a warm sugar cake inside it.

But there is no news the next morning or the morning after that. I cling to the hope that the letter is somehow delayed, and yet I cannot shake the fear that, as Don promised, I will never know my mother nor home again.

One morning, over five weeks after I sent my letter home, I wake to hurried shouts and the rush of footsteps outside. Ulf pulls hard on his tether, trying to turn and view the commotion. I quickly don my breeches and slip out into the main hall to investigate.

In the dim light of the late winter dawn, a procession of peasants carries a slain deer, a small flock of trussed and plucked geese, a giant slab of beef, bins of flopping fish, which slop water on the floor to the consternation of the house servants, and a great number of barrels of ale. The cook stands outside the kitchen, shouting instructions and kneading his plump hands in anticipation.

This is but the first sign that someone is coming to Uraniborg, someone important. I wonder if it is the Danish royals, for throughout the morning and into the afternoon, the servants are models of industry. The maidservants scrub the floors and set Tycho's table with three layers of lace tablecloths, the carver sharpens his knives, the cupbearer polishes the sterling silver vessels engraved with the Brahe family crest and shines a set of crystal glasses that I have never before seen. After Jonas and I walk Ulf through the grounds, the moose is banished to his room so as not to befoul the floors. After the midday meal, which we take in the kitchen instead of Tycho's chamber, Jonas is called away, and the cook tasks me with shucking oysters. Though the rough shells cut my hands, I find a rare moment of peace tucked away in a corner of the kitchen, watching the clouds of steam, the scaling of fish, the mixing of meat and spice.

As the three o'clock bell tolls, Jonas reappears and, spotting me with oyster in hand, shouts at the women who assist the cook. Before I know it, two of them have hoisted me into the air, one carrying me by the arms, the other by the legs as if I am some prize of the hunt. I fear that Tycho has discovered my forbidden letter and intends to add fricassee of dwarf to his banquet, until the women put me down in front of a basin of water and begin to scrub my hands with lime. It is only as they lean over to sniff my hands that I understand that Jonas must have informed them that today Lord Tycho's dwarf must not smell as briny as the sea or reek of moose.

As Jonas leads me out of the kitchen, he hands me the same clothes I wore when I arrived from Coudenberg, carefully washed and mended, along with my jingling jester's cap. My old costume seems a relic of a different life and yet, as he directs me to dress in the servants' sleeping chamber so Ulf's stench does not spoil my costume, it reminds me of how little my life has changed. With each garment I don, I feel more certain that my fortune will not improve, that I will always be some rich man's toy, that I will never be allowed to advance my station or cultivate my mind.

An hour later, Jonas leads me into Tycho's chamber. Even to one as heavyhearted as I, it is a grand sight—the table bedecked with crystal, silver, and lace and vermilion cloth; every candle on the wheel-sized brass chandeliers aflame; a trio of musicians I have never seen before playing trumpet, viol, and lute; footmen bearing enormous platters heaped with the sea's harvest— mountains of oysters and crayfish, mussels and shrimp, crabs and eel. The scholars are dressed as if for a holiday—Severinus cuts a dashing figure in an embroidered cape with gold buttons, and even Longomontanus, whom I have little cared for since he chased me out of the library, has donned a slightly ill-fitting doublet. Tycho, occupying his usual seat above the others at his table, wears a plumed beret, ruff collar, and gleaming silver nose. But the person who shares his perch is not his wife, Lady Kirsten, but a woman dressed in lace coif, enormous ruff collar, and velvet gown. I assume she must be a Danish royal to unseat the lady of the house, indecorously relegated to a place among the scholars. But this powerful lady seems to have no retinue beyond a sandy-haired gentleman with a gold medallion around his neck and an easy smile. He sits on Tycho's other side, sucking on crayfish tails.

"Welcome to my beloved sister, Lady Sophie Brahe, and brother-in-law, Lord Erik Lange," Tycho says in Latin for the benefit of the assembled scholars. "Sister and Brother, this is my new dwarf, Jepp."

After some exclamations in Danish, Lady Sophie summons me to her side. But just as I reach her, a tiny dog springs from her lap, and I stumble backward in surprise. Laughter rises up from the table as my cheeks color.

"He must be a big dog to you," says Lange in Dutch, with a tip of his crystal glass. He ponders the glass a moment and then, swishing the red wine inside it, holds it down to me. "Have a sip—that is, unless your master wishes it not."

Tycho shrugs and says in Latin. "He will only turn into more of a fool, not less."

My fists clench, but I force my countenance to remain blank as if I have understood nothing. I look at Magdalene to see if she, like the rest, is enjoying this game, but she is seated beside her mother, whose arm she rests her hand upon as she engages in animated discussion with Severinus. The sight of her stokes my anger further, for she is most certainly wrong. My fate is a bleak one. Yanking the glass toward me, I drink greedily, certain that the only place that I might find some solace tonight is at the bottom of it. Tycho's strong wine is nearly as bitter as Maria's hippocras but, after the first swallow, its pungent flavor tempers, and I am able to drain the glass.

"That-a-boy!" shouts Lange and pats me roughly on the back. "Ready for another?"

"Enough," Tycho says gruffly in Dutch. "Jepp, under the table."

As I assume my familiar place, I feel my limbs grow slack and my cheeks flush with the effects of the wine. Sucking down an oyster that my master offers me, my anger fades, replaced by a drowsy resignation. Above, Tycho begins to make his customary Latin proclamations about the great work of Uraniborg—how eternal fame awaits all, how the brilliant minds of Tycho Brahe and his scholars will expose the very secrets of the universe. I flip Matheus's useless copper, barely listening.

More courses arrive, more wine, I am briefly summoned to perform the French dance and take Lady Brahe's dog as my partner, who shivers with fright. As Tycho laughs, his silver nose takes the first of many tumbles to the ground, and I must stop the dance to retrieve it. Back under the table, I feel the snap of a finger on the back of my head and turn to find a goblet of wine clutched in Erik Lange's downy hand. As I wordlessly accept this gift, I hear the welcome clop of hooves, then cheers from the table, that signal Jonas is leading Ulf through the door. As Ulf noisily consumes his tankards to the shouts of encouragement and guffaws above, I quietly drain my goblet below, feeling a particular kinship with my thirsty bedfellow.

Tycho, under the same saturnalian influence, stumbles to his feet and begins once again to declaim the great work of Uraniborg in Latin. I am just about to fall asleep to the deep timbre of his voice declaring "To a thousand stars!" when Erik Lange interrupts him.

"You do know you're wasting your time, Tycho. It is alchemy that will change the world."

Though Lange's tone is playful, I have never heard anyone belittle my master. I sit upright, my old alehouse instincts awakened.

But Tycho only snorts as if he has heard such rubbish before. "Always this obsession of yours! Riches of the earth instead of the perfect harmony of the heavens! I hope you do not invest my sister's fortune in your harebrained schemes."

"I've invested nothing—" Sophie Brahe protests.

"Your sister will be handsomely recompensed," interrupts Lange cheerfully. From my vantage point beneath the table, I can see him finger his gold medallion.

Tycho hiccups, then sighs dramatically. "You have always plagued me, Erik, bringing misfortune like some comet. First you foist upon me that scoundrel Ursus, who ends up stealing the planetary system of *my* invention, then you refuse to temper your obsession with alchemy, though it threatens to bring not just you, but my beloved sister, to ruin. If you were not such an old friend, perhaps my very dearest—"

Tycho's voice breaks as his nose clatters to the floor.

"I would never wish to bring you ill, old friend!" interrupts Lange. "Was it not I who recommended to your service young Severinus, the son of a great mathematician and a great mathematician in his own right?"

"Now, now, gentlemen," Severinus says. I imagine him shaking his handsome head as if such praise is unnecessary.

"This is true," Tycho says. He settles back in his chair and takes his nose, which I have been dutifully holding out. "But remember, brother, gold is a false idol."

It has become clear to me that this argument will not end in fisticuffs; Tycho and his brother-in-law seem accustomed to engaging in such spirited banter. I stop listening and look into my own goblet, which lies deplorably empty. Before I can stop myself, I have tapped it against Erik Lange's knee in the hopes that he can perform the alchemy of turning air into wine. To my delight, he takes the goblet and, a moment later, slips it back to me filled nearly to the brim. I begin to drink.

Some time later Magdalene leans down beneath the table to stare at me. I turn away from her. There are cheers as Ulf slurps yet another tankard. Jacob plays his lute, though I am certain that it is not he but Lia. If I can only summon the energy to open my eyes, I will see her.

"Jepp!" Tycho calls.

I wake and crawl out from under the table. Half the company has departed, but Tycho, Erik Lange, and a half dozen red-faced scholars still linger over their cups. My master's noseless face resembles a keyhole. I wonder if, were I to open it, I would find inside his head a fleur-de-lis.

"I said you were dismissed!" Tycho says in Dutch.

There is a clatter as Ulf rakes the table with his antlers, knocking down several goblets.

"And take that moose with you."

I head for the door, which seems to have changed position from where I last recall it being. Ulf stumbles on a goblet in his haste to follow, and Jonas rushes forward to grab his tether. Once in the hall, my bedfellow catches up to me and shoves my head with his muzzle. Jonas looks fearful that Ulf means to trample me and tries to yank him back. But I know that, in the same rough spirit as Tycho and Erik Lange's banter, the creature means only to convey his affections.

"You old rascal," I say in Dutch, patting his slippery nose.

Inside our room, Jonas ties Ulf to his post, then leads me to my pallet. For a moment he stares at me with concern, before I smile and wave him away. As soon as he departs, I look for my bedfellow. But the room is spinning, and it seems as if there are several Ulfs looking down at me with their gentle, dark eyes.

"You are a good beast," I tell them.

As if accepting my benediction, the Ulfs snort warm, fetid air at me.

I drift from sleep to wakefulness, the room tilting like a ship at sea, then righting itself. Hendrika grasps me to her breast as Don chases us, but we are tangled in the chain that holds Sebastian's key and cannot escape. Then I am in the orchard with Lia, who teaches me the French dance—but it is not a dance at all but a series of kisses. I wake to Ulf nudging me with his muzzle. I push him away. He nudges me again, and I notice his tether lies on the floor. "Be free," I command, imagining his freedom to be my own.

Chapter 28

When I next wake, light sears my eyes. As I sit up, I realize I am still dressed in my wine-stained costume. My head throbs, and I feel a terrible sense that I have done something regrettable. I am so busy trying to remember what it was that it takes me a moment to realize that Ulf is not hovering over me. I sit up, though this action makes my gut roil, and look frantically around as if such a massive creature could somehow be hiding in the straw. Then I remember how he stood over me, unloosed from his post, and how I encouraged him to wander. I stumble to my feet, hoping there is still time to find him before Tycho discovers my neglect.

I race into the hall, alarmed to see servants already about, the morning further advanced than I had imagined. I dash toward the fountain—hoping that Ulf may have come to rest beside it, if only to quench the heinous thirst I myself now feel. But there is no sign of him. As I hurry into the corridor that houses Tycho's chamber and library, my stomach feels queasy with dread, and I pray that I may discover Ulf there before Tycho does. But instead I see Tycho, Jonas, and a small group of servants standing around Ulf, who lies motionless on his side by the staircase to the scholars' garret. His antlers rest upon the ground like the wings of a great fallen bird.

"Ulf!" I say, running up to him. "Does he live?"

But my own question is answered at the sight of a gaping wound in Ulf's side where a sword has entered and stained his hide with blood.

"What did you do to him?!" I shout.

Jonas catches my eye and shakes his head, but it is too late, for Tycho glares down at me.

"*We* did nothing," he says in Dutch. "He escaped your room last night and tried to climb the stairs to the scholars' garret. But he was too drunk for such antics and broke his leg. There was no choice but to return him to his maker."

I glance at Ulf's hind leg, which is bent at a most unnatural angle, confirming Tycho's story. I am the one who has done this to Ulf. I imagine him lying at the bottom of the stairs as I lay in my drunken stupor, his leg shattered, bellowing in pain. I feel my stomach rise, and race to the fountain where I disgorge the remnants of last night's supper into it.

I do not wait to see how my master responds to the befouling of his prize fountain. Instead, I run to my room and collapse on the straw, still redolent of Ulf's musky odor. My tears flow freely as I think of the gentle creature never again following me through the halls, or shifting in his standing sleep beside me. If only I had not been drunk, I would have tied him back up and saved him.

I expect to be punished, indeed I long to be punished. But as the hours tick by, Jonas does not summon me. Perhaps Tycho thinks it punishment enough to leave me in this cage of memories, or perhaps he means never again to feed me, for the dinner hour comes and goes. But this is hardly penance, for I have no appetite for anything beyond my own sorrow.

The darkest moments can be fertile ground for a humor black and consoling. At least this time, I tell myself, I have caused the death of a moose instead of a girl. Perhaps next time, it will be merely a chicken—though doubtless one I have also come to love.

As the afternoon lengthens, a shadow darkens the door and for a moment, I imagine it is Ulf returned. But the creature that enters does so on two legs not four.

"You seem little improved," Tycho remarks in Dutch.

I sit up swiftly. "I am . . . a bit better."

"Good," Tycho says, though I notice he keeps his distance as if he fears that I may yet heave upon him. "Now that Ulf is gone, we must find some additional duties for you."

That Tycho wishes to discuss such quotidian matters confuses me.

"Do you not mean to punish me?"

"For what? The fountain has suffered worse abuse. As for Ulf, you were obviously in no condition to prevent his death. Lord Lange saw to that. We should have sent Jonas in to watch over him. Ah, well. Poor Ulf was a merry creature."

After a moment's pause for this epitaph, he continues. "You had a way with Ulf. Perhaps you can help in the kennels. . . ."

I should be relieved that Tycho's mood is merciful. But all I can think of is how this gentle creature, my loyal friend, is gone. I envision the lonely years ahead, crouching in the shadows beneath the table in my jester's cap, being trotted out for the amusement of men who think me nothing but a fool. This wretched life, it seems, is my fate. No one has come to rescue me and, with each passing day that no letter arrives from Astraveld, it seems more likely that no one ever will. But I recall how Magdalene said I have a mind. Did not Tycho himself write that a soul with a mind can change his fate, can bend the very heavens to his will? I remain doubtful, but I decide I have nothing to lose.

"Give me a task that befits me," I say in Latin.

Tycho shakes his head as if trying to make sense of this familiar tongue. Then he leans over and peers at me in confusion. "What in hell?" he says in Dutch as his nose tumbles off and clatters to the ground.

I am almost as surprised as he and immediately wonder if I have made a terrible mistake by so boldly ordering about my master. But in spite of this, I am also tempted to laugh, for it is a rare day when Lord Tycho Brahe is caught unawares. His nose lies on the straw between us. I make no move to pick it up.

"I am not the fool you think I am," I say in Latin. "Fate has cast me here, but I wish to learn and better myself. I am tired of sitting idle."

For a few moments, Tycho says nothing, merely fingering his reddish blond beard as he stares down at me. If he didn't intend to punish me before, I am certain he is considering it now. I glance at the copper nose, knowing that I might temper his ire by retrieving it. But I do not move.

"Very well," Tycho finally says. "Jonas will fetch you tomorrow."

He leans down to pick up his nose himself, and departs.

Chapter
29

hough I am most exhausted by the emotions of the day, I cannot sleep, in anticipation of the following morn. Will Tycho permit me to be something other than a fool and so Uraniborg prove different, as Magdalene claims it to be? Or will he condemn me as defiant and, after reading the full contents of Don's letter, deliver me back into my tormenter's hands? It is not until late at night that I finally fall into a slumber as heavy and dreamless as death. When I wake, I am no longer fearful but resigned to whatever the day may bring. I dress in a clean smock and breeches, finding a small measure of assurance in these simple garments and the sugar cake Liv has once again left me.

At half-past seven, Jonas appears and, with a nervous glance, beckons me to follow. As he knocks on the library door, hope stirs that Tycho means for me to join him there. But when I consider Jonas's wary mien, I remind myself that it is just as likely that he brings me to the heart of his kingdom to inform me that I will be returned to Don for my secrecy and insolence. Despite this, I do not regret my request. Hearing myself make such a demand has reminded me who I am. I am not a curiosity or a clown. I am a boy with an agile mind and aspirations to use it. We are nothing if not our hopes and dreams.

The door swings open, and Tycho impatiently waves me inside.

"Come," he says in Latin.

As he closes the door behind me, I realize that this is only the third time in the three months I've been at Uraniborg that I have beheld the library by day. It thrills me to see it so occupied—the scholars bent over their calculations or arguing quietly around the great brass globe, their books and papers strewn across the desks, a rousing melody of lute and viol filling the room, though no musicians appear to be present. Outside in the aviary the birds twitter in song. It does not seem the same shadowy place where Magdalene and I discussed my fate. At the thought of our conversations, I find myself wishing she were present, though I know she does not work in the library by day. I wonder if she has heard about my revelation and imagine she would applaud me for it.

"Now you look better," Tycho remarks, appraising me.

"I am."

"Good. We can proceed."

Tycho turns away, leaving me to wonder what exactly he means to proceed with.

"Longomontanus!" he shouts.

Longomontanus detaches himself from the group by the globe. Upon catching sight of me, he briefly smiles, no doubt remembering the drunken fool I so recently was, and hurries over, lowering his eyes to the ground in his obsequious manner. "Yes, Tycho?"

"I have discovered that Jepp, my dwarf, speaks Latin."

Longomontanus kneels down as he did the first morning at Uraniborg when he presented me with my contract to sign. "How do you speak Latin, Jepp?" he says, addressing me in that tongue.

I wonder if some inquisition has begun.

"I studied it at Coudenberg," I say carefully. "But only a little over a year."

"You speak it most excellently if that is all the time you had to study," says Longomontanus.

Though his words are ones of praise, his cautious delivery makes them sound like an accusation.

"Where did you study before Coudenberg?" he continues.

"My mother has an inn," I say. "I did not study at all but schooled myself."

"Most excellent!" says Longomontanus, though I wonder if this answer truly pleases him or whether he is a man like Don, who pretends to be affable when he intends to be cruel.

"What shall we do with him?" Tycho asks.

Although I am relieved that they have made no mention of sending me back to Don, I feel as if they are playing some game with me. I stare nervously at Longomontanus, half expecting him to suggest punishments for my duplicity as exotic as Uraniborg itself—counting every star in the sky, testing potions that confer nightmare and madness, being held under the waters of the fountain.

"Inkpots?" says Longomontanus.

I burst into laughter. I am not being punished at all. I am being promoted to filling inkpots. Even if such a task hardly requires knowledge of Latin, Tycho is allowing me to labor alongside him and the scholars in his library. Longomontanus peers at me with concern. He no longer seems the inquisitor I imagined.

"What did you expect?" Tycho says with irritation, having mistaken my laughter for disdain. "You may know Latin, but you know nothing about the stars."

With this my master departs, disappearing through a back door of the library.

I force myself to stop laughing and assume a dutiful expression. "I shall fill the inkpots," I say. "Keep them filled."

Longomontanus seems satisfied with this show of humility and gestures for me to follow him.

"I have one other task for you as well."

As we walk past the desks, the scholars lift their heads from their work to stare at me, no doubt wondering what Tycho's dancing dwarf is doing in their domain. But only one voices his curiosity.

"What is Jepp doing here?" asks Severinus.

"He will be assisting us," Longomontanus says, as if my presence here is most natural. "He speaks Latin."

"Does he, now?"

I care not for the way Severinus says this, and wonder if he read the entirety of Don's letter before filing it away and has always known my secret. It occurs to me that he and Magdalene also converse freely at dinner. Would she have told him I speak Latin? Does he suspect I am a spy? But he follows this comment with a grin that suggests he means no harm, and these worries fade as I follow Longomontanus to the brass globe.

"This, Jepp, is a celestial globe, a map of the heavens. Each of these dots represents a star and where it lies in the celestial sphere. When we have ascertained to the most accurate degree possible a new star's coordinates, we record it here. I need you to clean it, as the men's hands often leave marks upon it. But take care not to damage it or share the markings upon it with anyone, for this is the sum of our contribution to man's knowledge of the heavens. Tycho's rivals, especially Ursus, would be most glad for such knowledge to fall into their hands. We hope soon that the stars upon it will number one thousand."

I stare at the globe's curved side; it is so large I cannot see over the top. The zodiac is etched upon it, while dots representing stars perforate its brass face like tiny pockmarks. At Coudenberg I saw a globe that showed the New World, but it is even more miraculous to think that captured upon this globe is the sky I see at night. I can barely believe that I, like Atlas, have been entrusted with the very heavens. I gently touch the stars, wondering if they hold my fate or whether holding them, as I do now, allows me to create my own. I feel a growing boldness, surrounded by these explorers of the heavens, that the latter is possible.

By dinner, I have filled the inkpots several times and carefully polished the globe. As I work, I listen to the scholars argue about the workings of the heavens, the proper way to measure the stars, their ideas for new instruments of celestial import. Although I comprehend little of this learned discourse, I can at least endeavor to instruct myself by listening.

My mood is most jubilant as I follow Tycho and the scholars into his chamber for dinner. But at the sight of the long table, my spirits fall, for I cannot bear to crawl beneath it and assume my customary place. I resolve to no more be treated like a dog but instead to demand a seat at Tycho's table.

But I am not granted this chance, for before I can protest, Tycho orders me over and hands me a plate heaped with fish and turnips.

"You may eat beside me on the floor," he says in Latin.

Though this position is an improvement over being fed scraps under the table, it is not the chair I had been hoping for. But I wish not to irritate Tycho again so soon after my advancement and decide that for now it is promotion enough.

From where I sit, it is hard to see much beyond legs and feet. But during the second course, a fork clatters to the floor, and Magdalene bends down to peer at me. For the first time since the night in the library, I smile at her. She grabs her fork and hastily rises. As the cupbearers pour more wine and beer, and Tycho and the scholars become more raucous as they pass the tankards, I grow bold enough to sidle on my knees behind Tycho and Lady Kirsten to her side.

"Hello, Magdalene," I say in Latin.

At the sound of my voice, she assumes a wounded expression.

"So, you are talking to me now?"

I feel a sudden shame over how I have ignored her since the night in the library. "I am sorry."

Her eyes narrow as she smiles. "Anyway, I was right."

"Right about what?"

"About your horoscope. I hear my father is allowing you to assist the scholars in the library. Your fortunes have improved. I told you they would."

I think of Matheus's copper—perhaps it has given me luck after all? But then I shake my head, for I know that it is neither lucky star nor coin that have changed my fortunes. "It is I who have improved them. I told your father I speak Latin and asked him for new duties. The stars had nothing to do with it."

"Just because you choose something doesn't mean it's not fated."

"But if it's fated, it's not truly a choice! And God gave man free will."

I expect her to concede the rightness of my argument, but she juts her jaw defiantly. "What does that mean when one man is born with nothing and another with all the riches of the world? The exercise of free will depends on opportunity, and opportunity is a measure of fate."

I would have liked to continue this conversation had Tycho not called for me. But there is no ignoring his booming voice. "Jepp! Where have you gone?"

With an apologetic glance at Magdalene, I scurry back to find Tycho dabbing ointment onto his face and pressing on his copper nose, which must have fallen off in my absence.

"Magdalene dropped her fork," I say.

"You will retrieve her fork but not my nose. Is that how it is?"

"I suppose so."

I nearly clap my hand over my mouth, but Tycho tips back his head and laughs.

"A morning in the library, and you are more amusing already."

But my boldness surprises me less than the sentiment I have revealed. I wish Magdalene to be my friend.

Chapter
30

though at night, I still miss the comforting clop of Ulf's hooves, I find that my melancholy fades at dawn when the scholars return from the observatory, and I am called into the library to labor among them. I am soon most proficient at filling inkpots and cleaning the celestial globe. But even during idle moments, I pretend to work at a stubborn mark on the globe or check the ink in an already full pot so I can hover by the scholars and listen.

On one such afternoon, as I stand upon a chair, dragging my rag across the top of the globe, an argument breaks out between two scholars who have come to view it.

"The earth revolves around the sun," says a plump, pale Norwegian astronomer named Aslacus. "Copernicus wrote—"

"The sun revolves around the earth!" interrupts the Bohemian, Oswaldus, who spins one long finger around the other in demonstration. "It is the other planets that revolve around the sun. Tycho is right on this point. Copernicus is wrong."

I am so perplexed by this argument that I forget to keep moving my rag. For it seems to me that both men are mistaken. As Master Kees, my tutor at Coudenberg, averred, the heavens—planets and sun—revolve around the earth. It is so strange to ponder a universe ordered otherwise that it takes me a moment to realize that Severinus is staring at me. I hastily return to polishing the globe, but he calls my name and waves me over.

As I approach his desk, I look for his inkpot, hoping that he merely wishes me to attend to it. But the inkpot is full.

Severinus gives me a shrewd look. "You seem to take great interest in our conversations."

I can hardly deny my curiosity. But there is also something about Severinus's haughty tone—the birthright of a boy handsome and tall—that makes me wish to challenge him.

"Should I not?"

Severinus grins as if my retort is most clever. "I suppose there is no harm."

To my surprise, he lifts his elbow and pushes the piece of paper pinned beneath it toward me. "Tycho hired me to serve as a mathematician. One of my tasks is to try to determine whether the sun or Mars comes closest to Earth. The astronomers give me measurements from fixed stars to Mars at different times of the night, and I use geometry to help account for the parallax, which is the displacement caused by the viewer's line of sight."

I am tempted to pretend comprehension, but I truly wish to make sense of this.

"I do not understand."

Severinus looks pleased for the chance to explain. "Close your right eye and look at the metal lion."

I do as he instructs.

"Now, close your left. It will seem as if the lion has moved."

"Yes! It is true."

"But it has not. It is merely the change in your line of sight. Only when you use both eyes do you see an object for where it truly is. Imagine now the lion to be the planet Mars, the background of the library to be the heavens, and your two eyes to be different times of the night. You need to use the measurements from both times of the night together to account for parallax and place Mars correctly in the heavens."

I am most intrigued by this principle but also by Severinus himself. No other scholar has explained to me the nature of his work.

Severinus slides back his paper. "There, you have learned something new."

He picks up his quill and begins to write. I take this as a sign that our lesson has ended and return to my station by the globe. From this vantage, I sneak glances at Severinus, first with one eye and then the other. Finally, I look at him with both eyes. I wonder if I have misjudged him.

That evening, as the scholars depart for supper, I stay on in the library as long as I am able. I pretend to neaten up, but what I truly seek is a piece of paper, for I wish to send my mother another letter. Though I am still not certain that she ever received the first, I feel ashamed of it and of the writer who whimpered like a child over his misfortunes. I am anxious to acquaint her with a different Jepp, one whose courage and force of will secured him a place in Tycho's library, one who thinks that just maybe the universe does not revolve around the earth, nor the world around himself.

There are but a few scholars left, rushing to finish some last calculation, when I spot a stray sheet of paper lying on an empty desk. I have even more to lose now if my letter writing is discovered, so I make sure no one is watching as I filch the paper from the desk and tuck it into my smock. I still have a quill and inkpot concealed behind a brick in the wall of my room.

That night, as midnight approaches and stillness settles over the castle, I pry the brick from the wall and commence writing. But after a few lines, I become stymied over the purpose of my letter. Do I still wish to be rescued? I desperately miss my mother and Willem, long to go home to Astraveld, where I know I will be safe and loved. But I also wish to learn and better myself, and Tycho seems to have given me that chance. I want to escape, and yet I am curious about what the future holds for me at Uraniborg.

I am so deep in thought that by the time I become aware of the footsteps padding through the kitchen, as light as a ghost's, they are far too close to my chamber. I blow out my candle and shove letter, inkpot, and quill under my pallet, heaping myself in a sham of repose over them. I close my eyes tight, willing for the footsteps to retreat. For a moment, I no longer hear them. I am about to sit up, thinking them gone, when I hear a whisper.

"Jepp?"

The voice is a woman's, but too low to be Liv's.

"I know you are awake," she says in Latin. "I can smell the candle smoke."

I open my eyes and peer up at Magdalene. She stands in the doorway dressed in a long, hooded cloak, a sack slung across her shoulder. The flickering light of a candle casts shadows across her sturdy face.

"What are you doing here?" I whisper, sitting up.

Magdalene reaches into her sack and pulls out a small cloak much like her own, which she tosses to me. "Put it on."

"Why?" I ask.

Magdalene puts a finger to her mouth. Then she reaches back into the sack and pulls out a set of keys.

I know not where Magdalene intends to take me. I know only that I risk losing all I have gained by following her. If my absence is detected, my pallet will be searched and my correspondence discovered. I will be banned from Tycho's library, even imprisoned. But still I don the cloak, which judging by its snug fit belongs to one of Magdalene's skinny young brothers, and follow her out of the kitchen and down the darkened hall. Perhaps I cannot lose this chance to be with her. Or perhaps it is the keys, jingling softly in her sack, that entice the part of me that still longs to escape.

Chapter
31

As Magdalene leads me out through the front door of the castle, a gust of wind greets us, nearly blowing off our hoods and extinguishing Magdalene's candle. The air is cold but not freezing, the sky starry and swept clear of clouds, the spring cleaning of a March gale. Magdalene places her candle in her sack and looks up at the stars.

"Where are we going?" I whisper to Magdalene as we hurry past the ornamental gardens.

"For a walk," she says, as if taking a jaunt after midnight is perfectly natural.

I cannot see much of her face, which is concealed by her hood, but I notice she slows her pace so I can follow more comfortably at my own.

"Are we leaving the castle grounds?"

At this, Magdalene turns to face me. Her gaze is as direct as that of a child.

"Do you have any objections?"

I can think of a number, but instead of voicing them I say, "No."

"We won't get caught," she says, sensing my apprehensions. "I have done this before. But it is best to proceed in silence until we reach the gate."

As she mentions the gate, I remember the mastiffs kenneled above it and wonder how she will prevent them from raising an alarm at our presence. But I feel an instinctive trust in Magdalene and an even deeper curiosity about what she means to show me.

I have not been outside since Ulf died, and as we pass into the orchard, I am moved to see the silhouettes of trees in bud. Though this is but the barest sketch of the season, it reminds me of Coudenberg, and that perfect spring with Lia that I shall never have again. But my sorrow does not last as long as I expect. For as I look up at the bud-covered branches, I realize that this spring is lovely to me for a different reason, for daring to come back, for beginning again the work destroyed by autumn's sickle. As we pass the glass house, I wonder if Liv's herbs have been planted in the knot gardens and whether the shoots of my elecampane seeds are among them.

At the outer edge of the orchard, Magdalene turns and follows the wall toward the eastern gatehouse. Just before we reach it, I can hear the mastiffs stir on the rooftop kennel. As one of them begins to growl, Magdalene opens her sack and pulls out a dead hare. Grasping it by the ears, she eyes the kennel, takes a step back, and then tosses it over the top of the gatehouse. There is a dull smack, silence, then the sounds of flesh being torn, interspersed with growls.

"Hurry," Magdalene whispers, dashing for the gate.

I race after her, but by the time I catch up, she has already unlocked the gate and is waving me urgently through. I run, afraid that I have been too slow, that the dogs have finished tearing apart the hare and are about to bark at the sound of our footsteps and the creak of the gate. I dash to the outer side of the wall and collapse at a safe distance from the gatehouse. Magdalene runs so fast that, although she must have closed the gate and locked it behind her, she reaches me but a moment later. She falls to the ground beside me, laughing.

"What?" I ask, between breaths. "What is it?"

"We are out!" she says. Her hood has blown off and her pale hair flies about, loosened from its braid. She looks like some creature of the night, a witch drunk on moonlight. I find myself laughing too as my fear melts into the exhilaration of our escape.

She catches my eye and holds it fast. As if extinguished by a gust of wind, our laughter dies away. I am suddenly aware that we are out in the night alone. I feel short of breath, as if my run has just caught up with me.

"I am glad you came," Magdalene says.

She turns away and looks out toward the horizon. But I continue to stare at her, for I realize I have never seen her at my own level. Her face is not so much plain as elemental, with the forceful beauty of lightning or a winter storm. And yet there is an impishness to her, a freedom of spirit, that seems at odds with such an earthbound form. I wonder if she ever feels trapped, as I do, my feelings so much larger than the vessel that carries them.

"You must think me strange," she says. "Running about at night."

"No less strange than myself. Besides, I am glad you fetched me. I wanted to thank you."

"For what?

"For believing me to have a mind."

"I appreciate your gratitude, but this is not a question of faith. I simply observed you." Magdalene grins. "Regardless, your trust in me tonight shall be rewarded. I will show you Hammer Castle, the most legendary of the island's Viking ruins."

I have thought of this island as eternally belonging to Tycho, so it gladdens me to hear of this other age of stargazers and seafarers. I imagine Viking ships and Viking maidens gazing upon just such a sky and feel as if Magdalene and I have escaped not just through space but through time. I am eager to explore, but, as Magdalene rises, I realize I know not how far away this castle lies.

"Where is it?"

Magdalene points toward the sea. "You can almost see it. Atop the cliffs."

From our vantage on the hill, I trace the darkened lines of the peasants' fields, sloping gently down to the village. Beyond the village, fading into the darkness of the horizon, are the cliffs. I sigh deeply. It is as if Magdalene has asked me to follow her to the moon.

"It is too far for my legs."

Magdalene turns to me with a look of consternation. "I did not consider—"

"I fear you have chosen the wrong companion for your rambles."

She considers this. "I do not think so."

I am secretly touched by her words. "You do not mind that I am small?"

"So you must look up. That is no fault at Uraniborg."

As if to emphasize this, Magdalene throws back her head

and studies the stars. With her back arched, I can see the rise of her breasts, the curve of her neck where it emerges from the folds of her cloak. It is as if she is waiting for the heavens to embrace her.

"You will do well here," she pronounces.

"Is that what the stars say? To me they seem most indifferent."

Magdalene feigns a scowl, though our conflict over astrology is well established. As I watch her, it occurs to me that it is my own fortunes or lack thereof that are always the subject of our debate. For the first time, I begin to wonder about Magdalene's.

"What do they say for you?" I ask.

"I am a Sagittarius—inquisitive and blunt-spoken. I have three planets in my fourth house, which tie me to my parents and home. My second house—of wealth and possessions—is afflicted but improves when I marry."

I do not think Magdalene, daughter of Lord Tycho, could have any shortage of wealth and possessions. "And you believe this?"

"I know it to be true. As I know yours to be true. You wish to become a scholar, and you shall, even though you are different."

I shake my head, giving voice to my fears. "But it is not just a matter of height. I am not schooled as the others are. Nor is my family like theirs. There was but a single man who could read and write in the village where I was born."

"This is not what matters. You have interesting thoughts about the world. You question it—not only with your mind but with your heart. There are many, even here, who cannot do that."

I look down at my lap, hoping that in the dark she cannot see my cheeks color with the pleasure of hearing such praise.

"And to further quiet your doubts," Magdalene continues, "you must know that my father looks down upon the foolish, not the humble-born. Just consider my mother. He loves her most dearly."

"Your mother?"

"She is a commoner. She grew up in a village outside my father's ancestral estate." There is pride in Magdalene's voice, as she adds, "As a noble, my father was forbidden by Danish law to marry her."

Tycho seems even more of a mystery to me. He could have forged an alliance of wealth or power through his marriage but, instead, he chose love. I think back to the night when Erik Lange and Sophie Brahe visited and how Tycho's wife was seated with the scholars. Her placement there now makes sense. But Magdalene was seated there as well. I remember how she touched her mother's arm, as if in alliance with her. I suddenly recall what she said about her afflicted second house, of wealth and possessions.

"And you? Are you a noble like your father?"

"By law, I am a commoner, as are the rest of my brothers and sisters. My father cannot bequeath any of us his name or property, nor can we marry into noble families. These are silly laws but they govern our fortune."

She frowns, then catches herself and shrugs as if trying to convince us both that this is no great matter. But it sets me thinking. I understand now why she has the carriage of a lady but dresses like a peasant. She is caught between worlds, a creature of both and yet neither. I wonder about my own father and the mystery of his identity, for it seems as if blood so often determines our characters and fates.

"You must marry a commoner then?" I ask.

"A promising scholar, my father hopes. When he is not star-gazing he schemes tirelessly to secure our fortunes. But I am not an easy match, nor do I wish to be."

Magdalene cocks her chin defiantly, and I am struck again by how she and I are more alike than I imagined—limited by our births and with fortunes that do not entirely rest in our own hands. But at least Magdalene knows who her true father is. How can I know in which world I belong—the common one of heart and hands or the higher one of ambition and the mind—without knowing mine?

"My mother is a peasant, too," I confide. "But I know not who my father is. My mother would never speak of him."

Magdalene considers this. "Perhaps he is a noble as well? Perhaps that is why he left you both?"

I wonder again, returning to my boyhood fantasies, if this could be true. On occasion, fine travelers were known to stop at the inn. If my father were a noble, it might explain why he did not marry my mother or claim me as a son.

"That would make us alike."

"It seems we already are," Magdalene says.

I cannot be certain who my father is or what my future at Uraniborg holds. But I am certain that Magdalene and I are friends.

"Will you join me again?" she asks. "I promise not to take you walking."

I do not hesitate. "Yes."

Chapter 32

During my long days in the library, I make every effort to become the scholar that Magdalene believes I can be. I use my leisure moments to peruse Tycho's astronomy books and study any page of calculations I come across. I boldly ask Severinus to explain how Tycho proved that Aristotle was wrong and the heavens constantly change, how to use trigonometric functions such as sine and cosine to detail the positions of the stars, how to correct for refraction, the bending of light that makes objects near the horizon appear higher than they really are. Of all the scholars, he appears to take the most pleasure in my enlightenment, unlike Longomontanus, who seems always to be watching with an anxious eye that I do not neglect my duties.

Although the greater part of my inquiries concern the heavens,

I delve into earthly matters as well—namely the mysteries of Uraniborg. I ask Severinus about the music that daily fills the library and learn that it is borne through pipes hidden in the walls that connect to a distant room where the musicians play. "Tycho believes that harmonic tunes help his scholars perform mental labors but he thinks the musicians themselves a distraction," he explains. From Severinus, I also learn that the fountain in the hall runs upon principles first devised by the Romans and copied by Tycho and his fountain maker, Georg Labenwolf. "There is a well in the cellar and the water's own weight propels it through pipes that run through the walls of the castle," Severinus says. What I first took to be sorcery is actually science, man's own magic.

At night, I intend to finish the second letter to my mother, but I am oft distracted, thinking about the workings of the stars and wondering if Magdalene will come. It is not until a week after our first excursion, on the night of the full moon, that she finally appears in my doorway, tosses me a cloak, and beckons me to follow. As soon as we have cleared the gate, my spirits soar to have escaped, yet again, into the spring night. But outside the castle, I hear a loud snort and turn to see a riderless pony tied outside the wall. He is dun-colored and stout with a crested white mane like the helmet of a Roman legionnaire.

I fear we have been discovered until Magdalene walks over to him and unties his reins.

"His name is Aries," she says. "You can ride him so your legs do not tire."

I hold out my palm and let the pony nuzzle against it. He is not much taller than I. "You arranged this for me?"

Magdalene grins at her own ingenuity. "How else could I show you the island?"

I mount Aries and am pleased to find that, upon his back, I am taller than Magdalene. Like most ponies, he is stubborn, and I must kick him most insistently to pry him from the grass he would prefer to munch on; but once he starts up a trot, I find I can follow Magdalene at her natural brisk pace, a centaur by moonlight. We tramp over fields, both fallow and dappled with seedlings, past a hulking, solitary windmill, past the darkened houses of the village, where a dog barks and is silenced and a baby cries lustily, reminding me of Lia and her silent one. I wonder what it is like to die, whether it is anything like this—for I feel myself a ghost, a wanderer of the night, and do not mind it.

Past the village, up a rise, onto a plateau, and we reach the headland. Perched upon the cliff's edge sits the roofless fortress with crumbling stone walls I first saw from the skiff when I arrived. Atop one side is the sagging vestige of a tower that must once have provided a sweeping view of the sea.

"Hammer Castle," Magdalene says.

We tie up Aries and peer through the vestige of a door. The moon illuminates long grass, which shelters inside the fortress.

"To think there were once people here like you and me," Magdalene says. "But I suppose one day Uraniborg will be a ruin, too."

She sighs heavily. As I recall the conditions of her parents' union, I understand why this thought troubles her.

"You cannot inherit this island, can you?"

Magdalene shakes her head. "When my father dies, the king will take it back."

"Have you never before wished to leave and see the rest of the world?"

Magdalene shakes her head firmly. "The rest of the world would not know what to make of me. I am neither noble nor peasant. I am a woman raised to be as learned as a man. Here, I have a place."

I suddenly realize why she has always seemed to understand me so well. My fate as a curiosity is not so different than the one she imagines for herself.

"But you won't forever," I remind her.

I fear my comment to be cruel but, as it is also truthful, Magdalene takes no offense.

"I shall enjoy it as long as I can," she says. There is determination in her voice but her eyes blink uncertainly, and I realize that despite all her faith in the stars and the fates they foretell, she is afraid. But she has also come to this cliff to gaze out.

"Why do you come here and look toward the rest of the world if you do not wish to join it?" I ask.

I await her reply, but I already know the answer: Even in paradise, the world beckons. It is my curiosity about it that made me willingly follow Don and abandon the comfort and safety of my mother and home.

"You ask hard questions," Magdalene says, furrowing her brow. "I suppose I wonder about it. But what of you, Jepp? Do you wish to leave?"

In the dark abyss below, the sea laps at the cliff wall, singing Lia's song, reminding me of how I do not have the choice. I am tempted to explain to her about the letter to my mother, but I think better of it. I do not wish to reveal Liv as my accomplice, but there is also a deeper reason: to tell Magdalene about the letter is to admit that there is still a part of me that wishes to go home. I sense that this one truth would injure her, especially as she has bound herself to these shores.

"I did at first," I say carefully. "But now my station has improved."

"Did I ever tell you that this island was once known as the small people's island?" Magdalene says.

"You jest!"

Magdalene shakes her windblown reddish blond hair. "No, it is truly part of the island's lore."

"So perhaps the island is not the king's to give but mine?" I say with a sly smile.

Magdalene grins back at me. "Perhaps then you can give it to me?"

I strike a regal pose outside the fortress, holding my head high. "I shall. But first you must show me our kingdom."

Throughout April, as the northern night continues its retreat, this is precisely what Magdalene does. She takes me to all four headlands; to the village square; to St. Ibb's, the white-walled thirteenth-century church overlooking the sea, where Tycho on rare occasion worships. She takes me to the sluices and fishponds that Tycho has built outside the castle grounds and to the manor house, where Tycho lived when Uraniborg was being built.

I begin to save half of each morning's sugar cake for Aries, who nightly acquits himself a most stalwart beast. I also begin to save stories from my days in the library to share with Magdalene. She is an attentive listener and encourages my honest impressions while boldly challenging any she believes to be in error. In this way, she serves not only as my guide to Tycho's island but to those who inhabit it.

From her I learn that Longomontanus is, as I first surmised, not a noble but the son of peasants so impoverished that he could afford but a year of university at Copenhagen. I learn that Severinus is the son of an esteemed mathematician and astronomer in Heidelberg, a scholarly pedigree that further explains his self-assured manner. I even learn the fate of Tycho's nose, which, it turns out, was sliced off in a drunken duel when he was a university student.

But as much as I enjoy Magdalene's company, I still think often of the seashell in my pocket and fear that the growing measure of happiness I find with Magdalene is a betrayal of Lia. This feeling is most acute on the nights we pass through the orchard on our way to the gate. As spring advances, the trees are covered with a profusion of pink, white, and red blossoms—the promise of pippin and white Gylling apples; blood pears; yellow, blue, and green plums; morello cherries; quince and apricots and figs. There is a comfort in imagining Lia here, dancing so perfectly in my arms as she did at Coudenberg, that makes me want to ignore the much larger, living girl by my side.

One cloudy May night, Magdalene takes me to an alder fen. I am surprised she has not brought me here before. The tall trees are a curious sight, so unlike the rest of the scrubs that cover the island. As Magdalene raises her candle, I can see that pools of dark water surround the trees, so that they each sit, like Uraniborg itself, upon their own private islands of earth, sharing them with a few ferns and tufts of long grass.

"There is a legend that Lady Grimmel, who once ruled the island, buried a treasure trove here," Magdalene says, as I watch the reflection of her flame flicker in the water.

"Have you searched for it?"

Magdalene crouches down beside me. "There is no point. The only way to open it is with a set of golden keys that Lady Grimmel hid on the bottom of the sea. What is more disheartening than to possess a treasure you can never open?"

"It is like one of Lia's songs."

"Lia? Is she the girl you loved?"

I look down, not meaning to have mentioned her.

"What happened to her, Jepp?"

The words spring out of my mouth before I can stop them. "I killed her."

For a moment Magdalene just stares at me. Then she shakes her head. "I do not believe that."

"You thought me a spy. Why not a murderer too?"

"The stars suggest you are neither."

"I would not trust them."

Magdalene ignores this. "How did you kill her, then?"

"We tried to run away."

"Tell me."

Magdalene settles in beside me, an insistent audience.

For the first time since she died, I speak openly about Lia. I tell Magdalene about my first glimpse of her, how she sang and danced, her memento mori. I tell her about our tiny quarters and jumping out of pies. I tell her about Pim, the dance lessons, Sebastian, and Maria. I tell her about Lia's plight, Robert's ill-fated attempt to free her, the Infanta locking us in our quarters. I tell her about the night I stole Hendrika's key and helped Lia run away, the house on Rollebeek Straat, the dead child, Lia's good-bye.

When I am done, Magdalene's expression is stern, and I fear my tale has displeased her. But when at last she speaks, her words are tender.

"You did not kill her, Jepp. You must not punish yourself so."

I did not cry as I recounted Lia's story, but I feel the tears well up at these words.

"If I had not chosen to take her—"

"It is man's folly to think so much is under his control! If you had not taken her, she still would have died, but at Coudenberg, a place she deplored."

"How can you know that? The stars?"

I fear my tone has turned mocking, but Magdalene does not seem to mind.

"I am certain that one of the horoscopes I prepared for Don was hers, for it suggests such an undoing. But I will not belabor that argument, for you and I disagree on such matters. Forget the stars, then, and listen to Lia. She wished to die free; she thanked you for helping her do so on her deathbed. You cannot be the judge of another's wishes. If you love someone, you must believe that they know what is best for themselves."

There is only one fault I can find with Magdalene's words.

"But I miss her!"

A hand clasps my own. It is large and ill-fitting, but I am comforted by it. As we sit hand-in-hand by the edge of the fen, listening to the wind rustle the grass and ripple the pools around the alders, I realize that Lia is truly gone. There is no ghost to hang on to, no phantom to love. I slide Lia's shell out of my pocket and let it drop into one of the dark pools of the fen to lie beside the treasure that can never be opened.

As it sinks, a few bubbles rise upward, and I almost plunge my fingers into the murk and fish it out. But then the pool regains its stillness, and I feel my heart at peace. I am alive, and so is Magdalene, whose hand is warm around my own.

Chapter 33

For nearly a week after we visit the fen, Magdalene does not come to fetch me. In her absence, I find I cannot stop thinking of her and the touch of her hand. During the day, I am distracted from my labors. I fail to hear Longomontanus call for more ink until he taps me on the shoulder, and fall into an idle reverie as I polish the brass globe, my fingers tingling at the memory of hers.

Magdalene was right when she claimed that my heart would heal and I would love again. But, until now, I could never have imagined that the object of this love would be her.

All the qualities that once repelled me—her forthright manner, her disregard for decorum, her passionate insistence on what she believes—now engender in me the opposite emotion. In her presence, I am able to be my true self. She lets me be no one else.

The question, I begin to realize, is no longer whether I can love again but whether Magdalene can love me back. I fear that my affections for her, though newly revealed to myself, are already transparent. This is the torment of any undeclared lover, that every word he utters and every gesture he makes betrays his heart. Did I hold her hand too tightly at the fen? Was my farewell in the hall that night too lingering? I wish Magdalene to know but not to know my true feelings.

At last one night I hear footsteps approach my room and leap to my feet, then force myself to recline so as not to seem too eager. It is fortunate that I feign repose and do not call out Magdalene's name, for the visitor who appears in my doorway is Longomontanus. He face colors slightly, as if I am the one who has interrupted him.

"Gather your belongings, Jepp," he says. "Tycho wishes you to join us in the scholars' garret."

A few months earlier, I would have greeted this news most gladly, but now I fear losing the solitude that allows me to slip away with Magdalene.

"I do not mind it here," I say.

Longomontanus is silent for a moment, as if searching for words. "Some of us mind it for you," he says stiffly. "Please. Join us."

I wonder if he means Severinus, who seems fond of me in a way that Longomontanus does not. I cannot help but feel touched that Severinus has thought to convince Tycho to elevate me from Ulf's quarters. Although I wish not to be separated from Magdalene, I fear I will raise suspicions if I resist. I also think of how she must marry a scholar, and wonder if sharing scholars' quarters makes me that much closer to becoming one. Surely Tycho would not have agreed to it if he did not think me worthy of such bedfellows.

As Longomontanus is watching me, I leave behind my writing implements where they are hidden behind the brick. I toss my few other belongings into a sack and follow him up a narrow staircase just off the central hall. At the top of the stairs, he leads me into a warren of eight attic rooms squeezed in between the second floor and the dome of Uraniborg. In each of the rooms, three or four scholars lounge on straw mattresses, reading by candlelight, or debating some question of the stars. The rooms are simple but clean, swept free of dirt and not covered in straw like my own. The only curiosity I notice is a bell above each man's bed that is attached to a cord that vanishes into the wall.

Longomontanus shows me the washroom at the end of the hall, which has two basins with running water and the most extraordinary contraption of all, a chamber pot attached to a pipe, which Longomontanus claims serves the miraculous purpose of carrying away waste. He then leads me back to the first room off the staircase, which he says I will share. As I follow him inside I am pleased to see the likely architect of my promotion, Severinus, propped on one elbow over an open book, his long legs hanging off the bottom of his mattress. Aslacus, the Copernican, is hunched upon a mattress next to him, tinkering with a small astrolabe. Longomontanus assigns me a mattress beside his own, as well as one of the bells attached to the cords along the wall. Each man, he explains, has a bell that Tycho can ring from the library below to summon him.

"So, Jepp, you have agreed to join us?" Severinus says.

I take a seat upon my bed as does Longomontanus upon his own.

"Yes," I say. "Your invitation was most kind."

"I did not invite you," Severinus says coolly, turning back to his book.

I wonder if he means to disguise his affection for me though I know not why he would wish to do so.

"There is no reason why he should not be here," Longomontanus says.

The two men swiftly exchange glances and I realize they have disagreed about inviting me here. But I have been sorely mistaken as to who thinks me unfit to lodge alongside him. It is clearly not Longomontanus who objects to my presence but Severinus. I feel a new appreciation for Longomontanus, who I am reminded is also a man of humble beginnings. But it wounds me that my friend has turned against me. I wonder whether Severinus has always considered my education an amusement, never imagining that others might see in me the makings of a real scholar. I feel my old distrust of him return.

The others blow out their candles and, as curls of smoke scent the air, the room grows dark. I lie back on my mattress but find it hard to sleep. I am not accustomed to the stirrings and sighs of human bedfellows. Slipping past them to meet Magdalene will be no easy task. And I know not what excuse I could offer if one of them, Severinus in particular, were to rise in the middle of the night and find me missing. Still, I know that when it comes to sneaking, I am resourceful, and will find a way to venture out with Magdalene again.

The following day at supper, as Tycho and the scholars celebrate their success in positioning the latest star over their cups, I abandon my spot on the floor and sidle up to Magdalene. At the sight of her hand, I feel the blood rush to my face. For the first time, I find it a struggle to form words in her presence.

"I have been moved . . . I mean your father has seen fit to move me . . . to the scholars' garret," I whisper. "I am not sure how to . . . to join you."

Magdalene smiles but does not look at me.

"I have heard, Jepp, and meant to congratulate you," she says.

There is an awkward pause before she picks up her spoon and begins to eat.

I return to my seat on the floor, sorely confused. Was she simply being cautious in case we were overheard? Or did she mean to to signal that our rambles were but the dream of a few spring nights? I try to speak with her again, but our subsequent conversations also take place in the presence of others—usually at her father's table—and she continues to act formally. As the days pass, I fear that she wishes me to know that I can be only a friend. How could I be otherwise—a man half her size, a suitor with no fortune to improve her own, a figure even more solitary and strange than herself?

But I still have hope enough that each night I contemplate how I might escape the garret unnoticed and speak with her alone. This is an even greater challenge than I imagined for, late at night, I often wake and see Severinus staring at me. I hastily close my eyes and feign sleep, for I fear he means to catch me at some mischief so he can prove to Longomontanus that I do not belong.

Such is the state of my emotions on St. John's Eve, when Tycho holds a great feast to celebrate the midsummer. All day long the scholars are in high spirits and, as I follow them out to the garden at the end of the afternoon, I can see why. Tables, covered in colorful linen cloths and stocked with silver wine vessels, have been set beneath the Gylling apple and blood pear trees. A profusion of lanterns hangs off their branches, which bear the small green beginnings of fruit. Jacob and his trio of musicians play peasant tunes beneath a quince tree, while Jonas and some of the other servants feed a bonfire in a clearing just past the morello cherries, which glow red and ripe in the evening sun.

Erik Lange and Sophie Brahe have sailed in for the festivities, accompanied by a dozen other nobles and a peacock, which Lange presents to Tycho as a gift. Tycho gives a rambling speech on brotherly love, then releases the bird to strut in the garden, where it cocks its small head and unfolds its shimmering blue-and-green tail.

The day is indeed long—not only with light but with speeches, songs, savories, and wine. My table of scholars is a merry one—Longomontanus surprises me by telling a bawdy tale; Severinus wears a crown of flowers in his curly hair like a Roman god; Aslacus repeatedly falls asleep and is roused, to the amusement of the rest, by his own snores. When I think the others are not watching, I steal glances at Magdalene, who has been seated with her mother, brothers, and sisters, while Tycho dines with the visiting nobles at another table. Although she engages in lively conversation with Georg, the little boy who stuck out his tongue at me, I catch her casting a glance at her father's table and feel indignant on her behalf.

As midsummer's perpetual twilight falls upon the garden, the lanterns begin to glow softly in shades of blue and red, attracting fluttering white moths, which thud against them. Jacob sings a tale about the treasure hidden in the fen that makes me long for Magdalene and her hand around mine. Sophie Brahe speaks passionately about the importance of collecting herbs on Midsummer's Day when their healing powers are most potent. Erik Lange delights the children and frightens the more superstitious servants with tales of the witches, goblins, and elves who are said to roam freely on Midsummer's Night, when the sun turns southward.

As the bonfire blazes, Tycho's children join some of the servants' children to dance around it, their faces caught between fear and delight as the flames flicker, warding off the evil ones. Tycho takes Sophie Brahe's hand and pulls her to the fire, stopping to grab Kirsten's hand with his other. Magdalene, her face flushed with fire, wine, or simply the pleasure of this uncommon sight, cheers. For a moment, Tycho dances alone with his wife and sister before the rest of us join them to form a ring around the children—nobles and scholars and servants together. The motion is dizzying, and I lose my footing and am sometimes dragged along, but I do not mind. When I look across the circle, I see Magdalene in her peasant dress, stomping heavily upon the earth, her eyes gleaming, her hair flying loose from its pale braid. Like two planets, we are conjunct for a moment, then spin away. I feel the longing the spheres must feel as they forever pass in the heavens.

When the fire dies down into red and golden embers, Erik Lange offers a prayer to alchemy and then jumps over it. Tycho follows with a prayer to Urania and loses his nose as he leaps over the fire, so that Jonas must pull it from the coals with long metal tongs. Longomontanus laughs beside me.

"I am glad this is not your duty anymore, Jepp."

The affection in his voice emboldens me to speak honestly. "Inkpots are not much better."

"And yet you have learned much about our work filling them. Do not worry, Jepp. I am your friend here and will look after you. And I know you are clever."

"He is, indeed!" says Severinus, who has joined us. "Tycho

should take him up to the observatory. Let him train his sights on the stars."

I flush with their praise.

"I like you, Jepp," Severinus adds. "I do."

As his hand warmly clasps my shoulder, I forgive him his unkindness toward me in the garret. It must be easier for a son of peasants such as Longomontanus to imagine me an equal than for the son of a university scholar such as Severinus. But he seems to have overcome his haughtiness.

Severinus toasts me with his tankard of ale, then bounds over the bonfire with it, spilling not a drop and earning great applause for this feat. As others begin to leap in turn, Magdalene finds me and holds out her hand.

"Shall we jump together, Jepp?"

I nearly take her hand, elated that it has been offered, before I remember that my legs may not be equal to this task.

"I fear I cannot make it."

Magdalene furrows her brow. "I could carry you?"

The thought of Magdalene picking me up before the others, like a child or a doll, horrifies me.

"No," I demur. "I would rather watch."

Magdalene shrugs and lifts her skirt, boldly revealing a pair of sturdy white ankles. But before she can take her first running step, Severinus grabs her hand, and they leap over the embers together. They are well matched, both in height and vitality, and as Tycho roars his approval, they gladly leap hand-in-hand again.

I feel myself disappearing where I stand, as if I am no longer human but one of the spirits looking in from the shadows. Of course, Tycho would wish for his daughter to have a suitor such as Severinus, handsome, tall, the son of a scholar. As I watch them together, I am reminded of the times I have seen them in animated discussion at supper, and am certain that she thinks of me as no more than a friend. I step back into the midnight gloaming, repelled by the fire, by Magdalene and Severinus, by the warmth and heat of a world that cannot truly be mine. For being part of this world is not a matter of choice or will as I have imagined. It is a matter of nature and its vagaries—in my case, short legs that do not allow me to make the leap.

Just after one o'clock, Jonas throws a vat of water on top of the embers, which sizzle and steam. Servants take down the lanterns, the musicians disband, the garden is returned to the spirits, good and evil, who lurk in its shadows. Back in the garret, the scholars stumble into bed, sated and drunken, moonstruck and dreaming. Only I, it seems, cannot sleep, only I lie awake, wishing I had taken Magdalene's hand, wishing I had had the courage to be burned. I think of her white ankles and what lies higher up in the shadows of her thighs and, as I do, I feel flames against my cheeks and in places less decent to mention.

But before I can douse this fire, I hear someone rise. I lie still, feigning sleep, but allow my eyes to flicker open. Severinus stands beside his bed, gazing from face to face as if to ensure we are all asleep. I hastily close my eyes. For a moment, there is no sound at all, and then I hear Severinus's soft footsteps as he leaves the room and slips down the stairs. I do not follow him, for I cannot bear to find, for a second time, a girl I have come to care for in another's arms.

Chapter 34

The more I look, the more evidence I see that Magdalene and Severinus are in love. Twice more, late at night when the others are asleep, I observe Severinus steal away. It is several hours before he returns, a contented smile on his face. During the days, Magdalene appears tired and pale, yet she brightens at supper, especially during her animated discussions with Severinus. I sometimes catch her watching me, but I suspect that the searching look I had once mistaken for affection must instead be pity. Even the stars seem to point to Severinus, for I remember how Magdalene said they augered that her fortune would improve when she married. I begin to avoid her and do not often meet her gaze, for I feel a fool to have imagined that such a girl would ever love me as I am. I realize that there is but a single soul in the world who has.

One morning, before the others are awake, I sneak back to my old quarters, where I remove the brick, take out my quill and ink, and finish the letter to my mother. I jot a few lines about my promotion and duties in Tycho's library, but mostly I write about how much I miss and love her. I do not broach the subject of my escape. Though it pains me now to see Magdalene, I find consolation in Tycho's library, in the books and globe and the scholars' celestial quests. In the wake of St. John's Eve, Longomontanus begins to guide me in my studies, and the other scholars follow his lead, taking time to explain their calculations. Even Severinus, whom I wish to hate, continues to show me kindness—boasting of my intelligence to Tycho. Although Tycho has not invited me to his observatory, as Severinus argued he should, he appears to accept that my rightful place is in the library and does not interfere with my education. It is no longer rescue I seek but rather my mother's voice and her answer to a simple question: Who is my father?

But in order to get that answer, I must slip the letter to Liv. I have seen less of her since I moved to the garret, for I eat breakfast—and my fill of sugar cakes—with the scholars now. Nor has she sought me out, presumably so as not to give me false hope that a letter has arrived from home. But I know she sometimes assists in the chemical laboratory, which is located in the crypt below Tycho's library. One afternoon, I spot her slender form slip through the door that leads there. I wait until the scholars take leave to tidy up for supper, then pull open the door and race down the stairs to the cellars.

I have never before been down to the cellars, though I know a small group of scholars spend their days in this subterranean gloom. They are students not of alchemy—which Tycho refuses to practice—but of *ars pyronomica*, or the art of using fire to create medicines that can heal the body and soul. I pass what seems to be a storage room, laden with bags of salt and vats of fuel, and the room that houses Tycho's well until I reach a door at the far end of the passageway. As I open it, I am met with a blast of heat as if the room inside houses the very forges of Hephaestus.

"Jepp!"

Liv stands before a long table, covered with mixing flasks and vials. Behind her are over a dozen furnaces of different sizes set in niches in the wall. Just as I had hoped, she is the laboratory's sole occupant.

"The others have retired for supper," she says in Dutch.

"I am glad, for I wish to speak to you alone. Has there been any word from my mother?"

She turns away to adjust the setting of a furnace, and from the way she avoids my gaze, I can tell that no letter has arrived.

"It is nearly August. No word at all?"

She turns back and touches her hand to my shoulder. "I meant to speak to you. Your fortunes here have improved. Longomontanus tells me the scholars think highly of you, especially Severinus, and his opinion is much valued by Tycho."

Though it pleases me to hear this, it does not entirely raise my spirits. Liv seems to divine my disappointment.

"Here," she says, holding up a vial filled with brown liquid. "Chamomile, St. John's wort, gentian root. These herbs can help soothe sorrows of the spirit. Have a taste."

I wave her away. "I only wish to know my mother is well."

Liv sighs and returns the vial to the table. "You have a future here, Jepp. But you cannot embrace it if you think only of the past."

"She is my mother, not my past!"

"Our parents are our past."

"She is who I am."

But even as I say this, I wonder if, in the two years since I left home, I have become someone else. I am just not certain who. Am I my father's child? But I cannot answer this question until I know who he is.

"What if no letter ever comes?"

"Then—"

Liv has voiced my deepest fear, for which I have no answer. I know not whether Tycho would let me leave to find my parents or whether I could create a fulfilling life for myself here without them.

Liv studies my troubled expression, then holds up a volume of Paracelsus from the table. "There are some men, Jepp, whose lives are like this—a single volume. Their story is seamless, without fissures or breaks. They live but one life.

"Then there are others, like you and me, whose lives are a series of volumes. Their stories stop and must be started up again. They must accept this is so, and put one book away on the shelf in order to start another."

Though Liv's words ring true, I feel most indignant toward her.

"Why have you turned against me?"

Liv shakes her head vehemently. "I have not turned against you, Jepp. I remain your friend. I will continue to aid in your efforts to reach your mother. All I mean to say is that if they fail, you must not abandon your future here at Uraniborg. Will you promise me that?"

Her voice is pleading, and I am reminded that Liv's own mother is dead, that her father and brothers are off at sea. Tycho has given her a home and a future, for her pursuits in the chemical laboratory are ones no peasant, and certainly no woman, would be permitted elsewhere. Can I fault her for wishing me not to squander the opportunity she herself has found? My anger dissolves as swiftly as if I have swallowed one of her tonics.

"Yes," I say. "I promise. But my mother will answer. I have written another letter. The first may have been lost and did not reach Astraveld. This one will."

I take the letter from the pocket of my breeches and hand it to her.

"I shall pray it does," she says.

Chapter 35

Late one night in early August, I am awakened by the jingle of bells, chiming in unison. Longomontanus, Severinus, and Aslacus obediently rise and, with great yawns, prepare to join Tycho in his observatory. I lay back and watch them don their clothes.

"Do not linger, Jepp," Longomontanus says.

It is only then that I observe my own bell and realize it is taking part in the tinkling chorus. I leap up and begin to dress, elated that Tycho has at last deemed me worthy of joining him.

Severinus clutches his side. "I feel unwell," he says. "Tycho has an extra set of hands tonight. Pray tell him I must rest awhile."

I wonder if he means to use this opportunity to sneak off to Magdalene. But I try not to dwell upon this matter as I follow the others down the stairs and into the library, where Tycho awaits us. His copper nose gleams in the light of a single candle as he stands before the door that leads up to the observatory.

"Where is Severinus?" he asks.

"He begs to rest, for he feels unwell," Longomontanus says.

A look of annoyance crosses Tycho's face before he tosses it off with a shrug and waves us through the open door. The winding stairs are steep and poorly lit, and I must concentrate on keeping my footing. When I at last reach their summit, I find myself in what seems like a small cottage suspended in the air. There is room for only four or five men inside, so crammed is the space with a vast array of instruments—brass spheres, triangular wooden sextants, an enormous quadrant mounted on a swivel, and other clocks and sighting devices. I can feel a breeze overhead, and when I look up, I see that panels of the cottage's triangular wooden roof have been removed to reveal patches of starry night sky.

"It is a most propitious night for stargazing," Longomontanus remarks as all four of us look up at the swirls of stars, some like a dusting of sugar in the upper heavens, others as near and bright as jewels that we might pluck if only our arms were able to reach a little higher. It is humbling to see them, for they are more vivid and intricate than the diagrams and equations I have been studying that seek to capture them.

Tycho peers upward with the same eager gaze, his face void of the irritation that so often crosses it as he considers earthly matters. For a moment, none of us speak but only gape— transformed into children by our wonder.

"Jepp, who were the Wise Men?" Tycho says, breaking our silence, his voice resounding.

"They were kings of the Orient who—"

"They were stargazers," Tycho interrupts. "Such as we. Look. Look up, boy! God is up there."

I peer up as commanded, feeling the same sacred pull as my master. I have no doubt that the Lord is in that firmament. I imagine Him perched in the web of stars, spinning our fates, allowing only the wisest and bravest of men to alter their own.

"May the Lord bless our endeavors so we may do His work, revealing to mankind the artfulness of His creation," Tycho says.

"Amen," Longomontanus and Aslacus say together.

I think truly that this is the most affecting of sacred moments that I have known, more so than any in the Infanta's grand cathedral or even in the small village church in Astraveld.

"Tonight we take measurements of our nine hundredth star," Tycho declares. "These measurements, Jepp, combined with ones we recorded earlier, will enable us to determine the star's position in the heavens to an unprecedented degree of accuracy and allow us to properly etch it on the celestial globe."

Longomontanus and Aslacus move to the enormous quadrant, the frame of which they manipulate with counterweights and pulleys. I feel an excitement watching them, for I understand now the value of the missing pieces they seek.

"Where are you?" Tycho shouts into the darkness. "It is time!"

At first, I think he is calling to the star itself. But a moment later, a door in the wall opens from the outside and Magdalene walks in, as if out of the air. She greets the others, then nods coolly at me.

"Magdalene asked if she might observe our efforts tonight," Tycho explains.

I no longer feel like the wise man that Tycho has anointed me but a fool, for I think she must have hoped to find Severinus in my place. I know I should try to disregard her presence, but I cannot help but gaze upon her as she cranes her neck at the sky and throws back her head to view the stars. I admire how she is not timorous, how she is a creature of will and flesh. I know I should not speak, should not expose my heart, especially as we are not alone. But I wish to be the same, not the defeated spirit I felt myself to be around the St. John's Eve bonfire.

"Do you know which star they mean to observe?" I ask, breaking the silence between us as the others prepare their instruments.

Magdalene's eyes fix upon me as if I am a star and she is measuring the distance between us. Her observation made, she turns away and points to the Milky Way, tracing her finger in a Z. "That is the constellation Scorpius. Antares is the brightest star of Scorpius, and the nine hundredth star is two down from Antares."

I follow the sweep of her finger to a pale blue star that seems to pulse with light. It seems to me most beautiful, a relic of the day the Lord first created light out of darkness. Tycho hands me a clock and instructs me to call out the time as Longomontanus and Aslacus measure angles to the star, and Tycho transcribes them into a foolscap folio. Though my duty seems a simple one, I know that time helps give the scholars' measurements meaning. I feel emboldened that Tycho has entrusted me with such a task. Am I really less of a man than Severinus? I think that from God's view, up in the heavens, all men are small. It is the spirit He has given us that makes us giants, if only we choose to be.

When, after some fifty minutes of this labor, Tycho permits us to rest our eyes, I walk boldly up to Magdalene.

"Where were you when we came up?" I ask. "It seemed as if you flew in."

"The wind brought me."

I give her a skeptical look.

"There is a viewing platform surrounded by a parapet."

"May I see it?"

Magdalene raises a reddish blond eyebrow at my request, then rises and opens the door. I follow her out onto a narrow walkway that encircles the observatory. We walk around it until we are out of sight of the others. There is no roof here to encroach upon our view of the stars. When I stand on tiptoe, I can see just over the parapet all the way to where the heavens fade into the horizon.

"So you wish to be my friend again?" Magdalene says.

She smiles, but her tone is sharp. Before I can answer, she continues in a voice that is peevish and unlike her own. "I do not understand you, Jepp. You keep my company then shun me. You—"

I look up at the sky, finding it easier than to look up at Magdalene. "I do not wish to be friends."

"Why not?" she exclaims.

A star falls across the heavens, then vanishes. I take a breath, preparing myself for the same fiery tumble.

"I believe you care for another."

Magdalene looks down at me with a bewildered expression. "Whom do you speak of?"

"I have noticed . . ." I pause, suddenly feeling my suspicions ridiculous. "Affections between you and Severinus."

"Jepp, you are mad! He is but a friend."

"You do not spend nights with him as you once did with me?"

A great gust of wind blows through our hair, like a breath held and then exhaled. Magdalene crouches down on her knees so that her face is level with mine. "What do you speak of?" she whispers angrily. "I stopped taking you because you moved to the scholars' garret. I did not encourage you only because I did not want to risk your being caught or our plans overheard, not when my father thinks more highly of you by the day. I have taken no one else."

If Severinus has not been slipping out in the middle of the night to see Magdalene, where then has he been going? But I do not dwell on this mystery.

"So it is not Severinus you came here hoping to see?"

"Severinus told me that my father was planning to summon *you* here tonight. That is why I came." Magdalene looks at me with fierce, wet eyes. "You are a fool, you know."

I have never been so happy to hear myself called so. But there is still a doubt that holds me back—not about Severinus, but about myself. My voice catches in my throat. "I am a dwarf."

Magdalene frowns as if disappointed by such an objection.

"Is it not our imperfections that forge our characters?"

I have never thought about my stature this way—not as a flaw but as a source of strength.

She starts to rise, but I take her hand and pull her back down. "What?" she says with irritation.

I lean over and kiss her. Her hand grasps my own as she kisses me back.

Chapter
36

To be loved is the birthright of every mewling babe but, once grown, a man is not assured of such affection. This is why, after I kiss Magdalene and she, most wondrous creature, returns this kiss with her own, I feel as if I have recovered the happiness of childhood. This feeling of being most blessed, of being not alone, of being a newborn, twin-souled creature fills my every waking hour.

During the day we take care to conceal our affections, communicating in a language of our own, a code of sidelong glances and smiles. But on the evenings that Tycho summons me to the observatory to call out the time, Magdalene and I are able to snatch moments alone on the parapet. We study the heavens, silently pressing close together, or whisper our innermost thoughts and impressions. On these gentle nights, it seems as if we are the only people in the world.

As we grow closer, there is a secret I feel compelled to reveal. One night, I tell Magdalene about my letters home.

"Ha!" she says with a satisfied grin. "I knew you were not being honest with me that first night about why you were in the library."

"I was being honest," I protest. "I wished to look at your father's books, too."

"Never mind. You were wise at the time to deceive me. But you have received no answer to these letters?"

I shake my head. "I am anxious to hear from my mother, to know she is well. And I also need to know who my father is. Only she can tell me."

"Why does this question matter?"

I feel my old irritation with Magdalene's candor return. "You may not be your father's daughter by law, but at least you know who he is and that he loves you. I simply want the same, to be someone."

"You already are, Jepp. You don't need a father for that. And, anyway, the stars suggest—"

"What? That I do not try to find him?"

"Yes," Magdalene says quietly. But we both know that it is not the stars that want this. I realize that I have wounded her with this whole revelation, for if I am ever to search for my father, I cannot do it here. I must venture out into the world, a place she fears and wishes not to go.

Later that night, I lie in bed, pondering our future. Though I know Tycho to be a man who cares little for the conventions of society, I am dubious that he would consider me a worthy match for Magdalene. Surely, a boy limited both in stature and fortune is not the suitor he would wish for his daughter. But Magdalene has also made it clear that she will not leave Uraniborg.

In the midst of these troubling thoughts, I hear Severinus stir. Since Magdalene's kiss, I have nearly forgotten about his nocturnal excursions; but as he rises, my curiosity is once again aroused. I swiftly close my eyes and feign slumber. For a moment, all is quiet. I imagine he surveys the sleeping forms of Longomontanus and Aslacus as well as my own. I slow my breath and ignore the urge to open my eyes. My patience is rewarded for, a moment later, I hear the creak of the floorboards as he steals out of our chamber. His footfalls recede down the stairs.

Without another thought, I slip out of our room in my bare feet and down the stairs after him. At the bottom of the stairs, I peer out from behind the doorframe as he darts down the hallway. He knocks on the door to Tycho's library, waits, then knocks a second time. I cannot tell if someone answers, but I can see him turn the doorknob and slip inside, closing the door softly behind him.

There is only one way for me to see what Severinus is doing and whom he is with. I run to the castle doors. The late August night is warm, the sky mottled with clouds that obscure the stars. When I reach the aviary, it is silent; but with every step I fear the birds will awake and betray my presence with their startled song. By some lullaby of the breeze, they do not stir; and I manage to clamber atop a bucket outside their cage, one likely used to feed them, and pull myself up to look through the window.

Severinus sits at his customary desk alone. A candle illuminates a folio before him, which he gazes upon intently as he jots with his quill across a separate page. I feel ashamed of my peeping, for it appears that he is merely pursuing his studies, perhaps reviewing the scholars' labors to ensure their accuracy. But just as I am about to lower myself off the bucket and retreat, he rises and, page in hand, walks swiftly over to the metal lion. As he touches the lion's mane, the creature rises up on his hind legs and opens the door to its fleur-de-lis heart. Severinus gently removes this silver organ, rolls up the page, and inserts it into the empty cavity. Then he screws back the fleur-de-lis and places his hand upon the creature's head, so it closes the door to its chest and lowers down to its front paws.

But I have no time to dwell on these mysterious actions, for Severinus hurriedly returns to his desk and closes the folio. I realize he means to depart, and picture him returning to our room to find my bed empty. He could suspect that I have followed him. I scramble off the bucket and race around to the front of the castle. Once in the darkened hall, I stop in the shadow of Tycho's gurgling fountain and, gasping for breath, gaze down toward the library. Better, I think, for Severinus to find me out of bed and not know my whereabouts than to apprehend me here. But the hall is empty, and after catching my breath, I resolve to dash down it.

At first, I think I will make it undetected. But as I dart onto the garret stairs, I hear the creak of a door back in the hall. I drive my aching legs as fast as they can carry me up the stairs and stumble into our room. Longomontanus shifts in his sleep but does not appear to awake as I dive onto my mattress. A moment later, I hear footsteps as Severinus slips back in. I fear he will notice my rapid breathing, but there is a rustling sound as he lies down on his bed and adjusts his blanket, suggesting that he is not engaged in studying me. After some minutes pass in silence, I crack open one eye and see that his are closed and that he appears to have fallen asleep.

But sleep does not come to me. What has Severinus hidden inside the lion? There is no way for me to investigate when Severinus is awake or the library is occupied. I realize that I must go back and that it is wisest to do so tonight when I know Severinus has already made one trip and is unlikely to make another. I wait for some time, until I feel confident that he is truly asleep, then creep out of the garret and hasten down the stairs to the library.

Just as I observed Severinus doing, I knock softly on the door and, when no one answers, I spirit myself inside. It is a dark night, and as I light my candle, I feel the same menace in the shadows of the metal man and lion that I felt so many months earlier when I came in search of Magdalene but did not find her. I recall the pages of calculations I found scattered on the floor that night and wonder whether the presence I felt was no avenging spirit but Severinus.

I touch the lion's mane and watch it rise on its hind legs and open the door to its heart. Though my hands shake, I manage to unscrew the fleur-de-lis, as I saw Severinus do, and snake my hand inside the lion's chest. At the first touch of paper, I pull, extracting a folded page, which I open and study by the light of my candle. There, in a long row, are the measurements we made of the nine hundredth star. Atop the page lie some notes, but they are in German, a tongue I cannot read.

I stick my hand back inside the lion and fish out several more pages, only to find more stars and their measurements. There is only one reason why Severinus would be copying Tycho's work then concealing it. I think of Magdalene, of the pride she takes in her father and his work, and of Tycho himself and the trust he has placed in me.

My arms full of folded pages, I run out of the library and

down the hall to Tycho's chamber. I boldly open the door and race to his curtained four-poster bed. Drawing back the curtain, I whisper, "Lord Tycho."

My master jerks upright, his chest naked and covered with graying hair, his noseless face caught in a rare moment of surprise. Kirsten's startled eyes blink as she pulls her blanket over her bare shoulders.

"What the devil?" Tycho says.

I heave the papers onto his bed and thrust my candle into his hand.

"Severinus has been sneaking down to the library at night and copying your work. There is more concealed in the lion's chest."

Tycho takes the candle and opens one of the pages. As he reads, his face turns red as if the flame of the candle is roasting it. He yanks open a second page. I know that, unlike me, he reads German.

Kirsten says something in Danish, and Tycho spits back a single word: "Ursus."

Then he jumps out of bed without a stitch of clothing, taking my candle with him. "Jepp, return to the garret. Now!" he shouts sternly.

"But the library. I left the lion—"

"I am going there myself. Back to the garret before Severinus wakes to find you gone!"

I scurry out, wondering if Tycho will remember to don his clothes, so consumed is he by his rage. As I steal up the stairs and back to the garret, I realize he has failed to bestow upon me a single word of gratitude.

Severinus does not stir as I quietly lower myself onto my bed. It occurs to me, as I lie sleepless, that he wished me absent from the garret not because he thought me unworthy—but because he feared I might catch him. Though I do not regret my actions, I cannot help but think of the lessons he gave me and the faith he exhibited, before anyone else, in my intelligence.

Some fifteen minutes later, Severinus's bell begins to ring, tinkling out alone. As he rises, his handsome face marred by a nervousness I have never noticed before, I feel no triumph in having discovered him to be a thief, only sadness.

Chapter 37

The following morning, not only Severinus but Longomontanus is gone and, when the rest of the scholars and I arrive at the library to begin our customary labors, Jonas bars the way. As the others turn back in confusion, he reaches for me and pats my shoulder. This is the beginning of a most unusual day. The scholars, inexplicably parted from their quills and calculations, wander the castle aimlessly, whispering in groups, while I search for Magdalene. I am eager to tell her what I saw but fail to find her and wonder if she is sequestered with her father in the library.

Everyone waits anxiously for dinner, when it is assumed Tycho will reveal the reason for this mysterious disruption. But at the dinner hour Tycho's door remains closed, and a servant informs us that we are to eat in the kitchen. It is there, as servants and scholars mingle, the curiosity of both aroused, that rumors begin to fly—first in Danish, then translated for the benefit of the rest of the scholars into Latin. Jacob, the lutenist, claims that in the middle of the night he saw Jonas pass by the servants' quarters carrying coils of rope from the stables. Liv and several others report being awakened by a fearsome, banging noise from the direction of Tycho's library. Though I know Severinus to be a thief, these suggestions of violence dismay me.

Just before supper, a most startling piece of news spreads through the halls of Uraniborg. Jonas has been spotted standing outside Tycho's prison, seemingly guarding someone inside. But before either servants or scholars have a chance to speculate as to the identity of the prisoner, a boy runs through the halls, calling everyone to supper in the Summer Room, an airy chamber on the second floor of the castle that is surrounded by a series of great windows that look out westward to the sea.

As everyone rushes with great anticipation toward the stairs, Magdalene slips out from the library and pulls me aside. There are hollows beneath her eyes as if she has slept poorly. We wait until the hall has emptied.

"And you thought it was me Severinus was so eager to visit," she finally says in a chiding tone.

"And you thought it was I who was the spy."

Magdalene's eyes crinkle in appreciation of my retort. But her mirth fades with a sigh.

"I feel like a fool. I thought him a friend."

I understand this feeling of betrayal, for I share it. "As did I."

Magdalene kneels down and takes my hand.

"My father told me what you did, Jepp. You are loyal and brave. Thank you."

Magdalene's gratitude is more than ample recompense for her father's lack. I long to rest my forehead against her own, to feel the brush of our lips. But I fear someone will appear and see us.

"Come," she says, rising to her feet with an expectant smile. "Let us go to supper."

By the time we reach the Summer Room, Tycho and his scholars are already seated. I can't help but notice Severinus's absent place between Magdalene and Longomontanus and am certain the others have as well. As I hasten to my accustomed seat beside Tycho on the floor, I hope my tardiness will escape notice. But although his nose juts crookedly off his face, Tycho's eyes are sharp.

"Jepp," he snaps.

"I am sorry," I say, hoping to soothe his ire.

"Sit down."

I drop to the floor.

"Not there, Jepp. In your chair."

He points to the spot where Severinus always sat. I rise, confused, but as I walk toward it, I realize that in place of Severinus's chair is a small oaken one with four tall legs designed to elevate its occupant to the table. I am so startled that, for a moment, I simply stare at it.

"Go sit, Jepp."

The voice is Magdalene's, and when I hear the glee in it, I know the seat is truly my own. I climb up into the chair and survey the table from this novel perspective. After nearly nine months, my world is no longer legs and voices but faces—perplexed, kindly, and wondrously level with my own. I only wish this elevation had not come at the expense of another's fall.

Tycho rises and begins to speak, first in Latin, then translating himself into Danish.

"There has been a traitor in our house, one who was planning to steal our labors and deliver them to his true master, Ursus, who has robbed me before. I do not want to hear mention of this miscreant's name, now or forever. Jonas is punishing him accordingly. But let this be a warning to all—loyalty is the first principle of my kingdom."

Tycho pulls a scroll of paper from his vest pocket and grabs a candle. Touching the flame to its edge, he sets it on fire. I wonder if it is Severinus's contract, whether he means to destroy any trace of his existence upon this island. But, as the paper burns, Tycho turns to me.

"Jepp, you are hereby freed from this contract for your service as a dwarf. We hope you shall choose to remain with us as an apprentice scholar. You have shown yourself more than worthy of such a position in my house."

As the ashes of my former contract drift down onto a plate, Tycho holds it up and blows, looking like one of the bronze winds of his fountain, as they scatter across the floor.

My eyes fill with tears, which shames me, so I look out at the white-capped sea. For so long, I have dreamt of crossing it, of escaping this island. But perhaps Liv is right, and that it is here, upon it, that I have found my true home. None of it is what I imagined for myself when I was but a dreaming boy—not this world of stargazing, not a girl such as Magdalene—and yet I realize that I have found exactly the life that suits me.

I turn back to Tycho. "I am most honored."

Longomontanus, who sits beside me now, passes me a tankard, and I take a draught of ale to the cheers of Tycho and my fellow scholars. As libations are poured and the kitchen servants begin to carry in great platters of fish and game, the pall of Severinus's villainy seems to fade, replaced by merriment even more robust than usual. Jacob plays a most rousing tune upon his lute, as if to celebrate a battle won; Tycho recites his poem to Urania; the scholars compete to call out constellations as the stars begin to pierce the slowly darkening late-August sky.

For the first time, Magdalene and I talk at the table—not under or beside it—and I feel a burst of hope that Tycho could actually accept me as Magdalene's suitor. For I am now one of his scholars, a man of intellect whose future rests in only one set of hands—not his master's, nor even God's, but his own. This intoxicating blasphemy so fills my head that I have no need for ale.

As the others wander off after this drunken supper to sleep or take in a breath of night air to discuss the day's events, Magdalene and I slip back into Tycho's library. There, in a pile of dented metal pieces, are the remains of the lion. I now realize the source of the banging and am much relieved that this creature, rather than Severinus, suffered Tycho's violence.

Magdalene drops to her knees beside the lion.

"It is a shame my father destroyed him," she says.

"It was not the lion's fault," I agree. I grin sidelong at Magdalene as I sit down beside her. "But no doubt such a fate was in his stars."

Magdalene returns my smile. "You mock me, Jepp, and yet everything the stars predicted for you has come to pass. You have found advancement here at Uraniborg; you have made a powerful ally in my father. You have even found a woman helpful and true."

I take her hand, for these last words touch me deeply.

"This was all fated to be," she concludes.

"I do not think so."

Magdalene pulls away her hand, and I fear she confuses my rejection of fate with a rejection of her.

"What I mean to say is that it is not fate that has brought us together. It is our own will, what we choose to do with the chances we have. I worked hard to become one of your father's scholars. I endeavored to discover whether you could care for me. Is not our capacity to choose, to chase, to dream of becoming other than we are, more powerful than the patterns of the stars?"

Magdalene's face softens, though I know not whether it is because she takes this as an assurance of my affections or because she at last sees some sense in my argument. Before she can reply, the door to the cellars opens, and Liv emerges. At the sight of us, she startles. Though Magdalene and I are doing nothing indecorous, I feel my face color at being discovered alone with her.

Liv says something to Magdalene in Danish, then turns to me.

"Congratulations, Jepp," she says in Dutch. "I knew you would have a great future here."

"Thank you," I say. But it is not my future her words make me think of but the letter that has never come and perhaps never will. I think longingly of my mother and Willem. They hold the mystery to my paternity, the one piece of my fate that I seem unable to control.

"What is it?" Magdalene says once Liv has left.

I am tempted to tell her, but I do not wish to trouble her as I did last night.

"Nothing."

Magdalene studies my face with care, as if she does not believe me. Then she picks out the lion's dented fleur-de-lis heart, and hands it to me, wrapping her hands around my own.

Chapter
38

I s it a fool or a wise man who questions his own happiness? I ponder this as autumn approaches, for in so many ways, and as never before, I can count myself happy. I have a future at Uraniborg, one based not on the limits of my stature but on the infinite possibilities of my mind. I have earned the respect of a powerful man, who sees the world as few are able, and has promised to share with me the vast sum of his knowledge. Stargazing suits me—both the rigor of the scholarship and the Promethean allure of mapping the heavens, bringing to my fellow man the light of the Lord's ingenious design. And it is not only my mind that has found a home at Uraniborg; it is my heart. For Magdalene seems to me my missing piece, the harmony for my song, the singular voice that answers my own. I cannot imagine willingly parting from her.

And yet, I still find myself yearning for an answer to the question of my paternity. When I next catch Liv alone, she reluctantly confirms that there is still no word from Astraveld. Could both letters have been lost? Or is my mother unwilling to tell me the truth about who my father is? I find myself thinking about Don, how my mother deferred to him that evening at the inn, allowing him so meekly to take me from her. I wonder if he holds some power over her I do not know. I can only hope it is not a paternal one, for I would rather be the child of the turtle my mother saw at the well or even fatherless than have such a man as my sire.

I think often of Liv's words—how some men's lives are many-volumed, how they must close one book and put it away to start another. But I am not sure that I can stop chasing the ghosts and shadows of my past and embrace the happiness that my future promises. I decide to seek the advice of one other friend who must surely have wisdom to impart on the subject of whether the past is important.

Late one afternoon, Longomontanus shows me how to use the coordinates Tycho and my fellow scholars have meticulously determined in order to etch a new star onto the brass globe. Only Longomontanus is permitted to alter the face of the universe, an honor that astounds me when I think of his humble origins. More than any other man I know, he has escaped the destiny of his birth.

"Does a man's past matter?" I ask, when we have finished depositing our star in the sky.

He studies me with the watchful eyes I have come to trust and love.

"Yes, a man's past matters. But it is not all that matters."

"What do you mean?"

"Our intelligence, our will, our perseverance. These qualities matter more."

Does it matter where I came from, who begot me? As I consider what Longomontanus has said, I tell myself no, it does not, not in Tycho's kingdom, not here upon this island where a man is judged not by his birth but by his ability—like Longomontanus and myself—to surpass it. The year 1600 is nearly upon us, and there are more miracles than ever before—new lands, new ideas, new inventions—and they are less the work of God and His angels than they are the imaginings of men, dreaming forward. Just like them, it is the future I should be chasing, for it is therein that paradise lies.

And yet, and yet . . . I am drawn, with a force as primal as sin, to the past. Like the thought of Severinus, bound in Tycho's prison, it pricks my conscience.

"I know not who my father is," I tell Longomontanus. "I think I wish to go and find him."

It is a relief, after weeks of hiding my true feelings lest they hurt Magdalene, to finally reveal them.

Longomontanus passes no judgment upon me, for which I am grateful. "But you are not certain of the worthiness of this quest?" he merely asks.

I think him most wise. "Yes."

Longomontanus gently spins the celestial globe, his fingers brushing against the stars he has set there. "The past always has a pull on us, especially if we have journeyed far from it. The life I had as a child could not satisfy me now, nor would the people I grew up with even comprehend me. But I still think about my parents and home often.

"I wish I could tell you what to do, Jepp. But every man must make peace with his own past. That is his work alone. Is it better to let it recede or chase after it, in the hopes of gaining some understanding? You must answer this question yourself."

I must appear disappointed by his refusal to advise me, for Longomontanus pats my shoulder.

"I do not want you to leave. But you are a man of intellect and will. If you do go, you will make sense of whatever you find."

By burning my contract, Tycho has given me my freedom. But it is this assurance that provides me with the courage to take it.

On a cloudy, early September night, with a cool breeze that portends fall, I ask Magdalene to join me on a midnight walk through Tycho's gardens. Just as Severinus once did, I have learned the sleeping habits of my bedfellows, and am able to slip out of the garret unnoticed. Magdalene joins me in the hall, a silent companion, shrouded in her cloak.

As soon as we pass through the ramparts and into the knot gardens, Magdalene turns to me. "You are leaving."

I am not surprised that she seems to read my heart as well as she does the heavens.

I light a candle, illuminating the shrubs cut in their patterns of stars and circles, a universe ordered by the hands of men. Arranged in rings about them are the medicinal herbs, transferred long ago from their pots in the greenhouse, now hardy and flowering. Tallest of all are my elecampane, some of which tower even above me, some still topped by large, yellow flowers. Gazing upon them, I wonder if what I am about to say is a mistake.

"I must do this. I must learn who my father is."

Magdalene shakes her head and turns away from me. I suddenly feel frantic. I can easily part with the stars for a few months, but I cannot bear to lose this girl.

"I cannot leave you. Will you come with me?"

Magdalene turns swiftly to face me.

"Do you not intend us to marry first?"

"If you wish it."

Her face darkens and, like a sailor caught in a storm that blows in with little warning, I realize I have erred.

"Of course I wish it too! But it shames me to ask your father for your hand when I have nothing to offer, no fortune to sustain you when he no longer can."

"So you meant not to ask at all but to have us run away?" Magdalene says angrily.

"I am sorry. I do not mean to dishonor you. It is just—"

"My father will accept you, Jepp. You have become one of his favorites."

"If he does, as you say, then will you come with me?"

Magdalene looks away, and I realize I have caught her in an evasion of her own.

"You cannot live in fear of the world judging you as different, of having no place in it," I say. "Anyway, the world will find you, even here."

"Someday, perhaps. But why go looking for it?"

There is a silence between us as we walk past the knot gardens and into the orchards. There are over a dozen varieties of apple trees, all of them laden with musky fruit, including exotics from the far corners of the earth. It is as if Tycho means to suggest that there is no need to go anywhere, because all the world's treasures have been brought to Uraniborg. It is tempting to stay in this paradise with Magdalene at my side. But I know I cannot.

"Magdalene." I pull her down beside me beneath a tree of golden apples. "You once told me that if you love someone, you must believe that they know what is best for themselves. I know this is best for me. But I am not leaving you. I am going to find a lost part of myself. But I will return to you, and when I do, I shall ask your father for permission for us to marry."

I speak these last words with a confidence meant to reassure her, though I inwardly fear my journey may not be so easy.

Magdalene bites her lip and blinks, but her eyes spout tears like one of her father's fountains.

"I know you must go."

Her understanding has a more potent effect upon me than her anger. I find I cannot speak, can only throw my arms around her.

"Oh, Jepp," she says as she returns my embrace. "What if you don't come back?"

"I will. I promise. And, in the meantime, I shall write to you."

We cling to each other until, at last, I pull back to stroke her face, seeking to imprint upon my memory the lively eyes, the reddish blond hair, the constellation of scars upon her forehead. I feel she is already becoming the ghost that absence makes, though she is warm and present. For a moment, I am again tempted not to leave, to be satisfied with such a perfect companion. But as an autumn wind stirs the apple trees, I feel myself blowing with it toward the sea.

Chapter 39

The following morning, I find Tycho in the library and inform him of my plans to leave Uraniborg. He seems surprised, as if it never occurred to him that I might wish to go elsewhere. With a scowl, he sits heavily upon a chair. For the first time, I notice the shadows beneath his eyes and the gray creeping up his temples.

"So you mean to abandon us, Jepp?"

"No. I wish only to go home. I have not seen my mother in two years, and there is a matter I must resolve. But in a few months I shall return to you."

"To me, eh?"

Tycho regards me with amusement, and I realize that the observant eyes that miss no star in the heavens have also not missed the conjunction of bodies here on earth.

"Go, Jepp," Tycho says. "You have my blessing."

"It is not only your blessing I seek. I have not the means to make the trip."

I look down, shamed by my need to make such a request.

"You have certainly saved me much hardship by exposing Severinus," Tycho says.

He disappears and returns a moment later with a small but heavy purse and a key.

"This key opens the gate to Uraniborg. There are twenty silvers inside the purse, which should be sufficient for your travels. And if you have greater purposes here," he says as he catches my eye, "I would advise you to find your own means to refill it."

I bow my head. "Thank you most kindly."

As he hands it to me, I think that Magdalene and I are both right. That Tycho will accept me as her husband, but that he wishes me to bring some purse of my own to the table. As lofty as his ambitions and ideals are, Tycho is as frightened as the rest of us by penury and the specter of it for his children. I do not blame him, though I fear that I, like Erik Lange, will be drawn to alchemy in the wild hopes of turning these silvers into gold.

I know I should see Liv before I go, but I have not the heart to tell her; I fear she will try to change my mind. Instead, I leave her a letter, thanking her for her help and kindness, and promising her—as I did Magdalene—that I will be back. Since I cannot bear to part from Magdalene again, I decide to leave Uraniborg, the Castle of the Heavens, as somehow seems fitting—under cover of night. I prepare to depart in the dark, starry hour before dawn. To Tycho's purse I add Matheus's lucky copper, though I intend not to spend it. Only Jonas and Longomontanus rise to see me off, the former pressing upon me bread and ale, and the latter a slender volume of Copernicus that I know to be one of his few possessions.

The darkness not only shrouds me from those I love and must leave behind, but from a world I have come to think of as my own—the castle and observatory and gardens. How far I have traveled from the winter's day when I arrived, forlorn and heartbroken, to what seemed a prison! Though I have pledged to return to this paradise, there is a part of me that fears, despite what I have promised Magdalene, that I will not see it again.

I have taken a hare from the kitchen for the dogs so as to unlock the gates without raising their chorus. I have also arranged with the stable master to ride Aries to the village, where I shall catch a morning skiff to Elsinore. But as I make my way toward the stables, I pass a small building set into the north corner of the wall with iron-barred windows and a heavy wooden door. It is Tycho's prison.

There is no light inside it and I am not tall enough to peek through the bars, yet I know Severinus has been there for nearly a fortnight. I can easily envision the horrors of his captivity—the stale air, the stench of one's own waste, the close, damp walls— but I remind myself that Severinus has committed a true sin against Uraniborg; that he made such a choice knowingly and is deserving of such a fate. And yet when I think how he was the first among the scholars to teach me how to see the heavens, I cannot force my feet to hurry past and abandon this Judas. Does not every man deserve the chance to redeem himself, to recast his destiny?

I inspect the heavy prison door, finding it, as I expected, locked. I can leave, my conscience assuaged. But as I step away from the door, I notice a key hanging on a nail in the wall outside.

If I stand upon my bundle, using the Copernicus and my other scant belongings to raise me up, I can just reach it. Am I abetting a thief or performing an act of mercy? Perhaps both. I put the key in the lock, turn it, and topple back off my bundle as the door creaks slightly open. The sound of it terrifies me as much as what I have done. I hurriedly gather my belongings and run toward the stable. Mounting Aries, I take off at a gallop down the hill, afraid not only of what I have unleashed, but of what I will unleash as I open the door to my own past.

The sun is just beginning to rise as I reach the village and give my sweating pony to a peasant who works at Tycho's stable. He agrees to tend to the pony's needs before returning him to Uraniborg. I pause to stroke Aries's nose as he gives his head a playful shake. Even this good-bye is hard to bear.

The same wizened peasant who ferried me to Uraniborg gives me passage to Elsinore on his skiff. As he pushes off from shore, the boat glides silently out of the shadow of the cliffs and away from the island. The sky fills with orange light, and a road seems to appear on the sea where the sun's reflection falls in a single glistening ray. I am a traveler on this road. But I am no longer certain whether I am going home, or leaving it.

Book III

PER ASPERA AD ASTRA

Chapter
40

Though the apprehension I feel upon leaving Uraniborg is most acute as I watch the island recede, in the days that follow, the rhythms of travel help soothe my nerves and restore my resolve. At Elsinore, I find a portly Danish merchant traveling to Utrecht and pay him seven silvers from Tycho's purse for a seat in his coach. This gentleman speaks just enough Dutch to understand I am a member of Lord Tycho's household but not enough to inquire into my affairs. This suits me, for though Don once said I liked to gab, I find a certain peacefulness in quietly watching the towns and fields go by—the reaping and the threshing, the warm harvest sunshine, and the cold autumn drizzle that signals winter's coming want. Although I carry the lion's fleur-de-lis heart next to my own and miss Magdalene dearly, she seems far away, a remnant of another world. I find that I am almost happy on the road, part not of a grand enterprise of scholarship but of simple, human life.

At night, we board at inns along the route. Though my stature draws stares, the merchant's presence at my side discourages derision. Besides, I am often too preoccupied to take much notice of the curiosity of others. For each inn, with its rough-hewn floors and tables sticky with ale, seems a stepping-stone to my mother. I see her in the girl who sweeps by, clenching mugs for thirsty travelers; in the hand of the woman who stokes the hearth flames; in watery porridge and lumpy pallets; in brooms and cats; and wanderers glad, for a moment, to be still. Though it troubles me that she has not answered my letters, these inns, like the churches on a pilgrim's route, bolster my faith that I will find her and solve the mystery of my father's identity.

As the coach reaches the Dutch lands and the tongue of strangers becomes my own, my excitement over seeing Astraveld becomes almost too great to bear. For two years, I have held the village dear in my mind's eye—its imperfections fading while its charms and comforts shine ever brighter. It seems as if I am returning not just to a place, but to a time, to my own innocence, to the boy I left behind.

Though I had planned to stay the night in Utrecht, when we enter that city I cannot bear to wait to make the final leg of my journey. After I bid farewell to the merchant, I buy a stout pony for three silvers from the stable and set off at a brisk trot for Astraveld. It is nearly dusk as I ride through the wild meadows and open fields, over streams and hills, toward my mother's inn. As I near it, I begin with swelling heart to recognize the landscape of my infancy, Farmer Helmich's field of hops—but was it this small?—Pieter the brewer's thatched-roof cottage—was it so humble? I make small corrections in my memory, feeling an even greater affection for these simple places.

There is no mile as long as the final one that leads back home. In the last minutes of my ride, I no longer look about but retreat deeper into my own memory. I clench the pony's reins in my sweaty hands, picture my mother's face, try to compose some words with which to greet her. I have a sudden urge to turn back for fear I am making a terrible mistake, then drive the pony forward with my heels so the interminable wait will be over. I am so lost in this rush of thoughts that I am taken by surprise when the very inn I have dreamed of for so long appears before me.

It is twilight, the time when most travelers arrive. The orange glow of a lantern hung outside the door beckons warmly. I tie up my pony in the stable and hurry to the door of the inn. Though the handle upon it is too high for me, the peg my mother affixed to the doorframe so I could boost myself up to reach it is still there. It gladdens me to find it, to think she has kept it there in the hope that I might someday return. I step up upon it and grasp the handle, pushing open the door with a familiar motion that recalls to me my childhood days. As soon as I step inside, I am met by that particular scent of burning firewood and hops, sweat and horse fur, porridge and steam that tells me I am home.

But as I look about, for a moment unnoticed in the shadow of the door, I realize with a wrench of my gut that time has changed more than just myself. Though in certain ways, the inn is still the same—a roaring fire in the hearth, mismatched chairs and tables, cats gaming beneath them—there are differences that make it seem a shadow of the home so carefully preserved in my mind. The floor near the hearth is black with ashes, the travelers few, the tables slopped with porridge.

I look anxiously about for my mother, certain she would never allow such disorder. But all I see is a thin man with graying hair who sits alone by the fire, absently stoking the flames. It takes me a moment to realize he is Willem, for his hair was still brown when I left, and such a task was never his. Even more troubling is the sight of Jantje, farmer Helmich's wife, idly sweeping a rag across one of the dirty tables. Though my mother had a certain fondness for her gab, she thought her hands did not move nearly as much as her mouth, and had never sought her help at the inn.

It is Jantje who spots me.

"Jepp!" she cries, abandoning her rag as she darts out from behind the soiled counter. "Is that you?"

Upon hearing my name, Willem drops the poker in his hand and springs to his feet. As I step out of the shadow of the door, he blinks rapidly as if he thinks me some apparition.

"It is," I say to an audience that now includes three travelers who stare with curiosity at my diminutive form. "Where is mother?"

At this, even Jantje is voiceless. My panic rises, but still I manage to repeat this question into the gaping silence.

"Where is my mother?"

It is Willem who at last answers, his long fingers gripped together as if in prayer.

"She is dead, Jepp."

These words strike me with no less force than Don's blows. And yet, as in the Infanta's dungeon, I do not rage or cry, only struggle to catch my breath.

"When?" I finally manage to ask.

Willem does not meet my eye. "A year after you left. Last fall."

It is then my grief breaks, like a great wave upon the shore, flooding everything in sight. I dash for the door, claw it open, and run out into the night. I do not know where to go but find my feet carry me to the barn where I once found solace as a boy. I climb up to the hayloft, startling a mother cat in the midst of nursing her kittens. That I have disturbed such a gentle scene— one my mother would have loved—pains me almost as much as her death, and the pitiful mewing that ensues coaxes out a torrent of tears as I grieve for the hungry kittens, for my mother, for myself.

Why did I ever leave her, she who loved me before all others? Nothing I have gained—a stargazer's wisdom, a girl's love— seems recompense enough for losing her. I see her in my mind's eye—the mole on her left cheek, the crinkly blue eyes, the sturdy arms and soft apron—but fear she is already less distinct, that I am forgetting, losing her to the fog of time. I try to imagine her, her hand upon my neck, singing the ancient nonsense of a mother's song, but there is only the rough scratch of straw and the plaintive cries of the barn cats. That is how death taunts us: the only one in the world who could comfort us is the one who is gone.

No one rushes after me, and for this I am relieved. I cry till my mouth is parched, till my sobs have wracked me like a fever. It is only sometime later, as I lie exhausted and numb, that it occurs to me to wonder why, if my mother died nearly a year ago, Willem did not write me to share this news.

Chapter
41

I do not ponder this question long, for soon merciful sleep overtakes me. I awake in what feels like the dead of night to a pair of arms tightening around me and lifting me up. For a moment, still under sleep's forgetful spell, I think my mother has come, that she is still alive or that I have died and joined her. I close my eyes, almost wishing it to be so. But the arms that carry me down from the hayloft are bony and thin, the face that brushes against mine rough with bristle. Still, Willem holds me with tenderness, and for this I am grateful. I feign sleep as he carries me back inside the inn and lays me gently in my mother's room, upon the pallet that was once my own. He stays beside me a long time.

The next morning, Willem appears with a mug of ale. He hands it to me and then crouches down beside my pallet, looking weary in dawn's light. He speaks in the slow, deliberate voice in which he once told me tales from the Bible or of the pagan heroes of Rome.

"Last fall, a traveler came to the inn, a young merchant, and fell ill with fever. Your mother nursed him, as was her way. But he perished, and the fever spread, reaping and sparing with a design only the Lord could understand. Your mother died on the second evening of the fever's scourge."

I had secretly feared that Don had had some hand in my mother's death, but I feel little relief that her assassin was a fever, common and black-handed. For sickness only reminds me how fragile our lives truly are—the warmth and vigor of our flesh fleeting.

"At the end," I stammer. "Was she . . . did she suffer?"

Willem shakes his head, but for the first time his voice quivers and catches. "She passed quickly that evening, as if death were just another task she meant to finish by day's end. She said your name before she died. She loved you, Jepp, till the very last."

He looks away as if the sight of me might bring him to tears, and so I am left to dab silently at my own.

"Where is she buried?" I ask.

"On the hill behind the old church," Willem says, still looking away. "With Helmich, and Pieter and his youngest son, and the girls who helped her run the inn. The dead here now outnumber the living."

I want to ask why Willem did not write to tell me of this tragedy as soon as it happened, but I can see how much even the recounting of this tale pains him. No doubt he only sought to protect me from such sorrow. There is another question, however, that I must ask.

"Is my father among them?"

Willem turns to me, his mouth falling open as if my question has startled him.

"She never told me who he was," I say. "I came home to find out."

I can feel my heart quake in anticipation of his answer, but Willem looks down at me sadly. "I do not know who your father is. I am sorry, Jepp."

"Surely, someone must," I protest.

Willem stands and makes ready to depart. "None of us knows."

I lie upon my pallet after he has left, mourning not only my mother but the secret that has died with her. Am I already at the end of my journey? Is this all I am fated to know? I cannot comprehend why my mother did not tell Willem, whom she trusted above all others. I briefly wonder whether he has lied to me, but the way he looked me in the eye and told me he knew not my father's identity strikes me as genuine. I feel my grief blend with anger. My mother has left it so I will forever know only half of who I am.

It seems I have learned all the answers that are possible for me to find here in Astraveld. I could begin the trip back to Uraniborg and Magdalene this very day. Yet, I tell myself that I must stay a few weeks to help Willem, who is in dire need of capable hands at the inn. I write Magdalene a brief letter, telling her of my safe arrival and my mother's death; how I miss her but feel compelled to remain a fortnight to help Willem. I do not tell her that there is also a part of me that in my grief prefers this village of shadows and ghosts to the living world of Uraniborg.

Willem seems unsurprised by my decision to stay and gladly accepts my help at the inn, washing bowls, stoking the fire, and cleaning the floors and tables. I attend to these tasks with a zeal I lacked as a boy, for in bringing back some semblance of the inn she loved, I feel as if I am bringing back my mother. I work tirelessly, and at night repair to the room we once shared. There I lie awake, imagining that if I only turn my head just so, I will see her there across the room in the empty pallet opposite my own. Some nights, I read the volume of Copernicus that Longomontanus gave me, puzzling over the inscription he wrote, *Per aspera ad astra*, or "Through adversity to the stars." On other nights, I roam the inn and graveyard like a ghost myself and, as the lonesome hours pass, I begin to learn the secrets of my companions—how Jantje lies upon her husband's grave in the moonlight, talking to him and the white stones that mark her six dead infants as if her family sits before her; how, late at night, Pieter's eldest son comes from the brewery to lie beside Willem. It is no mystery why the travelers, once plentiful, are few and the coffers nearly empty. It is neither their comforts nor their riches that occupy the minds and hearts of Astraveld's remaining inhabitants.

During the long days, I endeavor to bring some cheer, telling Willem and Jantje of Uraniborg and all its man-made wonders. Willem exhibits great interest in this topic, asking questions that reveal he received my letters, and expressing wonder as I take him out one night and point out the various planets and stars. But when I start to speak of Coudenberg and the misfortune that befell me there, he invariably changes the subject. Thinking he wishes to hear no more of death and despair, I try to tell him only of the court's extravagances and curiosities but he finds excuses not to listen even to these harmless tales, which serve only to entertain Jantje. I worry that he blames me for leaving with Don, for abandoning my mother for the promise of court life and its riches.

One afternoon, a fortnight after my arrival, I help Jantje make porridge for the evening's supper in the cauldron that hangs over the hearth fire. I carry water and kindling, and clean up after her as she spills peas and barley in her usual careless manner. Since Helmich's death, Jantje has only become more voluble, as if she dreads her husband's eternal silence will become her own. When I am called to assist her, I know I will hear every impression and vexation of her day. I do not mind it though, for I find her chatter soothing, like listening to the birds or the patter of rain. Since she rarely demands a response, it is easy to drift away and think of Magdalene or my lost parents.

I am doing just this as Jantje recounts Helmich's many virtues, a topic of which she is most fond. She goes on for some time as I half listen, picking up the discarded pods, when I suddenly catch her saying something strange.

"He was as kind to children as he was to beasts, though the Lord did not wish us to raise a child past its infant years. I think this is also the nature of those who are barren, to love the smallest among us not as burdens but as blessings. It was true of your mother."

I look up at Jantje. "But my mother was not barren. She had me."

Jantje colors. "Of course, Jepp. I meant that after you, she had no more."

There is silence between us, and in this silence a doubt begins to grow, one that makes my fingers tremble as my nails scrape the floorboard for a fallen pod.

"You were such a happy babe," Jantje says, brightly. "How your mother loved you!"

But in this gay memory I hear her desperation. Though it takes all my effort, I smile at her, concealing the terror rising within. What if my mother was barren? What if I am not her child? With a wrench of my gut, I think of how easily Don took me from her, how he said that I did not know myself. I fear that Jantje's slip has revealed a most horrible truth.

That night, I wait till only Willem is left in the great room, counting the evening's meager earnings in the dying light of the hearth fire. I drag a chair beside him and watch him mark the book in which he has always kept my mother's accounts.

"Look," he says, flipping back some pages to the fall I left for Coudenberg, "how much more our labors then earned. Once plague has struck, travelers are wary of stopping, though it has been over a year since the last of the dead were buried."

"Why did you not tell me my mother died? You read my letters from Uraniborg. You knew where to reach me. Was it your intention never to tell me?"

Willem sits upright and the book falls closed.

"Was she my mother?"

I expect Willem to laugh at so outrageous a question. I long for him to dismiss it with a wave of the hand. But his shoulders begin to heave as he starts to cry.

"She was your mother, Jepp. She loved you as a mother."

I scramble off my chair, breathing hard. "*As* a mother?"

"We didn't want you to go back," Willem sobs. "You were ours. You were our boy."

I hear Don's words instead. *None of us would ever keep a boy from his mother's breast.* With a wrench of my gut, I realize it was never an assurance. It was a reminder to her that she could no longer keep me, that I had another mother at court. Lia was right. When Don came to take me, I never had a choice. I feel the room spin and grip the arm of the chair.

"Who is my real mother, then?"

Willem wipes his eyes on his sleeve. Then he rises and pours himself a mug of ale, which he drinks rapidly, as if for courage.

When he returns, his speaks calmly, in the voice of the storyteller who over the years has told me every tale but my own.

"Late one night, in the middle of a fierce February storm, a finely dressed young man arrived at the inn with a bundle. In it was a babe, not quite a year old, a curious thing with a large head and short arms and a beguiling smile. Your mother took one look at you, scooped you into her lap and fed you milk and porridge. She inquired of the gentleman where your home and mother was. He said you hailed from a great court but were a bastard and a dwarf. I did not lie to you in saying I know not your father's identity, for the man revealed nothing about either your mother or your father. He said only that he had been dispatched to find you a home. Your mother did not hesitate to offer up her own. She loved you, Jepp, from the first sight. This was true."

I wish to say that little else was, that my life was built on deceptions, but I hold my tongue, for I wish him to speak freely.

"He introduced himself as Don Diego de la Fuente," Willem continues, mimicking Don's grand presentation of his name with distaste. "He gave you no name, and suggested your mother christen you with one of her own. He offered nothing else and left promptly at first morning light. Your mother did not even learn the true day of your birth, so she made your birthday February seventeenth, 1583, the day you arrived. It seemed fitting, as your life began anew upon that date."

It takes me a moment to comprehend the import of this revelation. "But you say I looked to be nearly a year already upon this date? Does this mean I am a year older than I have been raised to believe?"

Willem touches my shoulder. "You were small, Jepp. It was hard to tell your true age."

I pull away. My mother is not my own. My name. My age. My birthday. And what of the fortune and love promised by the stars? I realize that despite my argument with Magdalene that a man's fate does not lie in his stars, I had put faith in her horoscope and the good life it promised me. Now I fear that life is no longer mine. Why did I ever leave Uraniborg? I had hoped to find my father, and instead I have lost both parents. I know even less about who I am. Although Longomontanus assured me that as a man of intellect and will, I could make sense of whatever I learned, I feel only confusion. I am not even certain I am such a man any longer.

"Jepp," Willem says, his pleading voice reaching me as if from afar. "Your mother loved you. She was your mother."

Although I know that she loved me, I still feel betrayed. But I conceal my anguish, for it seems cruel to punish Willem, who only sought to protect me, and wished not to be the messenger of my grief.

"Forgive me," I say. "I am tired."

I return to my room. My hands are shaking as I open a pot of ink and dip my quill. I take out one of the pieces of paper I have brought with me and write to Magdalene. I tell her about my discovery: that I am not who I thought I was.

It is the end of my letter that is most important for I have a request for Magdalene. I am certain now that among the five horoscopes Don commissioned from Tycho is one with a birthday of 1582 and a birthplace of Brussels. I beg her to tell me, with the honesty upon which our love depends, what the stars in this chart foretell—and who I truly am.

Chapter 42

Magdalene, the girl I have grown to love and trust above all others in the world, will surely help me make sense of this terrible discovery. She is my hope—and the bulwark against my growing despair.

An autumn chill has descended upon Astraveld—bringing with it nights of cold rain and falling leaves, gray mornings that bring a shiver to the bones. This bleak weather suits me, for after losing my mother a second time, my spirit feels as diminished as the season. Nothing will ever be the same—not I, not the place I once called home, not the people I once thought of as my family. Although Willem treats me no differently than before, I feel beholden to him now for his and my mother's charity in raising me. I seek to pay off this debt by helping him and Jantje at the inn and not troubling them with the tempest of my emotions. But it is hard to play the stranger among those I love.

A month after I sent my letters to Magdalene, I receive one in return, stamped with the seal of Uraniborg castle. With great anticipation, I take it to a chair by the hearth and open it.

20 October 1599

Dear Jepp,

It is with great joy that I received your letters only to be plunged into the depths of sorrow upon reading them. Your misfortunes, dear friend, are my own. Though you may think yourself alone, it is I who have been with you, mourning your mother as if she were my own, decrying the pestilence that raged through your village as if Uraniborg itself were at the Lord's mercy.

In this same spirit, I share your anguish over the revelations of your birth. The moment I finished your last letter, I hastily abandoned the royal horoscope before me to search for copies of the ones Don Diego de la Fuente had commissioned from my father. I was most certain there was one that fit the particulars you described, and I was not mistaken. Your true birthday was March 15, 1582, and you were born in Brussels. You are seventeen, the same age as I.

You wish me to write you what this chart augers with the honesty upon which our love depends. Not only is this love my greatest treasure—and I pledge to honor any request made in its name—but it has always been my nature to speak truthfully. I thus tell you plainly: The horoscope of March 15, 1582 appears less favorable than that of February 17, 1583. The native is not an Aquarius, as you once thought yourself, but a

Pisces, soft-hearted and whimsical. Mercury in the Second House connotes fluctuating fortunes; the Moon in the Third House indicates a studious but overly impressionable nature; Saturn in the Seventh House shows delays in marriage.

But before you let this drive you deeper into despair, consider first the core precepts of astrology. There is no such thing as a perfect chart. Every man on this earth has his strengths and his afflictions. And while the stars can bestow upon us a life of ease or of hardship, this does not mean such a life is ours forever. A chart that has too many favorable aspects can lead a man to be indolent and weak and to squander his good fortune. Likewise, a chart full of hard aspects can build a man's character, giving him the strength to create a better life than fate intended for him.

I can hear you now, almost as if you were before me, question whether I am finally conceding the argument between us about fate and free will. I do not think of the above as a rejection of fate, for I believe the stars shape us in ways that, like the wisdom of God, we cannot always comprehend—the bad becomes good, the good bad, and life, at some moment or another, confounds us.

But I must also confess that my love for you makes me believe that, no matter what the stars divine, you can choose the life you wish to lead. If this means I am conceding our argument, so be it. Come home, Jepp, to Uraniborg and to me! Though you have lost yourself, I know who you are. You will not find your true self in the past, but in the future you have fashioned here upon this island.

On a final note, some news of Uraniborg you will no doubt find of interest. Severinus escaped from prison the night you left and fled the island before he could be recaptured. Father has learned he is back in Vienna now with Ursus but has returned to his master empty-handed. I do not imagine Ursus was pleased with his failed effort. Nevertheless, Father was irate, especially at Jonas, who he believes must have left the key in the door. You should know that only I think Jonas did no such thing.

May God almighty be with you now and always and graciously preserve you from all harm. I thank you for the goodness you have shown me in writing. I will do everything in my power to serve you across the great distance of sea and land that I pray every night will diminish between us.

Magdalene Tygesdatter

I read Magdalene's letter three times and begin to read it a fourth when Willem joins me by the hearth.

"Have you word from Uraniborg?" he asks.

I nod but do not reveal the dispiriting contents of Magdalene's letter.

Willem studies my face. "You are not happy here, Jepp. Go back to Lord Tycho. You will prosper there."

I think of the fluctuating fortunes that my true horoscope augers. "I am not so certain of that."

"Why? Has Lord Tycho written you otherwise?"

I can no longer conceal my true feelings. "It is not that. I am no longer who I thought I was."

"Nonsense! Nothing has changed. You are our boy. This is your home."

I want to believe these tender words, but my new horoscope fills me with doubt. "Then why do you wish me to leave it? I am a burden to you. Perhaps I have always been—"

Willem's face tightens, and he bangs his fist upon the arm of his chair.

"You were never a burden, Jepp! Your happiness was the measure of our days!"

I gently place my hand over his own, and he grasps it hard. Only then do I understand how little he truly wishes for me to leave but how I must—if only to give him a parent's due, the illusion of my happiness. I remind myself, too, of Magdalene's plea to forget this mystery of my past and, regardless of what is written in the stars, choose the future that I want.

The following morning, I give Willem my pony—for this beast will be of use to him in his daily tasks—and pay a farmer who is heading to Utrecht with a wagonload of barley a silver piece for a ride. From Utrecht, I plan to secure myself a place in a coach traveling back to Denmark. Willem pretends to be most pleased with my decision and I, for his sake, pretend to be as well. But it pains me to leave, knowing how unlikely it is that I will ever see Willem or the inn or the grave of the woman I knew as my mother again.

Shortly after noon, I stand outside with Willem and Jantje as the farmer readies his horse and cart. Jantje's tears, which threaten to be more copious even than her parting words, touch me deeply. But Willem and I are both careful to shed none of our own.

"I will write to you, I promise, Jepp," Willem says. "And you must do the same and tell us more about the stars and your studies with Lord Tycho. They are the same stars we see here too, are they not?"

I smile, if only to stave off my tears. "They are no different."

The farmer is in no hurry, probably hoping I might give him

an extra silver for any delays, but I do not linger. Willem boosts me into the wagon and, with a flurry of good-byes, we set off into the dry and bright October afternoon. Astraveld looks as beautiful at this moment—the simple thatched cottages, stubble fields, and wild stretches of meadow—as in my first memories. But I know it is just a trick of the sun and of my own longing for my old past as I leave it behind me. Like Longomontanus said of his own childhood home, I no longer belong here. I also now know that I am no native, but like the rest of the travelers who have sought shelter upon this road, merely a passerby. Without a name or kin, I fear I shall always be that wanderer—perhaps someone to Magdalene, but no one in my own mind.

I cry out to the farmer to stop.

"What?" the farmer asks. "Need a piss?"

"No. I need to change our destination."

The farmer turns, viewing me with distrust. He has oily black hair and the paunch of a drunk—befitting the breed of traveler who now frequents the inn, either too careless or too cheap to mind the history of plague or present gloom.

"To where, then?" he asks.

"To Brussels."

"But we agreed upon Utrecht. I have no cause to make such a long journey."

He sulks, scratching his oily locks and sighing as if I have deceived him most grievously.

"You will find an even better market for your barley there," I say. "In addition to which, I will pay you two more silvers for your trouble."

But this fellow is most sly. "I will have to return you to your father's inn," he says, shaking his head. "I am sure you will find another driver."

Though he has mistaken Willem for my father, his ploy is most effective, for I do not wish Willem to know my new destination. I wonder if this is a sign that I should just continue to Utrecht and then north, as I had planned. After all, it seems a great mistake to have left Uraniborg in the first place. Had I remained I would have gone on thinking my mother was my mother and my birth date as auspicious as it once seemed. I fear I am making yet another bad decision, that the truth, if I even discover it, will not bring me peace but further torment. I reach into the pocket of my coat and touch the petals of the lion's fleur-de-lis heart, thinking of Magdalene, of how she begged me to return to her and Uraniborg. And yet, despite these doubts, despite the entreaties of those who love me, I cannot imagine not knowing who my true parents are. I must return to Brussels.

"I will give you four silvers, then," I say. "And pay for us at the inns."

The farmer whips his horse forward, signaling his approval. But as I count the coins in Tycho's purse, even adding Matheus's copper, I realize I may not now have enough to return from Brussels to Elsinore. I imagine Magdalene scolding me for my foolishness. Still, I do not order the farmer to turn back.

The afternoon is much like the one two years ago when Don and I first traveled to Coudenberg and, as I watch scythes rise and fall over the fields and the sunlit leaves so red and orange they seem to be aflame, I remember the consequences of that journey and feel my anxiety rise. I try to dwell not on what could befall me as I repeat this trip but on the mystery of my origins that I am determined to solve.

In order to discover who my father is, I must first find my true mother, and I have been thinking most carefully about who at Coudenberg she could be. Of the women I met there, Maria, Hendrika, the Infanta herself, and Annika, the midwife, are all the right age to have borne me, and all are connected in some way to the odious Don. I consider how the Infanta came to favor me—and how she would have had good cause to send away a son who was both a dwarf and a bastard. But would she take such delight in my humiliation were I her own flesh and blood?

Hendrika is a more compelling possibility, for I recall how she disliked my given name and defended me in the dungeon from Don. But she too participated in my abasement, ordering me my first day into the pie and keeping me imprisoned along with Lia and the others. My suspicions fall just as heavily upon Maria, and not only because she is a fellow dwarf. I remember how Maria averred that some dwarfs managed to give birth and how during our argument about Lia, she spoke—knowingly, it now seems—of my mother. I know Maria to be a gossip and a drunk who, worst of all, confuses the indignities and cruelty of life at Coudenberg for the best possible fate. I do not wish such a woman to be my mother and yet, if she is and sent me away as an infant, perhaps she understands more about the perversions of this life than she admits.

These musings leave me most unsettled for I do not relish the thought of any of these women as my mother. Truly, the best of the lot would be Annika, whose capable nature reminds me most of the mother I have lost. I think back to how she touched my face when she met me as if remembering someone from long ago and how the old cook, Mena, made a point of telling me that Annika had once worked at Coudenberg. Even if she is not my mother, as a midwife and nurse at the palace, she is still likely to have some clue to who I am. But when I consider how she betrayed my own and Lia's whereabouts, I wonder if I can trust her. Still, it seems far less risky to approach Annika in the city than to attempt to sneak back into Coudenberg to interview the others.

Three days later, as we approach the gates of the city, I give the farmer an address I never thought I'd wish to see again: Rollebeek Straat.

Chapter 43

Dusk begins to fall as our wagon rattles along the cobblestone streets of Brussels. Though the cool evening air suggests that autumn has found its way into the city, the sweet scent of dried leaves and overripe fruit is absent here. Instead there is a stench that only winter can dull—of horse and human waste, smoke and offal, the smells of a thousand cooking pots. This foul mix of odors makes me want to turn away, but I resist, for I wish to look upon even the most painful reminders of my former life. The peddlers' square is unchanged—jammed with carts and sallow men hawking their wares—no different than before. It is as if Lia's tragedy never played out upon this stage. It occurs to me that cities are like life itself—continual in a comforting way but also, in a more terrifying way, indifferent.

Rollebeek Straat exudes the comforting spirit, for its grand brick and stone homes with their colorful shutters seem testament to permanence and wealth. Here the stench of the city is milder, and the windows reflect the last rays of setting sun. I order the farmer to stop his wagon as we near the house with the tree upon its coat of arms and reluctantly forfeit to him the four coins I have promised. Despite having been handed this generous sum, he makes no effort to help me down from the wagon, counting his lucre with a childish smile as I scramble indecorously down to the street. I do not bid this scoundrel farewell, nor does he me.

The houses of Rollebeek Straat are connected one to the next, but between each adjoining pair is a small arched doorway. Not wishing to present myself at the main door of the Dubois family home, I slip through this open doorway, hoping to find a servants' entrance beyond it. The cobblestone corridor is neatly swept and appears to lead to an elegant courtyard of which I catch but a glimpse before I spot the servants' door.

I take a deep breath and then knock firmly upon it. No one answers. I rap more insistently. I am about to abandon my efforts when the door flies open and Mena appears, gripping in one hand the bloody innards of some fowl or beast. Her eyes bulge at the sight of me and she nearly drops the viscera.

"Jepp. What are you doing here?" she whispers.

Before I can answer, she pokes her gray head out the door, looking this way and that, then pulls me inside the kitchen with her unoccupied hand, closing the door behind us.

"What are you doing here?" she asks again.

There is little tone of welcome in her voice, but I do not let this discourage me.

"I have come to speak to Annika."

Mena releases the innards on a cutting block on a table, beside a hen's severed head and scaly feet. For several seconds, she does not move, staring at these entrails like some ancient soothsayer. At last, as if she has determined that this moment has always been inevitable, she sighs and wipes her bloody hand on a rag.

"I will fetch her."

I expect a similar wary reaction from Annika. But some few minutes later she bustles through the door, her stout face pink, though I know not whether with haste or the emotions of seeing me. As when I arrived with Lia, her broad hand reaches out to caress my cheek, then draws hastily back, as if afraid of her own impertinence. I think she must be my mother to touch me so. But then I wonder if I am mistaken—for why would my mother betray me to Maria and Don?

"Jepp, you are well?" she says, reaching to take my hands and looking me up and down as if searching for signs of ill treatment.

I nod, though I feel greatly troubled in spirit.

"We did not know where they sent you," Mena adds.

But I wish not to be reminded of my previous visit. "I have come because I believe . . ." I turn to face Annika. "Because I believe I may be your son. Is it so?"

Stout arms wrap around me as a soft bosom cradles me. I allow myself to succumb, thinking that my true mother has been found. But some part of me holds back, waiting for the words that confirm that our flesh was once one.

"I nursed you, child," Annika says, her face damp with tears, "from a few days after you were born to the day Don Diego took you from me."

I pull away.

"You are not my mother?"

"I was like a mother, for I fed and tended you for nearly your entire first year."

I look at her in despair, for I am not searching for another woman who was merely *like* a mother.

"But who is my mother?"

Annika meets my gaze with pained eyes. "I do not know," she says gently.

At this, I cannot help but lose patience. "How can you not know? You are a midwife! Surely you delivered me."

"I delivered many a child at Coudenberg, but I did not assist at your birth, nor did I know anything about it. Don Diego was the first to speak of you. He said you were a bastard and let me a room outside the palace where I could care for you. He paid me handsomely to keep you a secret."

Annika blushes, no doubt regretting this mention of recompense. I am surprised to feel—along with my disappointment at having failed to solve this mystery—pity for her. She seems genuinely fond of me and, even if we are not of the same flesh, it is hers that nourished me. But this also makes the night Lia and I spent with her that much more of a betrayal.

"Did he also pay you to return me and Lia to Coudenberg?" I ask in a bitter tone.

Annika frowns. "I did not send you back because of him. I care little for Don Diego. It was Maria. She told me that if you and the girl came, you were sure to be in trouble and to return you to the palace where you would be safe."

"You thought me safe at the palace? It was there I was beaten, then banished!"

Annika shudders. "Jepp, I swear I did not know. Maria never

spoke to me of such cruelty, nor did I imagine that the Infanta would ever mistreat one of her beloved dwarfs."

"How could you trust Maria?"

"She knew that I nursed you. She was the one person I told when Don Diego first brought you to me. She said she would never tell a soul."

I feel my suspicions mount. I wonder if Maria already knew about me and kept the secret because I was hers. Perhaps she betrayed us when we tried to flee Coudenberg not for Lia's sake but because she could not bear to let me go.

"Please," Annika says. "If there is any way for you to forgive me—"

Her eyes brim with tears. I cannot help being moved by this piteous display and the thought of the tender care she must have once given me.

"I forgive you," I say in a gentle tone. "But you must help me. Do you at least know my true name?"

"Don Diego called you *Bebito*."

But this is no name; only the Spanish word for "little baby." I am certain I was not baptized as such, but I conceal my disappointment.

"Can you give me lodging? I wish to stay for a few days but want no one from Coudenberg, including Maria, to know I am here."

The two women nod most somberly in agreement.

"You can stay in my quarters," Mena says. "No one will see you here."

Annika crouches before me and takes my hands in her own. "I will say not a word to anyone. You must believe me, Jepp, I never intended—"

"I know," I say.

At the touch of her rough fingers, I realize how weary I am and how truly thankful for a place to rest. Tomorrow I will go to Coudenberg and try to find a way to confront Maria. But tonight, I shall rest.

That evening, Mena makes me a dish of sweetbreads and turnips. After supper, she prepares a pallet for me in her room by the fire, and when I lie down upon it, Annika gently rubs my back, as she must have done some seventeen years earlier. Though the room is drafty and smells strongly of the tinctures of old age, the weight of her hand comforts me.

But when she departs and I am left alone, I am troubled by thoughts of Lia and her last moments in this forlorn chamber. There is only one way to distract myself from this melancholy. Pulling the lion's fleur-de-lis heart from my pocket, I study it by the fire's light. Unlike Lia's shell, the silver lily is not nature but art; the world as rendered by man. I wonder at the hubris of this trinket—the illusion it gives that we can control nature and our own fate. I take out the paper I have brought with me and dip my quill into ink.

1 November 1599
Dear Magdalene,

Please forgive the delay in my correspondence. I was most grateful to receive your letter and for the honesty of your reply. You are the lone voice I trust, truer even than my own conscience. Though we are at present divided, I assure you there is unity between our souls.

Dearest Magdalene, how I wish I could come running to you, how I wish I could cast away these shadows of my past for a future in your arms. But I cannot build myself up from

312

nothing, and it is nothing I have become—without mother or father or name. Though you are my compass—and true North lies always with you—I must find my own way. I must learn who my parents are, for I fear I will not truly know myself unless I know them, why they gave me up, and whether they love me.

I can hear you argue that I already know who I am, for a man is what he makes of himself. I should be pleased that you have adopted this philosophy, but I am no longer certain whether it is mine. For though I was able to earn a place as one of your father's scholars and win your affections, the pull of my past was so strong that I could not continue to be the man I made of myself at Uraniborg. Instead, I fear I have become the man you describe in my true horoscope—with fluctuating fortunes and delays in marriage. Perhaps the stars know more about me than I do about myself? But I cling to the hope that you are still the woman helpful and true and that I can order the universe with my intellect and will. I must take this trip not only to solve the mystery of my past, but to discover if it is possible to reclaim my future.

I will not trouble you with the details of my journey, of which I know you must disapprove. If you wish to write me, send your correspondence to Mena Berg at the Dubois home on Rollebeek Straat, Brussels. She is a friend and will see to it that I receive your letter. I beg only that you forgive me for not being the Jepp we both thought I was. And, most important, remember still that I love you. May God almighty be with you now and always and graciously preserve you from all harm.

Jepp

Chapter 44

Early the next morning, I slip out of Mena's room before she is awake, quietly open the kitchen door, and let myself out. It is barely after dawn. A mist blankets the street, lending to the city the same air of confusion that inhabits my own head. As I walk toward the winding road that leads up to Coudenberg, I see but a few fellow men, ghostlike figures who emerge from the mist, their eyes widening at the sight of me.

Near the bottom of the road, the clouds part, and a fair-haired young man in military dress appears upon a horse weighed down by saddlebags.

"Do you journey north?" I ask him.

He cocks his head at the sound of my voice then, upon spotting me so far below, laughs softly to himself.

"I do," he replies, "but I am not taking passengers—big or small."

"It is not a ride I seek. I have a letter. My master requests it be sent to Uraniborg, to the court of Lord Tycho Brahe."

At the mention of a master, one powerful enough to keep a dwarf, the soldier assumes a dutiful expression and reaches down for the letter. "Tell your master that Johannus Betker is headed to Hamburg and will see to it that the letter is passed to those who can bring it safely to its destination."

I bow, relieved that at least if some misfortune befalls me at Coudenberg, Magdalene will understand why I went and that I truly love her.

Though the mist obscures the landmarks of my journey, my feet know the way, and I begin to feel grateful for this cover, as if I am some ancient hero the gods are shrouding from his enemies. But the mist is filled with other perils, for in the changing forms of stones and trees, the cries of invisible birds, the soft-stepped rustling of other creatures through unseen leaves, I am reminded of Lia. It seems she sighs heavily beside me or that her footsteps tread behind my own but, when I turn back, I see no one.

Halfway up, I slip off the road and into the gardens. The ornamental ponds of Coudenberg have not escaped autumn's scythe. When I stop at one to drink, I find that orange leaves, fallen during the night, shroud it. I clear the foliage away and cupping my cold hands, take a sip of the water, which tastes of mineral and leaf.

My step becomes more vigilant as I approach the orchard, for I fear the Infanta's gardeners have started their morning labors there. I avoid the stunted trees altogether, not only for this danger but for the memories they invoke, and sneak round them to the back door that leads to my former miniature quarters. But a rumbling of my gut reminds me that though I have slaked my thirst, I have not eaten since the previous night, and it may be a while before I can sate my hunger. I sidle up to the outermost tree until I can see its small apples—a few of which are temptingly in reach.

I pluck one and take a bite. Though it is bitter, I am glad for the sustenance. But as I am about to take another, the mist parts, and down the row I see a strange vision—a long arm, seemingly disconnected from any body—emerge over the top of an apple tree. I look for the ladder upon which the gardener is perched, but there is only a pair of massive legs.

"Robert?!" I say before I can stop myself.

My old rival stands fully upright, his head emerging over the top of the tree, as he stares quizzically into the mist.

Wary that others are about, I slip from tree to tree toward him.

"It is I," I whisper when I have near reached him. "Jepp."

Robert stares down at me, his large eyes blinking and blinking as if he hardly believes what he sees before him. I smile to show I am no trick of the mist, but he does not return the smile, his shoulders hunched under the weight of memory.

"Are you angry at me?" I ask.

"No," he says in a voice more slurred than his former one. It is only then that I realize that his enormous jaw still lists to the side where it was broken.

"I would understand it if you were. Lia—"

But Robert does not allow me to continue. "She wished to leave. You tried to help her."

With Magdalene's encouragement, I have come to believe

that my choice to aid Lia was the right one. But it is the decency with which Robert says this that fully absolves me. As I gaze up at this gentle soul, I am seized by rage at the thought of those who have maimed him. "Why have you not left this place?"

Robert heaves up his enormous shoulders then lets them fall. "Lia is dead."

"And Pim?"

His eyes flash with menace. "He knows to not find himself alone with me."

I am glad to hear him issue such a threat, but the slurred tones of his voice remind me that he is still broken in body as well as spirit. I long to console him and wonder whether he had heard me as I tried to tell him what Lia, on her deathbed, wished him to know.

"Did you hear me call to you in the dungeon?" I ask. "Don Diego was dragging me away—"

Robert shakes his enormous head. "I did not hear you."

"Lia wished you to know that she loved you."

"I know she did," he says softly, blinking back tears. Though I feel disappointed that I was never the messenger I believed myself to be, I am still grateful for the chance to remind him of this fact. I think of Magdalene and hope we will always love each other as truly as Lia and Robert.

"Why are you here, Jepp?" Robert asks.

For a moment, I feel my sole duty is to return to Magdalene, and do not know. But then I remember that my name is not truly Jepp, and my resolve to unlock the mysteries of my past returns.

"I believe Maria to be my mother."

I tell Robert what I have discovered over the previous month—how the mother who raised me was not the mother who bore me, how Don brought me as an infant from Coudenberg, how I have come to suspect that Maria might be my mother.

By the perplexed look that crosses his face, Robert clearly knows nothing of this secret. "Maria? Your mother?"

"I must speak to her to be sure. I plan to slip into our quarters now before the palace rises. Through the back door—"

"That door is still kept locked, it is said for the protection of the Infanta's dwarfs. Besides which, Hendrika will be up, and perhaps Sebastian as well. Have you a home, Jepp? Go back to it. If not, be glad you have escaped your exile and start a new life for yourself. Go to Amsterdam. There are ships there that leave for all parts of the world."

I am surprised by the fervor with which Robert delivers this speech. But I will not let him dissuade me. I feel so close to learning the truth, to making sense of who I am.

"And yet you yourself have not left."

"I work here in the garden now," Robert says, turning away, for even he realizes this to be a weak retort. We both know it is Lia's ghost who keeps him here. But, as his threat against Pim revealed, there is still indignation left in him, and it is to this I appeal.

"We have both made unsuccessful escapes from this vile palace," I plead. "Help me at least to be successful at penetrating it."

Robert does not answer me and, for a moment, I fear my cause is lost. But when he at last turns back to me, his eyes squint with schemes, and I can see that I have kindled his long dormant spirit of rebellion.

"You must go in late at night," he says, in his low, slurred rumble. "After there has been much merriment and wine. The Infanta has a great banquet planned for a fortnight from Friday in honor of the archduke's name day."

Though I am disappointed that I must wait more than a fortnight to confront Maria, I am most glad for Robert's help and agree that this timing seems sensible.

"But I do not have keys to unlock the door," Robert continues. "So we must find another way to spirit you to Maria's chamber. It is far too dangerous for you to come through another entrance and walk openly through the palace. If the Infanta's guards were to spot you, or worse yet, Pim . . ."

We both ponder this. But then I remember how I have been concealed from the court before.

"There is a door outside the kitchens, is there not?" I ask.

Robert nods. "Where deliveries to the cooks are made."

"Meet me there on the archduke's name day at midnight. And bring a cart."

Chapter 45

A fortnight later, I climb Cold Hill. It is a night befitting the month of the Scorpion—a treacherous hint of winter in the chill air, which smells of coming snow. Though my feet are determined, my heart wavers. It seems madness to return by choice to the very place where disaster struck and is likely to befall me again. I picture the dripping walls of the Infanta's dungeon and the heavy blows of the guards' fists crashing into my jaw, so much easier to break than Robert's. I imagine Lia's ghost and Magdalene's voice, like warning angels, entreating me to turn back.

But I do not, even though my journey is further hampered by what I drag behind me—not only these fears but also an enormous pie pan. I spotted it some days earlier at the peddlers' square, where a keen-eyed tinker asked several coppers for it. Refusing to give up Matheus's copper, I convinced him to settle on a slightly lower—but still costly—price. I try not to think how this expense, added to the costs of my journey and the silver I have insisted on paying Mena and Annika for my board, brings Tycho's purse that much closer to empty. Resting on top of the pie pan is a crust reinforced with metal wire and as large and hard as a plaster. The night before, I had waited till Mena was asleep, then quietly baked it in her kitchen upon the pie pan, setting it to cool in a corner of the courtyard, concealed beneath a pile of leaves.

It is Mena who taught me how to bake and, as I settle in the shadows outside the door to the kitchens to wait for Robert, I long for Annika and Mena and the safety I have left behind. The past two weeks I have spent with them seem most dear, like the last temperate days of autumn before the arrival of the winds and rain. In her warm kitchen, Mena made dishes just for me and slipped me the tenderest bites of the family's meals. And every night, after putting her charges to bed, Annika would join us in the kitchen, where she would stroke my head and tell me the stories of my infancy—my wild excitement over a ditty about mice, my first tooth, the time I nearly crawled into the fire. Though faced with much larger perils, I found myself comforted by the very smallness of these moments, and the glimpse they gave me of my earliest self.

But in one respect I was not honest with Annika and Mena, for I concealed the true reason for prolonging my visit. Instead of revealing my plan to sneak into the palace and confront Maria, I told them only that I wished to inquire discreetly around the city into my mother's identity; also that I awaited an important letter from Uraniborg. I knew they would not approve of the danger I meant to put myself in, and feared that if I revealed my scheme, they would inform Maria, who would once again betray me.

The only soul who knows what I intend to do is Robert. But as the bells of St. Michael and St. Gudula Cathedral toll a quarter past midnight, I fear that he has reconsidered his role as accomplice. I cannot blame him, for when he last tried to help one of the Infanta's dwarfs, he was punished most severely. For the first time that night, I no longer despair that I will be caught but that I will never know the truth about who bore me and why she sent me away. I try to calm myself by looking up at the stars and finding the ones that Tycho has marked upon his globe.

It is at this moment that the door to the kitchens swings open and light floods my startled face. I have foolishly failed to step far enough back, and fear my adventure is over before it has even begun. But the hulking figure of Robert, followed by the rumbling wheels of a small cart, transforms my terror into joy.

"I could not come directly at midnight, for one of the cooks was about," he whispers in his deep slurring voice, closing the door behind him.

"It is no matter," I reassure him with a generosity born of revived spirits. "I have the pie right here. If you lift the crust, I shall crawl inside. If anyone asks, I am a gift to the Infanta's dwarfs, who performed most admirably this evening, from the Infanta."

Robert's eyes flicker with mirth at the sight of the pie pan.

"You are most clever, Jepp."

"It will be a wondrous dish." I am pleased by his praise and, for the first time all evening, I feel a master of my fate. "All you must do is wheel me to Maria's chamber. After pushing the cart inside, close the door and conceal yourself in the sitting room till you hear my call."

"Are you certain of this, Jepp?"

In an instant, my boldness vanishes. I am reminded that it is not just my own capture and punishment I risk but Robert's too. I think of how I left him to be beaten by the guards that morning in the courtyard after they caught him and Lia. I cannot, in good conscience, allow him to sacrifice himself again, especially when my suspicion that Maria is my mother could still prove to be mistaken.

I look up at his trusting face and misshapen jaw. "I am certain of nothing. Which is why I would not fault you if you chose at this moment to abandon this scheme. You have suffered enough for us."

Robert does not answer but easily bends over and lifts the pie pan onto the cart. He wears a stubborn gaze that reminds me of Lia as he fingers the edge of the crust.

"Are you ready?" he asks.

But I continue to look up at him, for I fear he has not seriously considered the consequences of his choice. The more I worry on his behalf, the more I am certain that he should return at once to his quarters. But from the look on his face, I possess little hope of dissuading him. All I can do is devise a way to protect him should tragedy befall us.

"Wait. You must promise to abandon me if there is trouble. Deny all knowledge of this plot. Curse or capture me if you must."

Robert regains his old smile. "I cannot do that."

"You must!" I plead, in desperation. "For I have abandoned you. I left you to be beaten by the guards after your escape with Lia. I should have told them that it was Pim who abused Lia, but I feared for myself first. No matter what you hear from the sitting room, do not come until you are called. You must promise me this, or I will go alone."

Robert leans down and puts one large hand upon my shoulder. "I promise, Jepp. But you did me no wrong—then or ever."

"Lift me into the pie."

I am relieved that he does this hastily, for I am overwhelmed both by gratitude and shame. I take one last glance at the starry sky before he slides the crust over my head. Just this once I am glad to be entombed for, muffled by pastry, I need not suppress my tears. Having seen so much of the world, I realize that it is no longer cruelty that makes them flow, but the persistence of kindness.

With wet eyes, I leave the realm of sight and enter that of sound. The door creaks open, and a rumbling vibration fills my ears as Robert pulls the cart into the maze of kitchens. I am certain that some of the cooks are awake and at their stations lest the Infanta or the archduke demand a midnight meal. But I hear no voices and suspect that Robert has selected a route through those kitchens that prepare meals for the servants and guards, as they would be abandoned at this hour.

As the rumble of the wheels grows softer, I understand that we have passed out of the kitchens and onto the smooth marble floors of the palace's central hall. There are voices here, distant yet echoing—shouts and laughter from revelers likely retired to nearby chambers. Far off, a woman's shrill wail sounds, then abruptly dies out, leaving me unsure whether it was issued in passion or despair. A pair of clattering heels approaches, then stops. I hold my breath. A courtier—tittering with drink—makes some gibe about Robert's tremendous appetite. But then, to my relief, his stumbling footsteps resume and fade.

A moment later, I hear Robert's labored breath as he carries the cart up the stairs toward my former quarters, a task that would normally require the strength of three men. As the wheels touch down on solid ground, I realize how far I have made it and how close I may be to the truth. But I am also trapped here, for I know that should Maria raise an alarm or once again betray me, the only door that leads outside from this wing of the palace is locked.

The wheels of the cart rumble beneath me, then slow to a halt as Robert delivers me to Maria's door. I hear him knock upon it softly, not wishing to wake Hendrika, whose own chamber is not far down the hall. No one answers; and I am beginning to fear she is not even there when the door opens, and Robert pushes the cart inside.

Chapter
46

"**Wh**o is it? Is it you?" Maria says, her voice slurred with sleep, or hippocras, or both.

The door closes behind me as Robert retreats. Then bed covers rustle, and I imagine Maria rising. For a moment, I wonder if she has been expecting me; perhaps Annika could not help herself and told Maria of my return to Brussels. But then I realize that the "you" she expects could be someone else entirely. In the silence that follows, I envision her donning her dressing gown and lighting a candle from the embers of the hearth only to discover the curious sight of a large pie set in front of her door. I tell myself to rise out of the crust while I still have the element of surprise, but I cannot will myself to move, even as I hear her footsteps, tripping ever closer.

I fear she heads to the hall to inquire about this strange gift, and so, as I once did, upon the count of three I lift up the crust and emerge from the pie.

"Jepp?!"

At the sight of me, red-faced from my confinement and with crumbs in my hair, Maria shakes her head as if she suspects I am not truly there but some phantom borne of drink. Her dressing gown is wrapped tightly around her stout body, her hair—threaded with gray—falls in loose waves past her shoulders.

"You do not imagine me," I say, clambering down from the cart and seizing her arm. "I am truly here."

At my touch, she jerks back, nearly falling. I right her, and she stares at me as if I have become one of the dangers from which Coudenberg is supposed to keep her safe.

"I need a sip of hippocras," she says.

She tries to pull away, but I do not release my hold on her, for I fear that like the ancient sea god Proteus, she may yet again change forms. I think back to our argument the day I told her I meant to help Lia escape, how knowingly she spoke of my mother, how certain she seemed that I belonged at court.

"You once said that Coudenberg is who I am. What did you mean?"

Maria's lumpen face softens. "Where have you been, Jepp? What has happened to you?"

But I suspect she already knows the answers to these questions and is merely evading.

"I know my true mother is here. You knew Annika was my wet nurse. You are a dwarf like me."

Maria casts a longing glance at the drawer wherein her tinctures and spirits lie.

"I need you to speak truthfully," I say, following her gaze. "Are you my mother?"

My voice is commanding, my fingers dig deeper into her arm. Maria sighs as if I have won and she can no longer continue to deceive me.

"I am not."

I stare at her in confusion, for this is not the answer I expected. "I do not believe you."

But even to myself I sound uncertain. Though I still hold fast to her, Maria looks at me with pity, as if I am the one who is caught.

"If I were your mother, Jepp, I would never have sent you away as an infant," she says, shaking her head in disapproval of this action. "I would have raised you here at Coudenberg."

Though this argument is consistent with her faith in Coudenberg, I know there is some part of her, buried deep within, that does not believe the illusion that these walls protect us. It is this part of her that could have sent me away. It is the other part that could have later schemed to keep me here.

"Perhaps that is why you made certain that Lia and I could not escape," I say. "You wished for me to remain here, with you, so you instructed Annika to betray us—"

Maria wrenches herself out of my grip then turns to face me. "I did no such thing! I wished for both you and Lia to be safe. You were to go to Annika's only if you were not. In that case only, I told her to inform the palace—"

I feel my old frustration with Maria's misplaced faith return. "What safety did you expect us to find at Coudenberg? You know the cruelty of this place. She still died, and I was beaten and sent away."

"I would not have brought you back if I thought you would be sent away." Maria blinks back tears, as if exile from Coudenberg is a fate far worse than bodily harm or even death. "But that was your mother's doing."

"Who *is* my mother then?"

"I cannot tell you."

Maria turns away and marches briskly to her drawer. Though I am relieved that she is not my mother, there is a part of me that is disappointed, if only because I had hopes that she had once rebelled against the injustice of her situation. But as I watch her snatch up a clear vial and pour the contents into a goblet of hippocras, I push these emotions aside for, even though she is not my mother, she clearly knows who this woman is. I vow not to leave her room before I can shake the truth out of her.

"It was my mother who sent me away then after Lia died, not the Infanta?" I ask, though I have long suspected the Infanta did not order my exile.

Maria takes a long draught, briefly closing her eyes like a suckling babe. "The Infanta is merciful to her dwarfs," she says, when she opens them. "She would have punished you but eventually forgiven you."

There is one more mother to consider, though I am loath to do so, for she is the least appealing of them all. But I force myself back to the morning after Lia and I escaped Coudenberg. I remember Don dragging me into the Infanta's dungeon, tossing me into a cell, pummeling my face till the blood pooled in my eyes and I tasted it on my tongue. It was Hendrika who came to my rescue, pleading with Don. Had she simply been entreating him, as the mistress of the dwarfs for whom she had come to feel pity, not to beat me further? Or had she been asking him, as a mother, to do something more?

You have ruined me with this business, Don had said. At the time, I had assumed this was directed at me. But I was a child then, only dimly aware of the real forces that shaped my fate. What if he had not been chastising me at all, but Hendrika?

But before I can ask Maria whether these suspicions are true, a knock sounds at the door.

"Who else knows you are here?" Maria whispers frantically.

I hesitate, uncertain whether to reveal Robert's role, though I realize it must be evident that only he could have wheeled me single-handedly through the palace.

"Hide!" she orders. "It may not be a friend!"

I look frantically about her chamber for a place to conceal myself. But just as I dash toward Maria's bed, the door opens.

"Wake up. I have brought you your . . ."

The voice is not Robert's deep slur at all but a jaunty tenor that I had hoped never to hear again. It stops midsentence, and I know in that instant Pim has spotted me. I take the opportunity that his surprise affords to race past him out the door, a feat in which I am aided by his arms' being filled with the vials that hold Maria's spirits and sleeping tinctures. But as I dart down the hall, I hear a crash as he throws them to the ground and bolts after me. I make it halfway to the stairs before his hand closes around my arm and drags me to a stop.

"Titus," Pim says merrily as I vainly struggle to free myself. "How kind of you to pay us a visit. And to come by pie!"

Chapter 47

I must call out for Robert. There is no other way. Only he can wrench me from Pim's hands. Only he can subdue my tormenter long enough for me to escape. The sitting room is just down the hall and I am certain that he will come to my aid, yet I cannot bring myself to cry out. I have pledged not to put him in such a situation. For if Robert intervenes and I escape, Pim will see to it that he is grievously punished. It is I who chose to return to Coudenberg, to risk my freedom. It is I who must suffer now, not he.

But then I think of Magdalene, how my imprisonment will distress her. To love is to value the happiness of another as much as your own, and I love Magdalene more dearly than anyone on this earth. I cannot bear to sadden her. But neither can I bear the thought of Robert being once again beaten and abused. I must protect him.

"Look!" Pim says. He grabs my ankle and hoists me upside down, as the drunken peasants once did at my mother's inn. "The Infanta will be most delighted that her wayward dwarf has returned."

At first I think he addresses this comment to Maria, who has chased after us and gapes at the sight of my being dangled in the air. But then, as he turns, I realize that he is speaking to Hendrika, who stands barefoot before us in a long nightdress in the shadow of her open doorway.

Hanging upside down, I can see her narrow face, her lips pursed with displeasure, though whether with Pim or me, I cannot surmise.

"Let him go," she says, her voice stern.

I look at her gratefully, but she avoids my glance. I wonder if I am wrong, and she is not my mother. Perhaps she is merely protecting the Infanta's dwarfs, as is her job, and still means to turn me in.

Pim assumes a vexed expression save for his eyes, which crease with amusement. "But then he will fall."

"Put him down now."

Though she speaks quietly, there is a threat to Hendrika's voice that even Pim seems to hear. With a pout, he lowers me to the floor and rights me, but is careful not to release my arm. "I shall take him to the Infanta now, on his feet, if you will."

But Hendrika steps in front of him and takes hold of my other arm.

"Do that, and I shall tell her the truth about Lia."

It is as if the moon has slid from behind a cloud, for I know, upon these words, that Hendrika is my true mother. Though she has no apron to catch me in, she means to rescue me with this threat, and her intention illuminates every clue. I remember how anxious she was to meet me when I first arrived at Coudenberg, how little she cared for my country name, how she told me I was home. I think of the night I dreamt she was in my room, watching me, and am certain now this was no dream. I remember her clutching me to her bony breast after Don beat me in the dungeon. It was she who sprang me from this prison then, just as she endeavors to free me now.

But why did she give me up as an infant? Why did she have Don bring me back? How could she have allowed me, her child, to be stuffed into a pie, or herself to be my jailor once we were imprisoned with Lia? I know not whether to love her or despise her.

But I cannot give voice to any of this for fear of what is about to happen to us both. Pim has also been robbed of his prodigious powers of speech. The bemusement that always bedecks his jester's countenance vanishes as his face erupts into red blotches that match his hair.

"I will tell the Infanta as well," declares a haughty voice behind us.

We all turn to gaze at Sebastian, who stands defiantly outside his door clothed in a red velvet dressing gown. Though he makes for a comical sight, I am most gladdened by his presence. I remember how he always swore to protect himself first, and feel touched that he has made this exception.

"The Infanta will never believe you chose Jepp to perform a dance over me without some darker purpose in mind!" Sebastian adds with a loud huff.

His saucy tone seems to loosen Pim's tongue.

"Do you think the Infanta cares about any of you?" he says.

There is no anger in his voice, only pity. But this pity is worse than any cruel jest, for I realize he speaks the truth. I remember what Lia told me, that even if the Infanta were to learn of his misdeed, Pim would be only lightly punished. And if he delivers me back into her hands, the Infanta will likely not even punish him at all. Our threat is no threat at all.

"Robert!" Maria shouts. "Help! Help us!"

Her cry startles us all. It is loud and fierce, as though she summons some avenging angel.

Pim wrenches me out of Hendrika's grasp and begins to run, dragging me down the hall as I kick and struggle. But Maria's plea raises Robert, who bursts out of the sitting room and down the hall after us, his face scowling and fearsome. His gait is loping and ungainly, but just as my own legs could never escape Pim's much longer ones, so does Pim fail to outrun Robert. With one enormous hand, Robert grabs him around the neck and yanks him backward as I tumble, released, to the floor.

I look up, expecting Pim to threaten Robert with ruin; but my old tormenter's face is red, and his mouth gapes as he struggles for breath. Robert stares murderously at him, his hand unrelenting as it squeezes Pim's neck. I look at Maria, who having summoned Robert, can surely stop him, but her eyes narrow and she turns away. I am certain she is thinking about what Pim said, the sacrilege of his words. I realize that it isn't just the illusion of safety she has cherished here at Coudenberg, but the illusion of being cared about, even loved.

"Stop!" I say.

But Robert seems not to hear me. He continues to throttle Pim.

"Stop!" I plead, running to Robert's side and reaching up to touch his free hand with my own. "We are all sinners."

As if a spell has been broken, Robert looks curiously down at me. Then he releases Pim, who falls to his knees, gasping and clutching at his throat. Beside the wheezing sound of Pim's breath, the hall is silent. I am vastly relieved that he is still alive and that Robert has not damned himself. Yet I am certain now that Pim will find a way to punish and destroy those who have protected me—not only Robert but Maria, Sebastian, and Hendrika, as well. I feel I have cursed them all by coming back. My mind whirls as I try to devise a way to stop Pim, but I am unable to think up a single ploy.

"Robert," Hendrika says, breaking the silence. "Pick Pim up. We'll need rope to bind him."

Her face is ashen, but her voice is steady, almost calm. It is strange to finally see this side of her, the one that schemes. Here is the woman who for so long pulled the strings of my destiny. But, at this moment, I do not judge her for that. I only hope she can save us.

Hearing her words, Pim, still gasping, tries to crawl away; but Robert scoops him off the floor as easily as Pim did me.

"After you tie him up," Hendrika continues, "take him to Maria's room. Maria—"

But Maria does not answer. The fury that had been etched on her face has subsided, replaced by a look of confusion that suggests it is impossible for her to act and then retreat back into illusion. I long to tell her that she is not alone or unloved, and that kindness does exist in the world beyond Coudenberg. But there is no time for such comfort.

"Maria!" Hendrika repeats, in a tone so harsh I feel my old revulsion for her return.

Maria quivers, then looks up at her.

"Listen to me. After he is tied, give Pim several cups of your hippocras and some laudanum."

"I understand," Maria says, her voice subdued.

"If he will not take it, Sebastian, hold his nose."

"If he still refuses may I cover his mouth as well?" Sebastian asks.

"Sebastian!" I say.

Hendrika ignores this devilish comment. "Robert, when Pim is asleep, untie him and leave him at the bottom of the stairs. I will discover him there early in the morning and alert the guards."

She turns to Pim, who sputters wordlessly, though whether it is with rage or breathlessness, I cannot tell.

"You will be drunk tonight, Pim. None of this happened. Some kitchen maid you forced yourself upon will say she left that welt upon your neck."

I must admit that Hendrika's plan is truly ingenious, but I am disappointed that there is no role in it for me. After all, it is I who put the others in danger.

"What can I do?"

Hendrika looks surprised as if the answer to this question is obvious. "You are to come with me."

Robert steps forward uncertainly.

"She will not harm him," Maria says, with a knowing glance at Hendrika.

Upon Maria's assurance to Robert, Hendrika takes my hand and leads me into her chamber.

Chapter 48

I have risked everything for this moment, but now, as Hendrika releases my hand and busies herself lighting candles, I do not know what to say or even how to feel. There is a part of me that rejoices that I have a provenance now. But I cannot bring myself to embrace this mother. I fear she is not the one I want. I fear she will push me away. I have finally solved part of this great mystery of my birth and yet, instead of satisfaction, I feel only indecision and uncertainty.

Her room illuminated, Hendrika turns to me. Now that we are alone, I notice that her commanding air has disappeared. Her expression is timid, as if she knows not how to proceed either. I am struck by her height. I might have shared it were it not for my fate or perhaps for my father who, it occurs to me, could have been a dwarf she tended to. As it is, I still share her dark hair and eyes. I feel as if I should call her by her true name, but the word *Mother* dies upon my lips. What mother would give up her child? What mother would allow him to be mocked and abused?

"There is nowhere to sit," she says, looking dismally at her single large chair.

It is a relief to put aside these questions and concentrate on a practical matter.

"I can sit on the bed," I say.

I begin to scramble up the side when long fingers grip me about the waist and hoist me up. I jerk around to face Hendrika, meaning to scold her for this unwanted assistance, but she clasps me to her bony breast, just as she did in the Infanta's dungeon when she rescued me from Don. I feel at once both comforted and suffocated, but with my arms pinned to my sides, I am relieved of the choice of whether to return her embrace.

"Why did you come back?" she says, rocking me, though her tone is more dirge than lullaby.

"My mother died and—"

Hendrika stops rocking me and stiffens, though I feel I have made no error.

"I know I was born here. That you are . . ."

But I still cannot bring myself to call her my mother. "Why did you give me away?"

Hendrika releases me and stands awkwardly beside the bed, her hands clasped together as if in supplication.

"You are my sin."

At first, I think she has said *my son*, and it pains me to have misheard. Like every child, I wish to be my mother's joy, not the cause of her perdition.

"Your father was married, Jepp. Our indiscretion was brief. When I discovered my condition, I was deeply ashamed."

Though I do not recall hearing that Don was ever married, I suspect him of such mischief. "You speak of Don Diego?"

At this, Hendrika shakes her head most vehemently. From her bedside table, she picks up the painted likeness of the gentleman in the fur cape and holds it out to me. In that instant, it occurs to me who this man truly is.

"Don Diego's elder brother?"

Hendrika nods. "He was a powerful courtier, a favorite of the Infanta's."

I have at last solved the mystery of my paternity. Just like Magdalene, I am the child of a nobleman who could not bequeath me his name. But unlike Magdalene, whose father raised her, I shall never know the man who gave me life. His death grieves me not because I knew him as a father, but because I never will. I take the likeness and study it, searching in it for a reflection of myself.

"What kind of man was he? Was he clever? Was he kind?"

Hendrika peers down at the likeness as if she too seeks in it the answers to my questions. "He was accustomed to fortune smiling upon him. He was sanguine and charming."

Although I see the resemblance in our dark coloring and heavy brow, this description suggests that my father was not much like me. Instead, he seems to have led a blessed life, one that, as Liv might say, would fit in a single volume.

"Did you tell him about me? Did you acknowledge me as his own?"

"He knew and provided for you. But he never saw you. It was Don Diego who found you a nurse and ensured her discretion so I could return to court before my absence bred gossip."

It pains me to think that I have spent so long wondering about my father when he exhibited so little curiosity about me, tasking his younger brother with the practical matters of my care. All at once, I feel sickened by this reminder that Don is my relation, as if I have eaten the entire pie in which I had just entombed myself.

"He has been a good uncle to you," Hendrika says, perhaps anticipating my objections.

"He beat me!"

Hendrika begins to pace beside the bed. "You do not understand. It was I who gave you away, who abandoned you! For nearly a year the nurse cared for you, but when Don Diego told me she suspected you were a dwarf, my shame deepened. I begged your father to find you a home far away from court."

My father was of the class of powerful, heartless men who would keep a dwarf as a plaything. I cannot help but wonder how such a man would feel about having me as a son.

"What did my father think of my being a dwarf? Was he also ashamed?"

"Our affair had long ended. He was busy man. He had his family, his legitimate children, his position and intrigues at court. He seemed little troubled by this news."

But I take no solace that my father did not mind I was a dwarf if he hardly seemed to care about me.

"He did not love me, did he?"

Hendrika shakes her head vigorously. "You must never think that, Jepp! He was generous and loved you in his own way. He sent Don Diego to find you a good family and give them fifty gold coins for your care."

I recall how Willem had said that Don had given my mother nothing, and feel my ire at him return. Fifty gold coins would have been a great fortune to my mother. But Hendrika seems so agitated by her confession that I cannot bring myself to strip her of the meager comfort she seems to derive from imagining this to be true.

"They were good people," I say.

Hendrika waves her hand as if this means nothing. "At first I was relieved you were gone. But as the years passed, I could think of nothing else. The sin of giving you away eclipsed that of my indiscretion with your father. I could not marry, could not envision bearing other children. I was on the verge of taking vows when I heard the Infanta was seeking a gentlewoman to care for her dwarfs. Looking after them, I could imagine you."

As she says this, I feel tenderness for her stir in my breast. I much prefer Hendrika's guilt to my father's blithe indifference. But then I remind myself that it was she who decided to bring me back to Coudenberg. It was this decision that caused the chain of misfortune that cost me Lia and the mother who raised me.

"But this was not enough?" I say, barely concealing my disdain.

Hendrika winces. "After your father died, I asked Don Diego to bring you back. So many years had passed, I felt there was little danger anyone would guess your true identity—"

I wonder why Don agreed to bring me back, for I little believe, as Hendrika seems to do, in his kinship or the kindness of his heart. But I put aside this question for another, more pressing one.

"Did you not think there would be a danger I would be stuffed into a pie?"

"The Infanta's dwarfs were well-tended, beloved. Until you arrived, there seemed little harm in such follies."

"Little harm—?"

"It was a mistake, Jepp!" she cries, dropping all pretense of conviction. "Bringing you here. I came to realize I had been selfish. It was a terrible mistake."

She seizes her rosary beads off the bed table and begins to pray, stopping this frantic exercise only to wipe a stray tear from her cheek. For a moment, I see her as I did the night of All Souls' when she alone among us truly prayed, fingering her beads on her knees in the cathedral. I wonder now if she was praying for me. Though I cannot disagree with her words, the harshness with which she delivers this judgment against herself makes me pity her. For wasn't her sin, as so many are, committed out of love?

I reach for her hand, trying to still its incessant motion. "You should have told me who you were."

Her hand clutches mine, releasing the beads to her other palm, and we remain silently like this. I think of Magdalene and Robert and how they forgave me for Lia's death in a way I felt the Lord himself could not. Though the fathers of the church would no doubt disagree, perhaps true mercy comes not from up on high but from those beside us.

At last, Hendrika slides onto the bed beside me and, with a surprisingly girlish motion, clutches her gown about her knees, revealing the bony, white feet I remember from the long ago Coudenberg night when she slipped into my room to watch over me. "I did not tell you because I could not care for you here as a son, only as a dwarf."

"But you did," I remind her. "Was it not you who had Don Diego send me away after Lia died?"

This she does not deny. "I knew by then you did not belong here, nor would you ever be happy among us."

I cannot argue with these words. But, once again, I wonder why Don agreed to honor Hendrika's wishes, especially at the risk of displeasing the Infanta.

"Did you know where Don Diego was sending me?"

Hendrika shakes her head, her eyes searching my own. "He found you a good home before, I trusted he would do so again. Was I mistaken?"

I am tempted to tell Hendrika of the indignities I first suffered at Uraniborg, but my eventual triumph there makes me think that, on this count at least, Don Diego truly did me no wrong.

"No. Lord Tycho is most fond of me."

The taut lines about Hendrika's eyes soften. "Why would it be otherwise?"

For a moment, I have a mother again and wish never to leave her. "Come with me!" I implore. "We could return to Uraniborg together. It is a most magnificent castle. There is a fountain the likes of which you have never seen. Lord Tycho will welcome you—"

She gently releases my hand and smooths a lock of my hair. "You are no longer a boy. You no longer need a mother."

It is my turn to protest. "But I do!"

Hendrika rises from the bed. "It is not safe for you here, Jepp. You must depart."

She waves me down from the bed but offers no embrace nor even a hand to help me clamber down. I think she fears that if she touches me again, she will not be able to let go. But I find it hard to pity her, for her words have left me most forlorn. Our interview is over, and I am still both motherless and fatherless.

I slide off the bed, my legs dangling, until my feet land hard on the floor. "I suppose it is safest for me to go back inside the pie."

"No!"

I look up, surprised by the vehemence in her voice. She walks across the room, opens a drawer, and fetches something from inside. Then she returns to me and crouches down. In her pale palm is a key similar to the one I stole from her so that Lia and I might escape.

"Take it," she says, placing it in my hand. "It opens the door leading outside, at the bottom of the stairs. But I beg of you, Jepp, do not come back."

I know she can little more be a mother to me now than when I was born. But it touches me that she gives me the key to my freedom, and I feel most injured that she wishes not to see me again. As if sensing this, she grasps my head between her hands and kisses my brow. "I love you, child. Now, go!"

But instead I throw my arms around her. Our faces press together. My cheeks become wet, though I know not whether it is with her tears or my own.

"Go," she whispers, though she does not release me.

I know it is I who must let go. And yet I cling to her for, though she has anointed me a man, I do not think I can be one. I can only choose not to prolong our parting, not to torment us both further.

With a muffled sob, I dash out the door, down the hall, and to the stairs. I know I should bid farewell to Robert, Maria, and Sebastian, but I trust Hendrika will protect them. Besides I have no more strength for good-byes. It does not take me long to reach the little door through which I first entered Coudenberg two years ago with Don. I shove the key Hendrika gave me into the keyhole and hear the lock click. Then I turn the knob and push open the door into the chill November night.

Swallowed up by darkness the world seems large, and I a man of little consequence in it. As I slip back through the garden toward the road, I realize that I did not even ask Hendrika my true name.

Chapter 49

By the time I reach Rollebeek Straat, I am numb with cold and exhaustion, which blessedly extends to not only my body but also my heart. I can think no more of what I have learned about my father, or of the mother I have left behind—only of my own longing for warmth and sleep's forgetfulness. As I slip through the kitchen door and into Mena's room, I do not even bother to undress but collapse upon my pallet, the key Hendrika gave me clenched in my hand.

I awake the next morning to Mena's concerned face looming over me.

"Are you unwell, Jepp?" she asks.

Her gray hair is coated with flour and her apron smeared with stains. Like a clock, this soiled garment tells me it is long past dawn.

"I am . . . just tired," I say, sitting up.

Mena studies the cloak still wrapped about my shoulders but says nothing. Instead, she reaches into her apron pocket and pulls out a sealed letter.

"It arrived for you this morning from Uraniborg."

I snatch the letter from her. There is suddenly nothing I want more than to hear Magdalene's voice. As soon as Mena departs, I tear open the seal.

21 November, 1599

Dear Jepp,

I did not intend to write you in anger but neither did I expect to receive such a letter as you sent me. You now act as if the stars are everything, as if the accident of birth is the only measure of a man. The stars, your parents, your past—none of them can tell you who you are. You know who you are by the choices you make and the feelings in your heart.

You ask me to forgive you for not being the Jepp we both thought you were. But there is nothing to forgive, because I know you are still the Jepp I love. I can only entreat you one final time to come home. It _is_ possible to reclaim your future, to build a happy life despite an imperfect past. We _can_ order the universe with our will and mind. For those are the dreams that God gave us, and which bring us closer to Him.

Lest you doubt this, I assure you that there is still a woman helpful and true. But I cannot wait for you endlessly. My nights are restless imagining the dangers you face and the cruelty of the world beyond this island. If you love me, you will choose to return so we may begin our life here together. Your actions will be your answer.

Whether or not we see each other again, may the Lord be

with you now and always and graciously preserve you from all harm.

Magdalene Tygesdatter

I put this correspondence down on my pallet and try to still the tumult of emotions it has unleashed. I knew my trip to Brussels would distress Magdalene. But it pains me to have worried her, especially when solving the mystery of my birth has not given me the answers I had hoped for. I had expected that my parents would tell me who I am, that their lives would guide my own. Instead, I have discovered that I am nothing like them. Last night seems to me but a dream, one that has left me little satisfied upon waking. I have no mother or father to help me, nor even a name.

I take the lion's fleur-de-lis heart from my pocket and begin to pace Mena's bedroom. In the love it signifies, it seems the most precious object in the world and, as I hold it up to my own heart, I think of how I must get back to Magdalene. She alone knows who I am. She is not only the interpreter of my stars but of my self. I cannot lose her. But Tycho's purse has grown so light that its meager contents would never secure me a coach all the way back to Elsinore. I think, too, of how Tycho advised me to return to Uraniborg with a fortune of my own if I wished to present myself as a proper suitor.

I must believe Magdalene—that the stars are not everything, that my actions can alter my destiny. I must reclaim the fifty gold coins that my father meant for me but that Don stole. This may not be a bottomless fortune, but it is enough for my passage back to Elsinore and to show Tycho I have secured some means of my own. I begin to tidy my disheveled appearance, for I have resolved to pay a visit to Don that very morning.

Chapter 50

It takes me much of the morning to find Don's house. I have only a poor recollection of it from the morning after Lia's death, when he brought me there to bequeath me to Matheus. But I remember that it stood near the Cathedral of St. Michael and St. Gudula and, after making some inquiries of the servants who work in the houses that surround it, I am directed to a grand house perched on the slope of Treurenberg Hill, where the upper city descends into the lower. Like the houses of Rollebeek Straat, it boasts many floors and a profusion of shutters, but it is freestanding and with its own stables. From this, I can only imagine the opulence of its interior. This further emboldens me to ask for the monies that are rightfully mine.

But as I draw a deep breath and march to the front entrance, I hear a familiar voice call from behind.

"Jepp!"

I turn around. Standing near the stables is Matheus. He smiles at me but, at the sight of him, I am reminded of my cage and the cruel ride that Don ordered him to oversee. If I confront Don, he could easily force me upon such a wretched journey again.

"It is I, Matheus," he says, perhaps thinking that I do not recognize him. His smile fades, replaced by a look of apprehension. "You are well?"

His gaze is most beseeching, and it occurs to me that he wishes to know not only whether I am well but whether I forgive him the role he played in my exile. I think of the small comforts he allowed me in defiance of Don's orders, and the genuine concern over my welfare he showed as he delivered me to a master as strange as Tycho. If my journey since first leaving Astraveld has taught me anything, it is the lesson of returning such compassion.

"I am well, Matheus," I say. "And I have something to return to you."

I take the bent copper from Tycho's purse and hand it to him.

Matheus studies the coin in his palm, then closes his fingers around it, clutching it to his chest. "I thought it lost," he says softly.

"May it once again bring you luck."

Matheus smiles. But then he looks over his shoulder at the grand home looming behind us, and his smile quickly fades. "You had best be going, Jepp."

"I have come to see Don."

Matheus's forehead creases with worry, and I once again fear what Don will do to me if I confront him. But I cannot let fear prevent me from being reunited with Magdalene.

"Be careful," he says. "And expect little from him."

Then, with a nod, he turns and vanishes into the stables.

This admonition leaves me unsettled, but I am determined not to turn back. I approach the front door and rap upon it. At first, no one answers but I persist until a woman's voice—shrill and common—shouts back at me.

"The master is not here!"

Unwilling to believe this, I continue knocking until the door swings open.

"I told you—" says a wisp of a woman with a disheveled mane of ginger-colored hair. Though it is near noon, she wears a dressing gown and the peeved expression of one disturbed. But when she catches sight of me, she seems to lose her voice. I take advantage of her astonishment.

"Where is Don Diego?" I ask. "I must speak with him at once."

She steps back, allowing me to enter a foyer through which I see a hallway leading to other rooms. But as I glance into the rest of the house, it is not what I imagined from the outside. No rich tapestries line the walls, nor velvet curtains to cover paintings. Nor do I see a single servant, save for this woman who seems neither mistress nor maidservant as she stands in her bedclothes before me.

"Don Diego!" she shouts. "There is a . . . a dwarf here who demands to see you."

There is no response. Then Don's voice echoes through the empty house.

"Send him up, then go."

"But I must dress!"

"Show him up, then," Don shouts.

I follow the woman up a staircase and down another barren hallway to a room at the back of house. This chamber conforms

better to my expectations, for here at least are traces of elegance—
a canopied bed covered with fur throws and rumpled linens; four
red lacquered armchairs; a small silver mirror. Don sits, his back
facing us, at a small desk covered with inkpots, paper, seals, and
quills. He ignores us as the woman gathers up her partlet and
gowns from one of the chairs, squeezes her purse to see whether
Don has replenished it, and rushes out.

As soon as she departs, Don turns to regard me. His bearded
face with its dark, piercing eyes is unchanged from the morning I
last beheld it, when he swore I would never know my mother and
home again. About this, he was both right and wrong. But now
I recognize in those eyes the resemblance between us, though it
once again disgusts me to think we share this bond of blood.

"What do you want, Jepp?" he asks wearily.

Though his mood does not seem violent, I remind myself
that there is no Hendrika nearby to protect me if I anger him.
But if I wish to return to Magdalene, I cannot let my fears dic-
tate my actions.

"I have come for the monies I am owed."

Don stares at me uncertainly, his face set in a wary mask.
"What monies?"

But I am little fooled by this show of ignorance. "The monies my father, your brother, gave you for my care! You never gave
them to the mother who raised me, as my father ordered you."

I expect Don to bristle at this charge, but instead he laughs
easily. As he procures the splinter of a chicken bone from his
desk, I wonder why he seems relieved.

"So," he says, scraping it against his teeth, "You have finally
discovered who you are! Congratulations, Jepp."

I feel infuriated that he does not even acknowledge me as his
kin. "I am your own brother's son! How could you steal from me?"

Don lunges out of his seat toward me. My boldness dissolves into terror, and I leap back for fear he means to let a fist fly at my head. But his hands remain at his sides as he glares down at me. "Do you not know the trouble you have caused me?" he says in a thunderous voice. "It was I who found you a nurse, then a mother who would have you when your own would not. Your father could not be bothered—"

This mention of my father revives my hope of paternal affection, for surely Don, his own trusted brother, knew my father's heart better than Hendrika. "Did my father ever ask about me? Did he ever speak of me before he died?"

But my questions serve only to further irritate Don. "Never a word! He left everything to his true family. It was I who retrieved you, who gave you a life of riches—"

It injures me anew to hear that my father never inquired about me, even on his deathbed. But as I listen to Don rave about my life of riches at Coudenberg, I realize that it was he who must have profited greatly from my arrival at court. Though I hear myself breathing fast for fear he may yet pummel me, I unleash the angry words that fill my heart. "The life of great fortune was yours, Don, not mine! Did not the Infanta handsomely reward you for finding her another dwarf?"

From the way he scowls, I know I have guessed his true motivation for agreeing to bring me back to Coudenberg.

"A dwarf who insulted her with his disobedience?" Don snaps. "Who helped kill her favorite? You caused me more misfortune than anything else. I angered the Infanta further by sending you away to Uraniborg against her wishes. It is *I* who should be demanding recompense from you!"

I stare at him hard, sensing an evasion in all this false outrage.

"Why did you send me away, then, if you knew it would cause you such suffering?"

Don collapses back into his chair and shakes his head as if I have failed to comprehend the most obvious of reasons.

"I am your uncle, Jepp. I want only what is best for you."

He flashes a disappointed smile, all traces of his violent mood of just moments earlier gone. This insane transformation of Don's character unsettles me, but even greater than my fear is my disgust at so transparent an attempt to disarm me. It only makes me more certain that he conceals some other, depraved motive. I wonder whether he has abused me in some other way I cannot yet fathom.

"I still do not understand why you sent me away," I press. "You have shown me little kinship, unless you count beatings and imprisonment in a cage as an uncle's love."

Once again, I fear my boldness will inflame him, but Don seems little affronted by this charge. "I have merely sought to correct flaws in your character, Jepp, to mold you."

His dark eyes crinkle with paternal affection and I realize that he is enjoying his own performance and has no intention of telling me the truth.

Don laughs at my unyielding frown. "You can glower at me all you want," he says with a shrug, "but there is nothing to return. Fifty gold coins is no great sum, and I spent it long ago. Without the Infanta's favor my own fortunes have declined, and the creditors bang on my door. I am finished here. I leave soon for Spain."

I do not doubt his honesty on this point, for it explains why this grand house is nearly empty and the servants gone. But even if Don's ruin is complete, I know he conceals some greater truth still, for I do not believe that he would have sent me away from Coudenberg without some selfish motive. And I cannot even take pleasure in his downfall for, once again, our fates are tied together. Though fifty gold coins may be no great sum to Don, without it, I cannot return to Uraniborg or dare ask for Magdalene's hand. I struggle not to betray the devastation I feel upon realizing this. But Don sees some flicker of it, for he opens a drawer and fishes around inside it.

"I am sorry, Jepp. I gave most of what is here to the girl. One must have a little happiness, you understand. But here is something for your trouble."

He holds out a handful of coppers, but this paltry sum is an insult when he owes me so much more.

"I do not need your charity," I say curtly.

Don shoves the coins toward me. "Do not let your pride intervene, Jepp," he says, once again assuming a fatherly manner. "I know it is not much, but remember you are now a Pisces, the sign of two fishes. Was it not with just two fishes that our savior, Jesus Christ, fed the multitudes?"

I push away his hand so violently that I overturn it, and the coins clatter to the floor.

His nostrils flare as he stares at me in disbelief.

"You, Don Diego, are a thief," I say.

I turn and walk toward the door, forcing myself not to run though, at any moment, I expect him to yank me back and beat me. But as I continue down the hallway, I hear no footsteps behind me. All is silent save for a light thump. I imagine Don falling to his knees, not to seek forgiveness, but to gather up the spilled coins.

I race down the stairs, nearly crashing into Matheus, who waits at the bottom. One large hand seizes my shoulder.

"I wish I could help you, Jepp," he whispers.

The look of anguish upon his face eclipses my anger at Don. I realize he must have overheard our quarrel over the fifty gold pieces. I reach up my hand and touch his own. "I know, Matheus. But by saying so, you have."

Matheus shakes his head as if he little agrees, but his hand releases my shoulder and he leads me to the door.

"Do not despair," he whispers, as he hurries me out.

But how can I not despair when the very outcome he predicted has come to pass? I have received nothing from Don. As I step out onto the street, my terrible fury returns. My plan has failed. My hope of a fortune is gone. I know there is some other reason Don banished me from Coudenberg, but I am powerless to discern what it could be. Like so much of my life, I am bedeviled by a missing piece, and without it, I cannot see the truth of the world clearly. I have tried to be the man of action that Magdalene insists I can be. Yet I am still helpless, a victim of fate.

That evening, after I have packed my meager belongings, I sit before the fire in Mena's room, thinking about my two horoscopes. Am I Pisces the fish or Aquarius the waterbearer? Am I dragged along by fortune's hook, or can I control the very elements, as Tycho does? When I take the lion's hard fleur-de-lis heart out of my pocket and think of Magdalene, I believe that I can use my will and mind to order the universe. But when I think of Lia's delicate shell, I am not so certain. I think instead how easily the universe can crush us.

I do not know the answer to these questions. I only know the feelings in my heart. I take out my quill and ink and write to Magdalene.

5 December, 1599

Dearest Magdalene,

How it pains me to have angered you! It was never my intent to do so. I assure you that our love is no illusion. To the contrary, during this dark fall, it has been my one true light.

I have, at last, solved the mystery of my birth. My father is Don Diego's elder brother; he died several years ago, but was a mighty courtier and already married when he sired me. My mother is Hendrika, the woman who tended to the dwarfs at Coudenberg; at the time of my conception she was a lady-in-waiting at the court. Finding them has taught me who I am—but only so far as it has reminded me of who I am not. Whereas my father was an uncaring man, I believe in treating every soul—regardless of form or station—with compassion. Whereas my mother is an unforgiving woman, I believe in extending mercy to every sinner, even myself. I never did learn my true name, but perhaps, as you have argued, it little matters. No matter who I was in infancy, it is Jepp I have become. Just as you once told me that our imperfections forge our characters, I think now that it is our misfortunes and mistakes that are our true parents.

I promised you that by taking this journey I would determine, once and for all, whether I could choose my own future. On this count, I have failed for I am still uncertain of the answer. I agree that you can use intellect and will to make sense of the universe. But you cannot always change what fate decrees.

To wit, I wish more than anything I could come back to Uraniborg! But though it is the path I most desire, at this moment I am unable to return to you. Your father gave me a purse for this journey and it is nearly spent. And, even if I had the means to return, I have no fortune to support us, which we will need when the Eden of Uraniborg disappears, as we both know it someday will. I had hopes of securing some monies toward that end, but fate has conspired against me and I will insult neither you nor your father by returning empty-handed.

I dare not ask that you find me for I know you fear the world beyond Uraniborg. In truth, there is reason to do so, for there is much cruelty and evil here as well as kindness and good. But one of the graces of this world is that there is always some opportunity to show through our actions—be they ever so small or humble—who we are and what we truly believe. This is why I plan to use what little is left of your father's purse to make my way to Amsterdam. I am no stranger to work, and when I have managed to save a respectable sum for our life together, I will seek passage back to Elsinore. In time, I promise I will come home to you.

Please wait for me Magdalene! This is my plea. For you were right: after all my discoveries, I am still the same Jepp. And the Jepp I am—and forever will be—will always love you.

May the Lord almighty be with you now and always and graciously preserve you from all harm.

Jepp

Chapter 51

On a gray, late December morning, I stoke the hearth fire at Reynu Martens's inn. It has been nearly a month since I arrived in Amsterdam. Christmas has passed. With several more days until the New Year, the flow of travelers is light, and the inn, for the moment, is empty. I pour myself a mug of ale, climb into a chair, and quaff a few sips of it.

It is a rare moment of repose. Martens's inn is on the Damrak canal, halfway between the mouth of Amsterdam's harbor and Dam Square, where goods from around the world are weighed, taxed and transported. Nearly every day, ships bearing Polish grain or Venetian glass dock in the canal, disgorging weary Dutch sailors eager for a savory meal and a motionless berth. In the inn's great room, they join merchants from neighboring cities and other travelers drawn by the inn's carefully selected pretensions—French wine, oil paintings of a winter storm at sea, and Jonah and the whale—and proximity to the port's burgeoning commerce.

Reynu Martens appears from the storeroom. She is a widow, some fifty years of age and rich as Croesus, judging from the shower of coppers she collects nightly. At the sight of her, I slip off my chair, for I do not wish her to think me idle, but she waves me back up.

"Better to rest now," she says. "The *Vrede* and the *Dolphijn* are due into port in the next few days."

Reynu always has an eye on how to improve her fortunes. When I arrived in Amsterdam nearly a month ago, it was she who envisioned that the presence of a dwarf, delivering bottles of wine and lighting pipes, would further enhance the status of her inn. She offered me lodging plus a decent wage of half a silver each week. The days are long, and the men I serve range from the cultured to the coarse, but Reynu does not brook any serious abuse of me, and I have learned from my experience at court to parry what jests and insults come my way. There are kind men as well, who slip me coppers and tell me of their adventures in the Orient or on the Wild Coast of the New World. All in all, the rhythms of tavern life revive in me my mother's spirit, the mother who raised me and taught me to live in this world—as beautiful and ugly and wondrous and uncertain as it is.

But in the few moments I have to myself, like this one, my thoughts invariably return to Magdalene. I long for the intelligence of her observations, the slyness of her humor, the tenacity of her faith when she argues against me. I miss the way she forces me to question myself but at the same time does not allow me to doubt myself. I miss her exuberance, even her fear, for I know myself what it is like to gaze at the world from the outside.

As soon I arrived in Amsterdam, I sent Magdalene a letter informing her that I had found employ at Reynu's inn and reassuring her that I planned to stay only so as long as it took to establish a small fortune of my own. But over the past month, I have only managed to save two silver pieces toward this goal, and it will take me ten times that number to replenish Tycho's purse, and two hundred fifty times what I have to call it a fortune. I have heard there are cartographers here in Amsterdam who will employ men skilled in Latin and stargazing to assist them in their labors. I have begun to inquire about these positions, eager to engage my mind and add to my purse, but I little expect they will bring me instant fortune. More worrisome still, I have received no correspondence back from Magdalene. I even sent word to Annika and Mena, informing them where to send along any letters from Uraniborg, but none has arrived.

Come March, I will turn eighteen—the stolen year moving me swiftly into manhood—and the thought of the many months, even years, beyond this it will take me to return to Magdalene and ask Tycho for her hand leaves me most forlorn. As I take another sip of ale, I find the lion's heart in my pocket and caress it softly. But although the silver fleur-de-lis will never wither or die, I cannot mend the deep dents that Tycho wrought in it. I fear I have likewise wounded Magdalene's heart beyond repair and am filled with doubt that she will wait for me.

The door to the inn opens with a gust of sea air and a hefty, red-faced man in a woolen coat stumbles inside and looks about. With a start, I realize I know him.

"Jepp!" Matheus shouts, grinning wildly, as he hurries over.

His hair is bedraggled and his eyes rimmed by shadows as if he has been on the road day and night. I picture Don waiting in his coach outside, ready to spirit me away to yet another court. I contemplate shouting for Reynu, who has retreated to the storeroom.

"Where is Don Diego?" I ask.

Matheus shakes his head. "Don Diego? I did not come here on his behalf."

"What brings you here then?"

Matheus takes the seat opposite my own and cocks his head toward my mug. "Might I get a drink?"

I fetch him a cup, frothy with ale, and watch him gulp it down. Only when it is empty does he speak.

"Don Diego spoke truthfully when he told you he spent the fifty gold coins your father gave him. But he did not tell you that, in his will, your father left you an inheritance of three thousand gold pieces."

I am staggered by this sum, for it is a fortune befitting a son of noble birth. But what touches me equally is that my father kept me in his thoughts. Though he never knew me, he loved me enough to provide for me as his son.

"Don Diego was your father's executor," Matheus continues, "He was supposed to bequeath you these monies."

It now makes sense why Don seemed uncertain about exactly what fortune I had come to claim and why his mood lightened when he realized it was only the fifty gold pieces.

"Instead he collected a fine sum from the Infanta for bringing a new dwarf to Coudenberg and then, when he feared you would soon discover your true identity and learn of your father's will, he sent you to Tycho. He beat you first, and put you in the cage because he wished you never to return to Coudenberg, to fear him and that place, so you would never learn the truth."

This is why Don smuggled me out of Coudenberg—not because Hendrika begged him to, but rather because he dared not keep me there any longer. He preferred to anger the Infanta by banishing me against her orders than to risk losing three thousand gold pieces were I to unravel the secret of my birth.

I recall my visit to Don's barren house.

"But Don Diego is ruined. He must have already spent this fortune."

Matheus grunts. "He pretends to Hendrika and the rest of his creditors that he is ruined. But I have learned that he has hidden away your inheritance and means to take it to Spain. Only he will not have all of it."

At this, Matheus reaches into his coat and places a small, stout purse upon the table. "It is far less than you are owed, but it was all I could steal back. Take it, Jepp. It is yours. You are a good man, even to those, such as I, who have wronged you."

I hoist up the pouch. Judging from its weight, it contains more than double the fifty gold pieces I once set my hopes on. It is not the grand inheritance my father meant me to have, but it is enough. With it, I can return to Magdalene and present myself to Tycho as a suitor with at least modest means. I can start to build the future I want.

I clasp Matheus's rough hand.

"You have more than righted any wrongs," I assure him. "Do you mean to return to Brussels? I fear Don will suspect you—"

"He is no longer my master. I have abandoned his service. I mean to seek a better life here in Amsterdam."

"Let me help you."

I grab a handful of coins and hold them out to Matheus, but he waves them away.

"I have mine." He flashes me his bent copper as he rises. "I will accept only the draught of ale."

Upon these words, Matheus hastens to the door.

"Thank you," I call after him. "Thank you!"

The door closes behind him. I lift the coins, let them fall, listen to them clink together. It is the sound of freedom, and of a future that moments before seemed but a dream.

Chapter 52

The rest of the day, I can barely contain my happiness. I have proof, at last, of my father's love, and the means to ask Tycho for Magdalene's hand. All that remains is the practical matter of how to make the swiftest possible return to her. That evening, I weigh various routes to Uraniborg. I could pay for a seat on a wealthy merchant's coach traveling north or I could purchase a pony of my own. But the winter roads are snowy and rough, and I determine that the fastest way to Elsinore is by sea. I seek out Reynu and find her writing in her ledger in the storeroom.

"Do either the *Vrede* or the *Dolphijn* sail the Baltic route?"

"The *Vrede*," she says. "Why do you ask?"

There is something of my mother in Reynu, the industrious innkeeper, which makes me feel I can speak openly to her.

"I have recently learned that my father left me an inheritance. There is a girl in Denmark I plan to marry."

Reynu closes her ledger. "I will be sorry to lose you, Jepp, but this is happy news. Does she know your intentions?"

"Yes. She has been waiting for me."

But as I say this, my elation gives way to my former fears. Magdalene did not respond to my last two letters. What if I return only to discover that she no longer loves me, no longer wishes to be my wife? What if, like my mother, some tragedy has befallen her? While my father's inheritance can buy me passage to Uraniborg, it does not assure me of Magdalene's love.

Reynu must see this shadow of doubt cross my face. "The seas are stormy this time of year. Perhaps you should stay a few more months, write to the girl first—?"

I am confident that I can survive the ocean's treachery. I am less certain I can bear Magdalene's rejection. But of all the questions that have troubled me, there is no way I can leave this one—so fundamental to my very happiness—unanswered.

"Thank you for all you have done for me," I say. "But I must go."

Though the *Vrede* is due into port by the New Year, the days I must wait for it seem an eternity. I distract myself by carrying on with my work at the inn. I decide it is safest to wear the pouch Matheus gave me, keeping my fortune snug as a babe against me. I consider writing Magdalene to inform her I am coming, but it is unlikely the letter would reach her before my arrival. Besides which, I choose to remain hopeful that my return will be a happy surprise.

At last, late on the afternoon of the thirty-first, sailors begin to pour into the inn and, when I ask one of them, he confirms that the *Vrede* has just anchored in port. I am about to ask him the name of the ship's captain, so I might secure my passage with him to Elsinore, when a bearded man with a weathered face approaches us.

"Jepp?" he says.

"Yes."

Upon my affirmation, he smiles. "I have come from the *Vrede*. I have been asked to give you this correspondence."

He hands me a letter. My fingers quiver as I take it from him for, if he has picked up this missive along the Baltic route, it must be from Uraniborg. I hastily thank him, then carry the letter over to a corner of the inn farthest from any company. I take a deep breath—trying to quell my roiling heart—and open it.

31 December, 1599
Dear Jepp,
Shall we jump together?
Magdalene

I remember how Magdalene asked me this question as we stood on one side of the bonfire on St. John's Eve. But whereas I could not jump then, I am ready now. I clasp the letter to my breast, relieved that she is well and still loves me. As I imagine taking her hand and making the leap, I read the letter a second time. It is only then that I realize what I at first failed to see. The letter is dated today.

I clamber up onto a chair and search among the sailors that crowd the inn. But there is no girl among them. I dash out the door and into the early winter dusk, for I know she must be near.

"Magdalene?! Magdalene?"

A woman standing by the canal turns around. She wears a

heavy black coat and a ruff around her neck, the costume of a lady, but as she runs toward me, her face flushes and her pale hair flies about like the Magdalene I know. I run to meet her. She tumbles to her knees, laughing, as we embrace.

"You left Uraniborg?" I ask in Latin, though it is clear she has done so, for the warmth of her flesh tells me she is no apparition. "For me?"

Magdalene juts her chin with pride, for we both know how hard it must have been for her to leave the paradise of Uraniborg and venture alone into the world. "Not only for you."

I gently stroke her face, touch her scars as I think of my own, and the long, hard journey we have both taken to be together. Then I take her hand and lead her along the wharf of the Damrak Canal.

"I have a fortune now," I say, showing her the pouch of gold coins.

"Jepp!" she exclaims, bending over to kiss me. "How did you manage this?"

I tell her about my father's inheritance and how Matheus recovered a portion of it for me.

"So," she says. "Providence smiled down upon you at last."

I shake my head. "But it was I who chose to find out who I am, to confront Don, to befriend Matheus."

Magdalene laughs. "Let us put this old argument to rest. After all, we are both right."

I nod in agreement, for I know exactly what she means. Our stars, and the fates they spell out, constrain us. But so, too, through our will and intellect—and, most of all, our heart—can we make our own luck. Which of my two horoscopes is truly mine? Perhaps both.

"I was planning to return to Uraniborg on the *Vrede* to ask your father for your hand," I say.

Magdalene catches my eye. "Perhaps we need not hurry back."

As we near the end of the wharf, we are rewarded with a view of Amsterdam's harbor, clogged with ships. In every one, I see endless possibilities. The new century is upon us—with astonishing discoveries and great hopes that could be our own. I have heard the sailors talk about a new route to the East Indies and the fortune soon to be made off cloves, pepper, and other spices from the Orient. We could invest in such cargo. We could even sail to distant lands ourselves, like the Wild Coast of the New World, where Dutch sailors seek adventure and gold. Our lives could be many volumes, but united into a single story by our love.

Together we gaze up over the dozens of masts to the sliver of a new moon and the faint glow of the first evening stars.

"The stars here are the same as in Uraniborg," I say, thinking of Willem and how he reminded me that home is always with us.

"I should not be afraid, then?"

Magdalene smiles playfully, but the way her eyes delve into mine, I can tell she does not ask this question in jest. I wish I could tell her there is no cause for fear, but the hardships and losses of the past two years have taught me otherwise.

"There is always uncertainty. No pouch of gold, or star can protect us."

Magdalene laughs. "This is hardly reassurance, Jepp."

"It is the truth. But this being so, as my mother in Astraveld—and the mothers I have found since—have taught me, is it not better to act out of love rather than fear?"

Magdalene crouches down, and as our lips meet, I care not whether the world thinks us a motley pair. I care not where we will go tomorrow or what sorrows fate will inevitably bring. I care not that we face adversity by daring to look upward. For I am no longer on earth but in a heaven of my own making.

Finis

AUTHOR'S NOTE

epp, Who Defied the Stars is a work of historical fiction and, as such, it features a number of real historical figures. Some of these are well known, but the character that truly inspired me to write the novel is not. The real Jepp served the Danish astronomer Tycho Brahe as his dwarf jester. But he is no more than a footnote to history and, beyond a few biographical details, little is known about him—including who he was or how he ended up at Uraniborg. This is the mystery that captivated me, and the story I set out to tell.

My Jepp arrives at Uraniborg after a failed stint as a court dwarf for the Infanta Isabella Clara Eugenia, the real-life ruler of the Spanish Netherlands. When I was growing up, my parents had a wonderful book of European art, and I remember being deeply drawn to several portraits of court dwarfs by Diego Velázquez. This seventeenth-century painter, who depicted the court of Philip IV of Spain, captured a dignity and directness of gaze in his dwarf subjects that made them seem more alive than almost anyone else around them. It is two of his paintings, *Don Sebastian de Morra* (a portrait of the dwarf who served Prince Baltasar Carlos, the future heir to the Spanish throne) and *Las Meninas* (which features the dwarf Maria Barbola in the entourage of the child princess Margarita), that inspired the characters of Sebastian and Maria. One of the Infanta's own portraits, *Isabella and Her Dwarf* by Frans Pourbus, provided the inspiration for Lia.

As Jepp learns from his tutor at Coudenberg, there is a long history of dwarfs serving royal courts around the world. Although some held positions of power or prestige, many more were collected as status symbols, mocked, and treated cruelly. The indignities that Jepp and his fellow dwarfs suffer are not, sadly, fictional but a composite of actual accounts from Renaissance-era European courts: the miniaturized quarters, Lia's birdcage, Jepp's pie—all were real experiences that court dwarfs endured. For those who wish to learn more, *The Lives of Dwarfs: Their Journey from Public Curiosity toward Social Liberation* by Betty M. Adelson is an excellent resource.

Jepp is not the only character whose fate I sought to alter by writing this novel. The real Magdalene Tygesdatter never did marry, although she most certainly wanted to. Her destiny was very much shaped by that of her father, Tycho Brahe. This Danish astronomer is best known today for his precise celestial observations—made before the age of the telescope—which the German mathematician Johannes Kepler used to derive his laws of planetary motion, the underpinning of our modern conception of the solar system. Less well known, perhaps, is Brahe's colorful, eccentric life. Born into a powerful family of Danish nobles, Tycho developed a passion for astronomy—and its sister art of astrology—as a teenager. An opinionated and rowdy student, he lost most of his nose in a duel and, for the rest of his life, wore a metal prosthetic. In 1576, King Frederick, wishing to keep the promising young astronomer in his native Denmark, awarded Tycho the island of Hven in the Oresund Strait so that he might build an observatory.

The result was Uraniborg, or the Castle of the Heavens. The castle, built to Tycho's own specifications, contained a number of wondrous and innovative features. There was running water (including the indoor fountain that captivates Jepp); state-of-the-art astronomical equipment—some of it personally designed by Tycho; a system of pulleys and bells that could summon servants and scholars from across the castle; the exotic gardens that Jepp describes, and much more. *On Tycho's Island: Tycho Brahe, Science, and Culture in the Sixteenth Century* by John Robert Christianson is an excellent and entertaining introduction to Tycho's realm and his research—including the project to map the heavens on his celestial globe, with which I have Jepp assist him.

While at Uraniborg, Tycho hosted and employed gifted scholars from all social classes and parts of Europe, creating one of the earliest international—and meritocratic—research communities. Modern in other respects as well, he insisted that his employees sign written contracts, partly as a way to protect his research and ideas. Tycho's concern about intellectual property theft was more than just paranoia. In 1584, the German mathematician Nicholas Reimers Bar, who went by the Latin name Ursus, or "The Bear," visited Uraniborg in the entourage of Tycho's future brother-in-law, the alchemist Erik Lange. Ursus was caught prying into data and writings and, two years later, when he devised a planetary system very similar to Tycho's own, Tycho was certain that Ursus had stolen his idea. (Neither planetary system, however, would prove to be accurate as compared to Nicolaus Copernicus's fully heliocentric system.)

Although Tycho took his astronomical pursuits very seriously (as well as his astrological ones—among his duties was drawing up horoscopes for his patron, King Frederick) Uraniborg was by all accounts a raucous place. In addition to bantering with Jepp, who sat at his feet, Tycho entertained himself and his staff with lavish banquets and his beer-drinking pet moose, which like Ulf, met an untimely end after falling, drunk, down a flight of stairs. And, although Tycho did not possess a mechanical lion (I based the lion on Leonardo da Vinci's own lion automaton, which had a fleur-de-lis heart), he is said to have kept a collection of automata, or mechanized statues, with which he liked to frighten guests.

Tycho was unconventional in other ways as well: as a young man, he set up a household with a non-noble woman named Kirsten Jorgensdatter, who had grown up in the village outside his family estate. As Jepp learns, Danish law of the time allowed only a common law type of marriage between nobles and non-nobles, under which Kirsten and Tycho's children would remain commoners and could not inherit their father's name or his estate. As a result, Tycho worried incessantly about his children's future and attempted to find them worthy—and legal—matches. Magdalene, his eldest daughter, was briefly betrothed to a promising scholar, but the young man backed out of the engagement and spread rumors about her character—possibly because he feared he could not afford to maintain the type of household Tycho imagined for her. Although Tycho and his family fought the young man's innuendo—even suing him in court—Magdalene's name was sullied and she never married. I wanted my Magdalene to escape this fate and find a spiritual, as well as material, partner of her own in Jepp.

Although I tried to hew closely to the historical record, which provides such a bounty of colorful characters and details, I did take some liberties as a novelist. In 1597, after falling out of favor with King Frederick's successor, Tycho left Uraniborg and spent the last four years of his life in exile with his family, mostly in Prague. The Infanta Isabella did not ascend the throne of the Spanish Netherlands until 1599. But in the interests of Jepp's story, which takes place from 1597 to shortly before 1600, I allowed Tycho to remain at Uraniborg and the Infanta to make an earlier ascension to her throne. Historians may find other examples of poetic license taken in the interests of narrative, but hopefully I have captured something of the spirit of the times and the people who lived them.

On a final note: as I wrote this book, set over four hundred years ago, I was surprised to discover that what initially seemed like a remote past has, in fact, resonances with our own. Although astronomers are hardly ever now also astrologers, questions of fate and free will, faith, and reason, belonging and otherness, still occupy much of our public discourse and private struggles. In this respect, I hope readers will find in Jepp's story not so much a relic of history but the more universal tale of growing up and finding one's way in an uncertain and wondrous world.

A CONVERSATION WITH KATHERINE MARSH

Q: Would you tell us about your inspiration for *Jepp, Who Defied the Stars*? For you, what was the first spark of the story?

A: *Jepp* was inspired by my mother's passion for astrology. In fact, when I was growing up, it was basically the family religion. My mother can read an ephemeris and even draw up charts, and over the years she made many decisions, both large and small, based on it. I was due to be born on November 22, which would have made me a Sagittarius; but she saw better aspects for a Scorpio, so she helped her labor along with homeopathic remedies (I was born on November 11, a Scorpio, Aquarius rising). We cut our hair by the cycles of the Moon and tried not to travel when Mercury was retrograde. I even took my SAT based on the stars, on a particular date offered only in a neighboring state.

My mom and I are incredibly close; I'm an only child, and she's a late-in-life mother (she had me at forty-two). Save for the astrology, she was actually a fairly strict and traditional parent who emphasized hard work, education, and intellectual life. Because of this, I grew up half believing in astrology—and appreciating the sense of security it gave me—and half rejecting the entire premise that there were things about my life and others' that were predetermined. It's this struggle that is at the very heart of *Jepp*. Though my upbringing is admittedly unusual, I believe there's something universal about loving and deriving comfort from the belief system you grew up with and, at the same time, wanting to buck it in order to feel your destiny is your own.

Q: Sounds like you started with an interesting and personal theme. How did you then find the story?

A: Initially I had no idea what story or character would allow me to explore the struggle between fate and free will. But I knew I wanted to write about astrology, and so I began to read more about it. As I did, I became fascinated by the period in which astrology was a respected sister art to astronomy; but at the same time, Renaissance thinkers were beginning to grapple with a new sense of individualism, science, and free will. This led me to Tycho Brahe, and as soon as I began reading about his eccentricities—his futuristic castle, prosthetic nose, and beer-drinking moose—my inner novelist began to get excited. Then I saw a footnote about his dwarf jester, Jepp. It was at that moment the story snapped into focus. Jepp would have been witness to this emerging world of science and self-determination, but as a court dwarf, who might also have been exposed to a more traditional Catholic court, his own existence would have been more constrained. He seemed the perfect character to bridge these worlds and embody the fate/free will theme.

Q: Previously, you've written more fantastical novels for a slightly younger audience. What was it like to transition to a historical setting? Did you have to do a lot of research to feel confident writing in his voice?

A: Even in my fantasy novels, I've always incorporated a lot of history. My background is as a journalist, so I enjoy research and certainly made it a big part of this book (see my historical note). But at the same time, I tried not to let the history clutter or detract from the story. For example, in one scene, I became obsessed with how many furnaces Tycho Brahe had in his basement lab and was very insistent that Jepp notice there were exactly sixteen. It took me several drafts to realize that Jepp would not stand there counting furnaces. I also reconciled myself to the fact that I wasn't going to capture the period with perfect accuracy. Not only am I a novelist, rather than an historian, but I think we always see history through the veil of our own era and sensibilities. More important, I felt, was to give the reader a texture, a feeling, an impression, of how Jepp's world could have been. So, for example, while Jepp obviously would not have spoken English, I spent a lot of time with the etymological dictionary making sure the English words he spoke were in use before 1600 in order to give his voice a distinctive and antiquated feel. Paintings from the sixteenth and seventeenth century— Dutch/Flemish and Spanish art—also served as inspiration for the feelings and moments I wanted to re-create, for example, the amazing Dutch still lifes that inspired Lia's memento mori.

Q: Tell us about your writing process. Which parts of the novel were easiest and hardest to write? How much of the plot was clear in your mind when you first began?

A: I started the novel by writing a few chapters in Jepp's voice. I was actually supposed to be writing a fantasy novel for younger readers, but Jepp immediately felt so real to me that I couldn't abandon him. Soon after, I devised the basic plot of the story. I knew from the beginning that I wanted the book to feel like an adventure story, in the spirit of Charles Dickens, with lots of twists and turns and memorable secondary characters, some of whom return in surprising ways. I also envisioned the novel as having three sections, with each one, almost symphonically, having a different tone and pace. The hardest section for me to write was the second, at Uraniborg, even though I was more excited to write it than any other. It's my adagio section—more contemplative and slow-paced, and proved the most technically difficult in that I had to interweave a number of different plot strands. It was also a challenge to show Magdalene and Jepp falling for each other in a way that felt organic and convincing. It was so important for the rest of the book to get their relationship right.

Q: On a personal note, what aspects of Jepp's character and life experience do you feel are most like your own? Do you relate to any of the other characters in this book as strongly?

A: Obviously, Jepp's struggle over whether to believe in fate or free will is based on my own. Beyond that, I drew on my own experiences as a teenager and young adult—leaving home at a similar age, falling in love, feeling like an outsider, having my heart broken, making mistakes that felt irredeemable at the time, realizing who I was apart from my parents—to create Jepp's. I also relate to Magdalene and her contradictory mix of boldness and fear of the outside world.

Q: Did writing *Jepp* help you resolve the fate/free-will issues of your childhood? Having written the book, where do you stand on astrology?

A: There's a moment near the end of the book where Magdalene basically asks Jepp for reassurance that life will be okay. It's a question we ask ourselves all the time, and Jepp answers her honestly. He says he doesn't know. It's a terrifying answer, and it's no wonder that, faced with it, we turn to systems of belief (in my mother's case, astrology), that provide a sense of order and certainty. This is why I'll probably always think of myself as a Scorpio and want to know how the stars align for me during times of trouble or uncertainty.

But while I started *Jepp* as a letter to my mother, the writing of it ended up being bookended by the births of my own two children, and the novel also became a message to them. In that very last scene, Jepp concedes that life is uncertain, that "no blessed star can protect us." But then he asks us to reframe the question. Rather than searching for certainty, how do we live with uncertainty? It's a harder but ultimately more constructive question, because it points us to where we truly have a measure of choice—in how we treat others, in how we handle the inevitable moments of failure and loss, in how we value our dreams and ourselves.

DISCUSSION QUESTIONS

YOU MIGHT ENJOY SHARING THESE QUESTIONS
AND DISCUSSING YOUR ANSWERS WITH
FELLOW READERS, OR WITH A BOOK CLUB.

- Explain the significance of the title *Jepp, Who Defied the Stars*. In your opinion, does it accurately describe the events and relationships portrayed in the novel? Do you believe it's possible to control your destiny? Why or why not?

- After being accosted by travelers visiting his mother's inn, Jepp states, "And so I learned the word that would come to supplant my name. But I thought not of myself as a dwarf." What's the significance of this incident? In what ways is Jepp changed by this experience? In your opinion, why is labeling him so cruel? Have you ever had a similar situation happen to you? How did you choose to deal with it?

- Considering what happens to Lia, do you think Jepp's decision to help her is the right one? Was he a good friend? Has a friend ever asked you to help them do something that you worried wasn't in their best interest?

- Describe Magdalene. What makes her a dynamic character? Is she the type of person you would want to befriend? Why or why not?

- *Jepp, Who Defied the Stars* contains a number of characters who exhibit a variety of strengths. Which character impresses you most (or least)? Explain your choice.

- Jepp offers, "To be loved is the birthright of every mewling babe but, once grown, a man is not assured of such affection." In what ways does Jepp's relationship with Magdalene change him? How would you compare this relationship with the one he forms with Lia?

- Do you believe Jepp makes the right decision to leave Magdalene in search of answers? Why or why not? Do you think it's necessary for people to understand their history to be at peace and happy? Why or why not?

- In *Jepp, Who Defied the Stars*, at times, fear both motivates and incapacitates Jepp. Consider how he deals with his fears. Does he acknowledge them? In what ways do we witness him turning to others for assistance? Who are the people you seek out to assist you when you are afraid?

- *Jepp, Who Defied the Stars* is told in the first person; how would the story be different if another character (besides Jepp) were telling it? Do you think changing the point of view would make the story better or worse? Why?

- Jepp wonders, "Perhaps true mercy comes not from up on high but from those beside us." Discuss some of the moments of forgiveness in the book. Who is the hardest person for Jepp to forgive? Whose forgiveness means the most to Jepp? How do mercy and forgiveness shape the narrative of Jepp's life? What is the importance of forgiveness in your own life?

This discussion guide was created by Rose Brock, a teacher, school librarian, and doctoral candidate at Texas Woman's University, specializing in children's and young adult literature.

ACKNOWLEDGMENTS

A number of wise, generous, and loving people helped align the stars for Jepp. Lyda Phillips, my tireless Aries critique partner, read more drafts than I can count; her enthusiasm for the story never let me doubt my own, while her suggestions enriched every version. Alex Glass, my agent, let me follow my heart while looking out for the rest of me. Abby Ranger performed acts of literary alchemy while never changing the essence of the tale; every writer should be so lucky to find an editor like her.

Jennifer Besser was an early and ardent champion of Jepp's story. Copy editor Monica Mayper made many eagle-eyed catches and improvements. Fact-checkers Anna Hetherington and Robert Fucci helped me stay true to history on subjects ranging from astronomy to sixteenth-century drinks. Chloe Schama kindly helped me find them. Gibson Reynolds generously took the time to read the manuscript with a sensitive eye toward its dwarf protagonists.

I am grateful to the many friends, fans, and colleagues who provided companionship and encouragement during the writing of this book. Particular thanks goes out to the team at Disney-Hyperion, Maura Reynolds and the Chick Hacks, Frank Foer, Caroline Hickey, Pam Ehrenberg, the Children's Book Guild of Washington, D.C., Gussie Lewis at Politics and Prose, the students and teachers at the Washington Latin School, Miranda "Juliet" Schanner (in memory of her mother, Julie Ann Schanner), Amie Hsia and Ben Harder, and Erica Envall and Lisa Trovato, "the moms" club of Chevy Chase.

As a mother of young children, I am indebted to my family for providing me with a room of my own. My husband, Julian E. Barnes, gave me the precious gifts of extra hours, endless encouragement, and a patient ear. He was never too tired to talk about Jepp, our third child, and even paid a visit to the ruins of Coudenberg for me. Elaine Milosh Marsh served as my astrological consultant and rarely missed a day as mother's helper. Ken Marsh provided support for both children and chapters. Donna Barnes and Richard Barnes gave generously of their time.

Finally, my deepest thanks go to the Aquarius and the Pisces around whom my own world revolves. Aleksandr Barnes and Natalia Barnes, you were constantly in my thoughts—and in my heart—as I wrote this book. Love, Mom.